MW01154912

The Skeleton King
Dartmoor Book III

Lauren Gilley

This is a work of fiction. Names, characters, places and events are the products of the author's imagination or are used fictitiously. Any resemblances to persons, living or dead, is coincidental.

Names and characters are the property of the author and may not be duplicated.

THE SKELETON KING

ISBN -13: 978-1516905874

Copyright © 2015 by Lauren Gilley

Cover photograph Copyright © 2015 by Lauren Gilley

HP Press®
Atlanta, GA

All rights reserved.

The Dartmoor Series

Fearless
Price of Angels
Half My Blood
The Skeleton King
Secondhand Smoke (coming soon)

The Lean Dogs

Ghost – President
Walsh- Vice President
Michael – Sgt. at Arms
Ratchet – Secretary
Hound – Tracker
Rottie – Tracker
Mercy – Extractor
Aidan – Ghost's son
Tango – Aidan's best friend
Dublin
Briscoe
RJ
Troy
Carter
Littlejohn
Harry
Collier – incarcerated

The Old Ladies

Maggie – Ghost
Ava – Mercy
Holly – Michael
Nell – Hound
Mina – Rottie
Jackie – Collier

THE
SKELETON

KING

Atlanta

Brighton Racecourse
Brighton, East Sussex, England
24 Years Ago

The trainer was a broad man, with a full dark beard. He stood wreathed in mist beside the rail, gaze sweeping along the downs and the irregular track. His breath plumed like smoke. Dawn just breaking, and the ocean lay hidden under a white shroud, the crash of the waves a dull murmur.

An indistinct sound drew closer, and then became the fast drumming of hooves. Walsh felt the turf vibrating beneath his boots the moment before horse and rider burst from the mist. The horse at a sleek gallop, neck extended, legs driving like pistons. The jockey crouched low over the animal's withers, hands white-knuckled on the reins.

To see a horse gambol through an open field was beautiful. To watch a Thoroughbred breezing on the track – that was breathtaking.

Horse and jockey flew past, disappearing once more in the mist.

"Ha," the trainer said to himself, clicking his stopwatch. "Fast," he murmured. "Jesus, the beast is fast."

He jotted figures on the clipboard he carried, and then made to turn away from the rail.

Walsh felt his grandfather's hand between his shoulder blades, giving him a little shove forward.

Gramps cleared his throat. " 'Scuse me, sir?"

The trainer turned toward them, squinting to see through the fog. "Aye?"

Gramps gave another shove and Walsh was standing right in front of the trainer, head tilting back on his skinny neck so he could look up at the man.

"My grandson here," Gramps said, "is a right fine rider. He wants to become an exercise rider. Wants to work the horses." He gestured to the track.

The trainer leaned closer, inspecting Walsh from the top of his pale head to the scuffed toes of his outgrown boots. "I do need a new a rider. Had one broke his foot 'bout a week ago. How old are you, boy?"

"Eighteen, sir," Walsh lied.

The man grinned. "Sure you are. Can you sit a horse?"

"Like he's glued in the bloody saddle," Gramps said.

Walsh could only nod.

The trainer studied him a long moment, eyes hooded. Then he nodded. "Come back to the barn then, lad. Let's see what we can find for you to do."

One

Knoxville, TN
Present Day

"They're back, *chica*."

Of course they were. It was too much to hope for that they'd forgotten the way out here. "Good job, Kelsey. One more lap – keep those fingers light. Thumbs up. Atta girl. Then a nice, easy downward transition…there ya go. And walk him out. Let him have the reins." Her final instruction of the lesson delivered, pleased with her young student's progress, Emmie twisted around to face Fred.

The groom stood at the rail, hands folded over the top board, his expression one of resigned concern.

"How many this time?"

"Three." He pushed back his straw sun hat and scratched at his forehead. There was a deep crease where the hatband had been. "Fancy men, with shiny new *botas*." He lifted one of his dusty cowboy boots with a wry grin.

Emmie snorted. "Trying to look the part. Bastards." She sighed. "Alright. I'll head up and meet them. They're at the barn?"

"*Sí.*"

She turned back to face her student. Kelsey was ten, scrawny and tenacious in the way of all blooming equestrians. Emmie's favorite student, if she was allowed to have favorites. Kelsey would die of heat stroke before admitting defeat; Emmie was the one who had to insist on water breaks.

"Great job, girlie," Emmie told her, smiling. "Can you walk Champ out for me?"

The girl was beaming. "Yes!" Something as simple as cooling out a horse was thrilling for a kid with this kind of equine addiction.

"When he's cool to the touch, bring him back to the barn and Fred can help you untack and put him away, alright?"

"Okay!"

"Great job, baby!" Kelsey's mom called from the rail. She turned to Emmie and said, "Is she really ready to unsaddle him by herself?" Her brows plucked together with worry.

"Totally ready," Emmie assured her. In an undertone: "And the worst thing Champ's ever done is raid the Apple Wafers bag. If y'all need anything, ask Fred."

"Thanks."

Emmie wanted to walk alongside the horse as Kelsey cooled him out, discuss the highs and lows of the lesson, map a course for next week's lesson. It was her habit, a way to bond with her students and further their understanding. She liked to go up to the barn with them, instill good post-ride habits.

But she had three dicks in suits waiting on her, and wasn't that a mood-killer?

"Thank you," she told Fred on her way out of the arena, and he dipped his head in response.

Sweet Fred – she couldn't run this place without him. Originally hired on by Mr. Richards as a landscaper, he'd come running to her aid one afternoon when Brett left a gate open. In his soft-spoken, gentle way, he'd explained – after the horses were all safely back in their paddocks – that he'd worked with horses in his native Nicaragua before immigrating north to the US. He'd told her to call him Fred, because his real name was difficult for Americans to pronounce.

He'd been promoted to head groom, and his help was indispensable. Because there were horse farms...

And then there was Briar Hall.

As she mounted the hill toward the stone and timber barn, Emmie had a view of the farm bathed in amber evening light. Verdant fields dotted with oaks; two 100'x200' natural sand arenas with lights and sprinkler systems; outbuildings for hay and shavings in dark cypress wood; four-board black fencing across the property. The barn was a masterpiece: twenty stalls, tongue-and-groove wood on the interior, industrial fans over each stall, with four wash racks, massive tack room, office, and the loft apartment above, where she lived. Three cupolas set at intervals along the peak of the copper roof housed heating units that warmed the barn in the winter.

The property rolled gently upward from there, toward the pale stone house on the hill where Mr. Richards lived, alone since the passing of his wife last year.

All told, Briar Hall was sixty acres of horse heaven, a strip of forest hiding the property from its neighbors. It was more a home to Emmie than any house had ever been. From hangaround kid, to student, to stall-mucker, to groom, to working student – she'd poured her heart, her sweat, her blood, her life into this farm, and now, at twenty-nine, she was its manager.

And it was for sale.

Three men stood beside the black BMW X5 parked in front of the barn. Black suits, muted ties, and, as promised, shiny black cowboy boots with crazy-pointed toes. Two conferred, holding iPhones; the third scanned the front of the barn with obvious distaste.

Emmie felt sick.

She wiped her hands on the thighs of her breeches and forced a chilly smile. "Gentlemen," she greeted as she approached. "You're back."

Phones were pocketed and one of them stepped forward, his smile detached, professional. "We're here to talk with Mr. Richards again. He said you could show us up to the house, Ms. Johansen."

Vultures, she thought. *You awful bastards.* "I can." But she didn't oblige them right away. "You guys have new boots."

The man in front of her – she thought his name was Gannon – glanced down at his shoes. "Well" – he shrugged, made an attempt at a wry grin – "if I'm going to own a farm, I might as well get used to the attire, right?"

"Right." She sighed. "Come on. We can take the Rhino."

~*~

"Ratchet, what did your courthouse guy say?"

13

The secretary made a comical face, like he didn't want to have to say what he was about to. "His girlfriend was the one who pulled the plat. The names match. The guy looking to buy Briar Hall is the same guy who called and talked to Ethan about the cattle property. Lance Gannon."

Everyone at the table said "fuck" on the same breath.

"What do you know about him?" Ghost asked.

The zippered notebook came open, pages rustling. "He's co-owner of a land development firm, with two other guys: his brother, Neal, and a cousin, Don Harmon. The housing market's knocked 'em on their ass, but they had a successful build about six months ago, that retirement condo village down near Spring City."

"I've seen the place," Dublin said grimly. "Four condos to a unit, real nice, with their own grocery store, gas station, restaurant, that kinda thing. All self-contained, so the old farts don't ever have to leave. No offense to the elderly, mind," he added, a glance thrown toward Troy's empty chair.

"I don't care what the amenities are like," Ghost said. His face was thunderous. "I wanna know if they've got enough bank to buy out old man Richards."

"Bank and then some," Ratchet said with a wince. "These guys don't mess, boss."

"Shit."

Walsh turned his silver lighter around and around in one hand, watching the lamplight slide across its surface and fracture on his rings. Biding his time. Waiting until this clusterfuck was inevitably turned toward him. It was a stick of financial dynamite, and he was the one-man bomb squad.

Michael was the one who'd seen the sign. Almost a month ago, he'd taken Holly up to the cattle property to work on her target shooting, and he'd come back to report that there was a For Sale sign up at the street in front of Briar Hall, the cattle property's long-standing neighbor.

Two weeks ago, someone had called Ethan Briscoe's office, wanting to talk to the owner of "that piece of land beside Briar Hall." Since Ghost had finagled the property deed around

14

and set up a dummy corp as the land's owner, Ethan's office handled all phone calls and mail directed toward the place. The property wasn't for sale, Ethan had told Gannon, end of story.

But now plats were being pulled for Briar Hall. And if a developer bought the horse farm, that would mean earth movers, construction crews, and eventually a whole boatload of nosy neighbors right next door to their shooting range and body dump.

Comforting thought.

"We gotta talk to Richards," Aidan said, pulling in a deep drag off a fresh smoke. In the dim interior of the chapel, the scarred-over tats on his forearms looked darker than normal. "Convince him to hold out for a real buyer."

"Pretty sure Gannon's got *real* money," Rottie said with a snort.

"I meant somebody who's gonna keep it a farm," Aidan clarified, rolling his eyes.

"Yeah, but that place's gotta cost, what, at least a mil," Tango said. "Not a lot of wannabe farmers walking around with that kinda change in their pockets."

"We could advertise," Briscoe said, tone only half-joking. " 'Wanted: Rich Fucker Looking to Buy a Horse Farm.' "

Ghost shook his head. "Richards and his people have been quiet. No one comes over the fence, no one cares that we shoot out there. Even if Briar Hall stays a farm, who's to say new neighbors won't get nosy?"

"We convince them that's a bad idea," Mercy said with an elegant shrug, leaning back in his chair, looking satisfied with his logic.

"Cute." Ghost smirked. "But I don't think we're to the fingernail-prying stage yet."

"Aw, but boss, I've been so bored." Mercy pretended to pout.

"Which would explain the reason I've got another grandson on the way, right?"

Chuckles rippled around the table.

"Seriously, though." Ghost sobered, and the laughter died away. "We're gonna have to figure out something." His eyes flicked toward Walsh. "Everybody put your thinking caps on. In the meantime, I think we're going to have to reconsider our go-to remains disposal techniques."

Groans all around.

He ignored them. "I need you guys" – he gestured to Walsh and Michael on either side of him – "to head up to the property, get me a ballpark figure for how many bodies we're talking. Make sure they're good and deep underground. You" – Ratchet – "see what kinda dirt you can find on Gannon and his crew. You" – Mercy – "get a hobby that don't involve gettin' people pregnant, alright?"

A chorus of "yes, sir" and a big grin from Mercy dismissed the meeting.

~*~

Emmie had been inside the house countless times, but it never stopped impressing her. She led the developers around to the back entrance, up onto the wraparound porch, through the French doors of the library. The place had a *library*. The interior smelled of old pages and oiled leather, the cigars Mr. Richards enjoyed every evening while he read.

A door surrounded by bookshelves led into the adjoining office, and Emmie knocked once before opening it a fraction, peeking in.

Davis Richards sat at his massive marble-topped desk, scowling at his computer screen. He wasn't a big man, but there was a Churchillian pugnacity to his broad face that lent him an air of total authority. He was seventy-six, looked sixty, and oversaw his operations – all of them – with a brusqueness that would have been cliché if not for the occasional burst of unexpected levity. He'd always treated Emmie well, and at times, he felt more like a grandfather than a boss.

His head swiveled toward her as the door opened. "What? Oh, Em, it's you. You brought Gannon up?"

"Yes, sir." She pushed the door wide. "They said you had an appointment with them."

"Yeah, yeah, I do." He waved the three suits closer with an impatient gesture. "Come sit down." As she was backing out of the room, he said, "Thanks, Emmie. Everything going okay today?"

She gave him a quick smile. "Just fine."

Except for the fact that you're selling the farm to real estate developers, everything's fucking peachy.

It felt wrong to stay, and press her ear to the door, so she went back outside, pausing a moment at the top of the stairs. The stone house with its heavy timber trimwork seemed to glow in the evening light, the façade gleaming gold. From the porch, she could see most of the farm stretched out below. Tranquil, drowsy in the faded heat.

What would she do without this place? There were other farms, other students, other places she could go. But the landscape of her heart bore the image of *this* place, *this* farm.

The Rhino was waiting for her in front of the garage doors and she climbed behind the wheel. Let the flashy suits walk back down to the barn, she thought, cranking the engine.

Briar Hall was in its usual evening uproar: horses pawing at gates, whinnying, calling to her as she parked. The steady sounds of buckets rattling and pellets sluicing into feeders signaled that Becca was pouring dinner.

Emmie passed Tonya on her way into the barn. The leggy brunette led her gelding, Chaucer, out through the double doors, looking more like a Dover catalogue model in her fawn breeches and white poplin shirt than a serious equestrian. But serious she was, Emmie's most talented student, cool and beautiful and elegant.

"Running through your tests tonight?" Emmie asked.

Tonya nodded. "The transition after the second half-pass needs work."

"You want me to come watch for a bit?"

Tonya shrugged and tossed a disinterested glance over her shoulder toward the busy barn aisle. "If you have time, sure."

She'd known the high-dollar socialite too long now to be offended by her tone. " 'Kay," Emmie said, and kept moving.

Kelsey and her mother were saying goodbye to Champ, Kelsey flinging her arms around the stout gelding's neck for one last hug. Then Kelsey hugged Emmie, and Emmie felt that rare warm stir of emotion that sometimes left her lamenting her lack of children.

"Good job, today, I'll see you next week."

"Okay!" Kelsey was all gap-toothed smile and girlhood exuberance when it came to the horses; in truth, she reminded Emmie of herself at that age.

Becca came down the aisle, tower of eight-quart buckets in her skinny arms. "They're back," she said, wrinkling her nose, and Emmie nodded.

"Unfortunately, yeah. I just took them up to see Davis."

"Assholes."

"Ditto that."

"Though, actually," Becca dropped her voice, "this is really all Amy's fault. Her dad builds her this barn, and she up and runs off to Kentucky. Ungrateful–"

"I'm still not one-hundred-percent sure there aren't cameras in here," Emmie reminded, smiling despite herself.

Becca clamped her lips shut, eyes bugging. "*Oops.*"

Emmie laughed, hollowly. "It's okay. I ditto that too," she whispered, "but let's try not to get fired before our jobs are eliminated."

"Right." Becca nodded and walked off. "I'll start with the left side of the driveway," she called over her shoulder. "I'll let you get the Beast's pasture."

That would be Emmie's horse, Apollo. Who Becca and Fred referred to as either the Beast, Widowmaker, or *El Diablo*. He was the first one at the gate every night, no exceptions, and none of the other horses challenged him.

Emmie grabbed a carrot from the tack room fridge and took her first deep, relaxing breath of the afternoon, heading out the front doors. It had been one shock after the next lately – Amy announcing she was marrying and moving all her horses to

18

Kentucky; Davis deciding to sell the farm; developer after developer making their way up the drive in low-slung black cars. In the midst of the whirlwind, she was losing touch with the part of her that thrived on the even keel of farm life, forgetting to enjoy the quiet moments. She hadn't ridden in days.

She took a deep breath of summer-scented air as she headed down the driveway, resolving to shove all thoughts of leaving Briar Hall out of her head.

In the dressage arena, Tonya warmed Chaucer up at a swinging trot, horse and rider in perfect sync. Emmie watched them a moment as she walked, mentally approving of the way Tonya's hands rested light on the reins, letting the horse stretch.

"Em!" Becca shouted, startling her. "He's doing it again! Tally!"

Emmie glanced toward the pasture she was headed for…and sure enough, there went Tally, leaping neatly over the five-foot fence and taking off at a mad gallop toward the trees.

"Shit."

Two

It was early when church let out, and after a brief discussion in the common room, Walsh and Michael decided to head up to the cattle property now, avoiding the heat of the day tomorrow and getting a jump on whatever was to be done there. They shared an intolerance for waiting, in that regard.

The sun was at its sharp evening slant when they parked their bikes in front of the falling-down farmhouse and dismounted.

Walsh was slow about tugging off his gloves, straightening his rings. He took a moment to let the country air fill his lungs; he traced the rolling pastureland with his eyes. The grass rippled in gleaming waves as the wind caught it. Clusters of doves lifted from their hiding places and took awkward flight.

He loved it here. Nothing but the animals and the faded whispers of the dead to disturb the quiet. One of the few places in his brother-crowded world where he could feel his insides unclench.

"You good?" Michael asked. There was the faintest edge of impatience in his normally flat voice; he wanted to go home to Holly, and Lucy, and whatever hot dinner awaited him in the oven.

"Yeah." Walsh laid his gloves on the seat of his bike and pulled a notepad and pen from his inside cut pocket. "You were the last one to have a burial up here. Lead the way."

~*~

Tally was short for Tally-Ho, a name that had left the entire barn staff in stitches…until they'd realized how appropriate the name was for the Thoroughbred. On an almost weekly basis, Tally went over a fence. For a while, they'd turned him out in the round pen, because its eight-foot solid board walls couldn't be leapt. But it had been a cruelty, keeping such a large, energetic horse in such a small enclosure. They'd swapped pastures, putting him in with

Apollo's herd, and for a few weeks, the change seemed to please him, and he'd stayed put. But tonight showed him back to his old ways.

"I'm sorry, Fred, you're sure you don't need our help?"

"*Sí*. You better catch *Loco*, before his *madre* shows up and yells at us."

"No kidding." Emmie dropped the saddle flap and ran down the stirrup. "Don't worry about Apollo's fly sheet; I'll take it off when I get back."

"*Sí*."

She buckled on her helmet and glanced toward the neighboring wash rack, where Becca saddled her gelding, Mocha. "Ready?"

Quick *click* of Becca's helmet strap. "Yep."

Emmie draped Tally's halter and lead-rope over one arm and gathered the loose reins of her mount. She adored Apollo, but search-and-rescue wasn't his strong suit. She'd saddled her favorite lesson horse, Sherman, almost seventeen hands of solid, level-headed Quarter Horse with a knack for just about everything.

Sherman turned to regard her through sleepy brown eyes, the lopsided blaze on his face giving the impression that he was lifting one nostril in question.

"Let's go find your dumb friend, okay?" she told the horse, patting his shoulder and leading him from the barn.

Tonya was on her way back into the barn as Emmie and Becca left. "Tally got out again?" she guessed.

"He wanted to make sure I got a ride in today," Emmie said with a fast, false smile. The prospect of wrangling the wild Thoroughbred left her exhausted. "Good ride?" she asked Tonya.

"Better than the one you're about to have."

"Too true."

She and Becca mounted and steered their horses down the driveway, toward the run between two pastures where Tally had disappeared. The grass needed cutting and it swished around the horses' fetlocks as they walked. Mocha and Sherman stepped with coiled energy, necks stretching forward as an evening breeze ruffled their short manes.

It wasn't the ride Emmie would have chosen, but there was no fighting the magic of being in the saddle. Sherman had an easy, swinging walk and the motion of his shoulders rolling soothed her nerves. She pulled in a deep breath and let it out slowly, felt the tension bleed from the backs of her legs as his ribcage pushed at them.

"It's really happening, isn't it?" Becca said quietly beside her. "They're really selling this place. And those dickheads are going to turn it into a freaking shuffleboard court."

Emmie heaved a deep sigh that caught in her throat; her eyes burned and she blinked hard as she stared between Sherman's ears at the grass ahead. "I've gone through so many scenarios in my mind: What if we bought it ourselves?"

Becca made a gasping sound of shock beside her that quickly turned into an excited squeal.

"What if we started raising money? Hosted a tack sale. A 4-H show, and put all the proceeds toward a collective purchase of Briar Hall? What if we all chipped in – you, me, Fred – and we went to the bank to take out a loan? What if we tried to get Tonya's family to buy it?"

"Tonya!" Becca exclaimed. "That's it! Her dad's loaded. We'll get him to buy it, and she wouldn't have any reason to fire us, and we could....You're shaking your head."

"Because I already asked Tonya, and her family already has a farm; they don't want this one. And because no tack sale, or benefit show, or loan in the world will get our three broke asses enough money to buy this place." Emmie cleared her throat and hoped it didn't sound like she was on the verge of sniffling. "This is the problem with falling in love with someplace that isn't yours – it won't ever be yours."

"It's not fair," Becca said fiercely.

"Davis is old, and this is a lot for him to handle," Emmie said, knowing it was the truth.

"What does he handle? You run everything, and he just signs the checks."

Emmie snorted.

"You know what I think it is? I think he just doesn't want all his kids fighting about it when he finally kicks off."

She started to protest...but nodded instead. "I'd say that's a big possibility."

"I just don't want to leeeeaaavvve," Becca groaned, bending at the waist and draping her torso across Mocha's neck. The gelding snorted in annoyance but otherwise tolerated her theatrics.

Emmie smiled faintly at the display, feeling chilled and depressed inside. She knew, when the inevitable departure came, Becca would land on her feet. Eighteen, fresh out of high school and taking a semester or two to work, she was personable, responsible, bubbly, and could meld easily into a new barn and a new situation. She and Mocha would find another boarding or training facility to take them, and she'd swap chores for her board, and she'd start college, and in less than a year's time, the heartbreak of Briar Hall would have faded.

Emmie, on the other hand, was going to be scraped off the side of this place like bubbled-up lead paint, and wherever she went, she'd be starting all over, back to square one; no longer a trusted decision-maker, but the new-girl. The new, almost-thirty, boring, dry, workaholic girl with the difficult horse no one wanted to bring in from the pasture. Not to mention she couldn't afford to board Apollo; she needed to work off his rent. And, now that she thought of it, she'd need a place to live, because going home to the folks just wasn't an option.

Dwelling on it was getting her nowhere fast.

With a firm mental shake, she cleared her head. "Which way did he go, you think?" she asked as they reached the end of the run and had to choose to follow the property line to the left or right.

"Well, all those briars Brett was supposed to trim back are to the left," Becca said. "So..."

"He went left," they said in unison.

~*~

"These'll be the two kids who were bothering Ava," Michael said, gesturing to the innocuous patch of grass between two sapling pines. A good spot; the trees were small, still, so the roots hadn't provided much obstruction, but as they grew, the roots would further till the bones.

"Ronnie and Mason," Walsh said, writing down the location on his pad and putting two tally marks beside it.

"That should be it." Michael folded his arms and didn't seem to know what to do with himself, then, mouth curled sharply with distaste for this whole business. At least, that was how Walsh read his expression. What seemed a deep frown for Michael was just a facial twitch on someone else. "How many you got total?"

Walsh ticked through the list and whistled. "Thirty-seven."

"Christ."

"The Carpathians were a...large deposit."

"Yeah."

"But"- Walsh stowed his pen and pad away, straightened his cut and dug out a smoke – "the graves look good. Not too much erosion, no odor. All of it was done by the book. Digging 'em up would be a bloody nightmare."

"It's not possible," Michael agreed. "Some have been here for fifteen years. Nothing left but bone and dust. And you get that stuff up in the air, on the ground – dogs can sniff that out."

"Hmm," Walsh agreed, taking his first drag. "Better to leave 'em."

By unspoken agreement they headed back for their bikes, the walking slow in the rough grass. Twilight was hitting hard, and the farm around them was pulling on its blanket of shadows as the first stars flared to life overhead. It would be full dark soon, and then the property would become a whole other world, one that belonged to the quiet things that watched them now from the trees; things that slunk along on silent bellies, with yellow eyes and strange calls that echoed across the empty pastures.

It was a good dump ground, and Ghost had used it wisely. Not one body had been buried before the farm had been "sold" to the dummy corporation that now owned it. As far as the city knew, Ghost Teague didn't own shit aside from his home and business. The club was careful with its comings and goings, and up till now, their activity on the old cattle farm had been invisible.

But if a whole village of retirees moved in next door…

If there was shopping and entertainment and all sorts of staff…

It was something that bothered Walsh more than he'd said aloud.

All his Tennessee chapter brothers had grown up in the States; several had visited London, but they hadn't been raised there. They knew nothing of the din and stench and jostle of a city that size. Day in, day out, London had eaten at him, like acid rain crumbling away his hard edges over time, until he'd become this smooth, emotionless shell.

Until Gramps died, summers in East Sussex with his grandfather had been the highlight of his childhood life. His mother had fretted over him, worried that he had no father. "A boy should spend some time with men, learning how to be one," she'd told him, and when he was four, she'd begun packing him off to her father's house for two months out of the year.

It was in Rottingdean, East Sussex that he'd realized he was a boy misplaced in the world. He could close his eyes now and return there, to the bedroom that overlooked the back garden, the nubby clean-smelling blanket beneath his cheek, weak sunshine warming his bare arms, the scent of Gram's roses beyond the open window being swept up in the salt tang coming in from the beach. He could hear the ham frying and hear Gramps singing and he could hear *birds*. Real, actual songbirds, on the window ledge and in the garden, calling to one another.

Summers became his life, and all the months in between merely his existence. Rottingdean was roses and cottage gardens;

it was fumbling, pleasant-faced tourists and friendly locals. Cozy pubs, fingers sticky with candy, a belly full of Gram's fatty cooking. It was games of chase through walled back gardens with boys who didn't tease him for being so small. It was his bare sun-browned toes digging into the cool sand on the beach, and the sun striking off the white cliff face high above. Day trips to Brighton. Endless walks outside the town, into fields that fostered his wildest boyhood imaginings.

He didn't belong in the cheek-by-jowl world of cities. He belonged somewhere drowsy and soft. It was why he loved Tennessee. It was why something as sad as an abandoned cattle farm meant something to him outside its body-hiding attributes.

"Did you hear that?" Michael asked, startling him, slamming him back to the present.

He halted, going still all over. The wind touched his face. "What?"

"I heard—"

And there it was: a scream.

It wasn't a human one, though.

"What the hell?" Michael asked under his breath. His hand went to his waistband, the gun stashed there.

Walsh put his thumb and forefinger in his mouth and whistled, one sharp blast that made Michael wince and flushed doves from the grass.

A moment later, a figure emerged from behind a stand of trees partway up the driveway. A snorting, head-tossing, four-legged figure, who stepped to the center of the path and stared at them, nostrils flared. The horse was a dark, gleaming bay, rangy and long-necked, black tail cocked like he was prepared to bolt.

"Ghost got horses up there in the barn we don't know about?" Michael asked dryly.

Walsh whistled again, and the horse took a few steps toward them, threw his head up, and snorted explosively.

Walsh started up the driveway, toward the horse and the old vacant barn beyond it, pace steady so he wouldn't spook the animal.

"What are you gonna do?" Michael asked behind him, and he sounded annoyed.

He didn't know. But his feet were taking him up the hill.

~*~

"It's locked," Emmie said grimly, surveying the gate in front of her. They'd found hoofprints in the deep mud right at the property's edge, and they'd fought their way through honeysuckle and low-hanging tree limbs up to the fence. They'd found this gate that separated Briar Hall from its neighbor. And they'd found it locked, with a padlock that only bolt cutters could overcome.

"Is there a key at the barn?" Becca asked behind her, where she held both horses out from under the dense cover of branches.

"Not that I know about." Emmie gave the lock a tug, and the rusty chain scratched at the tubular gate. She had a sinking suspicion the neighbors had been the ones to put the lock in place.

She tilted her head back and looked up at the sky through the latticework of leaves above. It was almost dark, the landscape a miasma of purple shadows and indistinct outlines. She had a small flashlight and her cellphone in her breeches pockets, Tally's halter still slung over one shoulder.

Doubtless, all the horses were in by now. Tally's owner had probably arrived, and was wondering where her baby was.

"Stay with the horses," she said, stepping onto the lowest rung of the gate. "I'm going to go have a look around and see if I can find him."

"No!" Becca protested.

Emmie glanced over her shoulder and found the girl staring at her with horror.

"You can't."

"Why not?"

"Who even owns that place over there? What if, like, some crazy old farmer dude with a shotgun and a pitchfork is just waiting to…fork somebody to death," she finished, face going red with distress. "You can't go *alone*, Em."

"Someone has to stay with the horses." *And,* she added to herself, *if one of us has to get arrested for trespassing, better me than the kid with the bright future.* "I won't be gone long, and I'll call you if I need help." She touched her phone where its outline showed through her pocket. She grinned. "You know, if I almost get forked to death."

"You are *not* funny."

"And it's not getting any lighter. I'll be back." Without leaving room for argument, Emmie climbed up and over the gate, landing in a soft crush of ferns, and started off at a brisk walk before Becca could talk any sense into her.

There was evidence of Tally's passage: trampled undergrowth, more moon-shaped tracks in the soft soil, visible as Emmie passed the flashlight across the ground.

The sky retained color, but down low along the grass, it was already nighttime.

Something skittered in the brush and she jumped, sucked in a breath, berated herself. She was no stranger to the dark, or to the woods, for that matter. With the exception of Fred, Briar Hall was seriously lacking in the white knight department, and she'd learned to just suck up her worries and soldier on.

Still…

A little chill went down her back, light as the stroke of a finger. There was something about being five-feet-tall and wandering alone on someone else's land as night fell. She knew nothing about the people who owned this property, only that she heard the muted crack of distant gunshots on occasion. Becca's description of a farmer bearing a shotgun and pitchfork was a real possibility, one that left her mouth dry.

The clump of forest began to thin as she walked, last year's leaf litter crunching under her feet. Big flashes of indigo sky became visible, and then, swatting a cypress branch aside, she was striding into a pasture, a broad expanse of tangled grasses swaying in the wind.

Off to her right, a barn loomed as a dark shape stamped against the sky. It gave off that distinctly abandoned vibe: overgrown at its base, one massive door flapping idly. There were no lights, no vehicles, no homey scents of animals floating toward her.

What was this place?

A shrill whinny pierced the gloom, and she started, jogging forward a few steps through the tall grass. "Tally?" she called. She puckered her lips and made a loud kissing sound. "Tally, come here, man. I don't wanna hike all over this damn place looking for you."

"Don't suspect you'll have to, love," a male voice called out to her. "I've got him down here."

Emmie froze, heart slamming up into her throat. Her skin shrank tight over her bones, the sensation painful, as panic coursed through her in sudden, hot currents.

She felt like one of the horses she cared for: Stranger Danger! And a strange man, at that. She wasn't afraid of men, but being five-foot-nothing had its strength disadvantages when you were talking strange men in dark pastures.

She wrapped her hand tight around the flashlight and let the beam precede her as she stepped over the small rise ahead, and surveyed what lay below.

Two men stood in the center of a dirt driveway, both in dark clothes, one dark-headed, the other pale in the glow of the flashlight. The blonde had a belt looped right behind Tally's ears, holding the horse beneath his throatlatch with a makeshift collar.

It was the blonde who glanced toward her, squinting against the glare. "Put that away before you blind everybody," he said, and it confirmed her initial impression. He was English, the accent unmistakable. The words were said kindly, but in a way that suggested he meant to be listened to.

Emmie aimed the flashlight down at her boots. It was dark, but she could still see both men, and the white of Tally's eye as he glanced at her and snorted.

"Easy," the Englishman told the horse, stroking his neck. Something flashed on his hand. Rings, maybe?

29

Emmie pushed down the fear rising in her belly and took a deep breath. "I'm so sorry he bothered you," she said, pulling the halter down off her shoulder and stepping forward. "I hope he didn't damage anything. He's a boarder's horse, and we can't seem to keep him inside a fence."

The blonde man held onto the belt until she had the halter secure on Tally's head, then pulled it free and stepped back; slow, deliberate movements like he'd been around horses before. Greenhorns all shared a certain clumsiness. This man eased back smoothly, sliding the belt back through the loops on his jeans.

"No harm done," he said. "Gave us a bit of a start, seeing him come over the hill. I thought somebody'd be along to find him eventually."

She took a firm grip on the leadline, acutely aware of the dark-haired man's stare off to the side. His malevolence was visible even in the failing light. "Well...thank you for catching him." She clucked to Tally and began to turn him away.

The Englishman spoke again. "You came over from Briar Hall, yeah?"

She paused, skin still prickling, nerves rattling her breath. "Yes. I wouldn't have trespassed, but Tally–"

He waved off the explanation with a dismissive gesture. "If you don't mind me asking, how'd you get over here?"

She swallowed, and her throat felt sticky on the inside. "There's an old gate, just up that way. It was locked, so I climbed over."

"Ah."

When he said nothing else, only continued to stare at her, she cleared her throat and said, "Well, I'd better get him back...Come on, Tally."

She had her back to the men when Mr. English said, "How're you gonna lift the beast over, love?" He breathed a sound that might have been a laugh.

"I'll figure something out," she said, face burning, glad of the concealing darkness.

"Hold on," he told her. "I've got the key." A metallic jangle proved his point.

He moved up on her left, and Tally tugged at the line. She started walking again, feeling trapped between the two of them.

Her British horse-catcher wasn't tall, she noted as they moved. His chin was on eye-level.

So maybe, if he was a psycho rapist, she stood half a chance of kneeing him in the jewels and making a break for it.

His friend, though...That guy ought to be interrogating mafia rats somewhere.

"Briar Hall's for sale, isn't it?" the blonde asked beside her.

Warning sirens pinged in her head, sirens she would have heeded on a normal day. But she was tired, frightened, and emotionally taxed. "Unfortunately."

"Hmph." God knew what that sound meant. "How much does old man Richards want for it?"

"More than is polite for me to ask him about."

"You work for him then?"

"I'm the barn manager."

"So you run the place."

"Yeah."

"You turning a decent profit?"

"*Excuse* me?" She shouldn't be talking to him. She should just close her trap, let him unlock the gate, and then get the hell out of here.

"Does the barn make money?" he continued, unabashed. "All your horse-keeping, and lessons, and what have you. Is it profitable?"

She scowled at the dark trees ahead of them. "You'd have to ask Davis." A thought struck her. "Why?" she asked with a snort. "You interested in buying the place?"

"I might be."

That shocked her into silence.

Before she could gather a comeback, a low whicker issued from the brush ahead of them.

"Friends?" the blonde asked.

"Yeah."

"Em?" Becca called. "Is that you?"

"Yeah," she called back. "I've got Tally. Everything's fine."

"Who are you talking to?" Becca asked, voice uncertain.

"Your pitchfork-wielding farmer," Emmie shot back.

The Englishman made another of those indecipherable sounds in his throat and they ducked beneath the branches to get to the gate.

"No, for real," Becca insisted in a loud, frightened voice.

So done with this entire ordeal, Emmie said, "I have no idea. Some dude. But he's got the key, so he gets props for that."

She thought her English savior was laughing as the key slid into the lock and the thing came apart with a loud, rusty sound.

"Is he, like, a total serial killer?" Becca asked.

"Probably," Emmie called back. "My working student," she explained to the blonde. "She gets a little dramatic."

In answer, the gate squealed as it was forced open, long weeds and brambles catching at the lower rungs.

Visible only as shadows, Becca, Sherman, and Mocha appeared on the other side.

"Oh my God," Becca said. "I was so worried."

Tally whinnied to his friends and they answered.

Emmie hesitated, turning to her gate-unlocker. "Thank you," she told him, and meant it.

"Go on," he said. "Don't be losing hold of that nag."

She wasn't sure, but as she walked through the gate, she thought she caught the quick gleam of white teeth as he grinned.

Three

Dolly's quiet chuff of greeting from the porch was the first thing he heard as the growl of the engine died away. The Aussie/Border Collie cross was laid out across the top step, mismatched eyes trained on him, tail thumping the boards.

"Dolly-girl," Walsh greeted, climbing off his bike, taking the two steps up onto the porch and bending to stroke the dog where she liked it best, behind the ears. She licked his wrist and made a happy sound.

Home sweet home. Arriving, petting his dog – it always set things to rights inside him, eased the tension across his shoulders.

He'd left a lamp on in the front window, and it shone out on the porch, illuminating his keys as he found the right one and unlocked the front door. Dolly pressed in behind him, heading for her bowl and sitting in front of it expectantly. She knew the routine: lock up, set the mail on the table, hang up his cut, boots off – and then chow time.

It was a tiny house. Three rooms encased in time-eaten white clapboard, quaint front and back porches. Room enough only for one man and one dog. But the kitchen was fairly modern and the back porch was screened in. It sat a stone's throw off the railroad tracks, and the trains rattled the windows at night when they passed.

The front room was part-kitchen, part-den, the stove and accoutrements on one side, his one fat chair, the dog bed, and TV on the other. The back room was his bedroom, and off that the bathroom, with its wall-mounted sink and narrow fiberglass shower stall.

Walsh went to the cabinets, pulled down a can of Purina wet food and opened it for Dolly, pouring it and a scoop of dry Chow into her bowl and leaving her to it. He grabbed a Newcastle for himself from the fridge, leaned back against the counter and drank half of it standing up.

His mind was whirring away like a computer.

Of all the possibilities, there was one he hadn't considered until right this moment. Briar Hall falling into the wrong hands spelled discovery for the Dogs. No one was aware of the connection between the club and the cattle property. At least...that had always been the case. But if that little barn manager had gotten a good enough look at either of them...

The girl came back to him, what he'd been able to see of her. Small, well below his own insubstantial height. Pale hair – it had seemed to glow in the gathering dark. And that faint sharp edge he'd always associated with horse women. Handling animals that large and dangerous had a way of washing all the silliness out of a person.

But even the most practical of civilians could prove a liability.

He pushed her out of his mind for the moment. Now wasn't the time to try and recall the exact golden shade of her hair. She'd done something more impactful than provide him with a few moments' entertainment. She'd pressed home the urgency of their situation. That farm couldn't fall into anyone's hands but theirs.

~*~

Emmie pulled off her left boot with a sharp tug and a grunt, then fell boneless onto the bench just inside her front door, too exhausted and harried to face the task of showering just yet. Catching Tally had been only the beginning.

She and Becca had returned to the barn spotted with beggar lice, sweaty, and grumpy from managing Tally on the ride back, only to find that the barn had been beset upon by not one, but two problems. First had been Tally's owner, Patricia Cross, red-faced and frantic as she demanded accommodations for her horse. The fences must be built higher. The pasture situation must be re-evaluated; surely Tally jumped because he was being chased, not because he was making mischief. More food, that's what he needed; his rations needed increasing because he was jumping to get to better grass, the poor hungry baby.

Becca, stressed and eighteen, had said, "We can't change the whole freaking barn for one horse." She'd clapped her hand over her mouth, eyes closing in regret the moment the words left her lips, but it was too late. Damage done. Patricia exploded, words pouring out of her in an angry tirade. It had taken Emmie fifteen minutes to smooth things over, and even then, there was still no solution to the Tally problem.

Then there'd been Brett.

Brett Richards was Davis's ne'r do well grandson, her mentor Amy's son, and had been given the title of groundskeeper and an undeserved paycheck as a means to (unsuccessfully) keep him out of further trouble. He mowed the grass when it suited him. Most of the time, he was meddling in barn business and making life difficult for the Briar Hall employees he deemed lesser than himself, him being related to the owner and all that.

Tonight, he'd taken the tractor and manure spreader, who knew why, which meant Fred couldn't empty the spreader and prepare it for the next day's stall-cleaning. Emmie spent a half hour tracking the equipment down, only to be told by Brett that she'd get the tractor back "when he felt like giving it to her."

What she should have done was march up to the house and inform Davis of the problem. What she did was flip Brett the bird, conduct one last sweep through the barn, shut out the lights and lug herself up the stairs to her apartment.

Exhaustion fell across her, made it hard to breathe. Not just physical, but mental, emotional – total exhaustion, the kind that left her unsteady. She let her head fall back against the smooth plank wall and stared up at the rough-hewn beams of the slanted ceiling.

She loved her apartment. It was a large loft space, with dark timber and plank walls, so it gave the feeling of living in a cabin. Her bed was tucked beneath one eave, leaving plenty of room for her small kitchen, café table, dresser, steamer trunk and desk. Her clothes were on open, wheeled racks, pilfered from a going-out-of-business Dress Barn. The bathroom was hidden in the far corner. It was cozy, comfy, perfect for her.

And she'd have to leave it behind when the farm sold.

Her phone rang and she groaned. "What now?" She checked the wall clock as she pulled the cell from her pocket. Ten till nine. "Hello?" she answered.

"Emmie, it's Joan," a familiar voice said on the other end. Deep sigh. "I'm sorry, doll, but you're gonna have to come get your daddy."

She closed her eyes, fighting the scream that welled in her throat. She swallowed and said, "How long's he been there?"

"Since three." Which meant he was good and pickled at this point.

"Right. On my way." She disconnected and reached for her boots.

Maybe, she thought, if this horse business didn't work out, she ought to go into bartending. If nothing else, her dad would enjoy the family discount.

~*~

It was five-forty-five the next morning when Walsh pulled into the Lécuyer driveway. The little white house was ablaze with light already at this early hour. Parents of one-year-olds didn't sleep late.

Ava answered his knock at the back door, her narrow face appearing in the window to check his identity before the latch turned. Her hair was up in a towel turban, and she'd just done her makeup, the mascara still wet in the glow of the mudroom lamp. She cinched her black robe a little tighter over the round protrusion of her pregnant belly and waved him in with a tired smile.

"Bit early for house calls, isn't it?"

He ducked his head in apology as he followed her into the kitchen. "Yeah. Sorry, love. I wanted to talk to your man about something."

She glanced at him over her shoulder, brows going up. A silent question.

"Thought I'd catch him before he got to the shop."

Before he got to Dartmoor, after which whatever they discussed would feel more like official club business, and less like two friends chatting.

"Ah," Ava said, and her smile became knowing. "He should be out of the shower by now. I'll send him out."

She managed to move elegantly, despite being seven months pregnant, leaving him to wait in her coffee-scented kitchen.

The house hummed with quiet morning sounds: a radio murmuring down the hall, rush of water in the pipes, low notes of voices. There was an untouchable warmth in the air, one his own small house lacked. That energy of two people and the bond they shared; it marked everything, from the hand-print on the frosted steel of the fridge to the multiple jackets hung up at the back door. There was a love in this house the likes of which he'd never lived with.

Mercy's slightly uneven footfalls announced his approach, and he stepped into the kitchen scrubbing his long black hair with a towel. The portrait inked into his right biceps seemed alive as his arm flexed, like Ava's seventeen-year-old face was winking.

"What's up, brother?" the Cajun greeted, setting the towel on the counter and going to the gurgling coffee pot. "You want?"

Walsh nodded. "I wanted to run something by you, see how it hits you."

"I'm intrigued." He handed over a full mug.

"Ta."

"Should I get the whiskey out for this?" Mercy grinned as he poured his own coffee. "Or…"

"Not yet, I don't think."

When they were settled at the table, Walsh thought maybe he should have waited for daylight, because this felt like a nasty confession under the glare of the overhead lamp. He took a deep breath.

"I think the club ought to buy Briar Hall."

Mercy blinked. "Come again?"

"I want to get a look at the old man's records, first, talk to him about net profit and all that – but I think a farm that big, and that exclusive could make decent money, if it's run right. We already said it has to stay a farm, and it has to go to an owner who won't cause trouble for us." He shrugged. "Who better than us?"

Mercy took a long swallow of coffee. "Okay, so nobody can make something profitable like you. I give you that. But how are we gonna come up with the cash to buy the place? We're not exactly...*liquid*, routinely."

Walsh made a face. "Still working on that part. Sort of. I've got good enough credit to take out a loan for three-hundred K."

"How much is the farm?"

"One-point-six million."

"Jesus." Mercy whistled. Then his expression froze. "Wait, you're not – I mean, I've got the mortgage on this place—"

"No. No, of course not. I don't want your money. I think the club can swing it, between Dartmoor, and if we take a loan from Texas, shift some stuff around, sell that strip club Lorenzo's been after us to buy. He's offering cash; that'd be a nice little bump."

Mercy took a deep breath, massive shoulders lifting. "You're the Money Man," he said. "I trust your judgement on all this. Even if I don't know what the hell we're gonna do with a horse farm." He snorted.

"Never say no to a money laundering opportunity," Walsh said, and Mercy grinned.

"Nah. Guess not." He sobered. "Ghost's gonna be the one to convince."

"I know. That's why I wanted to talk to you first. See if I've lost my mind – or if I'll have some support when I bring it to table."

Mercy set his mug down with a decisive thump. "Long as my girl and my kids are alright, I'll support whatever you need, brother, you know that."

A comforting assurance, one Walsh didn't take lightly.

~*~

The thing about being largely silent was that when you finally opened your mouth, everyone shut their own and listened. Walsh presented his farm-buying idea at a mid-afternoon church meeting, in front of the entire club, even Troy, who'd been dragged in for the occasion. He'd put together a logical plan after leaving Mercy's that morning, and he outlined it point by point, touching on questions before they could be asked, walking through all the risks.

"I want to talk to Richards about profits and losses first," he said, in conclusion, "but I'm optimistic we could make some money off the place. Not too different from running a strip joint or a restaurant."

Then he was done, hands curled on the arms of his chair, waiting for his brothers to come back to life.

Ghost was the first to speak. With deceptive calm, he said, "So the Lean Dogs would run a horse farm – which, by the way, none of us have any idea how to do."

"I do," Walsh said, and heard the creak of chairs as people sat forward in surprise.

Ghost's brows went up, an expression a lot like the one his daughter had given Walsh that morning.

"I didn't run the place, exactly. I was a jockey. But I know how it works, generally. And there's already a manager in place. Maybe we could keep her on."

"Did you just say you were a jockey?" Aidan asked.

Beside him, newly pathed and mostly silent at church, Carter said, "Like, as in the Kentucky Derby?"

Ghost waved for them to be quiet. "Isn't it gonna look real damn suspicious if the club up and buys something like that? What the hell would we need with a farm?"

"Which is why I buy it privately," Walsh said. "Everybody in this city knows I'm a recluse who likes it out in the country." He shrugged. "And I do have a reputation with money."

His bluntness drew a small grin from Ghost. "Yeah, you do."

"I like it, boss," Mercy spoke up. "It's the only fool-proof way to keep the developers the hell away from our place. Nothing like being your own neighbor."

"Horses can't be as high-maintenance as dancing girls," Rottie said, earning several chuckles.

Ghost still didn't look convinced. "This would be a *big* purchase. A lot of risk for us. Look into it. Go by and talk to Richards, tour the place, see what you make of it. Then we'll vote."

Four

"Dad, please go home." Emmie pressed the phone close to her ear and dropped her voice to a whisper, not wanting anyone in the barn to overhear her. "I can't pick you up tonight; I have evening lessons. Please, please just pay your tab and go home."

There was a long pause on Karl's end, the sound of his labored breath rushing across the receiver.

"Where's Maryann?" Emmie asked quietly. "She was supposed to be home today."

"Well, she ain't."

"Dad. Go home—"

There was a loud throat-clearing behind her and she jumped. "I gotta go," she told her dad. "I'll call you later, and you better be at home." She disconnected knowing that he'd be a puddle on the floor of Bell Bar in a few hours, feeling helpless as hell and sick to death of it.

Fred stood behind her, looking apologetic. "Someone asking about the farm, *chica*. Wants to talk to you."

She took a deep breath that didn't do much to fortify her. "Where is he?"

"At the tables. I told him you were busy, said he might need to wait."

"I've got lessons later, so might as well get it over with." Another breath. "Thanks, Fred."

The "tables" were the picnic tables around the side of the barn, in the shade of the roof's overhang, with a nice view of both arenas and whatever was happening in them. A man sat at the nearest, sitting with his back to the tabletop, elbows braced back against it, watching Melissa Harper put her horse through its paces. He was blonde, that rich wheat color that always seemed to come with a really thick headful of hair. He wore a faded chambray shirt with the sleeves rolled up past the elbows, jeans, and an impressive pair of scuffed black boots. He reached to scratch at his bristly chin and Emmie caught the flash of metal on his hand: heavy masculine rings, one on each finger.

His head turned toward her as she approached, and her step faltered.

His *eyes*. She'd never seen such wintry blue eyes, almost colorless, and luminous though he had them narrowed. She would have said his face was sharp and foxy, and it would have been a compliment.

"Hi," she greeted, recovering, stepping up to the table. "My groom said you wanted to talk about the farm."

He nodded, and something about the set of his mouth looked like he was about to smile. His eyes raked over her, top-down and then back up. "That's right."

The voice!

There was no mistaking it. This was the guy from the other night, who'd unlocked the gate for her. The mystery Englishman neighbor.

Thrown by the realization, wanting to squirm under his scrutiny, she kicked her chin up and said, "You really need to talk to Mr. Richards. I'm just the barn manager."

"Right." His gaze lingered a moment on her breasts then came finally back to her face. "I'll get to that. I wanna see the place first. If you've got time for a tour."

"I…" She did, but he'd set all her nerves on edge.

He stood, hands going in his pockets, and she saw he wasn't much taller than her. Five-six at the most. A compact little guy, but well-built. She liked how casual and very un-developer-like he seemed, standing in front of her with patient expectation.

"Can I ask why you're interested in the farm?" she asked.

He shrugged and glanced down toward the arena, giving her a look at the precise stamp of his profile against the barn wall. He was very cute, in a scruffy, weathered sort of way. "I like horses; been wanting a place of my own for a while now."

It felt like she'd touched an electric fence, the jolt that went through her. "You'd keep it a farm, then?"

He nodded, turning back to her with a wry half-smile. "Be looking for someone to run it, too, if you know of anybody who does that sort of thing."

She didn't want it to, but a bright spot of warmth bloomed to life in her chest. "I'm Emmie Johansen," she said, extending a hand toward him. "Barn manager and trainer."

His other hand was loaded with rings, too, and the metal was warm and smooth against her palm as he accepted her shake. "Walsh."

~*~

He was impressed. With the farm, yes, because it was gorgeous and leagues beyond the places where he'd ridden in a past life. But with little miss Emmie Johansen, too.

She was a tiny thing, prettier in the face than he'd guessed, with the full hips, ass, and breasts that made someone her size ultrafeminine. She was dressed for riding: black breeches with suede on the ass and inner thighs, tank top, boots that had seen lots of use. Her hair was a rich honey-shot gold, and though it was pulled back in a knot at the back of her head, he could see that it was wildly curly, little stray corkscrews loose around her summer-flushed face.

Older than she looked, he decided, because there was nothing young, dumb, or kid about the way she showed him around her barn. That's what it was – it didn't matter if someone else owned the place; this was her domain.

"We did away with the manure pile about three years ago," she said, gesturing to the spreader and tractor rig parked on a concrete pad beside the round pen. "Best decision we ever made. It cut way down on the flies, and there's no smell; Fred fertilizes the pastures on a rotation, so the grass doesn't get burned."

"Hmm," he murmured. The only answer he'd given thus far. He was mentally calculating all of it, running figures…trying not to stare at her ass when she had her back to him.

Emmie folded her arms loosely, gaze landing on him, expression closing up. Cautious, not sure what sort of game he was playing, but clearly in love with the idea of the farm staying a farm. "That's pretty much it. If there's anything else you want to know—"

"How much is board?"

She blinked, but didn't miss a beat. "Seven-hundred just to board; eight-fifty for board plus weekly lessons; nine-fifty to have your horse in full training."

"Moneyed customers, then."

Her grin was wry. "A broke girl's gotta eat somehow."

"Wouldn't want you getting too skinny now."

She started to retort, thought better of it, and her cheeks darkened with an embarrassed blush. "It's competitive pricing," she defended.

"A better bargain than Hawkshill," he said of a farm about thirty miles east of Briar Hall. "And rumor has it you run a tighter ship than them."

This time, the blush was pleased. "I do my best."

He nodded. "Call your boss-man, love. I want a word with him."

~*~

"Okay, who is that, and is he really going to buy the place?" Becca asked when Emmie joined her in the tack room.

Through the window, Davis and Walsh were visible down the driveway a hundred feet or so, sitting in Davis's red golf cart, red Solo cups in hand. If the old man was having a drink with this guy, then talks must be going well.

"He's some kinda weirdo perv, I think," Emmie said, frowning to herself. During their tour, the man had seemed both removed, and overly interested, a strange juxtaposition of energy coming from him. "But he's talking like he wants the place, yeah."

"My God," Becca breathed. "You think he'll really buy it? And let us keep working here?"

Emmie swallowed down her hope, trying to keep it contained. "Maybe. We'll have to wait and see."

~*~

Of all her roles at Briar Hall, teaching was by far her favorite. To let go of all the mundane problems of operations, get out in the arena and focus on nothing but student and horse, the dance, the knowledge that she could impart – that was the best part. That was why she mucked stalls and administered wormer and fielded a million questions a day.

She taught three lessons, and then checked her voicemail. Joan again. Daddy was falling off his stool at Bell Bar and needed to be picked up.

Emmie called her stepmother, got voicemail, and with a resolute groan went upstairs to change.

Forty-five minutes later, she was in jeans and a t-shirt, nosing her F-250 into a parking place in front of Bell Bar. She stared at the darkened windows and their cheery neon a long moment, gathering the resolve she'd need to go in there and walk her stumbling father back out to the truck.

It was a sticky night, and the sidewalk smelled like greasy bar food. Of all the bars in the city, this one was a hybrid of dive and gentleman's retreat, populated by blue collar types and tired suburbanite fathers. The college kids tended to go for the flashier haunts. And because it was usually a thirty-and-over crowd, this was the one public spot where the Lean Dogs MC seemed to congregate on a regular basis. There always seemed to be a black Harley or two out front, and tonight was no exception.

Telling herself that bikers only broke bottles over people's heads in post-apocalyptic eighties movies, she entered and went straight to the bar against the back wall, her father's slumped shape unmistakable on his stool.

Matt was behind the bar, and greeted her with a nod. "I'll tell Joan you showed up," he said of the owner's wife.

"Thanks." She sent him a tired smile, then turned her attention to her father. "Dad." His head swiveled precariously around when she touched his arm. "Come on, it's time to go home."

Karl Johansen had been a handsome man. Once. Medium height, thinly built, the only child of Scandinavian immigrants, he was the source of her blonde hair and blue eyes. He'd been happy. Once. He'd had a crackling laugh that startled anyone else in the room with its sharpness.

But what life the divorce hadn't stomped out of him, Emmie's mother's second marriage had crushed to dust. He was a shell of a man, and nothing seemed to matter to him anymore save filling himself to the brim with gin.

He searched her face a long, uncomprehending moment, his red eyes moving sluggishly. "Em," he finally said. "What are *you* doing here?"

The same thing she'd done the last two nights. "I'm taking you home. Can you stand? Here, I'll help you."

"But I don't want to go home," he protested, sliding down off the stool and nearly collapsing as his knees buckled.

"That's the only place that'll admit you, I'm afraid. You're about one more sip from being a fire hazard." She kept her tone light, even as her chest clenched tight. He was a sad sight, swaying and leaning into her, fighting to keep his balance. "Slow and steady, Dad," she cautioned, putting an insubstantial arm around his waist. "One foot in front of the other."

"But I wanted another drink. Em, hold on now – wait just a minute!"

"No, Dad." She squeezed his arm, praying he'd quiet down and keep moving forward. She could feel the eyes of patrons, their open stares. "You can have something at home," she lied. She'd thrown out his home stash weeks ago.

"Are there waitresses in hotpants at home? No," he said, much too loudly. "I gotta have something to look at while I drink."

"Oh, Jesus," she whispered.

Someone off to her right laughed. A waitress in said hotpants sent a glare their direction.

"Let him stay," a voice called, and someone else said, "Don't take away a man's hotpants."

This was a freaking nightmare.

"Dad, please, try to think beyond the gin-fog," she whispered. "We need to leave."

"Don't tell me what to—"

"Mr. Johansen," a familiar voice said, and Emmie snapped her head up.

The Englishman, Walsh, stood in their path, hands in his jeans pockets, head cocked at a curious angle. His expression was carefully blank.

Surprised to see him, Emmie didn't have a chance to respond to his quick glance before he focused on her father.

"Mr. Johansen," he repeated, "what were you drinking? Gin?" He gestured to the door and lowered his voice. "The gin in this place is nothin' but piss, yeah? Why don't you come with me, and I'll get you some of the good stuff."

Emmie opened her mouth to protest…and Walsh shot her a covert wink.

"Who are you?" Karl asked rudely.

"Friend of Emmie's." Walsh stepped to the man's other side and took a solid hold across his shoulders. "Here we go. Let's walk."

A hot flood of shame washed through Emmie. She wanted to crawl behind the bar, latch onto a bottle of anything, and try to wipe this embarrassing moment from her memory. Just perfect – the man who might be her new boss was seeing her dirty family secret in the flesh. Not even Davis and Amy knew about Karl's drinking problem. What a *perfect* impression she was making on this guy.

She wasn't going to turn his help away, though. He made quick work of hustling Karl out onto the sidewalk.

"Which one's yours?" he asked, scanning the vehicles in front of them.

"Tan Ford," she told him, and saw his brows twitch as he turned that direction.

Between them, Karl burped in a suspect way, and Emmie cringed.

"Puking is imminent, I think," she said.

47

"Right." Walsh took a firm grip under her dad's arm and sat him down on the curb, his feet in the gutter.

Karl pitched forward, put his head in his hands and groaned.

"You need a good heave," Walsh told him. "Have at it." And then he stepped back onto the sidewalk and took up a post beside her.

"I'm sorry." Emmie brushed loose wisps of hair off her face. "You didn't have to help with him…but thank you." She turned to look at him, trying and failing to smile. "Not exactly the impression I wanted to make on my new boss, but…"

Now that she was really looking at him, one aspect of his wardrobe leapt out at her. He hadn't been wearing it during his visit to Briar Hall, but now wore a black leather vest over his western shirt. A black leather vest covered in white patches. Over his breast pocket, she caught the words *V. President.* He was…

Oh shit. He was a Lean Dog.

~*~

Walsh saw the tension whip through her. In a flash, she went from tired and embarrassed to tightly-wound, even nervous. Alarm flickered through her blue eyes, their shine caught by the neon signage on the windows behind them. Her gaze wasn't on his face…but on his cut.

A typical reaction. So many people in this city – in any city – saw cuts, saw bikes, and thought *criminal*. Thought *dangerous*, *violent*, and *lawless*.

They weren't wrong.

But there were worse monsters than him on these streets, and those blended right in. Those were the *most* dangerous – the ones you couldn't spot.

"Something wrong?" he asked her.

She swallowed; he saw her throat work. Her mouth twitched in a halfhearted smile. "You mean aside from the fact that my father's a raging alcoholic?"

Johansen chose that moment to curl forward and deposit his liquor onto the asphalt.

Emmie's nostrils flared as they listened to the retching. Her eyes were laser-focused on him, though, a question and a rejection building in them. "You're one of those bikers," she said. "I didn't know that."

He snorted. "One of those bikers?"

She pulled back inwardly, composing the fear out of her expression, fiddling with her hair again. It was fast trying to come down and the dramatic curls were more noticeable than they had been earlier. "I meant…I don't think of…someone like you buying a farm like Briar Hall."

"Because I can't possibly afford it? Or because it's too fancy for me?"

She blushed and looked away from him, but her voice was strong. "You know the sorts of stories that get told about the Lean Dogs. You grow up in Knoxville, you're either fascinated by them…"

"Or?"

"Or you wonder if you can bring yourself to work for one." She gave him a cold sideways glance. "Thanks for helping with my father, Mr. Walsh. Don't take this the wrong way, but I hope I don't ever see you again."

Some inner stirrings of chivalry left him wanting to manhandle her father into the truck for her. But there was such a proud lift to her chin as she stepped off the curb, he stood back and watched instead.

Apparently, Johansen felt better after puking, and managed to stumble to his feet, crawling up into the truck with minimal help from Emmie. Walsh waited for her to glance his way once more, as she walked around to the driver's side and climbed in.

She didn't. He could sense the tightness in her, the way she was making an effort not to look toward him.

But as she put the truck in reverse, her gaze came through the windshield, and he had one fast glimpse of the raw panic in her face. Then she turned away and didn't look back.

49

Back inside, at their tall table, RJ looked like a kid awaiting the arrival of Santa Claus, about to burst with curiosity. "So," he said, tone mock-casual as Walsh climbed back on his stool. "Who was that?" He hid a grin in his mug as he took a swallow.

Rottie rolled his eyes.

Walsh gave RJ his flattest, most disinterested stare and said, "What?"

Undeterred, RJ wiped the beer foam off his mouth with a sleeve and kept grinning. "Do you have a girlfriend? Or is it more of a fuck buddy situation?"

"Bro, you have nothing but restraining order situations," Rottie said. "Leave off."

"I'm curious, though," RJ persisted. "I was starting to think you didn't like chicks or something, man." He lifted his brows with mock sternness.

Idiot.

"That's the manager from Briar Hall," he explained without enthusiasm. "And she runs a tight ship, and she already spotted Michael and me over at the cattle property, so it'd be nice to keep her on and not have to hire someone new, yeah?"

RJ seemed to deflate. "You mean you're not hitting that?"

"No."

"Why not? She's got a great ass."

"Why don't you go tell her that," Walsh shot back dryly. "And see if she can be a little more biker-phobic while we're at it."

"Ah," Rottie said with a little nod. "The cut freaked her out?"

"Women fall into three categories, mate." Walsh heard the grim note in his voice. "The ones who think it's hot" – he touched the front of his cut – "and the ones who can't get far enough away from it."

Rottie made a thoughtful face. "And the third kind?"

"Old lady material."

~*~

50

Karl's second wife wasn't at home, and there was evidence she'd been gone for a few days: stacked dishes by the sink, overflowing laundry hamper, pizza boxes on the coffee table. The place was a shambles, and smelled like alcohol and body odor.

Emmie helped her dad shuffle to his room, deposited him on the bed, and went into the kitchen in search of the booze he'd so obviously restocked.

She found a bottle of gin wedged behind the kitchen trash can, and she carried it to the sink, unscrewed the cap and poised the bottle to pour it all down the drain. She was swamped by the stink of unwashed dishes. Through the window above the sink, the outdoor security light was an ugly smear against a greasy night sky.

An outlaw biker wanted to buy Briar Hall. Wanted to hire her. Wanted to save her farm…

And do what to it?

She put the bottle to her lips and took a long swig, relishing the burn.

Brighton Racecourse
Brighton, East Sussex, England
20 Years Ago

The roar. Not the crowd – never that. He couldn't hear that roar for the one that had swallowed him whole. The drum of forty-eight hooves digging up the turf with each lunging stride; the great inhale and exhale of air as the Thoroughbreds dragged oxygen down into their massive lungs. It was the roar of the race, and this time, it was a real race, and not just a practice run.

Walsh was nineteen, and still growing, but still small enough to make weight as a jockey. This was a claims race, with low attendance, but his horse was quick out of the gate and he wore real silks, instead of jeans and chaps.

The reins bit into his hands, the horse was an undulating lightning bolt beneath him, and the wind scraped his face as they hurtled down the slightly-curved track toward the grandstand.

Lost in the track, he didn't notice the horse coming up on his left at the rail until the other jockey was angling his mount sideways. The horse's shoulder slammed into Walsh's horse, and his animal shuddered, staggered…then rebalanced.

Walsh shot the other rider a furious look, only to realize that another collision was coming. Forget pace, forget safety – this bastard was trying to unhorse him.

Without thinking, Walsh brought his whip down across the other jockey's face, with all the force in his small arm.

The jockey jerked backward, hauling on the reins –

The horse stumbled –

Walsh felt the bottom go out of his stomach as he watched the other horse go down on its knees, falling from a full gallop, somersaulting. The jockey went flying –

Straight into another horse's path.

Five

She was dreaming. Gin always made her dream. Knowing that it wasn't real, that it was only an illusion, Emmie lay still as Walsh climbed onto the bed beside her. He was still wearing that vest with all the patches, and he smelled dangerous, and his eyes were narrow, bright, and penetrating.

She was naked, but that seemed natural. She eased onto her back as he climbed over her, opened her legs so he could settle between them. She was the one to initiate contact; she took his hand in hers and brought it to her breast, jerked upward into his touch because his rings were cold against her skin.

He stared at her a long, unreadable moment, his expression blank.

"Please," she whispered. "I…"

And then he was thrusting inside her, and it was even better than she'd expected. They were well-matched size-wise, and his hips flexed generously against hers, creating a delicious friction as counterpoint to the heat and weight of him inside her.

Emmie closed her eyes and gave into the rhythm, let herself relax and enjoy it. She –

Her eyes slammed open and she was in her apartment, in her bed, alone. She'd kicked her covers off and rolled onto her stomach. Her face burned when she realized she was grinding against her mattress, flushed and damp all over, physically affected by the vision in her dream.

It had been a long time since she'd been with a man, and before that, it had fallen flat and been less than stimulating. She'd known the day before that she was attracted to Walsh – she was a big girl, she could admit that.

Apparently, she hadn't known *how* attracted. And apparently, dream-her was all hot and bothered about the biker angle, even if awake-her found it irresponsible, immature, much too dangerous…

And Jesus, hot as hell.

She rolled onto her back and exhaled loudly toward the ceiling. She was falling apart. The fatigue, the worry, this wet dream – all symptoms that a breakdown was in her future.

What she needed was a ride. And not of the biker playboy variety.

She checked the clock – five. Still dark, but that's what arena lights were for. She dressed in riding clothes and slipped downstairs to the dark barn, greeted by the contented, sleepy sounds of resting horses.

And by the stink of cigarette smoke.

She had no doubt who she'd find in the office, and when she flipped on the lights, Brett cursed, sitting forward in the chair he'd been reclined in, coughing on a drag of smoke.

Emmie folded her arms and propped up in the doorway. "You're smoking in the barn."

He kept choking and gave her a dismissive wave.

"So either, like I suspect, you can't read all the No Smoking signs out there. Or you're trying to burn the barn down."

Recovered, Brett scowled at her. "What you gonna do about it if I burn the place down? It's not your barn. Not any of your business."

"Considering I get paid to ensure the health and safety of all the horses in here – yeah, it's very much my business. There's over three-hundred-thousand dollars' worth of horseflesh in this barn," she reminded him. "That's three-hundred-thousand dollars you'll get sued for if you start a fire."

He shrugged with one shoulder, putting the cigarette back to his lips. "They'll sue my grandfather, not me."

"And that doesn't bother you?"

"Why should it?" he sneered. "What's that rich old fucker ever done for me?"

"Um, for starters? Posted your bail, got you sent to that rehab program instead of *jail*–"

"Shut up and get the fuck out of my business. You're just the goddamn hired help."

Inwardly seething, outwardly composed, Emmie turned away from him, and her now smoke-scented office. "Put the cig out, Brett," she called over her shoulder in parting.

"Get fucking laid and loosen up," he shot back.

Her face felt scarlet and hot to the touch as she flipped on the tack room lights and went for her brush box. Everything that ever came out of Brett's mouth was poison. He was an uneducated, unmotivated, and mean little screwup with nothing but insolence and thievery to his name. Exposed to it since childhood, she was long used to his nastiness. Other girls came and went, part of the revolving door of boarders, mistakenly thinking he was some sort of tortured bad boy with a genuine soul hidden behind his harsh outer shell. Emmie knew better; with Brett, there was nothing but shell.

So why was her face on fire after his last comment?

Just the dream, she told herself. Just her inappropriate subconscious hunger that had nothing to do with an attractive stranger, and everything to do with her stress level.

Yeah, getting laid would be a godsend. Only, she didn't do casual hookups, and she hadn't been on anyone's radar in a long time.

So saddle therapy it was.

Apollo whickered a deep greeting as she let herself into his stall. She had an apple wafer in her pocket and he nosed her hip impatiently, already smelling the treat.

"You brat," she scolded, feeding it to him on a flat palm. "You only love me for the food."

The big gelding snorted as if in agreement.

Grooming her horse went a long way toward relaxing her. The repetitive brush strokes down his sleek sides, the careful detangling of his tail, the struggle with a pebble lodged against his shoe – all of it slowed her heartrate, lowered her blood pressure. She was humming to herself by the time he was saddled, and her stomach gave a happy twirl as she led Apollo through the darkness down toward the arena, and its glowing flood lights.

The second her butt hit the saddle, every extraneous, nagging thought flew out of her head. "Alright, 'Pollo," she said, gathering the reins in a light warmup contact. "Let's see how rusty you are."

On horseback, she was distracted by nothing. Her mind was totally clear, occupied only by the loose swing of Apollo's walk, and then trot. Without thinking, her body adjusted, compensated, steered and corrected. It was like dancing, the perfect harmony of working together with the horse.

Her father had asked her, in one of this rare sober moments, if Briar Hall selling was a sign: She was too stressed and tired, and long overdue for a career change. But Dad didn't understand the way this right here made all the stress worthwhile. Nothing could compete with this.

~*~

The sky was lightening when Walsh parked in front of Briar Hall's barn. The morning was a pearly gray, thick drifts of mist hugging the grass. There was a rider in the arena, and he sat on his bike a moment, watching.

He recognized Emmie, the way her posture in the saddle made her seem taller than she was, her little gloved hands held lightly above the horse's withers. A big horse – her legs extended only halfway down its deep barrel. A heavy-bodied giant of a horse, black and shiny beneath the arena lights, his movements powerful rather than fleet.

At the top of the arena, the horse turned down the center line, and then began to track sideways and forward at once. What was that called again? A half-pass; yeah, that's what it was. A dressage move, executed with no obvious cues from Emmie.

She sat the horse well, neither hampering, nor over-helping its movement. There was little tension in the reins – she and the horse had a good working bond; he was listening to his mistress.

Walsh scanned the front of the barn, searching for movement or a watchful presence. When he saw none, he dismounted and walked down to the arena, pushed a hand absently through his hair, tidying it by some impulse he didn't understand. When he reached the fence, he braced his forearms on the top rail and waited.

She executed another smooth half-pass before she noticed him, and then it was only a flicker of head movement. She slowed the horse to a walk, patted its muscled neck, and took her time ambling over to the rail.

"You're back," she said without inflection, but there was a bright flare of interest in her eyes, their blue electric under the manmade light.

"Your boss is a busy man and an early riser," he said, voice equally blank.

Her gaze moved over him. "Where's your vest thing?"

"It's called a cut, actually. And I left it at home." Before she could ask anything else, he said, "How's your father?"

She cringed. "Asleep still, I'm guessing." Shame colored her face. "Thank you, again, for helping me with him."

"Always happy to help a beautiful damsel in distress. Twice," he added, grinning a little. "I think that's two favors you owe me, counting the night the horse got out."

She fixed him with an annoyed look, which he found more attractive than he would have thought. "I'm not loving the word 'damsel.'"

"Damsels never do."

"And even if I owed you ten times over, I've got nothing you want, trust me."

"Hmm. Not sure about that, lovey."

As hoped, her eyes popped wide and her lips pressed together. Something passed through her eyes, something that wasn't shock, disgust, or rejection. Like maybe she was feeling the pull same as he was.

Yes, definitely. He'd been around enough women to know when one was put off…and when one was interested.

Even if this one didn't want to be interested.

Emmie opened her mouth to reply –

And in a feat of bad timing, Davis Richards' golf cart came whirring up behind him.

The horse flicked its ears and let out a deep breath of mixed curiosity and surprise, but didn't spook.

"Good morning, Mr. Richards," Emmie said, before turning her mount and walking off.

Walsh took a deep, bracing breath and turned to greet the farm owner.

~*~

"Lean Dog. You mean, like, *the* Lean Dogs? The biker dudes with all the leather and all the riding together and that stuff?" Becca asked.

"That would be them, yeah," Emmie said, adding a scoop of electrolyte granules to the next bucket in line.

Walsh was still up at the house with Davis, it had been almost two hours now. Emmie had no idea if that boded well for negotiations – or if she wanted them to go well in the first place.

"I'm confused," Becca said as she scooped Farrier's Formula into the proper buckets. "Is he gonna kick us all out and use the barn as a motorcycle garage?"

"He says he wants to keep it running as is," Emmie said, frowning to herself. "Says he likes horses."

"Is he lying?"

"No idea."

"God, I hope he buys it," Becca said. "I so don't want to leave."

Emmie felt agreement wasn't necessary.

A quick rap at the doorjamb brought her head around, and she was surprised to find Amy Richards lingering in the threshold. "Em, can we talk?" she asked, expression almost hesitant.

"Uh…"

"I'll go feed," Becca said, stacking up the buckets.

"Thanks." Emmie dusted the orange granules off her hands. "Coffee?" she asked her mentor, and they headed for the office.

~*~

Though doubtless a maid service came to clean the house, Davis Richards didn't have a housekeeper or homecare worker. He made his own coffee in his massive, stainless-everything kitchen, poured it, and invited Walsh out onto the wraparound porch where they settled into white rocking chairs, overlooking the barn and arenas below. The silence stayed companionable for a while, and then filled up with expectation.

"That's a nice Harley you've got down there," Richards said in the deep, gruff voice that seemed to leave his throat with a lurch, like he was trying to surprise whoever he was talking to. "I didn't know you Lean Dogs could afford bikes that nice."

Walsh twisted his mouth in a wry non-smile. "You know I'm a Dog, then."

"I asked around. Talked to a buddy who knows there's somebody named Walsh who rides with that crew." He glanced over with shrewd assessment. "Figure there's not too many British bikers around here named Kingston Walsh."

"You figured right."

He made a phlegmy, old-man sound in the back of his throat. "So what's going on here? The MC wants to buy my farm? Why? Y'all need another crack house? A brothel? Gonna start selling turns with horses?"

Walsh couldn't suppress a low, dry laugh. "No, sir. That we're not doing." He added, "This isn't for the club. Not to be used the way you're thinking."

"But a man like you can't afford a place like this. Not alone."

"You're right, I can't." Walsh shrugged. "I have the club's support behind me. We're a family – we support each other. Just like you," he said with a pointed stare that made the man scoot back in his chair. "But the plan is for Briar Hall to keep functioning as a boarding and training barn."

"Why?" Richards demanded.

"It benefits our interests to keep high-density housing developments to a minimum."

The old man snorted. "This isn't a small town, Mr. Walsh."

"You're right. But there's no sense letting this place" – broad gesture to the land around them – "get turned into retirement condos, is there? The MC's all about tradition. About history. We don't like seeing old things plowed over to make way for new."

Richards' face was set at a stern, bulldog clench, but he was listening intently.

"And truthfully," Walsh continued, "I don't want to see that happen. Personally. I'm a hermit, Mr. Richards. I like peace and quiet. I like animals. I like your farm. And I want to buy it. For myself."

~*~

Though equine-inspired, Amy's outfit wasn't suitable for the dusty inside of a barn. Designer jeans, glossy brown riding boots, airy gauze top printed with brown-on-brown horseshoe design. Diamonds sparkled at her ears and throat, and her dark hair was swept up in decorative leather combs.

She occupied the ratty swivel chair as a queen would a throne, manicured hands curved on the arms, legs crossed at the knee. She did a lazy spin, eyes roving over the photographs, ribbons, trophies that decorated the wall. Some were Emmie's. Most were her own.

This farm had been her father's gift to her. Her four siblings had been sent to college. She hadn't wanted to go, had instead wanted to marry the young man who'd knocked her up with Brett. Davis had made her a deal: don't marry the young man, and he'd build her a farm. She'd accepted the deal.

And now, almost thirty years later, she was leaving the farm for a new husband, new life, new farm in Kentucky. And there was nothing Emmie could do about it.

"How's the farm coming?" Emmie asked, proud that she didn't sound too bitter.

Amy nodded. "Fence is all done. We're planting trees this week. A whole bunch of silver maples going down the drive."

"That'll be pretty."

"Yeah." Amy stopped spinning and pinned Emmie with a glance. "How're you doing?"

"I'm..."

She always said "fine" in these instances. But today, the word got stuck against the roof of her mouth. All her horse-related life, she'd worked to be easy, compliant, uncomplaining. She wanted to be a help and never a hindrance. She'd seen her quiet acquiescence to everyone else's wishes as a way to gain some career karma. That her dedication and unfailing good spirits would give her a leg-up professionally.

It had gotten her nowhere.

"I'm not great," she said, and Amy looked surprised. "I'm..." She glanced up and saw a faded photo of herself at age eleven, grinning hugely as Amy held her old lesson pony's bridle. She'd won her class that day at the pony club show. "I'm depressed," she admitted. "I'm exhausted, and I hate what's happening."

She offered her boss a sparse smile. "But what can I do, huh?"

Amy studied her a moment, head cocked. "I think you're burnt out, is what I think. When the builders close on this place in a few weeks" –

Emmie's breath caught in her throat.

– "you can take some time off. Go on vacay or something. You need a break. This place is killing you."

What was killing her was the loss of her childhood home-away-from-home. She swallowed down that retort and said, "The builders? I didn't think anything was decided yet. There's another buyer–"

"Brett told Dad he ought to take the developers' offer, and I think he's right. They'll pay the most, everything will happen quickly, and we can get this place off our hands."

"But..."

But what about Walsh? What about keeping it a farm? What about...

A little fucking emotional understanding, damn it?!

Emmie felt her face settling into a cold mask. "You aren't going to be upset when they turn your farm into a retirement village?"

Amy shrugged. "It's just a place, Em."

~*~

He knew he shouldn't, but Walsh just had to stop down at the barn on his way out. Something about Emmie's authenticity – that non-club realism that knew nothing of flirting and flashing skin – the way she took her job seriously: that called to him the way strippers drew the attention of his brothers. He'd had whores; he was done with them.

He wanted something...more than that.

He found her mucking a stall the old fashioned way, pitching the manure into a wheelbarrow parked at the door. Quick, efficient movements with the rake as she sifted through the shavings. She'd done this a lot. Could do it in her sleep. The easy way he handled his guns.

Walsh propped a shoulder against the tongue-and-groove, fancy-ass stall paneling and watched her a moment. She was agitated, the tension in her arms speaking to more than hard work. She was dressed as she had been on his last visit: black breeches, a tank top – this one pale green and tight.

"Where's your tractor?" he asked, and she spooked, bad as one of the horses she cared for.

With a gasp, Emmie spun toward him, stall fork lifting in an automatic blocking maneuver. Like maybe she'd bash someone over the head with it, if she needed to. Defensive. He liked it.

She calmed when she recognized him, but then her lips thinned in an unhappy way.

"Didn't mean to scare you," he offered.

"You *startled* me, is all."

He snorted. "Tractor busted?"

She made a face, nose wrinkling. "No. It's not here." She scowled and stabbed at a horse apple with the rake tines. "Brett has it."

"And Brett is...?"

"Davis's grandson. He's offered to till up a patch of his girlfriend's yard for a garden, and so he took the farm tractor to do it."

"Ah. Spoiled rotten little tosser, is he?"

A surprised smile split her face, turned it sunny and beautiful. She coughed a small laugh. "Exactly. The one thing I *won't* miss about this place."

"Miss?" He folded his arms across his chest. "You planning on quitting on me?"

Her smile collapsed fast, and her gaze came up to meet his. "You aren't going to get the farm. Brett talked his grandfather into selling to the developers, apparently. You're standing on the future site of Briar Hall Retirement Village."

Six

"Everything's all set," Walsh assured.

On the other end of the cellphone conversation, Ghost said, "Good. I'll see you in the morning."

The line disconnected with a click.

Walsh set the phone on the plastic patio table at his elbow and picked up his beer. The fridge in his little cottage ran about five degrees too cold, and there was a crusting of ice on the Newcastle bottle, the ale itself frigid on his tongue.

Beyond the screens of the porch, insects, frogs, and nightbirds filled the black night with music. Dolly lay at his feet, half-asleep, one speckled ear cocked for threatening noises.

It was a perfect, tranquil night. Which meant something was bound to screw that up.

As if on cue, his phone rang. It wasn't one of his club brothers this time, but one of his *actual* brothers.

"Shane," he greeted, slouching down lower in his chair.

A deep breath was taken on the other end of the line, from all the way across the pond in London, then Shane's deep, kind voice came across. "Hi, King. How are ya?"

Walsh was an only child. On his mother's side of things, anyway. He'd been twelve when she'd sat him down for biscuits and chocolate he'd been too old for, and haltingly explained to him that his father had sown his seeds all over the city. At the time, she'd known six half-siblings. In fact, there were eight, and even if Phillip was the London chapter's president, the man who'd recruited Walsh into the Dogs and by far his most influential brother, it was quiet, careful Shane who was his favorite.

"Can't complain," he answered. "Everything alright with you?"

"Aye." But that was a lie. The tension in one word told a different story.

"What's wrong?"

Another deep breath. "I saw your mum today. She and my mum were having tea at the Black & Tan, and I stopped by and...King, she's talking to Dad again."

Walsh sat upright, a jolt going through him. "*What?*"

"I know, I know, I never woulda believed it myself, but she slipped up, and mentioned him. She blushed this awful color red. She's lonely, I think. And she's been talking to him on the phone." Shane sighed. "For now, anyway."

"Jesus." Walsh took a fortifying sip. "What's she thinking? That bloody – She's having lunch with your mother. I thought that was a 'Girls United Against Devin Green' sorta thing."

"Me too."

"Shit."

"I'm sorry, mate. I didn't wanna get you worried–"

"No, it's good you told me."

The night sounds seemed to swell to a roar in the silence that followed. Walsh could think of no reasonable explanation for his mother to go back to the man who'd broken countless hearts – unless she was lonely. And he knew she had to be. In every phone conversation, she asked when he'd be back for a visit; wasn't he tired of the States yet? Wouldn't it be better to come home and serve under his brother Phil? If he insisted on this biker business at all. Why couldn't he be nice and calm like his brother Shane?

The beer wasn't doing the job. Walsh stood, Dolly's head lifting in question. He motioned for her to stay down and went back in the house, heading for the liquor cabinet.

"You still there?" Shane asked.

"Yeah. Still here."

~*~

The atmosphere was sharp, that crackle of static in the air before the lightning came.

There. Emmie spotted it through the stall window: a narrow white ribbon crackling across the sky. The thunder that followed was distant, but close enough that she knew she had to get moving if she was going to make it up to the house and back.

"Good boy," she murmured to Apollo, patting his neck in farewell. She'd meant to drive up to see Davis an hour ago, and had instead loitered in the barn, delaying the unpleasant conversation they were sure to have. Becca and Fred had gone home for the night; all the horses were put away. Nothing stirred but the cats after mice. The horses chewed hay, stamped the occasional fly, but it was otherwise quiet, the freshly swept aisle full of warm artificial light. Outside, the night was oily and sinister. She didn't relish going through it. Even in the Rhino, with the headlights on.

But that's what she did, swapping her boots for leather barn clogs, giving her hair a fast tidy on her way out.

The wind picked up, raking across her, dashing felled leaves through the Rhino's lights. The trees bowed around the big stone house, giving the impression it was heaving, like a ship at sea. Lights burned on the first floor, beacons drawing her through the gale toward the parking pad. When she climbed from the ATV, she felt the first spit of rain, a few drops against her face.

She needed to hurry.

But there was no hurrying Davis Richards. He did everything in his own time.

This was probably an intrusion, she thought, as she climbed the back steps onto the porch. Davis was probably ensconced in his favorite chair with a cigar and the latest Patterson novel.

Nerves made her pause at the library door. She took a deep breath, smoothed her shirt, reached to knock –

The door was open.

A stream of light poured out around the disengaged lock. It was only open a crack, but the door was still open, and the sight of it twisted her stomach into a tight ball.

"Mr. Richards?" she called, rapping once before pushing the panel wide and stepping into the library. "Mr. Richards? Hello. It's Emmie."

The room was empty, lamps burning, illuminating the walls of books, the vacant chairs.

"Mr. Richards, did you know your back door's open?" she asked, turning a slow circle, searching for a sign of life.

When she got no response, she went to the door to the study. Knocked. Got no answer.

Her pulse thumped in her ears. Her breathing quickened. The sense that something was wrong crawled across her skin like insects, tickling up the back of her neck.

"Mr. Richards?"

She turned the knob and pushed the door open in a rush, fighting dread. The office was as tidy as always, both green lamps on the corners lit, the light falling across –

Davis, his arms and white head down on top of the desk.

"God," she whispered, rushing to him. "Mr. Richards? Mr. Richards?"

Emmie touched his shoulder and gave him a light shake. He was warm to the touch, so that couldn't mean that he was...

"Davis!" she said, dropping to her knees beside his chair, pressing her fingers into his neck, searching for a pulse.

There was none.

Seven

The storm lashed the house, the thunder like fireworks exploding overhead, the lightning appropriately dazzling.

By contrast, the kitchen was tomb-like, its sterile stainless appliances watching her with blank faces, the drone of the fluorescent tubes drowning out the shuffling voices down the hall in the study. There were so many people: police, fire rescue, the EMT crew. And none of them could do anything for poor Davis.

Emmie had been standing, frozen, still clutching her cellphone when the fire rescue team came barreling in through the open back door. One of them had draped a blanket across her shoulders and told her to go wait in another room. "Most likely a heart attack," he'd told her with a sympathetic frown.

That's what happened to old people, right?

She had no idea why she'd come into this cold, heartless room. It was industrial and uncomfortable, but her innate Southern roots had drawn her to the kitchen. That's where you went in a crisis: the kitchen. And you made coffee and you looked for cookies in the pantry, and you soldiered on through the pain.

She was sitting at the butcher block table, an untouched mug of French roast and plate of Oreos in front of her. Waiting.

She knew Amy arrived when she heard the ragged, gasping breath coming down the hall, the sharp rap of boot heels. "God!" she exclaimed when she burst into the kitchen, arms already outstretched as she plowed toward Emmie. "Oh God, Em!" Her face was wet with tears, streaked with mascara.

Emmie stood and caught her oncoming hug, getting squeezed tight and squeezing back in return.

Amy dissolved into wrenching sobs, her face buried in Emmie's shoulder.

"I'm sorry," Emmie said, voice too-calm. None of this felt real. How could it possibly be happening? "I'm so sorry."

~*~

68

"I just..." Becca said, sniffling into a crumpled tissue, and summed up everyone's thoughts on the matter.

Just...

Because none of them could come to grips with what had happened.

Emmie reached over and patted the girl on the shoulder, earning a grateful, tear-stained smile in return. She herself was in shock. Physically cold, shivering, and detached in her mind. She'd been like this before, the day her mother announced she was leaving Karl and marrying someone else. The day she'd buried her first horse beneath a sweet gum tree out in the pasture beyond the window. She was no stranger to shock.

Fred stood leaning against the barn office fridge, arms folded, head bowed. He was stoic in the extreme, but his face had been grave when she told him.

Gruff and stern though he'd been, Davis had also been a fair, kind-hearted boss. This was the loss of a friend. For Emmie, it was like the loss of a grandparent.

"But he was so healthy!" Becca said.

"He *looked* healthy," Fred said sadly. "But he was old, *chica*. It happens."

"But..." She jerked upright, grasping on an idea that popped her eyes wide. "The door! Em, you said the back door was open. What if...okay, hear me out. But can't like, you murder someone and make it look like a heart attack? I saw that on TV, I think. Someone left that door open. Someone *murdered* him." She glanced around wildly, searching for the killer as if he might be hiding behind the desk.

Emmie shook her head, but inwardly, she clung to that open door, terrified of what it might mean.

Fred said, "He was sick. He went in, and his chest was hurting, and he forgot the door. It wasn't murder." He looked sorry to have to say that.

Becca curled in on herself. "Oh. Yeah, maybe."

A heavy silence descended again. They had chores to do, horses to exercise, stalls to muck – and they'd been in here ever since they'd finished turning out, wanting to be near one another. Shocked into total stillness.

A sudden knock against the open door startled all of them.

Becca gasped.

Emmie whacked her shin against the desk and she bit down hard on her lip to keep from cursing.

Walsh stood in the threshold, in his cut, jeans, a green and white plaid shirt. Sunlight coming in from the open barn doors struck highlights in his wheat-colored hair. His expression was unreadable, his eyes white-blue and bright.

His gaze moved between the three of them, lingering on Emmie, and she crossed her arms, feeling like she ought to cover herself for some reason.

"You heard?" she asked.

He nodded. "Saw it on the news."

Another trowel full of sadness got heaped on her grief pile as she realized what Davis's death meant. "Then you'll know the developers are going to get the farm for sure. His family's going to fight and wind up carving this place into bits; they won't have any option but to all sell to Gannon."

Stone-faced, Walsh said, "Hate to break it to all of them, but the paperwork's already signed, and we closed yesterday afternoon. The farm's mine."

~*~

Dolly had nosed him awake for her usual six a.m. trip outside, and he'd turned on the TV like always, and there had been Davis Richards' photo up on the screen. Local millionaire found dead in home. Suspected heart attack. An autopsy would be performed. Everyone's thoughts and prayers were with the family.

Walsh's first thought had been *Thank God*. Because the accelerated closing, the quick transfer of property into his hands had ensured that Briar Hall was his, and couldn't be contested by any of the family.

His second thought had been *Emmie*. Because his little barn manager with the T&A was going to be devastated by the loss.

He was pleasantly surprised to find her dry-eyed, consoling her coworkers. She was in shock, he saw, as she stared at him. It hadn't penetrated yet that Richards was dead, and she was coping.

He was impressed again. Women like Maggie Teague, like Ava Lécuyer, hell, even Michael's Holly – they coped, shoving the grief down in the heat of the moment and handling what needed to be handled. Like he'd told Rottie and RJ – the old ladies.

He wouldn't have blamed Emmie Johansen for sobbing like the teenage Becca beside her, but he was glad she wasn't.

He opened his mouth to ask her if she'd step outside with him a moment, but she was on her feet before he could form the question.

"Let's go out to the tables," she said as she walked toward and then past him, her stride brisk, boot heels clicking over the concrete.

Walsh followed her out the front doors and around to the pavilion. Emmie sat not on the bench of a picnic table, but the tabletop itself, small hands gripping the edge hard. Her face was grave, her eyes tired, but she didn't have that red, puffy look of a woman who'd been crying.

With all professionalism stripped away, she stared at him with obvious suspicion. "How the hell did you manage this?"

"The process started before I ever showed up. Richards said over the phone he wanted to sell to anybody besides those developer wankers. Even," he said with a wry half-smile, "an outlaw biker."

She looked like she'd been punched. "*What?*"

"We closed yesterday afternoon."

"How?"

Walsh wasn't the international Money Man for every chapter of the Dogs because he was slow on the uptake. Before he'd ever talked to Ghost, he'd initiated contact with Richards, set the closing process in motion, set everything up with Ethan as

71

if the sale would be green-lighted. He'd figured it better to back out than drag his feet, and he'd been right.

He wanted to smile at her again. "You do know how real estate works, right?"

She waved a hand, like she wanted to swat at him. "I don't understand. Amy said Brett had talked everyone into selling to Gannon."

"He was trying to do that. Richards didn't want this place to get bulldozed. Turns out, he was as sentimental about it as you are. When I agreed to keep all his staff on, that was the final push – he sold to me without contest. I didn't even have the house inspected. Wham–bam, and all that."

"I…" She rubbed at her eyes, wincing as if they hurt. If she'd found the body last night, then she hadn't slept. She was too tired to make sense of this.

"You own it?" she asked, voice strained. "You really, legally, honest to God own Briar Hall?"

"I do."

"Shit," she said, dazed. "Shit…" And then in a flurry, she burst up from the table, leapt down, and flung her arms around his neck. She trembled all over, the shiver passing into him as her breasts pressed into his chest. "Thank God," she whispered, and he felt her breath against his neck, warm and gasping. "Thank you, thank you."

His imagination conjured an alternative scenario, one in which her arms were wrapped around him, and she was gasping against his neck for a very different reason.

"Thought you couldn't work for a big scary biker."

She pulled back, and then seemed to realize what she'd done and withdrew her hands, pressing them together in a nervous gesture. She smiled though – one of those breathless relieved smiles that had little to do with joy. "Finding a loved one dead tends to change your perspective," she said. "And…" Her brows went up. "Biker, maybe, but you're not very big."

"I could resent that, you know."

She snorted.

"I'm big where it counts."

72

"Ew," she said without inflection. Her smile dropped away, eyes widening in sudden dread. "Oh, man. The family. Amy and her brothers and sisters."

"What about 'em?"

"They're going to be *pissed*. Shit." She rubbed at her forehead like she had a stress headache and paced away from him. "They wanted to sell to the developer. They thought Gannon would give them more money." She glanced over. "How much did you give him, by the way?"

"Full asking price."

She whistled. "Not that it's my business."

"It's not."

"But that'll help. It's all about the money with them, so that'll definitely help." She dropped onto the picnic table bench with a deep sigh. "Okay, so…"

"Emmie?"

"Yeah?"

"Who gives a shit if the guy's bastard kids are pissed off?"

She stared at him. Blinked.

"They can't do anything. This isn't their farm."

"It's…" She sucked in a breath. "It's not, is it?" Her smile was exhausted and wobbly. "It's not."

"Leave the kids to me. You don't have to worry about any of that anymore."

She shivered hard, a full body chill moving through her.

"You alright?"

She kept smiling, shaking her head. "Fine."

~*~

Emmie felt relieved. A big, overwhelming, muscle-relaxing relief that she couldn't blame on the hot shower she was taking. It bothered her – she should be sobbing like Becca – but there was nothing to do about it. All the dread that had lay coiled in her belly like a snake for the past weeks was gone. Briar Hall was staying Briar Hall. She was keeping her job. Nothing was changing…

Well, she assumed nothing was changing. She hadn't asked Walsh about her salary, or talked much about barn policy, or inquired as to any changes he might want to make.

Assuming he wanted to make any. Assuming this was a legitimate venture for him, and not some strategic MC move –

Shit. She'd seen that on TV. Clubs like the Lean Dogs owned all kinds of business that served as fronts. Hell – the Dogs had all those shops down on Industrial, that big Dartmoor complex.

What if Walsh was going to run drugs out of Briar Hall? What if…

Stop, she told herself. Be glad for the moment, and worry about the rest later.

Becca and Fred had told her to go up and grab a nap, that they'd take care of all the afternoon chores, but Emmie knew that would be impossible. She was always too tense to sleep during the day, and she felt guilty taking any time off from work. She couldn't remember the last time she'd gone on vacation.

After her shower, she dressed in cutoffs and a tank top, not worried about saddle time today. Today was all about muddling through and handling the inevitable fallout with the Richards clan.

She only made it as far as the bottom of her apartment steps when the shit hit the fan. Becca was waiting, nibbling at her lower lip, bouncing one foot with the toe braced on the concrete. Her eyes flared unhappily.

"Amy and Manny are in the office waiting on you."

All the muscles that had relaxed under the hot water immediately tightened. "Awesome."

Eight

There were five Richards siblings, it turned out, each one more distraught than the last: Manfred, Junior, Gail, Jan, and Amy. Manny and Amy, from what Walsh could tell, held one another in extreme contempt, and had been shouting, screaming, crying – on Amy's part – for the better part of an hour.

They wanted the sale contested on account of Richards' mental stability. They wanted to see all the documents, talk to the lawyers. They thought Walsh was a swindler who'd used grifter-magic to talk their father into selling to, as Manny eloquently put it, "a fucking white trash loser who couldn't even fucking talk right."

It had been halfway amusing at first, but now, Walsh was done with the lot of them.

He put thumb and forefinger in his mouth and whistled loud enough to burst their eardrums.

"Ah!" Amy yelled, clapping her hands over her ears. She was a beautiful woman in a physical sense, but she'd cried off all her makeup and her face was blotchy and swollen beneath. Listening to her talk to her siblings had turned her truly hideous in his eyes.

"Who the hell do you–" Manny started.

"Shut up," Walsh said in his calmest, flattest, most emotionless voice. With his accent, it always got under Americans' skin. It was the voice that had launched prospects into action. The voice that had sent club sluts stumbling out of his bed in search of their clothes.

"If you wanna cry about it, do it somewhere else," he continued. "This place – not yours. And you" – he pointed at Manny – "and you" – the rest of them – "just lost your goddamn father, and you're bitching about where his estate ended up? Shame. Shame on all you assholes. Take the money I gave him, and get the fuck off my property before I call the cops."

The women stared at him agog, mouths falling open.

"Go on." He gave them a little wave. "Off you go."

75

They fumed a moment, but ultimately turned around.

Manfred lingered, glaring.

"Oh," Walsh told him, "and if I hear of you down there yelling at my manager again, you're gonna find out the difference between a biker and a *real* biker, mate. We clear?"

Manny said something that sounded like "fuck you," and stalked off after his brother and sisters.

Walsh was then alone, in his new front yard, looking down at his new farm, more than a little stunned with the turns of life that had led him to this point.

Technically, it was the club's farm, and the Knoxville crew was going to do a major run as favor to Texas for their loan.

But in this moment, he felt proprietary and peaceful inside. He did love farms. Oh, how he loved farms.

It was evening, and the low sounds of horses nickering floated up from the barn. He watched the Richards all leave in their various cars, and then climbed the porch steps, went into the expansive house, its industrial kitchen, and found the champagne he'd left in the fridge earlier.

He glanced around the room as he stripped off the foil. The appliances would probably stay, but the table, the dishes, the pots and pans – all of the furniture in the rest of the house – would no doubt be hauled away by Richards' children. It was theirs, after all. The house hadn't been sold furnished. And Walsh wouldn't miss any of it – it was just stuff. But he would be in the lurch furniture-wise. His own bed, table, and TV wouldn't go far toward filling this cavernous home.

Any regret he felt over Davis Richards' death was slotted in his usual Unpleasant Things mental drawer, and he went back out to the porch to enjoy his chilled champagne on the porch, overlooking his new domain.

He'd just gotten settled in a rocking chair when he noticed a lone figure cresting the driveway, cutting across the flagstone path toward him. Emmie had swapped her riding outfit for short cutoffs and another tank top, this one navy. Instead of boots, she wore a pair of those ugly leather Dansko clogs every chick at every barn wore.

Her hair was down, and that pleased him into a momentary stupor. It was sheared straight off at the ends just below her shoulders, and was a tangle of tight curls, a dozen different shades of blonde.

He liked for his women to look like women, and her combination of curvy and fit, small but emotionally sharp-edged was pushing all of his buttons.

She reached the base of the porch steps and paused, looking up at him. "Can I come up?" she asked.

He bit back a smile. "You don't have to ask that."

"I always did before…not because he asked me…I just…" She shook her head hard and walked up the few steps, clogs loud on the wood. "Sorry. Old habits."

"S'alright."

She came to the chair beside him, hesitated, then sat, arms braced on the chair arms that were really too tall for her, looking stiff and uncomfortable.

"No lessons tonight?"

"They all canceled. Because of what happened."

"Figured."

She looked down at her lap and fiddled with the frayed hems of her shorts, then gathered a breath and looked over at him. "I realized there's some things we didn't talk about. Important, boss/employee stuff. I think we ought to walk through it."

He couldn't help it: it was a small disappointment that she hadn't come up here just to see him. Then again, he wouldn't have wanted her if she'd been that kind of girl, would he?

"Yeah." He fitted a thumb at the base of the champagne cork and sent it flying with a fast movement. Emmie gasped at the loud *pop*. "I'm celebrating," he explained, taking a long swig of the foaming crystal bubbles. "I can drink and listen at the same time."

She looked flustered. "Okay."

He gestured for her to continue.

"Right. Okay. Well, we didn't discuss salary before."

He shrugged. "It won't change. I went over all that with Richards."

Her brows plucked in surprise. "Yeah, but I thought…" she trailed off, lips compressing like she'd thought better of it.

"You thought I'd shaft you?" he asked.

"No. I didn't think – this is just a bit of a change, is all. I sort of…" She gestured around her head with both hands.

"The salary won't change. Not for you or the other two. How do you pronounce Fred's real name, by the way?"

"He won't tell me."

"Well, I can copy it down on a check, at any rate. So it's all good. No worries for you."

"I can't help it. I'm a worrier."

"Anal retentive, are we?"

"No." She looked scandalized by the idea. "Practical."

Walsh nodded, trying not to laugh. Her presence left him in better spirits than anything had in a long while. "Alright, Miss Practical." He leaned toward her and offered the champagne bottle. "Stop raining on my parade."

She looked at the bottle, then at his face. He was delighted to realize she'd put on lip gloss for this little chat. Not so practical after all, was she?

"I don't have hepatitis, love."

Still staring at him, her hand extended slowly.

"You're not one of those no-drinking religious types, are you?"

Lips compressing, she took the bottle and lifted it to her mouth, took a healthy sip. His eyes followed the way her lips pursed around the bottle where his had been. The way her throat moved as she swallowed.

"At least, I don't think I have hepatitis," he said, and she choked, eyes going huge as she fought to keep the champagne in her mouth.

"Joking," he said mildly. "I don't fuck around with the club sluts."

Finally recovered, Emmie thrust the bottle back toward him, her expression angrier than it should have been. "Oh, *that's* a nice thought. Excuse me, I've got to–"

"Run go sit by yourself up in that apartment that smells like horse shit?"

"It doesn't *smell*," she insisted. She was getting to that adorable, indignant state of annoyance. "And I–"

"Just want to be a martyr?"

"Would you stop it?"

"Would you sit down and drink your damn champagne?" he countered, without inflection.

Emmie had been pitched forward in her chair, and all but threw herself back, lifting the bottle and taking another swig.

"You won, love," Walsh added. "You've got your farm, your job, your students, and you never have to deal with those pricks again. Be happy about that."

She looked like she wanted to say something, but took another swallow instead.

~*~

There was a reason she didn't drink very often. Two, actually, one being the fact that her father was an alcoholic and she was afraid that trait was hereditary. Secondly, because drinking always made her relaxed and chatty – and there weren't many people she wanted to be that way around.

Somehow, she'd managed to choke down half a bottle of champagne in the last half hour, and her worst nightmare was coming true – she was getting too candid with a hot stranger.

Because as her inhibitions were stripped away one bubble at a time, she admitted to herself just how wildly attractive she found him. No, screw *attractive* – he was *hot*. The weathered lines on his face, the thickness of his hair, the compact musculature under his shirt – hot. And he was just her size, too, which was an added bonus.

She stared at him, and he stared back with a narrow-eyed, unreadable gaze that she found unnerving at other times – completely enthralling now.

"What are you doing?" he asked, and she thought he almost smiled.

Shit, she couldn't tell him what she was sitting here thinking. She'd have to come up with a convincing lie. "I'm wondering what part of England you're from," she said. "And if everyone there is as hot as you."

Damn it! She wasn't supposed to say *that* part.

His smile was slow, sly, and pleased.

"Oh no." Emmie turned away and slapped her forehead down into her palm. The darkening lawn before her swayed. Way, way too much champagne. "Is there any chance you can pretend I didn't say that?"

"Not in the slightest."

She groaned. Gapped her fingers and twisted just enough to see his smiling face through them. "I didn't mean it, you know. It just came out. Like champagne-induced word vomit."

His laugh was quiet, but it did twirly things to her insides.

"Here." She thrust the bottle toward him, the liquid inside sloshing thanks to her unsteady hand. "Take this before it gets any worse."

"Worse? You gonna start telling me *why* you think I'm so hot?"

"I said 'hot,' not 'so hot.'"

"Big difference?"

"Huge." And for some reason, the word huge heated her cheeks until she knew they had to be pink. What had he said before? Something about not being small where it counted? "Shit."

He laughed again – what a smoky, wonderful sound it was; she had no idea a laugh could have a British accent, but it was making her blush all the harder. God, she'd lost all self-control.

She really did need to get laid apparently.

But then Walsh seemed to take pity on her, grabbed the bottle back from her and said, "So how'd you end up at this place anyway? Why's it mean so much to you?"

A nice safe, non-sexual topic.

Emmie lifted her head, squinted against the heaving of the lawn in front of them. Night was fast falling, and it made her vision even blurrier. "I was eight," she said, "and I wanted riding lessons more than I wanted to take my next breath. Mom finally relented, looked up Amy in the paper classifieds – that was back when people went to the newspaper for information, you know."

"Hmm."

"And I had my very first riding lesson on an Appaloosa named Cheyenne. He was a hundred-years-old, but he was sweet, and I – God, even though I was on the longe line, and all I did was trot a little, it was like someone had given me wings. Like I could fly. Like who I was, and what I was, what I looked like, how small I was – none of that meant anything. It sounds hokey, but it was electric. It felt like destiny clicking into place."

"You're right. That does sound hokey."

"I know, I know." She leaned back in her chair, pushed her feet against the porch boards to set it rocking. "But I get all hokey when I drink."

"And when you talk about horses."

She smiled. "Yeah."

They rocked in silence a moment, the song of crickets filling up the gathering darkness around them. She'd left the lights on down in the barn, in her apartment and the office; their glow was a happy one.

"So you didn't tell me," she said, "what part of England."

"You mean you weren't just trying to get in my pants?"

She snorted, finding his quip funnier than she normally would have. "Um, no. I really wanted to know."

"So you can come onto me?"

"So I can know who I work for," she said, shooting him a level look that was thrown by the way her head didn't want to lift off the back of the chair. "And for the record, I don't 'come on' to anybody."

"Shame."

"Not really."

"I think it is." His smile had dropped away, his expression more serious and thoughtful. It seemed to be his default expression: composed, emotionless, analytical.

Emmie liked looking at him – something about his features and the tight way he was put together drew her eye the way a well-built horse did at a show ground – and she was drunk enough to give into temptation. She stared at him without being too ashamed about it. "London, right? You've got that little bit of – something in your voice makes me think London."

"Familiar with the place, are you?"

"I cliniced with a trainer from London once. You sound like him."

He nodded. "London."

"Why'd you leave?"

His fast non-smile said so many things. "That's a very long story that doesn't need telling to a woman I'm trying to impress."

She felt her face grow warm. "There's not a lot that impresses me."

"Give it a bit. I expect that'll change."

~*~

Walsh couldn't remember the last time he'd been this cocky. Or talkative. Pre-club, he'd been earnest, awkward, kind with women. He'd hadn't wanted to be anything like his no-account, seed-spreading father. But then…after what happened with Rita…

By the time he'd joined the club, he'd become cool and detached with the ladies. Just enough effort to get what he wanted, and that was it. They were lucky if they got a goodbye afterward.

But somehow, now, the hard and soft sides of himself had coalesced into something snarky, talkative, and surprising. He was flirting with this woman, and he was enjoying the hell out of it.

She was watching him, her eyes a little glassy from the alcohol, her face flushed prettily, her breasts straining against her shirt every time she inhaled. He had a feeling she wouldn't be this talkative if not for the champagne, but he would take what he could get.

"Well…so much for being humble," she said, flustered by what he'd just said.

Walsh was afraid if he turned loose of the idiotic grin he wanted to flash, he wouldn't be able to rein it in. "You don't believe me?"

"You're not as charming as you think you are."

He started to refute her – and his watch beeped. "Ah, shit."

"What?"

"I almost forgot Dolly."

Emmie recoiled against the back of her chair. Too tipsy to hide her disappointment, she frowned. "Who?"

"Dolly. My dog."

She blinked…and then he saw the relief wash over her. So she was interested enough to be bothered by the sound of another woman's name. Score for him. "Oh. You have a dog?"

"You'll like her. She's a good girl. Good farm dog."

Emmie nodded. "We used to have a dog here, long time ago. An Aussie named Bert." Her smile was wistful. "It's been forever, but I still miss him sometimes."

Walsh would have happily sat there and watched her face cycle through one expression after the next until the drink eventually sent her off to dreamland. But Dolly was waiting, and that meant this moment had come to an end.

Unless…

"You want to come with me?"

She looked surprised.

"To get Dolly. You wanna come?"

Fear, just a touch of it, edged through the champagne fog. "How are you gonna get a dog on the back of your bike?"

"I have a truck, too."

"Oh."

"So do you?"

She swallowed with obvious difficulty, like a skittery teenager in a horror movie. "I probably shouldn't."

Walsh stood, wincing as every joint in his body cracked. "I only bite if you want me to, love. But stay here if you like. Be all lonesome."

"I'm not lonesome," she protested hotly.

"Sure you're not."

"I can't believe I'm doing this," she muttered behind him, and then the champagne bottle was plucked from his hand.

When he turned around, she was swallowing down the dregs and surging unsteadily to her feet. "Where *is* your dog?"

"Not far."

Nine

She was astounded by her own stupidity. No one in her right mind would allow herself to get into a truck with a confirmed outlaw, who was also a stranger, after dark, on the way to an unknown destination. Just stupid.

But here she sat, in the passenger seat of a Silverado old enough to have *Chevrolet* etched into the chrome bar across the tailgate, watching the headlights skim across mailboxes and shaggy roadside grass, breathing in the old tang of smoke embedded in the cloth seats.

She was quickly sobering up, the fizzle in her veins being replaced by an uneasiness that left her cursing her own slip. She couldn't believe she'd had so much to drink. Couldn't believe she'd agreed to go anywhere with this man.

A glance across the cab proved that Walsh watched the road with practiced ease, one hand cocked at a loose angle on the wheel, the other on the arm rest between them.

"Worried I can't keep on this side of the road?" he asked, and she glanced away, ashamed to be caught staring.

"Worried I'm about to be cut up into bits and bricked into a wall."

He snorted.

"No offense."

"Not real trusting, are you?"

"Not really."

"That's good."

Emmie took a deep breath and let it out in a rush, let her head fall sideways so her temple rested against the window. Her pulse pounded behind her eyes and she hated trying to make sense of the situation. At this point, she had to trust he wouldn't kill her, and accept the fact the she'd put herself right here, in this spot.

"What's it like?" she asked quietly. "Being a Lean Dog?"

He gave the vocal equivalent of a shrug. "It's like having loads of brothers. Lot of riding. Lot of work."

"Work?"

"Bein' part of a family that big isn't like being on vacation, love. Yeah. It's work."

Emmie frowned at her ghostly window reflection. She'd heard any number of things about the Lean Dogs MC: that they were ruthless killers, drug dealers, ex-cons, para-military types, anarchists. Some of the rumors amongst polite female society verged toward tales of baby-eating and satanic rituals.

She'd never heard it spoken of as a family.

"Brothers, huh? Is that why you joined? Are you an only child?"

This time, the sound he made was derisive.

"Take that as a no."

"Hmm."

"Do you have a family of your own? Is there a Mrs. Walsh who's gonna move in at the farm?"

"You've got a lot of questions, pet," he said, not unkindly. It almost sounded like he was smiling.

"I'm drunk, for one," she admitted. "Also, I'm getting to know you, remember? I've only ever had one boss, and he's dead now…And you're some sort of…well, I don't know what you are. Because I haven't decided what a Lean Dog really is yet. That's why all the questions."

There was a pause. Then, "Wait till your head's clear, love, then decide how much you really wanna know about the Dogs."

She was working to form a comeback – brain sluggish and heavy – when the truck slowed and lurched over a broken curb, into the patchy yard of what looked like a tiny shack of a house. The headlights washed across it and she saw that it was in good repair, the siding faded, but not termite-eaten. A lamp was on somewhere inside, its glow shining through a window. And on the porch, fluffy tail thumping and tongue lolling, was a black and white and blue Aussie-type dog, ears pricked up as she spotted her master's truck.

Emmie climbed out much more clumsily than Walsh – shit, she shouldn't have had that much to drink, for so many reasons – and heard him whistle.

"Dolly-girl," he called, and the dog barked in greeting, nails clicking as she scrambled off the porch to go to him.

When Emmie reached the front of the truck, standing in the headlights, she saw Walsh crouched down in front of the dog, ruffling the thick mane of multicolored hair at her throat. Dolly licked his face, panted happily – then turned to Emmie.

"Hi, baby." Emmie extended a hand to be sniffed.

Dolly did so, then licked her, and stared up at her with intelligent, mismatched eyes, one blue and one gold.

It was love at first sight, on Emmie's part. She joined Walsh, crouched down in front of Dolly, getting hit in the face with warm dog breath, smiling hugely.

In the headlights, Walsh watched her with what seemed like an approving half-smile.

Okay, she thought, a guy with a dog like this couldn't be all that bad. Right?

~*~

Walsh had never brought a woman to his house. It didn't matter that Emmie didn't go in, that they loaded Dolly up and turned right back around for Briar Hall – it still rattled him, a little. Nothing illegal ever happened at his little place. He held no ill-gotten gains there; the club had never touched it. So it was for purely personal reasons he'd been shaken to see this new pretty blonde in his life standing in his front yard.

He couldn't stop fantasizing about getting her in a bed somewhere, and that wasn't like him, dwelling on someone, wanting in this way; he hadn't been with anyone who wasn't a complete waste of hairspray in years. And years. Maybe ever, if he counted Rita among the list of nothing-specials…

It was one thing to have a woman at the clubhouse, where it was about the way leather, and smoke, and danger sharpened the sex drive. It was another thing to have a woman who was worth a damn see where he lived and pet his dog.

Dolly liked her right off. Of course she did; Emmie was an animal person. And when Emmie fell asleep on the ride to the farm, Dolly half-flopped across her lap and the two of them made a homey picture in the passenger seat. A picture that was less cute when they pulled up in front of the barn at Briar Hall, Dolly jumped out, and Walsh realized Emmie was out cold.

"Emmie. Em." He prodded her shoulder gently. Then less gently. Nothing.

She'd fallen asleep against the door, her hair across her face, and the blonde curls rustled as she let out a deep breath…and stayed asleep.

"Brilliant."

He got out and walked around – Dolly was already off smelling things, snuffling through the dark around the sides of the barn – hoping Emmie would stir before he reached her.

She didn't.

When he opened the passenger door, she fell out, or at least started to. He caught her and eased her back into the seat, so she was in a slouched, semi-upright position. She gave a very unladylike snort that made him grin, but again, didn't wake.

Walsh sighed. Tenderness was a dangerous, dangerous thing. It had made a complete fool of him once before, and he wasn't anxious to repeat the experience. Tenderness had served Ghost, and Mercy, and Michael, Rottie – all his married brothers – well. But for him, tenderness was only ever a trap. One he carefully avoided. One made less avoidable by what he was about to do.

Shit.

"Come on, then," he said to the sleeping barn manager, gathered her up in his arms, lifted her against his chest with one arm beneath her shoulders, the other beneath her knees. He was thankful for her smallness, her lightness. Not so thankful for the way she settled in against him and didn't stir.

The barn lights were still on, so he didn't have to stumble through the dark. The apartment stairs were alongside the office, narrow and steep, but he managed, even getting the knob turned and the door open without dropping his burden.

The lights were on up here, too, and illuminated a cozy, wood-paneled space that looked like a barn loft, despite the furniture. She had a TV and a computer, he saw as he crossed the room. The air smelled like shampoo, and lotion, and clean sheets, not like horse piss; a faint undertone of fresh-cut hay.

A comfortable, well-taken-care-of apartment. And a lonely one. He knew loneliness so well he recognized its taint here, the cold drafts of it that rushed across his skin.

When he set Emmie down on top of her quilt-covered bed, she rolled away from him immediately, tucking into the fetal position, spine curved like a protective shell against him.

Walsh braced a hand on the mattress, noting the way it dipped beneath his weight as he leaned forward to peek at her face. "You still asleep for all that?"

She was, and making a distressed sound in the back of her throat, brows crimped together like she was having a bad dream.

He didn't need this. He *so* did not need this.

Withdrawing, he found an extra folded quilt at the foot of the bed, shook it out, draped it over her. "Sleep in tomorrow," he said, though she couldn't hear. "Let the others worry about it."

Is that what he'd do? Sleep late in the massive four-poster bed the movers weren't coming to take away until the morning?

No. He wasn't sure he'd ever rest easy in that dead man's house. Davis Richards kicking off was much too convenient. And whatever the cause, he knew for damn sure the universe never shifted of its own accord in his favor.

Ten

"Michael…"

For almost forty years, his name had just been his name. The two syllables people used when they wanted to catch his attention; something scribbled at the top of his paychecks.

But when his old lady said it, when she was naked under him and he was touching her, his name on her lips was something to be savored.

Holly shifted, like his hand between her legs wasn't enough, lifting against him, the sheets rustling. Her nails dug into his shoulders. "Michael," she said against the underside of his jaw, that breathy, turned-on, helpless voice he loved hearing when he was inside her.

He grinned against her hair, the side of her face. "What?" he asked, fingers playing against her wet heat.

It was still dark, and so it didn't feel like morning yet. The birds were still asleep. The neighborhood was still hushed. No one awake but them, in this stolen moment before the day arrived and responsibility claimed their attention. A perfect, steaming moment to just be a man and a woman, instead of all the other things they were.

"You *know*," Holly groaned, and her hand slid between them, wrapped around his cock.

That put an effective end to his teasing.

He braced up on his arms above her, stared down into her flushed, heavy-lidded face – she was smiling, beautiful, hungry. God, he needed this. He –

A scream shattered the moment, carrying all the way down the hall and slamming into him hard as a fist at the base of his skull.

Holly closed her eyes, grimaced, turned her face into his wrist in a moment of pure sexual frustration. Then she composed herself and smiled up at him in quiet apology. "Hold that thought," she said, smoothing a hand across his chest. "After she eats, we'll pick things up again."

He nodded, knowing there was a fifty-fifty chance they wouldn't be picking anything up except the baby.

"Let me up," Holly said, grinning, giving him a little shove.

"I'll get her."

"Oh, you don't have to."

But he was already off his wife and dragging a pair of sweatpants on over his painful erection.

"You sure?" Holly asked, pushing up on her elbows.

"Yeah."

Holly probably thought that Lucy's sudden, shocking screams irritated him, but that wasn't the case. They freaked him the hell out. Whenever she started crying, especially if he wasn't in the room with her, he was already reaching for a gun, a knife – last week, he'd had the heavy silver picture frame that held their wedding photo in his hand and ready to brain someone with it when he realized it was simply time for a diaper change. No one was breaking in the nursery window, coming after his baby. Just routine kid stuff.

He'd thought, by six months, he would have stopped reacting with panic.

Wrong.

Every hair on his body had stood on end the first time she ever screamed, the day in the hospital when she came into the world. He'd been holding onto Holly's hands as she'd pushed, and then there'd been all this screaming, this pitiful baby-crying noise, and his heart had slammed against his ribs.

How did other fathers do this? How did they not camp outside their children's doors with AK-47s round the clock?

"Luce?" He flipped on the lights and the two lamps in the nursery came on, a muted glow that wouldn't hurt her eyes. "What's the matter..."

His automatic scan of the room took in the pastel yellow walls, the white dresser and changing table, rocking chair, pile of stuffed animals, photos and prints Holly had so lovingly hung on the walls, and Lucy squalling in her crib, red-faced.

He also saw, in the instant the lights came on, the pale oval of a face pressed to the window.

Masculine features, too little light to make out. And then he was gone, disappearing into the bushes.

"Fuck," he breathed. A jolt like he was hooked to a car battery shot through him, tightening all his skin, punching him in the sternum.

Michael bent over the crib and scooped his screaming daughter into his arms. Her face was wet with tears when he tucked it into his chest, but she calmed at the contact, settling into a dog-like whine that made him want to put baseball bats through people's heads.

"Shhh. I got you. It's alright. Let's go see Mama."

Holly was out of bed and cinching up her robe when he got to the master bedroom.

"Here," he rushed to deposit Lucy into her arms. "I gotta go."

Panic streaked through Holly's eyes. "Where?"

"Outside. There's something out there."

Holly gasped.

"Stay here." He pulled his .45s from his nightstand drawer, laid one on the bed for her, and palmed the other one. "I'll be back."

"Michael..." She looked like she wanted to tell him not to go, as she hugged Lucy and stared at him with huge green eyes. But she said, "Please be careful."

He left the house dark as he ghosted through it. Barefoot, he unlocked the front door and slipped out, the grass dew-drenched under his quick steps. His hand clenched around the gun until he felt the grip biting into his skin. The shadows down the driveway, heading into the backyard, were black and oily, statue-still in the muggy predawn air.

Lucy's bedroom was at the back of the house, shrubs and overgrown trees shading the window. Michael knew what he'd find when he got there, and wasn't wrong: nothing. Whoever'd been spying was long gone, no trace.

He didn't relax until he was back inside and heard the tumblers of the front door lock fall into place. Even then, *relax* was a relative term.

In the bedroom, Holly sat on the edge of the bed, trying to shush Lucy, the gun at her hip on top of the covers. "What was it?" she asked.

He didn't want to worry her.

But he hated the idea of lying to her.

"There was a man outside Lucy's window."

"Oh my God."

Michael hated the fear that crossed her expression, the way it was so much more than a typical frightened reaction. He swore he could see the memories cycling through her head, feel the way old traumas grabbed at her lungs.

He stepped up to the bed, sank down on his haunches before her, so his hands were on her knees. "Hey, don't worry about it. I've got this. He's not gonna get to you and Luce."

Her smile trembled. "I know, baby. That's really sweet. But it's not what I was thinking."

He lifted his brows.

"I was thinking I'd hate to have to shoot somebody."

Eleven

The sprawling stone house didn't echo as much with the Knoxville chapter of the Lean Dogs MC filling it up. In their usual grungy t-shirts, cuts, wallet chains and flashing jewelry, they looked out of place amid the plush, earth-toned furniture in the main living room. Furniture that was, thanks to the newly arrived moving crew, disappearing one piece at a time. The crew sent them darted, curious glances, but wisely kept their gobs shut.

Walsh stood with his back to the far wall, facing the opposite wall of floor-to-ceiling windows, his brothers limned in silver by morning light. He smiled inwardly to watch the very not-subtle way they couldn't stop gawking at the house around them.

"…so like I said," Aidan was saying, leaning back in a leather arm chair and kicking his feet up onto the ottoman, "you need a couple roommates. You know, keep you from getting all lonesome in this…" His eyes tracked over the stone mantle again. "Giant motherfucking castle."

"Just a couple?" Carter asked, unable to mask the hopeful lift to his voice. "Or more than a couple?"

"You can move in too, Jockstrap," Aidan assured him. "But dude, Harry, no. You blow too much shit up in the microwave."

"Not on purpose," the redhead protested.

"And we get first dibs on rooms." Aidan gestured between himself and Tango. "Seniority, and shit."

"Or," Ghost said, the only one not agog at his surroundings, "none of you move in, and then it doesn't look like this is a fucking MC headquarters, and we don't draw the cops out here on a regular basis to check in on things."

Aidan deflated. "Yeah."

Boots in the hall announced the movers were coming back in, and they all shifted topics as a seamless group.

"Is this place gonna turn a profit?" Rottie asked pleasantly.

Walsh hesitated. The movers were on either end of the couch where Mercy was sprawled, and when they tried to lift it out from under him, the thing only shuddered.

"Damn!" the big Cajun exclaimed in a show of mock outrage. "Warn a som'bitch 'fore you start stealing his seat! Fuck!" His expression had all the Dogs stifling laughs – and the movers tripping over themselves and the couch as they tried to navigate it out while scared shitless.

When they were gone, Mercy perched a hip on a sofa table and said, "You gotta keep 'em on their toes. A little fear's good for ya now and then."

Ghost snorted.

Walsh listened until the footfalls had moved out the front door, then said, "Actually, it's gonna turn a better profit than I thought. I went through Richards' books last night." Because he'd been too wired and restless, thinking about lonely girls with blonde hair to get any sleep, he'd sat up in the study with the ledgers most of the night. "The old man was taking most of what he earned off the boarders and giving it to his daughter. The youngest one, Amy. And to her son, Brett."

"To do what with?" Ratchet asked, frowning.

"To have. Dunno. It's listed as a charitable gift, which means he was getting a tax break on it. But he ought to be paying his barn staff a helluva lot more than he is. He could have afforded to make some barn improvements, get a second tractor, all kinds of shit. Instead, he was funneling all of it toward his family."

"His choice, I guess," Mercy said, but was frowning also. "Kinda makes you wonder why his kids were so anxious to sell."

"If he sells, then all five kids get an equal cut of his inheritance when he dies," Walsh said. "Which, well, yeah. The others didn't want him throwing everything he made away on Amy and Brett who, far as I can tell, are both fuckups."

The movers returned, giving Mercy a wide berth this time. They each grabbed a lamp and scurried back out.

"Either way, it's not our problem," Ghost said when the movers were gone. "We stopped the developers, and I trust you to make us some money off this place," he told Walsh.

As a general rule, Ghost didn't trust anyone, so his sentiment was deeply appreciated. Walsh never took for granted that, of all his brothers, he was the one who'd never endured censure or suspicion from the boss man. Had Aidan or Mercy or anyone else broached the subject of buying Briar Hall? It never would have been taken seriously.

"I'm off," the president said, pushing away from the mantel. "The rest of you losers don't forget you have to work today."

"I gotta head, too," Mercy said, "Ava's got a doctor's appointment."

"How's she feeling?" Ghost asked his son-in-law.

"Good."

They fell into step alongside one another.

"I'll go out with you," Michael said, following them. His expression had been darker than normal all morning. "I wanted to ask you something," he said to both men, and he was included in their knot as they disappeared down the hall.

Rottie, RJ, Ratchet, Dublin and Briscoe all had things to get back to at Dartmoor. Harry and Littlejohn were ordered to come along with them, still snapping to at commands even though they were patched.

Aidan looked like he had nowhere else in the world to be, which meant Tango and Carter were sticking around too.

"You know you're not moving in, right?"

Aidan made a face. "Aw, come on, Walsh. This house is big enough you can still be a hermit."

"Thought you were all about big life changes and taking shit seriously," he countered.

Aidan pulled his feet down and sat upright, some of the petulance dropping off his face. "I am. Which is why I think it's time I looked into branching out a little. Yeah, I'll still work at the bike shop, but maybe I ought to take on some new responsibilities."

"Like running a farm."

"I could help you."

"Do you know the first thing about running a business?"

He gave Walsh a shit-eating grin. "Nothing like learning from the master, is there?"

"He just wants to look at the girls ride horses in tight pants," Tango said, and grinned when he got a murderous glare from his best friend.

"Not true," Aidan said. Then, "Okay, maybe a little true, but I'm serious about the business thing too. I can't just be a mechanic forever."

"Dude, you told me there was nothing wrong with being a mechanic," Carter said. " 'No shame,' you said."

"There's not."

"He's moved beyond us," Tango said, grinning. "He wants to be *somebody*."

"Bite me."

But it was the truth, and Walsh knew it. Aidan had his sights set on becoming president one of these days, and in his own overeager, misguided mind, he thought becoming more financially successful was a step in the right direction.

Poor kid.

"Well, I've got a whole office of shit to sort through, and I know Richards' kids are gonna show up at some point today and gimme hell. So I gotta get to it."

"Is it okay if we look around a little?" Carter asked, genuinely curious.

"This is the club's farm, not mine. Do whatever you like. But" – he aimed a stern look at Aidan – "don't go spooking my staff, alright? I need them."

Aidan sighed. "Yes, Master."

~*~

"You didn't get a good look at him?" Ghost asked.

"Too dark and he moved too fast," Michael said. "I know it was a man, and I know he was white, that's about it."

It was a relief to be able to tell someone about this, and to be listened to in earnest by both parties. Holly had recovered better than he had that morning, feeding Lucy, showering, doing her makeup, fixing them both breakfast and packing their lunches like she did every other day, the only tell the mild haunted look in her eyes. But Michael's hands still shook, and he'd sucked down four cigarettes to no avail.

"Well that's shitty news," Mercy said. "Just what we need: peeping toms." He searched for his own cigarette in his cut pocket, as they stood on the shaded farmhouse driveway. "Anybody been paying lots of attention to Holly at work? She got a customer who's too friendly?"

That had been Michael's first impulse. "She woulda told me if she did. She doesn't like getting hit on."

Ghost and Mercy shared a look.

"Things've been real quiet, boss," Mercy said. "I hate to say it —"

"Then don't."

But they all knew: their fan had been shit-free for too long now. It was about time something sinister happened.

Michael was glad for the warm solid weight of Mercy's palm landing on his shoulder. "Call if you want help, bro. I could always use the target practice."

~*~

"That's really nice. Half-halt, bring him back, and then try another one down the long side," Emmie called, then forced another slug of ice water down her throat.

She'd awakened that morning dressed, sleeping on top of her covers, head pounding like someone had taken a hammer to it, and a telltale stale hangover taste in her mouth.

It had all come rushing back to her, and she'd buried her face in her pillow and groaned.

The champagne.

Sitting on the porch of the big house.

Telling Walsh she thought he was hot.

Telling Walsh she thought he was hot.

Going to get his dog.

And clearly, he'd carried her up, left her on her bed, and covered her up with a quilt, because no way had she been able to.

She felt like shit. But she'd showered, dressed, and was managing to teach her eleven a.m. lesson to Tonya with the help of big sunglasses and lots of aspirin.

"That's great, Tonya," she called, as horse and rider executed a lovely passage down the long side of the arena, Chaucer slow-stepping with high, snapping lifts of his knees and hocks. "Keep your hands relaxed, that's right—"

The rest of her instruction was cut off by the loud growling of motorcycles.

Emmie twisted around and saw a whole fleet of black Harley-Davidsons coming down the driveway from the house, cruising past the barn with a sound like thunder and heading on toward the road. The men riding them were all sporting the black leather cuts she'd spotted so often around town, their emblem of a black running dog on a white field clear even from a distance.

"What in the *hell?*" Tonya shouted, and Emmie whipped back around to see that Chaucer was spooking badly, shying hard to the left, tossing his head against the reins.

Emmie jumped off the rail into the arena. "Whoa, whoa," she called, approaching slowly as Tonya sawed on the reins and fought to get control.

"Easy," Tonya said, but it was a sharp command, and not a soothing reassurance.

One of the bikers revved his engine, as they headed out of the turn, a sharp blast of sound.

Chaucer lost it. Eyes rolling, mouth gaping as he jerked at the bit, he plunged his nose down and bucked. And no matter how talented a Quarter Horse bronc at a rodeo, a leggy, athletic warmblood could put any bucking horse to shame. Chaucer's spine curled the wrong way and his hind end flew skyward as if spring-loaded, kicking madly with both back legs.

Tonya was launched over his shoulder, managed to tuck, and landed hard on her side with a shocked grunt.

Chaucer, further distraught to have unseated his mistress, set off across the arena at a hectic trot, snorting and blowing.

Emmie rushed to her downed student, dropping to her knees. "Tonya, you okay? Can you move? What hurts?"

Tonya rolled onto her back with a big, deep gasp. "Fuck," she breathed, wincing. "Nothing, just..." Her pretty face with its smudge-proof makeup was dusted with arena sand. "Knocked...the wind..."

"Out of you," Emmie finished. "Hold on, let it pass. Don't move. See?" She smiled weakly. "This is why you always gotta wear a helmet."

"Is she okay?" a male voice asked, and she snatched her head up, shooting an automatic glare toward whoever had spoken.

Three men she'd never seen before in black Lean Dogs cuts stood on the other side of the fence, two blonde, one brunette, all wide-eyed and pale-faced.

Emmie couldn't keep the snarl out of her voice. "No thanks to you idiots."

~*~

As they'd walked down the hill toward the white sand-filled arena and the two women and one horse inside of it, Aidan's thoughts had been this:

Okay, that was a big horse. And it danced around like...well, like it was dancing.

The blonde was short, but hot. Nice shape to her. The sunglasses were very Hollywood.

Okay, the brunette? Ten times hotter, and that was with a helmet on and nothing but a dark tidy bun of hair hanging out the back. Her face was stunning even from a distance. Nice tits – perky, not too big.

Oh shit, was the horse supposed to do that? Was it...?

Yeah, definitely not.

Oh fuck, hot girl flying! Don't break your hotass face, baby. Or your hot ass either, actually.

She's moving, that's a good sign, right?

Blonde girl just lost ten hot points for being a bitch.

"No thanks to you idiots," she said, and he got twitchy on the inside. There was hot-bitchy, and then there was straight up I-wanna-cut-you-bitchy, and the blonde was the latter of the two.

He stepped forward, arms draping over the fence rail. "Is she okay?" he repeated. "Should I call 911?"

"I'm fine." The brunette sat up, and she was knock-him-out gorgeous this close. Even as she winced, took off her helmet, and stroked a hand across her sweaty, mashed-down hair. "I'm fine." Her gaze lifted, and her eyes were blue.

Really blue.

Without warning, Aidan felt attraction tackle him. Not the subtle, easy attraction of seeing a beautiful woman and wondering what he could get her to do. But the visceral need to have this woman's legs around his waist.

In a flash, he was over the fence and offering his hand down to her. "Here, let me help. I'm so sorry about all this."

"Then tell your friends not to rev their engines like they're in a freaking race," the blonde said.

Aidan ignored her. The brunette gave him a strange look, then grasped his hand. He saw her blood-red manicured nails, felt the softness of her skin, and he was sunk.

~*~

Emmie wasn't actually angry with the Dogs. She was angry at the very real possibility that her richest, best-paying student would be so pissed off that she moved her horse, or worse, started making demands around the farm.

Tonya, in a very unlikely move, let the dark-haired biker with the killer grin lead her up to the barn on the premise of "making sure she was okay," and Emmie caught Chaucer, took him inside, untacked and hosed him off. She was putting him away in his stall for a hay snack and a calm-down when the two blondes from before approached her.

Both were beautiful in different ways. One had the masculine, pretty-boy features of a former athlete and ladies' man. The other had a funky haircut, lots of piercings, even more tattoos, and that almost hid his delicate feminine prettiness.

The pretty one spoke, as she was latching the stall door. "Look, we didn't mean for the horse to get scared and do that. Sorry." He sounded and looked sincere, a graveness etched into his clear-cut features. "Is she okay?"

Emmie sighed, braced her shoulder against the stall, and focused all her weak patience into offering them a halfhearted smile. "I didn't mean to snap before," she said. "I'm…kinda hungover. And situations like that with the horses can be so dangerous…" She'd seen horrible accidents, yes. And she had been upset in the moment. But her new reality involved bikers, and if she had to choose between noisy tailpipes and no Briar Hall at all, she'd pick tailpipes in a heartbeat. "Anyway," she said, "it's alright. The horses will eventually get used to the sound of the bikes."

Obvious relief in both of them.

"We don't know anything about horses," the younger, more normal one said. "So…yeah. Sorry."

"Makes me wonder why your friend bought a horse farm," she said, and didn't mean it as an insult, was truly fishing for answers, because Walsh was a puzzle she wanted to solve.

"Because he does know something about horses," Walsh's distinctive English accent said, and she glanced sharply down the aisle to see him approaching. "He was a jockey, actually, so he knows a lot."

The sight of him set her face aflame. The skin heated until she knew her blush must be visible, even from this distance. Laying eyes on him – his blue and white plaid shirt, the battered jeans, the bedhead thickness of his hair and the narrow blue eyes – sent a keen awareness shooting through her. He'd touched her, carried her, been in her apartment, been next to her bed.

Her dream from a few nights before tumbled through her mind and made the blushing worse.

She cleared her throat and watched the other two guys step back, perplexed and amused expressions lighting their faces. They could feel the attraction coming off of her, and she hated that, but had no idea what to do about it.

"A jockey, huh?" she asked, and her voice sounded unnatural to her ears. God, what was wrong with her? Had to be the hangover. She didn't get like this with men. Ever.

He met her flickering glance with a solid stare that told her he knew exactly how much her insides were churning at the moment. "Till I got too tall for it."

"That'd do it."

He shrugged.

"So you swapped to bikes instead."

"More or less."

This was stupid, inane chatter, on both their parts. Stupid, she told herself. She hadn't expected anything to be different today. But had she wanted it to be? She wouldn't allow herself to dwell on that; it felt too painfully like she was hoping for something, and given what had just happened with Tonya, that wasn't a good idea.

Still…

She was suddenly more feminine, more lonely, more achy inside than she had been years, and for some reason, her body wanted this man. Maybe it was because he'd saved her farm. Maybe because of the way his shirt sleeves fit over his shoulders. Either way, she couldn't pretend that she wasn't wondering what his mouth tasted like.

"So you've met Tango and Carter," he said, like he was getting things back on track. "Boys, this is Emmie, and you're obviously bothering her, and you know what I said about that before. So." He lifted his brows expectantly and both younger men lurched into action.

"Right," the one he'd called Tango said. "We'll go see if Aidan's ready to leave."

In the wake of their departure, Walsh closed the distance between them, hands going in his pockets, gaze raking over her in a calculating way. He was cold and hot all at once in his regard, and it stirred up a deep tug in the pit of her stomach. It was a horseman's gaze, she realized; it had been all along. His mixture of intrigue and analysis was the careful, thorough look of someone used to measuring horseflesh.

And now he was measuring her, and trapping her back against the stall.

And Lord help her, she liked it.

"Problem with your student?" he asked, and his eyes were fixed on her mouth.

"Nothing an ice pack won't solve. And you can tell your boys to be more careful driving in and out."

He nodded. "I'll do that."

"You're the vice president; they have to listen to you, right?"

"They do."

"You put me to bed last night," she said quietly. All the logic was fast draining out of her head, and she was powerless to make a last grab for any of it.

He stared at her a long moment, then tilted his head toward the door. "Take a walk with me."

~*~

Dolly walked alongside them, her panting a sound that grounded them in reality, and in the farm. A sound that kept Emmie's brain from going too far afield. Walking side-by-side, she could smell the remnants of shaving cream, and the tang of morning cigarettes. A dozen personal questions bubbled to life in her mind, things she wanted to ask Walsh about his past, himself. But she held her tongue, because he had something he wanted to tell her; she could sense it.

"Richards should have been paying you more," he said as they moved slowly down the long outside of the barn.

She hadn't been expecting that. "What?"

"I'm giving you a raise. All of you. Most of Richards' cash was going...somewhere else. You ought to be paid more."

"Oh, you don't have to do that. I'm fine with my salary."

Walsh shot her a sideways glance. "He should have been paying you a lot more."

She frowned, and some of the arousal fog began to lift. "You looked at the finances?"

"This place could do better than it does, and I want you to make suggestions." He halted, and she turned to look at him, shocked. "I'm guessing Richards didn't take advice too well, am I right?"

"No, but..." She frowned. "He was a grumpy old man. Why are you doing this?" she added quickly. An unpleasant idea dawned. "You're not trying to buy my favor or something, are you?"

God, that would suck if he was that shallow. If he resorted to all those lame tricks the men she'd known before had used.

He twitched a half-smile. "No, love. I don't buy favors from pretty girls." He leaned forward, close enough for her to see the dark filaments in his eyes. His voice: low and thick, sending shivers across her skin. "I want to fuck you, trust that. And it would be very, very good for you. But I won't try to trick you into it. You'll have to say you want it."

Oh God, oh God.

He pulled back, totally composed, calm, dug a pack of cigarettes from his jeans pocket and went about the business of pulling one out, lighting it. "Think about it," he said, like he'd suggested she get her oil changed, or invest in a new lawnmower.

"Think about..." Her mouth was dry. She couldn't repeat what he'd just said, too stunned.

"How much of a raise you want." He flicked her a blank, heatless look. "Okay?"

"O...kay."

The sound of a car door slamming drew both their attentions toward the parking pad in front of the barn. Amy Richards, dressed to the nines, sunglasses masking half her face.

"I wanna talk to you," she said, and it was almost a shout.

Emmie gathered her composure and started forward.

"Not you," Amy snapped, dismissing her with a wave. She aimed a jeweled finger at Walsh. "You, biker boy."

~*~

Aidan had never really understood those *Penthouse* horse trainer fantasies. He didn't see anything sexual about horses.

But he was rethinking that thanks to the woman sitting across from him. They were in the "tack room," she'd said it was, in the AC, on folding chairs facing one another, and he would have been having a much easier time unwrapping the Band-Aid in his hand if he hadn't been so busy staring at her.

Holy shit, she was hot.

Tonya, she'd said her name was, with an O. Yeah, he could see that. He wanted to make her say "Oh!" Movie star perfect, all legs and tight-fitting clothes, her makeup flawless despite the dirt smudges, she looked exactly like the sort of girl who belonged on the back of his bike.

"You really didn't have to help me," she said. "I'm capable of putting a bandage on my face."

She was snippy, and he liked that. He imagined she'd be feisty between the sheets, the kind of chick who'd be just as into the sex as him.

"Yeah, but then I wouldn't get to play doctor." He gave her a wide grin and finally got the Band-Aid open.

"Wouldn't want to deprive you of *that*, would we?"

"Nah, that'd be cruel."

She had a small split at her hairline, where her helmet had banged into her head, and it had only bled a little, but Aidan had insisted on patching her up. Mainly as an excuse to touch her.

"Alright, hold real still." He leaned forward, bandage held by both edges, getting closer, closer, there, smoothing the little strip down onto her skin. Skin that was satin-soft. He could imagine the smell of it, its texture beneath his tongue.

He had to have her, there was no way around it. And lucky for him, he had ten years of chick-catching experience.

"Come out with me," he said softly, in that voice that always worked for him. He met her gaze head-on, the intent shining in his own.

"Come where?" she asked, and unlike so many of his conquests, she wasn't taking the bait so easily.

He grinned. "Anywhere you wanna go, baby."

~*~

Amy Richards was a pretty woman. The trouble was, she was the sort who knew it, and gave off the vibe that she'd used her looks to her advantage repeatedly. The cruel twist of her mouth, the dark misery in her eyes – this was a woman who bargained with her body, because there wasn't much of use between her ears.

When Walsh settled behind her dead father's desk, she tossed her Coach bag on top of it and squared off at him, hands on her hips. "The movers were supposed to take that out today."

"Too much for one truck. They said they'd be back tomorrow."

She snorted. "They said you and your buddies scared them shitless."

He lifted one shoulder in a half-assed shrug. "There's a lesson in not moving a couch when a man's sitting on it."

"Alright, cut the bullshit." The pinched look of her face suggested she didn't like bantering. Probably because she couldn't keep up. "What do you want?"

He made a show of looking around the office. "A vodka'd be nice, but I'm trying to cut back on the day drinking."

Her lips peeled back off her teeth – thick coat of red lipstick, white-white teeth, but an unsteady hand with the lip liner. Little smudges at the corners of her mouth. The aggression in her had a buzz to it, a frenzied, reckless energy.

But then she took a deep breath and worked the snarl into a smile. "Mr. Gannon and his people," she said in a brittle, cheery voice, "still want to buy this place. You and I both know that you didn't buy Briar Hall by yourself. This was the club. So

108

what does the club want with it? And what will it take to get you to sell to the developers?"

He leaned back and let the cushioned chair hold the weight of his head, taking an even more detailed look at the woman in front of him. There was something else. Some other motive. Something that had to do with the energy rippling through her. This was personal – her wanting the developers to have the land.

"Your inheritance will be the same either way," he said "I buy it, they buy – you get paid the same."

Her jaw tightened.

"So what I can't figure out is why you'd want your farm to get turned into condos."

"This place is a money pit," she said, and he could see the way the lie drew out the veins in her throat. "I don't want to watch anyone waste their time trying to do something with it."

"Concerned citizen, yeah?" He gave her an insulted glance. "Give the poor stupid biker more credit than that. No," he said, enjoying the way her eyes widened. "You're worried about you, Amy. Daddy was cutting you and your worthless whelp a check every month—"

"How did you—"

" – and that means whatever your plan, it involves keeping that allowance of yours. It means you" – God, he could get high off the rush of deduction – "are somehow gonna get an allowance off Gannon's people. It—" His eyes widened, a blast of triumph hitting his blood like coke. "*Ohhhh.* I got it now."

Amy gave him a peevish frown, but he saw the fear rattle through her, the doubt. "What?"

He felt a satisfied smile tug at his mouth. "Amy, where does this new fiancé of yours work?"

She stiffened. He had her.

"In Kentucky."

"No, I mean which company? Which…development firm?"

Her aggression did ugly things to her face, carved deep lines in it. "You don't—" She started to shout, then thought better of it, clamping her red lips together, drawing in a deep breath through her nostrils. She glanced up at the ceiling, smoothed her hands down the front of her cropped white linen jacket...and undid the top button.

"Did Em put you up to this?" she asked. "Is this for her?"

When he made an inquisitive sound, her gaze dropped down to his, and she undid the second button. "Are you fucking her?"

"How would that be your business?"

"It's not." Amy shrugged as she undid the last button, and the jacket slipped down off her shoulders, slid off her arms, so she was in a black see-through camisole that clearly had nothing underneath it. Her nipples were pebbled against the fabric. "It's just, I can't imagine how bored you've gotta be with her. Little good girl Emmie? Yeah, snore."

She hooked her thumbs in the straps and drew them down, pushed the camisole past her breasts and left it bunched at her waist. "Someone like you, living the life you do." Her voice was a deep purr now. "You've gotta want something more than that little snoozefest." She leaned forward, braced her hands on the desk, let her breasts dangle before his face. "I'm sure we can work out some kind of deal," she whispered. A heavy, overdone sex whisper. "So we both get what we want."

Walsh stared at her without reaction. "Have you ever been to one of the club parties over at Dartmoor?"

She cocked her head, scrambling to get a read on him and keep up her seductress façade. "No..."

"If you had, you'd know about all the strippers, the groupies, the poor lost lambs who turn up every time. Darling, I've seen everything and done everything. More than you can even imagine. Put your tits away; you're embarrassing yourself."

She exploded like a cat that had been hit with water: jumping back, covering herself, tearing at her camisole to get it back in place. "Fuck you!" she spat. "Fuck you, asshole!" She bent to retrieve her jacket, breathing in furious deep draws. "I want my dad's stuff!" she shouted as she stomped off in her stiletto boots. "All of it!"

"Talk to the movers," he said calmly.

His stomach didn't unclench until the front door slammed, and then the shiver that went through him was nothing short of revulsion.

~*~

After the day's minor excitement – and the swirling remnants of last night that wouldn't leave her mind – Emmie was glad for a chance to spend time with Apollo. Her gelding had his eyes shut in bliss as she curried his satiny coat, groaning occasionally and twitching his upper lip when she hit a favorite spot.

"There?" she asked, glad of the chance to laugh as she dug the brush into his withers and he arched his neck in reaction.

Grooming was one of those therapeutic exercises – for human and horse. The repetitive brush strokes and the rich scents of dust and horseflesh were better than any drink or any pill.

Apollo noticed Fred first, blowing a greeting to the man as he drew up to the horse's head.

"Hi," Emmie said, glancing over as she worked the tangles from Apollo's tail with a human hairbrush. "Everything alright?"

"*Sí.*" He stroked the gelding's nose, proving his equine magic; Apollo didn't like men as a rule, but got on well with Fred. "How 'bout you, *chica*. You alright?"

She made a face. "If you're wondering if I'm going to show up to work half-drunk again, the answer is no. I'm alright. Just had a momentary lapse in judgment." She laughed hollowly. "We're all allowed a few, right?"

But Fred didn't share in her humor. "The new boss has eyes for you. I see it." He tapped at his temple, alongside his own eyes. "I think maybe you have eyes for him too."

"What? Phshh." Her forced laugh sounded stupid to her own ears. "Yeah, right. Like I have time to worry about blonde-haired, blue-eyed bikers who…" She clamped her lips shut, and saw the knowing tilt to Fred's non-smile.

"You deserve to have a man," he said. "A good man. A marriage like I have with my Maria. But be careful, Emmie. This man is dangerous."

Emmie frowned. "I don't want to be with him. It's not like that."

He nodded, but the sadness in his eyes told her he didn't believe her.

"I need to spread the manure," he said, and walked off with one last pat to Apollo's nose.

When he was gone, Emmie found herself still frowning, suddenly cold inside. When she examined herself closely, she realized that she'd been keeping Walsh's words in the back of her mind all afternoon. *You'll have to say you want it.* She'd been gearing up to that, preparing herself to say those words. *I want you.* Because she did, God help her.

She'd never had what she'd call a successful relationship. So her logic had been, what did it matter if Walsh was the dangerous, bad boy type she was supposed to avoid? Playing it smart had only ever left her lonely.

But the way Fred said *dangerous* left her wondering. Because there were bad boys…and then there were men who'd kill you.

Twelve

Mercy loved evenings. Without all the rush of mornings, he got to be with his family in a more tranquil state. He got to play with Remy, and after dinner was done and all the dishes stowed away, he got to play with his woman, too.

"He's moving," Mercy said, pausing with his hands pressed to the sides of Ava's distended belly.

She sat in front of him, between his extended legs, resting back against his chest. "Hmm." One of her hands joined his. "He's more active than Remy was. He likes to use my bladder as a speedbag."

"Little monster," Mercy said affectionately, following the movement beneath the skin as his son squirmed in the womb.

"Mom thinks he'll come early. She keeps looking at my stomach like she's got X-ray vision and telling me he won't make it to nine months."

"Your mom *does* have X-ray vision."

"She does. But are we gonna talk about her?" Her hand closed over one of his, drew it downward along the swell of her belly, down between her legs. "Or do something more fun than that?" Her voice got husky on the end, dark with wanting.

He shifted forward, so he was curled around her, her sleek hair against his cheek, her ear at his lips. "Ava Rose," he said, laughing quietly. "I think being pregnant makes you even dirtier than you already are."

"It's the hormones." With an impatient sound, she dropped the vixen act and said, "God, Merc, I'm just really horny."

He laughed again, fingers dancing against her. "Don't worry, *fillette*, I've got you."

She twisted her head, like she was searching for his mouth, and he gave it to her, kissing her, taking over —

The loud crash that echoed through the house startled them both.

"What the hell?" Ava gasped.

"That ladder your dad dropped off," he said, searching for an explanation even as his heart galloped. He'd never known fear that wasn't tied to his girl, and now that fear had been doubled – tripled – by the babies. Loud sounds he could handle all day. Loud sounds when his family was around? Scared him shitless. "That had to be it. He left it up against the side of the house."

But then it crashed again.

"That's not the wind," Ava said grimly, surging awkwardly out of his arms and onto her knees. She was off the bed almost as quickly as him, tugging the straps of her cotton slip into place, heading for her nightstand as he opened the drawer of his.

Guns were drawn, her Glock and his Colt 1911.

Mercy caught her eye across the expanse of the king-sized bed and he couldn't help but smile, just for a second. His ferocious *fillette*, all ready to put lead in somebody.

"You okay?" he asked.

She nodded. "Yep."

He moved quickly, long legs taking him across the house, through the mud room, and out the back door in record time. The ladder had indeed fallen, and lay on the grass. But it wasn't the wind's fault – a man all in black was sprinting down the driveway, arms pumping as he raced away from the house.

"Hey!" Mercy shouted, bringing his gun up.

But it was dark, and they were in a residential area, and the guy was lost to the shadows already anyway.

"Shit," he muttered.

Ava was waiting in the living room, having pulled a sweatshirt over her nightgown, tied her hair back, eyes serious. "What was it?"

"I'm guessing it was Michael's peeping tom. He must have a thing for Dogs."

Thirteen

"Mum." Walsh closed his eyes and rubbed them with his free thumb and forefinger. The other hand held the phone to his ear. "You know how this is gonna turn out. You *know*."

Beatrice took a deep, shuddering breath on her end of the line. Walsh could picture her by the window in the lounge of her flat, hand clutching at the strand of pearls he'd given her two Christmases ago, watery afternoon sunlight touching every line time and worry had etched into her face. "He's changed, King," she said unsteadily. "It's been so long, and he's learned he went wrong, I think."

Jesus. "Learned he went wrong with ten women? I have eight half-siblings, Mum. The man's cock ought to have its own passport."

"Kingston!" she chided. "That's no way to talk of your father."

"He's not my father. He's nothing but a bit of DNA to me."

Rottie ambled past with a travel holder of steaming paper coffee cups, and lifted it in offering.

Walsh shook his head and picked his cigarette up off the edge of the table. "Look, Mum, I've gotta go. Will you – will you just promise me you won't put too much stock in anything he says? You won't go away with him anywhere or make plans, yeah?"

There was a pause. "Well, I'm lonely," she admitted in a small voice.

He drew hard on the smoke. "I know."

After promising to call her again later, with a stomach full of transatlantic dread, he disconnected and plugged himself into the present.

"Problem?" Ghost asked when he joined the rest of the boys in the common room.

"Nah." He climbed onto a barstool. "What's this about?"

Ghost gave a quick, tight smile. "It's about these two are gonna end up cellmates if we don't figure out who's spying in their windows," he said, gesturing to Michael and Mercy, who looked downright chummy sitting at a table together.

"I catch him in my yard, I'm turning him into a baby mobile to go over the crib," Mercy said matter-of-factly. All his Cajun joviality had dropped away. He was serious about killing someone, and beside him, Michael was his silent bookend, both of them holding up two sides of a frightening hostility.

"You might wanna tap the brakes a bit, boys," Dublin said. "All he's done is look in a couple windows, right?"

"He woke my baby up," Michael said, like that was valid justification.

Ghost glanced over at Walsh with a look that said *suggestions?*

In his head, Walsh set his personal issues off to the side with a mental sigh. He was tired. Damn tired, inside and out. "Set a trap for him," he offered. "Set out some tape on the windowsills, see if you can get prints off him. Use a trail camera, one that's motion-activated. Maybe you can catch him on film and Ratchet's guy can run facial recognition on him."

"Or how about I get a bear trap," Mercy said, snapping his palms together in demonstration.

"Or how about you calm the fuck down a little," Ghost said.

President and extractor went back and forth a few moments, Mercy's wish list of punishment growing more graphic, until finally it was agreed some of Hound's trail cameras would be set up at Mercy and Michael's houses.

Ghost seemed largely unconcerned, almost content, as well he should be. The new mayor had no interest in the Dogs, had instead been busy the past year and a half putting out all the previous mayor's fires. The drug business was good. The gun business out of Texas was good, and had helped majorly fund the farm purchase. Then there was the farm – another victory. Their burial ground safe from bulldozers and prying eyes.

116

But Walsh was stalked by an uneasiness he couldn't yet define.

Ghost turned toward him as the impromptu meeting broke off and everyone headed back to work. "Everything good out in the sticks?"

Sure, except for the fact that he wasn't entirely sure at this point that Davis Richards' heart attack had been natural, and he had a dead man's daughter trying to fuck him into selling the place, and he was overly distracted by Emmie Johansen at this point. But Ghost didn't want to hear any of that.

"Yeah." He nodded. "All good."

~*~

Whatever Emmie's feelings about Walsh, she was completely in love with his dog. It was lunch time, and she and Becca were choking down turkey sandwiches at the picnic tables, Dolly lying at their feet, looking at them adoringly until they felt compelled to offer her turkey.

"Who's a pretty girl?" Becca asked, tossing over a large chunk of meat. "Huh? Who's the prettiest girl?"

Dolly took the treat daintily and gave a tongue-lolling dog smile.

"Okay, she's the best," Becca said, returning to her lunch. "Can we keep her?"

"If we keep her owner, I guess so."

"Ah, the owner." Becca grinned as she chewed. "Do we *want* to keep him?"

"If we also wanna keep the farm, yeah."

Becca rolled her eyes. "I was trying to do a thing. Be all suggestive or whatever."

Emmie smiled.

"But, seriously, do you, like, totally want to let him in your pants?"

Emmie wanted to act scandalized, but it was a little late for that routine. "You've been talking to Fred, haven't you?"

117

"Just as your two concerned coworkers and friends. Well, only Fred's concerned. I'm more like 'Girl hasn't been on a date in forever, let her have some fun.' Plus" – she leaned across the table, voice going low and conspiratorial – "I think he's totally cute."

Emmie's stomach grabbed in a way it hadn't since she was still in school. "You do?"

"Definitely."

"That's…oh, hell. It doesn't matter anyway. It's really bad form to mess around with your boss. Plus, I don't even know the guy."

"So? You knew your last boyfriend, and look how *that* turned out."

She winced. "Yeah." She shook herself all over and tossed the rest of her turkey to Dolly. "Anyway, there's more important stuff to worry about right now."

Becca lifted her brows like she didn't believe that.

"Donna Murphy's sitting trot for one thing." She gestured to the boarder riding trot circles in the arena below them. "I don't know who's going to be more sore afterward – her or the horse."

Becca twisted around to watch. "Ouch. That's painful to look at."

Thankful to no longer be the center of attention, Emmie braced her elbows on the table, traced the condensation droplets on her water bottle with a finger. She'd lost sleep the night before, worrying about Amy's visit. All through the evening, she'd expected Walsh to come down to the barn and tell her what was said, but he hadn't shown. And walking up to the house felt like she was taking him up on his sex offer.

Which she wasn't thinking about *at all*.

The sound of a bike engine started as a low murmur and grew louder as it came up the driveway. Walsh was back.

Becca twirled around and gave her a wide, evil grin.

Emmie rolled her eyes…skyward, and then over to the side, so she could watch Walsh park, strip off helmet and gloves, and climb off the Harley. He wore his jeans just tight enough, and his boots were scarred and dirty. His wallet chain and all the rings on his hands caught the light in a dazzling glitter burst. He kept his shades on – smoked aviators that left her palms damp – but pushed his fingers through his hair, raising it up after the helmet had flattened it.

Damn, he looked good.

She was embarrassed by how much she wanted to slide her hands up into the rolled sleeves of his denim shirt, feel the crinkly hair on his arms and the muscle beneath.

He spotted them and walked over. In the shade of the pavilion, she could see that he hadn't shaved that morning, sharp edge of his jaw stubbly. He pushed his shades up into his hair and sat down on the bench beside her without preamble, leaning over to scratch Dolly behind the ears.

"Mr. Walsh," Becca greeted in a chirpy voice. "We were just talking about you."

Emmie wanted to kick her under the table, especially as the teenager shot her a wide smile.

Walsh looked between the two of them, expressionless. "Really."

"Emmie was, mostly," Becca said, getting to her feet. "I was just listening." She gave them another of her big fake grins. "I better get back to cleaning tack!" she chirped, and left them alone, with no buffer save Donna's awful sitting trot in front of them.

"I–"

"I–"

They both started talking at once, and Emmie felt her cheeks warm.

A tiny smile plucked at the corners of his mouth; his little almost-smiles were better than any of the widest, whitest male grins she'd ever seen. "Ladies first."

She dampened her lips and watched his eyes follow the passage of her tongue. "I wanted to ask how things went with Amy yesterday. Did she yell? She's kind of a yeller."

His little smile widened a fraction. "She yelled. After I told her I didn't want what she was offering."

119

She lifted her brows and felt her chest tighten. "What was that?" But knowing Amy as she had all these years, she had a pretty good idea.

"Your mentor's a bit of a whore, pet. A lot of one, actually. You think her fiancé would care she took her top off to try and get me to sell?"

Unbidden, anger coiled through her. "She did *what?*"

"I turned her down, love," he said quietly.

"I don't – that doesn't matter. I mean…" Her face was hot. She took a deep breath as he breathed a low laugh. "Why in the world does she want you to sell? She's got her money. God knows she doesn't have a sentimental streak about this place."

Walsh shifted to the side and dug a scrap of paper out of his pocket, setting it on the table between them. It read *Scott Palmer, G&G*, and included an address. "One of my brothers is real good at looking stuff up. Your girl Amy's fiancé? He works for Gannon & Gannon, heads up their division in Kentucky."

"No!" she gasped. "No way! I met Scott. He's…" She frowned. "Well, damn, I have no idea what he does."

"Now you do."

"So…what. If G&G is making money off the development, her new husband will, which means she makes more off the developer deal than off her inheritance."

Walsh nodded.

"Oh, she's cold." Emmie had a hard knot in her stomach. "I knew she was…well, kind of a bitch…but…" Words failed her. The hurt, the sense of betrayal, the idea that she'd studied under this woman, idolized her and wanted to become her – only to see all the pretty colors run in this time of crisis. It was too much to digest on a breezy summer afternoon. This sort of thing needed a bottle, a dark room, and a whole lot of self-recrimination.

Her drunken father probably would have said the same thing.

"This place," she said in a small, defeated voice. "The horses, and the pastures, and the stalls…and all our stories." She glanced over at him, unable to force a smile. "It never meant a thing to her. It was all about the money, always. I feel like an idiot." She glanced away, toward the arena. "An idealistic moron."

There was a pause in which she imagined him agreeing with her. Then he said, "Or you expect the best of people."

"Like a moron."

"A rare trait, I'll give you that. But the world's better for a bit of rare, I think."

She glanced over, her sudden burst of nausea subsiding. She finally found her smile. "You talk funny, Mr. Walsh."

"I know. The ladies usually like it." He lifted his brows in question.

"Yeah, I'd say they do."

There was a moment, a brief one, in which she should have torn her eyes away – but didn't. In which she should have said something snappy to negate her compliment – but didn't. The men she'd known in her life hadn't flirted; it had always been "hey, babe, I'm totally gonna rock your world." There had been no cleverness or intensity to them, and for that moment, she was trapped in Walsh's blue gaze and didn't want to be anywhere else.

It hurt, suddenly, how much she wanted a real man, a partner – and it hurt to know that she would probably never have one.

If she leaned forward, she knew, he'd close the gap and kiss her. It was a knowledge that fizzled through her, an assuredness so strong, her lips tingled in anticipation.

But then Donna shouted, "Hey, Emmie! Can you come look at this?" And the spell was broken.

Emmie lurched to her feet. "Coming!" she called to Donna. "I should get back to work," she told Walsh, not willing to meet his gaze again. "I have a lot to do." She made a vague, lame gesture that went nowhere and explained nothing.

I want you and it scares me was the truth.

"Me too," he said. "See you later."

And she hoped she did.

~*~

Later was after he knew all the horses were put away for the evening and Fred and Becca had driven off the property. He'd spent the day on his laptop, a makeshift desk of card table and kitchen chair making his back and neck sore, digging up dirt on the Richards. He'd gone back and forth on the phone with Ratchet, and after hours, he had a headache and a vaguely sick feeling in his gut.

Just went to show that money didn't buy love, class, good behavior, or loyalty.

But it paid off a lot of speeding tickets and sure got Brett Richards out of house arrest a few times.

It was a relief to get away from it, get out of the house.
The farm, draped all in gold this time of evening, rang with the soft silence of a day's ending. Quiet rustlings of horses in stalls, wind in branches, birds calling to one another. But the human noise had melted away as the sun faded, and it was his favorite sort of countrified stillness that he walked through, down the driveway, into the front doors of the barn. He breathed deep the smell of hay, dust, and freshly oiled leather. His blood pressure dropped, and his muscles unclenched. Just what he needed.

And then he spotted Emmie. She sat on a stepstool outside her horse's stall, the monstrous black gelding using his lips to daintily play with her ponytail. She didn't seem to notice, staring blankly into space, face etched with unhappiness, her cellphone in one hand.

"I'd offer a penny for your thoughts," he said, and she jerked, head lifting so she faced him. "But I think they'd cost more than that."

It tugged at his gut when she did nothing but turn baleful, exhausted eyes to him. He knew her well enough now to know she hated looking vulnerable. And well enough to feel a strong, uncharacteristic anger on her behalf. Whoever had turned her gloomy, he wanted to throttle.

"What's the matter, love?"

Love. That British term of endearment, like *sweetheart* or *baby* or *doll*, or all the other meaningless words men used to trap women. It wasn't a trap when he used it with her. It was a word *for her*. It was something about her quiet, respectable fierceness taking hold of him.

She dampened her lips – God, he wanted her tongue on him – and blinked once, but held his gaze. "My dad. At Bell Bar again."

Without knowing what he meant by it, he reached out a hand to her. "Come on, baby. We'll go get him."

~*~

Walsh spotted RJ and Briscoe sharing a pitcher at one of the usual Lean Dogs' high top tables the second they walked into Bell Bar. He made eye contact, sent them a silent signal with his eyes: *hold back, but be ready if I need you.* He let his hand float at the small of Emmie's back as they moved through the tables toward the bar, where her father was in the slow process of falling off his stool.

Emmie took a deep breath, her spine digging into his palm, feeling fragile and strong at the same time. "Dad," she said, stepping forward, separating them. "Dad, it's time to go."

The man looked slowly over at his daughter, head wobbling on his neck. "I didn't call you!" he said, too loudly.

"No, Jeff did. Come on. It's time to get you home." She laid a hand on his arm and he jerked it away, almost toppling from his stool in the process.

"I don't have to go anywhere if I don't want to, and I sure ain't going home to that bitch."

Emmie sighed. "Maryann's back, I take it."

"I hate her."

"Dad–"

Walsh stepped up to the bar on the man's other side and leaned in close, so he could keep his voice low. "Mr. Johansen, let's make this easier on your girl, yeah? Let's just walk out of here like gentlemen so we don't get her upset."

On the other side of her father, Emmie sent him a tight-lipped, mortified glance.

Johansen seemed to consider it a moment, then said, "Fuck her," and buried his nose in his tumbler of gin.

Emmie's eyes sparked bright with unshed tears and she bit down hard on her lower lip. "Dad." Her voice was shaky, uncharacteristic.

Alright, enough of this. Walsh stepped back and motioned to his brothers.

"Friend of yours?" RJ asked when he and Briscoe reached them.

"Not after this," Walsh said. "On three."

The others nodded.

"One, two, three."

They took Johansen under the arms and hauled him back off his stool.

"Oh shit," Emmie breathed.

"Hey!" Johansen shouted, kicking like an angry toddler. "You can't do that. Fuckers! Let go o' me!"

"Sorry, mate," Walsh said to the bartender, and captured Johansen's feet, holding them together up off the ground so he couldn't kick people's drinks off their tables as they hustled him bodily from the bar.

They turned him loose when they reached the sidewalk, and he collapsed in a cursing, incoherent heap, too piss-drunk to find his footing.

"Who's this charming individual?" Briscoe asked, chuckling as they stared down at the fuming, grumbling shape sprawled at their feet.

"My dad," Emmie spoke up in a pained voice. When Walsh glanced at her, he saw that her eyes were dry, but no less haunted. "I'm Emmie, by the way," she continued. "I'm the barn manager."

Briscoe shook her hand and said, "Very nice to meet you, darlin'," because he was an outlaw and a gentleman.

RJ leaned over the poor girl's writhing father and reached for her offered hard. "Hi." He gave her his favorite shit-eating grin. "For the record, if Walsh hasn't told you how hot you are, he's a dumbass."

124

Her eyes flew wide. "Um…"

"Fuck," Walsh breathed.

"*Um,*" Emmie said again, and it wasn't shock, but aggression tightening her expression. Indignation. She took a deep breath. "Guess I'm gonna have to take that as a compliment."

RJ's grin got wider, if that was possible. "You should."

"Have a little respect for the lady," Walsh told him.

"I apologize on his behalf," Briscoe told Emmie. "He got dropped on his head as a baby, and now the only head that works is the one in his pants."

Emmie hesitated…and then she laughed. A fast, unexpected laugh, like she was glad for the chance to find something funny as her father congealed on the ground.

"So, you guys are in the club?" she asked, folding her arms, pointedly not looking at her father.

"RJ and Briscoe," Walsh said of them, suddenly wanting her away from all this. He didn't like the way Briscoe kept shooting him those *you sly dog* glances. "And after they help me hustle your old man into the truck, they're gonna go back in and have another pitcher on me."

RJ grinned. "Yeah. Wouldn't wanna interrupt anything."

Walsh sent him a quelling glance that was listened to, for once.

Ten minutes later, Johansen was snoring in the deep backseat of the truck, and Emmie steered with a mechanical sort of awareness, pulled deep inside herself, frowning.

"I can drive," Walsh offered as she turned off the main strip and headed into the warren of neighborhoods that ringed the city. "If you're tired."

She ignored him. "Look, it was real nice of you to come along with me. Really, it was, because I couldn't have dragged him out by myself. But when we get there, you don't have to come in. My stepmother's probably here so…yeah. You can wait in the truck."

Because women who weren't club sluts, groupies and strippers didn't want to be seen with the likes of him.

125

"Alright," he said tightly, and pushed his head back against the seat, resolved to wait.

She pulled into the cracked driveway of a split-level house choked by overgrown shrubs. In the dark, the white stucco siding glared sickly beneath the glow of the streetlamp. In Walsh's experience, drunks weren't big on home and landscape maintenance, and Johansen seemed no exception.

Dim lights were on in the upper windows, and there was a bumper sticker-plastered Camry in the driveway.

Emmie took a deep, shaky breath as she killed the engine. She stared at the house with something resembling fear.

"You sure about me waiting?" Walsh asked.

There was a pause before she nodded. "Yeah."

It made him itch to sit still, hands clenched tight on his thighs as insubstantial little Emmie wrestled her half-asleep father from the backseat and let him lean on her as they limped up to the door. There was a long moment of fumbling with keys and then the door opened, light swallowing them up and then sealing off.

Walsh opened his truck door and sat sideways on the seat, digging a smoke out of his pocket. He'd taken his first drag when he heard the yelling start up inside. Harsh, angry yelling that carried through the walls and windows. He couldn't make out words, but he didn't need to.

He flicked the cig into the weeds and was at the front door in three jogging strides. He walked into a foyer with steps leading to the upper and lower levels of the house, and waded through the fetid stink of garbage in bad need of taking out.

The screaming came from above, so up he went, and when he hit the living room/kitchen combo there, the words became distinct.

"...your goddamn father, Emmaline! It's not my job to keep him sober! Christ, girl, can't you do a damn thing?"

Johansen had puddled again, this time on a rug in front of the kitchen sink, out cold. Standing over him was a woman built like an old-fashioned icebox with artificially black hair and one of the uglier scowls he'd seen in his lifetime. She was the one screaming, brandishing an empty gin bottle to emphasize her points. A lit cigarette perched beside her on the linoleum countertop, smoke curling up from its tip.

Emmie stood with her feet braced apart, hands knotted together in front of her stomach, spine brittle enough to break as the words crashed over her.

"Maryann," she said in a low, firm voice. Not shouting. Totally in control. But Walsh could see the tremor in her throat. "I do my best, but when I take his keys away, he walks, and when I take his wallet away, he bums money, and I have a job. I can't babysit him all the time."

"What, like I'm supposed to?!" Maryann screamed. "I ain't the reason he drowns hisself! He tricked me, 's what he did! Tricked me into thinking he's worth a shit, and he ain't nothin' but a goddamn drunk!"

Walsh's hands were curled into fists before he realized it. He didn't fight much, and he'd never in his life hit a woman – but his brain didn't seem to be aware of that at the moment.

"And where have you been this week?" Emmie asked quietly. "What have you been doing?"

Maryann's face screwed into even uglier angles. "Fuck you, little bitch," she snapped.

"No, fuck you," Walsh said, stepping into their bubble. Both women glanced at him in shock, just now noticing his presence, but it was Maryann he turned his coldest stare on. "Actually, go fuck yourself, 'cause any man with eyes in his head'd be hard-pressed to fuck *you*."

"You – who – what–" she sputtered, drawing herself up to her deep-freeze tallest.

"Em." Walsh reached blindly behind him and felt Emmie's small, rough hand slide into his grip. Calluses, from riding and mucking stalls, and working like a man. He closed his fingers tight around hers and headed for the door.

"You bitch!" Maryann shouted at their backs.

Walsh maneuvered Emmie in front of him, so he was a shield between her and her stepmother, so he could keep his hands on her shoulders as they walked back out to the truck.

She was shaking, and when he held out a wordless hand for the keys, she gave them to him.

~*~

"Can you pull over?" she asked when they drew up on Leroy's Gas 'n' Grocery, and Walsh turned into the Dartmoor-preferred convenience store.

Emmie hadn't said anything, and he hadn't pushed her. She was silent in a solid, tough-bitch way he admired. But he ached for her too, because when he stole glimpses at her eyes, he saw the awful hurt stacked up behind the pretty blue irises.

She dug around in her purse, came out with her wallet, and popped the door. "I'll be right back."

She didn't want company, and so he nodded, watching her with an uneasy, possessive lurch in his gut as she went into the store and moved through the aisles. She wasn't long, up at the counter a moment later, handing her purchases to the dead-eyed teenager behind the register. The glass was old and yellowing, and so he couldn't tell what the little box was, but he recognized the big bottle of gin she set up on the counter.

Her gaze was downcast, shoulders slumped as she walked out and came back. When she was in her seat, and the door was shut, she took a deep breath and let it out slowly. Then she reached into the paper bag, drew out the little box and set it on the console between them.

"I didn't know what kind you'd want," she said, tapping it with a fingernail.

They were condoms.

~*~

There was no speaking until they pulled into Briar Hall, headlights catching tree trunks and fence boards as they bypassed the barn and headed up the hill to the house.

"Wait," Emmie said, sitting upright. "I was thinking my place."

128

"I've got vodka," he explained. "I don't drink gin, pet."

She sat back. "Oh."

The condoms were back in the bag with the gin, and she hugged the crumped paper sack to her chest as they walked up the sidewalk, through the humid dark to the front door. He'd left lights on, and the foyer was bright, made them both blink. Their footsteps rebounded hollowly across the hardwood; all the furniture was gone now, and it was like a museum, cold and full of echoes.

Emmie halted in the center of the cavernous living room, the one that had been packed with overstuffed couches and chairs mere hours ago. She snorted. "At least I have a bed."

"I have a mattress."

"Ah, romantic."

She was utterly dead, dark circles smudged beneath her eyes, all the life drained out of her.

"Didn't think you were after romance, love," he said quietly, turning so he stood directly before her.

She wouldn't look at him, just kept hugging the bag. "No," she said, and it was an obvious lie. "Nothing about gin and condoms says 'romance.'"

"No," he agreed.

Her eyes finally came to him, and they were devastated.

That was his undoing. He liked women, enjoyed their bodies, the feel and taste of them – but nothing about sex made his chest tight, had him feeling like crumpled up paper inside. Realness, genuine human emotion – that broke him open every time. In the club there were women who were nothing but a collection of holes. And then there was Maggie, and Ava, Holly, Mina, Nell, Bonita, and Jackie. There were the women who were people.

And right now, there was Emmaline Johansen, and he'd be damned if she gave him her body to ease the sting of heartache.

He'd be damned if he acted like his father.

He stepped in close, reached to lay a hand against her face.

She startled, just a little, but then her eyes fixed to his mouth and went soft. She thought he was going to kiss her. Wanted it.

"Not yet, lovey," he said, stroking the soft swell of her cheekbone with his thumb. She shivered like she liked the cool touch of his ring against her skin. "Not yet."

Fourteen

She wanted to feel stupid, because technically, he'd rejected her. It didn't feel like a rejection though. There was such heat in him – she'd felt it in the gentle stroke of his fingers on her face. This was just them pressing pause. This was sitting in a numb fog and letting someone else be the industrious, responsible, in-charge one for a change.

She sat on the granite-topped island in the kitchen, because there wasn't a table, watching as Walsh pulled things from the fridge and slowly built up something that almost resembled a meal.

"Mr. Walsh," she said, smiling, taking a deep sip of gin from the bottle, "are you a jockey *and* a chef?"

"Former jockey, remember?" he said, tossing the crumbled breakfast sausage into the skillet. "I got too big." He grinned and waggled his eyebrows and she decided she *loved* what a few shots of vodka did to his charm.

"Hey, there's nothing wrong with a big jockey. Look at Red Pollard. They put his ass in a movie."

He tilted his head in concession and dumped the roasted red peppers in next.

Drinking made her talkative. "So where'd you learn to cook?"

"My grannie." He tossed in pepper and reached for the wooden spoon. "After she realized there'd be no granddaughters, she slapped my arse into an apron and dragged me into the kitchen."

She grinned and let her lips linger against the sticky mouth of the bottle, wondering what it would feel like to kiss him. "She was a good cook?"

"As good a cook as any Englishwoman can be, I expect. If that means anything." He shot her another grin that killed her. He had dimples; oh God, the dimples when he really smiled.

"So what's this gourmet concoction?"

"Eggs and such." He cracked the first one in and it hit the meat and peppers with a hiss.

"So like a cowboy omelet."

"If you wanna call it that."

Emmie took another sip of gin while he worked and felt the liquor swirl lazily down into her stomach, sending her head on a slow trip.

"I'm sorry you had to see that before," she blurted, before she could catch herself. "My stepmother—"

"Is a fucking bitch? Yeah, I picked up on that," he said dryly.

She smiled, warmed more by his support than by the booze. "She gambles," she said. "She was at Harrah's all this time she wasn't at home, and then she comes home, and expects Dad to be sober."

He made a sound in his throat she took to mean *not fair*.

"She's nothing like my mother, and just as awful for him. Jesus." She sighed. "Dad isn't a bad guy. Except when he's drinking."

"Known a few of those in my time."

"Known any who kicked the habit?"

"There's plastic forks and real plates over there," he said, dodging the question, motioning toward the far counter. "This is done."

They ate sitting cross-legged on the hard tile floor, and his "eggs and such" was the tastiest thing she'd ever eaten – or so she thought in her depressed, buzzed state. She was starving, she realized, and ate half the plateful before sitting back, taking another big swig of gin, and deciding there was something she *had* to know.

"Walsh is your last name, right?" The room was fuzzy around the edges and when she looked at him, he was the only thing in focus.

He nodded and set his fork down, like he didn't like where this was headed.

"What's your first name?"

A beat. Then, "Kingston."

Emmie didn't want to, but she laughed. "Kingston? Is your mom Gwen Stefani?"

He frowned. "Who?"

"No, nothing. I'm sorry. It's not funny...well, it is, sort of. That's like, a name for a stripper, or a romance novel character. It's good, though," she added in a rush as he continued to stare at her. "It's sexy."

He kept staring at her, chin tucked, eyes penetrating. "I didn't pick it out you know."

"Like I wanted to be Emmaline?" She snorted. "Kingston's better than that. *You* can be in a novel. You ever read a steamy book where the heroine was named Emmaline? Didn't think so."

"To be fair, I don't read that kinda shit, so I wouldn't know." He almost smiled.

"Yeah, well..." Feeling ridiculous and girlish for admitting to her reading habits, she decided it was time for the next topic. "So I never asked: that night Tally got out, what were you doing next door? That's your land I'm guessing, since you had the key and all."

"You're just full of questions," he said, spearing a fat chunk of sausage on his fork.

Instead of coming up with a smart reply, she took a sip of gin. "I've never slept with a stranger before," she admitted.

Walsh went very still.

She forced a dry, humorless chuckle. "So do I call you King now or what?"

He swallowed, took a hit of his own drink. "Everyone just calls me Walsh." His voice was softer now, the harshness leaving his face. "And it's my friend's land. I was just scoping it out, realizing it was a lost cause to try and turn it into something."

She nodded, glad he'd skipped over her little admission. "It's been abandoned for a long time."

"Too long to make a farm out of it in less than two years." He mopped up the last of his eggs with a bite of bread and then pushed his plate to the side, its bottom scraping against the floor. "Done?" he asked, reaching for her plate.

She nodded. "Is this your stuff? The china and pots and pans?"

"Yeah. Had to make a run after they cleaned everything out. You know, that bitch stripped the fancy showerhead outta the master water closet, so now I gotta take a bath like an old woman," he said with a rueful non-smile. "Guess I'm lucky she didn't have the floors pulled up."

"I still can't believe what a sellout shallow bitch she is. Underneath all the pretty." *And underneath all my misguided ideals,* she added in her head.

"Probably shouldn't talk about her anymore, then."

"Probably."

They reached for their respective bottles at the same time, took long sips. Emmie watched the way his throat opened for the vodka and swished the gin around in her mouth, all between her teeth. It wasn't mouthwash, but it was better than nothing.

She lowered the bottle and closed her eyes, felt the floor tilt beneath her, felt the heavy ache inside her that was too complicated to describe. When she opened them again, Walsh was right in front of her, on his knees. His hand came up slowly, as if in a dream, and cupped the side of her face. He pressed lightly at her lower lip with his thumb.

"You're sure?"

"Yes." She closed her eyes again. "I want it."

~*~

She didn't feel anything until he kissed her. Getting up off the floor, walking through the house, up the stairs into the cavernous master bedroom. She'd never seen it before, but she didn't have eyes for it in the moment, only verified that, yeah, he had a mattress on the floor, and it even had sheets on it, the covers still messy from where he'd slept the night before. She was numb and fuzzy-headed for all of it. But then he caught her gently around the throat, drew her in, and kissed her.

134

All her senses lit up at once, a circuit board flaring to life. It was an easy, clinging kiss. A question. And she opened her mouth in answer. She felt the alcohol burn out of her blood as his tongue passed between her teeth; it sizzled as it left her raw, sober, and shaking, grabbing at the soft front of his shirt and twisting it in her hands.

She'd never wanted a man so bad in her life, and it didn't matter that she didn't fully understand why, only that she needed him inside her. *Now.*

Emmie flattened her hand and passed it between them, finding the bulge in the front of his jeans and curving her palm around it.

He pulled back from the kiss and she was gasping for breath.

"Easy, love," he murmured. His hands were at her hips, and he flicked his thumbs beneath the hem of her t-shirt, rubbed at the bare flushed skin of her hipbones. "There's no rush. You want it to feel good, yeah?"

A hard shiver stole across her skin. When had it ever been good? When had it ever been anything besides two bodies slamming together? "Yeah," she whispered, leaning into him, closing her hand more tightly against his cock. "Yeah, but…"

But she didn't know what. She was humming with inner electricity, and all grace had left her.

He took her lower lip between his teeth, pulled at it *slowly*. At another time, she might have been embarrassed by the sound that stirred in her throat.

He chuckled again, a dark breath of sound against her face. Then kissed her jaw, the tender spot just beneath her ear. "Stop trying to be in charge for once," his English-accented voice said against her skin, moving through her body like a tremor. "Right now, I'm in charge."

Holy shit, *yes.*

She felt the tension leave her – the unproductive kind – and she settled against him, caught at his shoulders to keep herself upright, because he was kissing her throat and his hands were moving under her shirt, and she didn't trust her legs to hold her up.

He lifted her shirt off in one fast maneuver, barely breaking away from her skin with his mouth. And then he was at her bra clasp, and then the straps were sliding down her arms.

When she was bare, he pulled back, his breath warm and uneven as it fanned across her chest. The moonlight turned his hair silver, cast deep shadows between their bodies.

"Ah, love, that's nice," he said in a strained voice.

His hands slid up beneath her breasts, cupped and lifted them. His thumbs flicked across her nipples. And then his head dipped and he kissed her there, passed his tongue across one hard bud and drew it into his mouth.

She speared her hands through his hair, marveling at the texture of it, the way it was thick and slippery all at once. But it wasn't about his hair – it was about curving her fingers against his skull and holding him to her as his tongue drew lazily across her nipple. Once and then again. It felt so amazing, but –

He moved to the other, taking it between his lips, touching it with his tongue.

God.

Her pulse vibrated wildly in her wet nipples, between her legs. She ached there, empty and hungry and needing him.

His mouth left her and she hated the loss of sensation, the way his hair was sliding out of her grasp. But then he was on his knees in front of her, and his rings caught the faint moonlight with fast glimmers as he unfastened her cutoffs. The sound of the zipper gave her gooseflesh. The feel of his hands curling in the waistband, tugging shorts and panties down together left her breathless.

"Walsh." She wasn't sure she wanted him looking at her up close like this. Hadn't expected it. The air was a shock against her bare, heated skin. "What are you doing?"

"Shh. Shut your eyes." His breath was a warm rush of air against her pubic bone and it startled her into compliance.

Her eyes slammed shut. "Walsh–"

136

He touched her, and it was only one finger, stroking lightly across her sex. Teasing at her.

She reached blindly for something to grab onto and found his shoulders, braced both her hands on them.

His finger pressed more firmly, parting her, finding where she was slippery and scalding hot. It was a careful, deliberate probing, unlike anything she'd ever felt. Not the rough pawing of a boy, but the sure slowness of a man.

A finger entered her and her inner muscles contracted. Exactly what she needed, wanted, but yet not enough.

"What does that feel like?" he asked.

"Good...it feels good." So good her fingertips were digging into his shoulders.

"More?"

"More."

He pressed in and in, and then she felt his ring, the heavy ornamental metal warm from his skin, sliding into her entrance.

She took a deep, ragged breath, and he chuckled, a low dark sound.

"Not just knuckle dusters, yeah?"

He stroked her inner wall and she felt the movement so acutely, in every nerve ending. There was a stretching – he added a second finger. All the way to that ring, and its ridges and raised designs.

He withdrew a fraction, and then pushed in again. Back and then forth. A thrusting rhythm, driving his rings into her, mimicking what they'd do later, when he was joined with her.

His thumb found her clit and she was lost. She let her weight sag against him, braced her feet on the floor, and let her hips move with the rhythm of his hand, overcome by the winding tension of pleasure.

When she came it was shattering. She bit down on her tongue and tasted blood, leaned down onto Walsh to keep from falling, made a sound deep in her throat that made him say, "That's a good girl."

It was a slow, blurry fall from grace, and in the midst of it, Walsh stood and gathered her up in his arms, lowered her down to the mattress and stretched out beside her.

"Oh my God." She rolled toward him, put her hands on his chest, and swore she could feel his self-satisfied smile through the dark. "I…" She didn't even know what.

His hand settled in the curve of her waist. "When was the last time you did that, love?"

"You mean, when was the last time I did that…or when was the last time I came?"

He kissed her. "When did you last come?" he asked against her lips, and those words said with his accent made her shiver.

"A very long time ago."

"Really?" There was no imagining the satisfied lift to his voice.

"And even then, it wasn't that good."

He made a low deep purring sound in his throat, and his hand slid down to her ass, pulled her in tight against him so she had to hook her leg over his hip.

"You've got too many clothes on," she said, flexing her fingers into his pecs.

"Wanna help me with that?"

In a clumsy rush, she lifted his shirt over his head and he managed to work off jeans, boxers, and boots, all of it going off the edge of the mattress in a heap.

The moonlight silvered his skin, shadows marking hair and the grooves of muscles. When he gathered her to his chest again, she was shocked by the heat of him, electrified by the scratch of his legs against her smooth ones, the tickling of his chest hair against her breasts. He kissed her and it was amplified by the skin-to-skin contact. The small, unconscious movements of her hips pushed his erection against her belly.

She reached to take him in her hand. "You bragged," she said, smiling against his mouth, and felt him smiling back.

"Disappointed?"

"Oh no. I'm a very little girl. You're just perfect."

With a pleased growl, he rolled her onto her back, settled between her legs.

Emmie caught herself in the act of lifting toward him. "Condom," she reminded.

"Shit. Yeah." He twisted around, fumbled with his jeans. She heard the foil tearing and imagined the sight of him rolling it on. All she could see was the white shine of his shoulders, the mess of his hair.

Then he was lowering over her again, kissing her mouth, bracing himself. One of his hands slipped between them, found her still warm and wet from his fingers.

He entered her with one sure thrust, and being suddenly filled like that overwhelmed her in the best way. She'd told him it had been a long time, and so he waited, breathing in strained gasps against her throat until she slid her hands down his back and latched onto his ass.

"I'm good," she said, wrapping her legs tight around his hips. "I'm ready—"

He took it slow and deep, more of that assured maleness that had nothing boyish about it. Thrusting, rooting into her with a depth and force that lifted her hips up off the mattress, had her whimpering deep in her throat.

"I want to feel you come around me," he said in her ear, and the pleasure arced through her, lighting her up from the inside out.

He grunted and stiffened, and she knew her pulses had kicked off his release.

They lay on their backs afterward, the echo of their breathing filling up the empty room. Through the drowsiness, Emmie could already feel the low sizzle of wanting more, a banked fire in the pit of her stomach.

"You okay?" Walsh asked, voice husky with aftermath.

"Very much so." Except it felt vast and lonely over here on her side of the bed suddenly. With the sort of bold familiarity that only existed in the dark of night between sheets, she reached over and found his hand on top of the covers. He let her lift it, arm pliant and unresisting, so she could take his palm between both of hers and angle his knuckles toward the weak haze of moonlight above their heads.

"I have to know about these," she said of his rings, passing a fingertip across their ridges. "Do they mean something? Or did you just like the way they looked?"

"Little of both. Mostly it's because when you're my size, it never hurts to have a sharp punch."

She grinned.

"But that one there on my thumb?" It was the face of a snarling dog, wrought with incredible detail. "I got that when I patched in London. Everybody gets one."

"It's...well, I won't say pretty. That's probably not the effect you're going for."

He snorted. "The Union Jack's to remind where I come from, not to get too above my means." It was on his ring finger, and though colorless, the distinct bars of the British flag were visible. "The W my mum gave me." It was done in masculine but elaborate font. "I've got the eagle on the other hand, for the States. And the skulls I just liked." He shrugged and the sheets rustled.

She rubbed her thumb slowly across the laughing face of one of the skulls, flushing with heat as she remembered the feel of it against her sex.

"Any tattoos?" she asked, not sure if she wanted there to be any.

"No." His voice became reflective. "There just wasn't anything I wanted in my skin."

"Hmm."

"Okay, my turn for a question. How long do you need?" he asked. "Before we go again."

She rolled toward him, smiling.

Fifteen

The sun woke her. Not her alarm clock, not the chirp of her phone, not a hungry horse pawing at its stall door below, but the sun's bright early rays, stabbing at her closed eyes and sending her into a little ball beneath the covers. *Five more minutes*, she thought. *Just five more minutes, and then I'll get up.*

And then she remembered where she was.

"Oh shit."

The covers slid off her naked skin as she sat up, and she grabbed for them as her eyes skipped across the bare room. Mattress on the floor. Her clothes in a puddle a few feet away. Memory of Walsh, neon all over every part of her skin.

Damn.

It had been nothing like she'd been expecting. It had been so much more than that.

But now she was faced with the reality that she'd slept with her boss, and that she had to go to work and pretend the world hadn't been knocked askew.

Fuzzy-headed and vaguely sick from drinking, she scrambled to her feet, determined not to stare at the marks on her hips and thighs where finger-shaped bruises were going to darken over the next few days.

She hurried into her clothes, a little breathless, heartbeat pounding in her temples, and not only because of the drinking. The wide room with its knotted pine floors and heavy moldings felt too empty, too cold.

The en suite bath, trimmed in modern chrome fixtures and sensible but expensive porcelain, echoed with the sound of her breathing. In the mirror, she looked pale, drawn, muddled. Like a ghost.

What had she done?

She didn't have rash, frenzied sexual encounters with near-strangers. She didn't have sweaty, gasp-inducing, spectacular —

Don't go there. Just don't.

Part of her hoped Walsh would be gone, off on his bike to do whatever bikers did first thing in the morning. But as she took the stairs down to the first level, another part of her hoped to see him. Laying eyes on him, all disheveled the morning after what they'd done, would be the real test. The thing that determined how much of a mistake it had been.

She got the chance to find out, because he was on the front porch, sitting down on the far end at the built-in wooden breakfast table, laptop open in front of him. He'd pulled on his jeans from yesterday, but the belt was unfasted, his feet were bare, and without a shirt, the morning sunlight was catching in his golden chest hair, highlighting his truly awful farmer's tan. Dolly lay at his feet. A cup of coffee sat beside the computer. The utter absorption as he stared at the screen was both boyish and cynical, the lines in his face harsh, his focus adorable.

Dolly lifted her head and let out a single low bark of greeting.

Walsh turned, and the sharpness of his eyes froze Emmie in her tracks. Whatever he meant to convey, she was powerless against the onslaught of heat that poured through her, turned her stomach to molten gold. The night before flashed through her mind like a slideshow, and she knew then that she wanted it again, and again. Wanted *him*.

Damn it.

She wasn't ruled by her hormones, though. "Morning," she said, closing the distance between them, striving to look as unaffected as possible.

His eyes flicked over her, and she knew he was looking right through her clothes and remembering. "Mornin'." Then his eyes went back to the laptop and he turned it toward her. "You're gonna want to see this."

It was a video streamed from that morning's local Fox affiliate news cast. Walsh clicked play and it jumped into motion.

"Davis Richards died Tuesday evening, found in his home, unresponsive by an employee," the grave suit-wearing anchor said to the camera. "Authorities initially believed cause of death to be a heart attack, but we're just learning that's not true.

142

According to the coroner's report, Richards' death was the result of a drug overdose..."

Emmie didn't hear the rest of it. It seemed like her ear canals compressed, like sound was coming from a long, long way off. "What?" She turned to Walsh. "*What?*"

~*~

The coffee was helping. Emmie took another long sip, drew her legs up into the chair and watched over her knees as Becca and Fred led the horses out one at a time to their pastures. She wanted to feel terrible that she was abandoning them to the morning feeding routine, but she was too shocked to feel much of anything.

She got more hot coffee down her throat and glanced over at Walsh, still shirtless, still gorgeous, much less distracting now. "That door," she said, frowning. "I knew there was something fishy up because the back door was open a crack."

"Bloke's having a heart attack, he might forget to shut the door."

"But he didn't have a heart attack, did he? I know for a fact that man didn't have a secret drug habit. Drinking, sure. You hardly saw him without his Solo cup of hooch. But drugs? Enough to OD? No. Never."

"Well you know what that means, then."

"Murder."

His brows gave a jump that seemed regretful. "Think about what you wanna say, pet, 'cause that story got leaked, and we aren't supposed to know about it yet. Coppers are gonna be talking to you and me."

She blinked. "Why us?"

"You found the body." He pulled a cigarette from the pack on the table, put it between his teeth while he lit it. Smoke curled through his words when he spoke again. "And 'cause I'm living in his house."

The coffee congealed in her stomach. "We're suspects." Except she knew she wasn't. Which meant... "*You're* a suspect."

And she'd been alone with him, been in bed with him, had him inside her.

He met her wild eyes with a steady, calculating look. "Do you think I killed him?"

Did she?

Davis had sold the farm without fuss. And the way Walsh had been with her, the blunt way he was asking her now – she couldn't think the worst of him, biker or not.

"No," she said, her inner tension easing. "I really don't."

His mouth twitched. "Woulda been a shame to have my girlfriend thinkin' I was a murderer."

His what?

She opened her mouth to protest, and caught a flash of shine down on the driveway. A police cruiser pulling up down at the barn.

Emmie took a deep breath and got to her feet. "The 'coppers' are here."

~*~

Walsh had no personal feelings toward Sergeant Vince Fielding. From what he'd seen, the guy was a standup cop who took his job seriously, who tended toward fussy when rebuffed. Not the enemy, just someone whose path he didn't love crossing.

"I wasn't here," he said with a shrug. "Not much else to say."

Fielding propped his hands on his gun belt and looked beleaguered. "Walsh, you know this doesn't look good."

"It doesn't?"

"Considering you're the only one of this bunch with an IQ, yeah, you do." Pointed look down the length of his nose. "So tell me your whereabouts, with decent alibis, and don't gimme a buncha shit, alright?"

"Fair enough." Walsh was still at the table on the porch, working on his second cigarette and third cup of coffee. He'd gone in to shower, shave, and draw on clean clothes while Fielding was busy down at the barn, talking to that crew.

Respectability lending itself to credibility, and all that. He tapped the ash off his smoke and took another drag.

"We closed on the sale that afternoon," he said, and the cop lifted his brows in surprise. "Richards knew loads of people at the banks, so he got it all accelerated. We closed, I left from there 'bout four, went to Dartmoor. Security cameras should clock me in the clubhouse till eight. Then I went home. Old home," he clarified. "Had a beer, talked to my brother on the phone – you can check my mobile for the time stamp. Give Shane a call if you want. He'll tell you we talked about my mum's terrible love life. That's when Richards bit it."

"And you can say all that on record for me at the station later?"

"If you need me to."

Fielding sighed, but nodded. "Thanks."

It always paid, Walsh kept trying to tell Aidan and the younger ones, not to be a smartass with law enforcement. No sense making trouble for yourself.

The sergeant paused at the top of the porch steps, glancing back over his shoulder. "Your barn manager was very defensive of you, by the way."

"Have to give her a raise then."

Fielding snorted. "Yeah."

~*~

"Oh my God, I heard it on the news!" Tally's owner said, grabbing Emmie by both shoulders in a way that was meant to be concerned, but came off as manic. "Overdose! Who knew? Did you know anything?"

Emmie tried unsuccessfully to back out of the woman's grip. "We had no idea."

"None of you?" She looked at Fred and Becca, then swung her gaze toward Walsh, who stood propped against the stone façade of the barn. "Who are you? Are you the new guy?"

"No, ma'am," he said, straight-faced. "Just a groundskeeper."

145

Emmie rolled her eyes before Patricia whirled to face her again.

"I just can't believe it!"

"None of us can," Emmie assured her. She pried the woman's hands off her and was thankful no offense seemed taken. "The police are looking into it."

Which meant they'd shooed Walsh out of the house and were dusting for prints, taking lint-rollers to everything, and accomplishing nothing because any evidence had to be trampled at this point. Drug overdose, sure, but it was being investigated as a homicide. No needle found? That meant whoever had pumped the drugs into Davis had taken it with him.

"*Señora* Cross, Tally is ready," Fred reminded, gently.

"Yes, of course." Patricia seemed to shake herself. "Just shocking," she muttered, heading into the barn.

When she was gone, Becca said, "Mr. Walsh, did you kill Mr. Richards?" in an innocent voice Emmie knew to be an act.

She elbowed her working student and got a muffled chuckle in return.

Walsh didn't take the bait, eyeing Becca flatly. "Gonna turn me in if I did?"

"Yes! I always wanted to be on the news."

Even Fred had to laugh at that.

Emmie smiled and saw the echo of a grin deep in the centers of Walsh's eyes.

"Fred!" Patricia called from inside the barn. "I need you!"

"*Ay Dios mio*," he muttered. "*Si Señora*, I'm coming." He tapped Becca on the shoulder. "You have horses to ride, *amiga*."

"I know, I know." She got reluctantly to her feet and followed him inside.

In their absence, Emmie became very aware of the fact that she hadn't showered, probably looked like hell, and hadn't had a moment earlier to spend any kind of real time with Walsh. The news of Davis's murder had eclipsed any morning-after stuff.

"Busy day?" he asked.

"Lessons start back up, so yeah. Pretty busy."

This was awkward, and she didn't want it to be.

"Fielding didn't scare you, did he?"

"Of course not."

He grinned. "Of course not." With a glance down the barn aisle, he pushed off the wall and walked toward her.

Her eyes went to the way his shoulders shifted inside his plain gray t-shirt.

She wasn't expecting him to lay hands on her, to put one on her hip and cup the back of her head with the other, kiss her like he had every right to.

Her breathing was shaky when he pulled back.

"I gotta go into Dartmoor. You'll be alright, yeah?"

"Yeah," she said, hollowly, gaze trained on his mouth.

He kissed her one more time and she had a bad feeling she'd be back in his floor-bed again very soon.

~*~

"He just left here with our camera feeds for the past week," Ghost said of Fielding, scowling. "Jesus Christ." His eyes flipped up to Walsh. "Who killed the old fucker?"

"My guy at the lab," Ratchet cut in, "says it was H. Nobody deals heroin 'round here that we don't know about it. So it's no one in the underground."

"My guess is one of his lovely family members," Walsh said, taking a hard slug off his Newcastle. He filled Ghost in on Amy's proposition, much to the amusement of his brothers. "And then Em says the grandson's a total prick."

"Em?" Ghost asked.

"That'd be the little blonde, right?" Briscoe asked, grinning.

"Totally hot," RJ put in.

Ghost made an inquiring face.

"My barn manager. The one I kept on from Davis."

Ghost nodded. "And I'm assuming you're fucking her?"

"Dude, I would be," RJ said.

Walsh shrugged. "She's a nice girl. We get on well."

Ghost smirked. "Which has gotta be you-speak for 'I'm hitting that.' Alright. Whatever. She's got your back?"

He hesitated a moment. Sex didn't turn a staunch MC supporter out of a woman like that. But he wanted to trust her. He thought he could. "Yeah, she does."

"Good. You keep the heat off of us. Whatever happens with the investigation happens." And there was more of that unquestioning trust. So precious and rare coming from Ghost Teague.

The president then glanced over at Mercy. "You got yourself a peeper trap yet?"

Walsh tuned them out. He was worried, and since he couldn't remember the last time he'd felt that way, it was consuming him. He was being trusted to handle the Briar Hall situation, and while he could – that was starting to sound more and more difficult.

Sixteen

"What a big girl you're getting to be." And a squirmy one, too. The first time Lucy rolled over, Holly celebrated with exclamations, clapping, and a little dancing around the room. But by the two-hundredth time, while she was trying to diaper her, it was much less cute.

Not that she was finding fault. She wasn't sure there was anything more wonderful in the world than the tiny girl she'd made with Michael.

Lucy stopped trying to roll over long enough for Holly to get the clean diaper secure, then decided she was done with that game, smiling and cooing up at her mother.

Holly smiled back. "There, isn't that better?" She scooped the baby up onto her shoulder and carried her out of the nursery, down the hall into the main part of the house. "How about lunch? Hmm?"

Most days, Lucy was at the Dartmoor Trucking office with her, in her Pack'n Play, fawned over by customers and employees alike. Sometimes, she had Remy Lécuyer for company, when Ava was at school and Maggie couldn't watch him. So Lucy was never starved for attention, but Holly loved her days off, when it was just her and her girl, waiting on Daddy to get home at five-thirty. Lucy lit up like Christmas when Michael picked her up every evening, and his mixed bag response of terror and adoration melted Holly's insides.

"What should I make for dinner, Luce?" Holly asked as they entered the kitchen. "That roast needs to get cooked before it goes…"

There was a man standing on the back deck, visible through the glass insets in the door.

"…bad." Holly's heart slammed into her ribs. "God," she breathed, a hand going to the back of Lucy's head on protective reflex, tucking the baby in tightly beneath her chin. "Oh, God."

He had flipped the tops off their rolling trash cans and was poking around in them. *Homeless* was her first thought, but then she looked more closely at him. Clean white sneakers, new jeans, a plain black t-shirt. Hair buzzed close to his head. He was young – younger than Michael at least – and tan, appeared to be in good health.

So not homeless, which ratcheted her panic another notch. Had he been in search of a meal and a trash find, she would have felt sympathy. Now she felt like someone was stalking them. And that never went anywhere healthy.

As if he'd sensed her presence, he froze, turned around, stared hard through the window panes. He was wearing sunglasses, but she could see the anger in his face; she knew that emotion too well to ever mistake it for anything else.

Then he flashed her a brilliant smile that was not even a little sincere, and stepped in close, until his nose almost touched the window. "Good afternoon!" He was shouting to be heard through the glass. "Ma'am, I'm with Knoxville PD, and we've gotten reports of strange activity in your neighborhood. Have you seen anyone who's out of place? Heard anything unusual?"

Yeah, you she thought, frowning. "You're police?" she called back, and Lucy started to fuss. "Where's your badge?"

He gave her an over the top regretful face. "I'm afraid I'm off-duty and it's in the car. Do you mind if I step in and we have a word?"

"Yes." She kicked her chin up. "I do mind. And my husband would too."

He stared at her, perplexed. For a moment, the anger caught hold of his blunt features again, but then he put the fake charm back on. "Okay, well, thank you anyway."

Her breathing didn't return to normal until he was out of sight, and then her heart was running like a jackrabbit.

Michael answered on the second ring, voice gruff and low, like he was glad she'd called, but was never going to be one of those guys who made a big deal about it. "Hi, baby."

She took a deep breath. "Michael, I think I just met our peeping tom."

Seventeen

Years after the fact, Walsh could look back on that day with Rita and know that the outcome had been for the best. At thirty-nine, he could say with confidence that a life attached to her in any way would have been nothing but miserable. Anyone related to her, who carried her DNA, would have been poisoned from conception. Just as well a life hadn't been allowed to grow to fruition. It was better all around that they'd never become a family.

But at nineteen, fresh from his banishment from the track, holding onto nothing save the ghost of the life he'd tried to make for himself in Brighton, Rita's betrayal had been one of those tidal shifts in his history. Gramps was dead, and Gram had moved to London to be with Mum, where she could be cared for. It had been just him, all alone in Brighton, pretending he wasn't a street rat and that exercise riding and stall-mucking was somehow better than the urban heritage he wanted to deny. After all, he hadn't been alone, not really – he'd had Rita.

If he opened up his mental file cabinet and pulled out that day, he could see it in aching detail. Could smell the ammonia stink of horse piss and the mold of the straw bedding. He could hear Rita's footfalls coming down the barn aisle: *rat-tat-rat-tat.*

His heart had leapt for a moment, just a moment, before she came into sight and the sheer cold wall that her face had become told him what he couldn't bring himself to ask. *"I had it taken care of,"* she said. Just like that. Like it was a carpet stain, or a shirt that needed mending, rather than a baby in her belly. *"I can't be having a baby by the likes of you,"* she'd said. Because her father was a partial owner of one of the horses, and he was just the hired help.

With one quick trip to the clinic, she'd had his future stripped out of her womb.

How did a man grow tender with a woman after that?

151

Walsh closed his eyes a moment, cleared the memory, and opened them again to see the road unfurling ahead through the lenses of his sunglasses. He didn't know why he was thinking about Rita now, when there were so many things on his plate.

He didn't want it to be because of Emmie. He couldn't afford to go there with her. He wasn't Ghost, wasn't Mercy, wasn't Michael – wasn't the sort of man who magnetized a woman to his side. He lacked their magic.

He shoved it all away.

The scene he arrived upon at Briar Hall wasn't a welcome one. Cars jammed the parking pad and a knot of people stood in the threshold of the double doors. Lots of movement, arms waving. When he killed the engine, he heard the shouting, and he leapt off his bike, fighting the impulse to reach for the gun in his waistband. It was knee-jerk, but liable to get him arrested in polite society.

All of Richards' kids were present, all red-faced and furious. At the center of the group, Manny Richards held his youngest sister Amy back, while Amy gesticulated, raved, cried, screamed…at Emmie. Emmie, who was ashen-faced, eyes glittering with unshed tears. Fred had stepped in front of her, and little skinny Becca had a stall fork in her hands like she meant to use it on someone. But Emmie was staring at Amy, and she was devastated by whatever was coming out of the woman's mouth.

Walsh didn't need to hear the words to know what was happening, but they assaulted him anyway.

"…you killed him!" Amy screamed. "You always wanted this farm for yourself. You and your boyfriend. Your little fuckbuddy! You killed my dad. You *killed him!*"

Oh hell no. This wasn't going to go on. His farm, his woman.

His woman?

Walsh gave his shrillest, loudest whistle, and all heads came his direction. "Oi, cut the shit, the lot of you," he said. He didn't demand explanations, because he didn't want them. "All of you" – he gestured to the Richards – "get the hell off my property 'fore I have you arrested."

152

Wouldn't Fielding love that? An outlaw calling the cops.

Amy rounded on him. "You!" she screamed. Mascara and snot poured down her face. "You and that stupid little bitch killed my dad!"

Her son stepped around her, bowed up with aggression. "Fuck you!" he yelled. A vein leapt in his forehead. "Foreign prick, fuck you, I'll kill you!"

"That's original."

"Walsh," Emmie said, and his heart grabbed, the way she looked at him like she was worried about him, the withheld tears.

Walsh refocused, trained his gaze on Brett Richards and his bloodshot eyes. Drug user, he thought. Hmm…and Richards was killed with H? Wonder where that came from.

"Kill me," he said calmly, "and you'll have an army of men on top of you. This ain't a bar parking lot fight, mate. Recognize that you've lost, and move on. Yeah?"

Brett lunged forward, but Manny caught him, whispered something in his ear, frowning harshly.

"Yes," Walsh continued, "if you could all just leave, that'd be brilliant."

There was a lot of mumbling, fussing, and arguing, but en masse, the group headed toward their vehicles.

"This isn't over," Manny said ominously. He thought it was ominous anyway.

Walsh didn't react, waiting stone-faced until all their vehicles had headed down the driveway.

His three employees sagged with obvious relief.

"Oh my God," Becca said. "Those assholes think Em killed Mr. Richards. I mean, seriously." She snorted. "If anybody did, it was Brett."

Emmie turned toward her working student like she meant to chastise her, but didn't follow through. She swallowed hard, eyes still glimmering.

"Fred," Walsh said, "are the horses all put away for the evening?"

"*Sí.*"

"And the lessons all over?"

"*Sí, Señor.*"

"Good. I'll you see you tomorrow."

And then his eyes were only for Emmie as he stepped toward her. "Come on, love," he said quietly, sliding an arm across her shoulders. "Ignore it. Just put it out of your head."

~*~

Easier said than done. Emmie put the wineglass to her lips, saluted her drunken father in her head, and drank deep.

"Why the hell'd you drink gin last night when you had a decent white up here?" Walsh asked, filling his own glass.

"'Cause liquor is quicker," she said, shaking her head. "And because I'm doomed to my DNA," she muttered.

He cocked his head, staring at her in that penetrating way that left her frightened and turned on at the same time. "You think that?"

"You don't?"

He made a considering face. "If I did, I'd have about nine kids by now."

"You're one of nine?"

"Half-brothers and sisters, all."

"Ah." She felt a quick stab of sympathy for him. "I always thought being an only child was the worst. Maybe it's not?"

"Definitely not." He set the wine down on the small café table between them with a soft thump. "They aren't all bad. Some I get on with. But knowing my father's a useless piece of shit? Not the best feeling."

"I'll drink to that."

The wine went down her throat with a crisp kick and a warm afterburn in her stomach. Worlds better than gin, but it left her soft and sensitive. Gin could dull the pain, but wine could make it worse, if she let it.

Walsh had lingered down at the barn after the Richards mess was swept out onto the road, undeterred by Fred and Becca's questioning looks and raised eyebrows. Emmie had known where the night would end up, and wasn't going to fight it. When they were alone, she'd said, "Come on up," and here they were in her loft, the smell of frozen pizza beginning to waft over from the oven.

"It's nice," he'd told her.

"You've seen it before," she'd said, and he'd ducked his head in acknowledgement.

"You know these assholes better than I do," he said, slumping down against the back of the chair. "How far are they gonna take things?"

"They're mostly talk. The kids anyway. Davis was the bulldog. None of those five have ever had to take care of anyone or anything, so chances are slim they'll push much further."

"Good. We don't have to talk about them, then."

"Isn't that what you said last night?" she asked, grin tugging at her lips, warmth tugging even harder in the pit of her stomach.

His golden brows lifted. "You want to do things differently than we did last night?" A tiny hint of a smirk sent her pulse skyward.

"Depends on what you mean by *differently*."

The oven timer chose that moment to go off with a loud droning buzz. The last thing she wanted was to get up and walk away from the table – more like crawl across it to get in his lap. But the touch of his eyes on her body made her regret it a little less.

It hadn't ever been like this for her, this mutual, mature attraction. The patience in him, the way he could eat and drink with her and talk about things, all the while he was simmering on low, ready to get his hands on her – that turned her on more than *anything* ever had.

She cut the pizza and carried the plates back to the table, let him top off her wine. When she was settled, blowing on her slice of pepperoni to cool it, he said, "Can I ask you something?"

"Sure."

His face grew serious, the sexual gleam leaving his eyes, replaced with something that looked raw in the low light. "Where will you go," he said carefully, "when you're done here?"

"Um…to the dishwasher, I guess. To put the plates in it."

"No, I mean: when you're done with Briar Hall, when you move on, where then?"

The question hit her like a fist. "Why would I be done with it?"

He made a face that said *come on*. "You're young, you're talented – aren't you trying to get in with some big name trainer? Set up your own barn? Get married?"

"I…" Her bite of pizza felt lodged in her throat. The anxiety that always accompanied such questions turned her hands clammy, tightened her chest.

"I'm not saying you ought to do those things, love," Walsh said. "It's just, in my experience, good things don't stick around very long. So I'm wondering if you've got plans. If you're planning on leaving me." He smiled, but it was false and sad.

She set her pizza down, heart pounding. "And I better jump on those good things before they go away?"

His voice grew softer, gentler. "No, pet. *You* are the good thing."

She couldn't breathe. She lurched to her feet, paced away from the table. When she turned around, Walsh was watching her with that appraising look of his. The words tumbled out of her, lubed up by the wine.

"I was supposed to go to Florida," Emmie said. "All the good dressage trainers winter in Florida or California. I was going to go work for an Olympian, ride his horses, get myself a sponsor." She shook her head, pain prickling her skin at the memory. "I applied to be a working student with four different trainers. Sent resumes, videos. Even rode in person for one of them. You know what they said? They said I didn't have 'it.' I didn't have the 'wow factor.' 'She's a good rider,' they said, but I wasn't ever going to be anything 'special.' And what the hell does that mean, huh? 'It'?"

He shook his head. "No idea."

"Amy was my only reference – I've ridden here all my life, never worked anywhere else, thinking *loyalty* would count for something. And you know what? Loyalty isn't shit, because now

156

Amy hates me, won't give me a good recommendation, and I wasted my whole life on a family that's accusing me of killing one of them." She shut her eyes against the tears and they pressed hard at the lids.

"Loyalty counts."

"No, it doesn't." She sighed deeply, years' worth of devotion and incredibly hard work scraping against her lungs. She dropped back into her chair. "And marriage?" She snorted. "Men don't like me. Men don't want me."

"I do."

God, his face, with its intensity and sincerity, the blue of his eyes in the dim light. The tears came back, blurring her vision.

"You don't want me to leave, do you?" she whispered. "Because I have nowhere to go. All I have is this farm."

"No, love. I'll never want you to go."

Emmie wasn't aware of moving, knew only that he was suddenly right in front of her, and that she was crouched before him, her hands on his denim-covered thighs. "I'm sorry. I don't mean to cry—"

He caught her face in his hands and kissed her, drew her up against him and pulled her astride his lap so he could get better access, crack her jaw wide with his lips and taste the inside of her mouth.

His hands moved down her neck, her shoulders, until they were on her hips and pulling her in tighter. His tongue flicked against the roof of her mouth the same moment his hips lifted into her.

Maybe he was lying about wanting her long-term, but he wanted her now; she could feel the evidence against the inside of her thigh. And maybe she shouldn't have, but she wanted him just as badly.

His hands slid forward, skimming beneath her shirt across the sensitive bare skin of her belly, finding the button of her shorts and thumbing it open. He teased the zipper down, slid a thumb into the opening, found her clit through her panties with devastating accuracy.

She tilted her hips forward, seeking his touch, urging him to go further.

He pulled back from her mouth, pressed a kiss to her jaw, beneath her ear, his stubble prickling at her skin. A low, throaty whisper, right at her earlobe: "Do you ride anything besides horses?"

She didn't recognize her own voice, the ache in it. "*Yes.*"

She hated that she had to climb off of him and stand to ditch her shorts. But then she was straddling his lap again, knees against the seat of the chair so she'd have leverage, and his hands were sliding up her bare thighs. "I have a magic trick for you: get a condom out of your pocket while you're sitting down, 'cause I'm not getting up again," she teased, wrapping her arms around his neck.

He grinned and lifted one hand, Trojan packet held between two fingers. "Way ahead of you."

Her fingers trembled with anticipation as she unfastened his belt and jeans, took him in-hand and did the honors with the condom.

It had never been this way with a man before, like that persistent emptiness inside her shifted, so she needed more than a hug, a kind word, those small tokens she limped along with. With Walsh, it became this acute need; she wanted him inside her, wanted the pleasure to be her comfort, her stand-in for love. Wanted him specifically, just him, his hands on her as she sank slowly down, taking him deep, relishing the sense of being filled, loving his sharp indrawn breath as her sex gripped his cock tight.

"Jesus," he whispered, and his fingers bit into her hips.

Emmie flattened her hands on top of his shoulders and lifted, and lowered. Found a rhythm. It was nothing and everything like riding, and her thighs knew the tension to hold, and her muscles were primed for this kind of joining. The tension built in slow, gossamer tides, and she felt like she could have spent hours building it, little by little, sustaining the teases of pleasure without reaching the crest.

She didn't want it to be over.

But apparently, Walsh wasn't going to let her do all the steering.

He hooked his hands behind her knees and pulled her legs straight on either side of his hips, so she was sitting on his lap, fully impaled, the penetration impossibly deep, and wholly within his control.

"Walsh," she said on a gasp, not sure if it was a question or a plea. She didn't want it to stop. She wanted –

"Trust me, love," he murmured, and eased her upper body back, back, back…until she was lying across the tabletop.

Completely vulnerable. Stretched out. At his mercy.

"Walsh," she said again, and he rolled his hips, lifting into her, the penetration at a new angle. "Oh," she said, and then she bit down hard on her lip as he moved again.

His hands glided up beneath her shirt, bundling it, pushing it above her breasts. He unclasped her bra with an efficient move and pushed it up too, so she was naked to his eyes, bent back like a sacrificial offering.

She was more than ready to play the lamb, especially as his hands closed over her breasts. He shaped them in his palms, teased her nipples to tight buttons.

She lifted into his touch, shameless and gasping.

Endless teasing, petting. And when she thought she'd shatter with waiting, he lifted her with two firm hands on her thighs and surged to his feet, driving forward hard with his hips, pinning her down to the table.

It was a small table, and her head hung off the far side, but she didn't care. The first real man to come into her life was about to make her come, and it was going to be earth-shattering.

She clutched at his shoulders as the spasms hit her, wrapped her legs around his waist.

Mind-blowing was too polite a word.

And after – after, he was so sweet, and cradled her in his arms, carried her to bed. He stripped naked and climbed in beside her, pulling her in close, tucking her head beneath his chin.

All her life, Emmie had wondered why women allowed themselves to become entangled with heartbreaking, poisonous men. Law-breakers and chain-smokers.

Now she knew. As he switched off the lamp and darkness bathed their sweat-damp bodies, she understood completely.

~*~

One second Walsh was deep asleep, dreaming about soft, feminine sounds of pleasure, and the next he was fully awake, staring through the dark, his arm wrapped around a warm, narrow waist.

"What was that?" Emmie whispered, and he knew she was awake too.

"Dunno. Sounded like one of the horses maybe."

As if on cue, the sound echoed again below them, and it was indeed equine: a short, unhappy snort. Followed by the strike of a hoof against a wooden stall door.

The covers rustled and Emmie slid away from him, sitting up as a dark shadow against the timber wall. "I better go check."

Given Michael and Mercy's peeping tom complaints, Walsh wasn't betting on a coincidence. "Not alone you're not." His head reeled as he sat up, but he told it to cooperate.

He fumbled around and managed to pull his jeans on, found his gun in his cut, where he'd left it.

When Emmie flicked the lights on, he saw that she was wearing his shirt and had tugged on a pair of soft cotton shorts. She pushed her hair back and stepped into her ugly brown clogs. "You don't have to come," she insisted.

"Yeah, I do. And I'm going first." Belt done up, boots on, gun in hand, that was the best he could do for the moment. "You got a torch?"

"A – oh, a flashlight, yeah." She produced one from a kitchen drawer and handed it over. "You're armed?" Her face compressed and became impossible to read as she stared at the Glock in his right hand.

"That a problem?"

"Just unnecessary."

"We'll see."

A black stretch of shadow lay at the bottom of her staircase. The moon was up, and pale light lit every window and both wide doors at either end of the aisle, but the center was blackness, filled with the restless shifting of animals, at least most of which were horses. Walsh had a prickling up the back of his neck that told him at least one human was here, too.

"Stay behind me," he whispered.

She snorted. "Yeah. I'll do that, Hercules."

"I'm serious, Em."

There was a scuffle of noise like footsteps on the concrete aisle.

Walsh clicked on the torch and flashed its beam in a fast arc, his Glock at the ready below it, police-style.

Nothing.

But still, his skin crawled like someone was watching him, like maybe someone lurked just out of sight. He was never wrong about that sensation, and so he stood, sweeping the aisle with the light, hand tight on the gun.

"Good Lord," Emmie said and ducked around him. "We're not in a detective movie." She hit the lights and they came on with a dull hum, flooding the barn with fluorescent glare.

He winced against the onslaught. "I thought I told you to stay behind me."

"I need to make sure the horses are alright." She paused in her walk down the aisle, turned and gave him a wide-eyed look. "Does this sort of thing happen to you all the time? Does being a Lean Dog inspire a lot of nights like this?" She gestured toward him.

He lowered the gun and torch. "No," he lied. "But it's best not to be an idiot about weird noises in the middle of the night."

She gave him a funny look, mouth tucked to one side.

"Check the horses. I'll have a look around."

She nodded.

Nothing struck him as out of the ordinary as he circled the barn. He flushed a fox from the shrubs around one of the outbuildings, but otherwise all was still. He walked through the back barn doors and found Emmie standing in front of her horse's stall, tickling at his chin with her fingertips and saying something low and baby-talkish to him. She filled out his shirt in a completely different way than he did, the chest stretched tight, the shoulders, sleeves, and everything else too baggy for her. She looked tan, fit, young and wholesome, with a little edge of freshly-fucked around the edges.

Reaching above your means again, he told himself. So what if she didn't have any plans now. Was that any excuse to take her future for himself?

His phone rang, the sound blaring in the quiet, startling Emmie. Her finger-raked curls flared around her head as she turned to face him, and he was struck by the urge to wrap them around his hands again.

Later.

The screen ID'd the caller as Mercy and his stomach tightened. It was almost midnight, which meant this wasn't a social call.

"Yeah?"

Mercy's normally-jovial voice was grim on the other end of the line. "Fisher's dead."

"Shit. How?"

"Someone put a bullet through his brain. He was supposed to meet Ratchet tonight, and when he didn't show up, Ratch went looking. Found him at his place, very dead, very fresh."

"Ah, Christ…"

The little dealer had his faults – housekeeping and personal hygiene among them – but they all bore a certain affection for the weasel. "What's to be done?" Walsh asked, mindful of the way Emmie's eyes rested on him.

"Ghost doesn't want to call the PD – too many connections with us. And the guy's got no family to cry for the news cameras. We're gonna bring him to the property. Meet us there in fifteen?"

"Yeah."

When he disconnected, Emmie stepped toward him. "What's wrong?"

"Nothing." He slipped the phone in his pocket and met her halfway, settled his hands on her hips and pulled her in close. "Club stuff."

"Oh." The way she said it was like cold water across him, her doubt and apprehension.

But he loved the dewy look of her bottom lip and the way her eyes tracked all across his face like she was trying to read him. She wouldn't be able to do it successfully, but the effort was nice.

"You go back to bed, love."

Her hands landed on his bare chest, small and warm. "You're not coming with me?"

Damn, he wanted to.

"No, baby." He leaned in and kissed her. She had a soft mouth, and she liked to kiss. She was eager and pliant. "I've gotta go somewhere. Which means" – he reached beneath the shirt, wrapped his hands around the narrowest part of her waist – "I'm gonna need this back."

He drew the shirt up so fast she had no choice but to lift her arms free with a startled gasp.

She didn't cover herself, though. She matched his stare and hooked her fingers in the front of his belt, titling her upper body so her raised nipples brushed his chest.

"Will you be back before morning?" she asked in a throaty, thoroughly aroused voice that rubbed hard against his self-control.

He gritted his teeth against temptation – and then finally gave in a little. He covered her breasts with his hands, kissed her again, let her feel the warm slide of his tongue in her mouth. "Yeah," he said as he pulled back, feeling out of breath. "Yeah. But you go back up." The situation pushed back against his lust. "And for Christsakes, don't go wandering around in the dark by yourself, yeah? Be careful."

She nodded and composed herself, stepped back. "Yeah. Okay."

He forced himself to move away from her, tugging on his shirt and heading for the doors before he could change his mind.

One last glance back showed her shirtless under the bright lights, watching him go, her lip caught between her teeth.

~*~

About five seconds after he disappeared, Emmie became aware that she was mostly naked in the middle of the barn aisle. "Shit." She covered herself and dashed up the stairs, pulled on the first shirt she found, an old unisex rag that had the United States Dressage Federation logo printed on the front.

This was so unlike her. All this need and want and being overtly sexual. God, what was wrong with her? And worse yet, why didn't she want it to stop?

Maybe there was some truth to that whole sexual frustration theory, she thought with an eye roll.

She was collecting their forgotten dinner dishes from the counter when she realized she hadn't heard Walsh's bike start. Or the truck. She hadn't heard anything.

She set the dishes down and walked to the window, the one set in a deep dormer that overlooked the main fields. A small light was bobbing its way down the run between the pastures, heading for the tree line. The flashlight she'd given Walsh, had to be.

"What the hell?" she muttered. Why would he go wandering through the fields at midnight?

Club stuff, huh?

She argued with herself a moment, watching the flashlight progress toward the trees. Go back to bed, he'd told her. Be careful.

Yeah right.

She pulled on thick socks, stepped into her muck boots, and grabbed the spare flashlight. Around her neck and shoulder she slung a cross-body leather bag. Inside it was a .22 Magnum revolver.

~*~

"Poor Fisher," Mercy said. "He died like he lived: real shitty."

Aidan made a sound like he was smothering a laugh, then cleared his throat. "It's not funny, bro."

"No, it's not," Mercy said in all seriousness. In the wash of the truck's headlights, the big Cajun was unusually somber. "You know we gotta find out who did this, right?"

"We will," Ghost assured. "Ratchet, you got all the pictures you needed?"

"Yep." Apparently, the secretary had acted as MC CSI back at the trailer, recording what he could, even pulling prints off the front doorknob that his buddy in the lab would try to run for them.

"I don't believe in coincidences," Walsh said. "Someone's been lookin' in our windows, spying on us, and our main dealer turns up dead? That's related, boys, I'd put money on it."

"And Walsh doesn't fuck around with money," Mercy said.

"How's that hole coming, boys?" Ghost asked.

In answer, a shovel heaved up out of the grave, followed by another, followed by Carter and Littlejohn heaving themselves up onto the grass. Dirt-smeared and panting, they stretched out on the ground and stared up at the stars.

"Shit," Carter said. "It's ready."

"Thank God for seniority," Aidan said, nudging Carter in the head with his toe.

Carter swiped his boot away but it was an exhausted, uncoordinated effort.

"Alright," Ghost said. "Let's get him out of the truck."

The mood went somber again in a flash. Drug dealer, scrawny redneck – whatever else he'd been, Fisher had been loyal to them, and he deserved a little respect at his unsanctioned burial. Especially considering they were more than likely the cause of his death.

Mercy and Michael opened up the camper shell on the back of the club truck and carefully pulled out Fisher's burlap-wrapped body. A nice touch, Walsh thought, because the burlap could be burned and leave no DNA evidence behind. They laid him in the grass and pulled back a square of the fabric, revealing his face, the bloody hole in the center of his forehead. As moths danced across the headlight beams, it almost looked like he was moving, like his mouth lifted in a smile.

Awful, every part of it.

"Anyone want to say anything?" Mercy asked.

"You're the Catholic, Merc. Why don't you take 'er away," Ghost suggested.

"Alright." He cleared his throat, stared up at the sky for a moment. "Okay, here we go. 'Dearly beloved–' "

Walsh saw the glowing sphere of a torch just above them, at the top of the small rise they were parked beneath. Before he could react, he heard a sharp feminine gasp of shock, and then the tall grass rustled as someone fled.

Not *someone* – Emmie. She'd seen his light and followed him.

"What the–" Ghost said, swinging around.

All heads turned.

Walsh knew what he had to do, and he hated it.

Eighteen

A dead body. That was his club business – a dead body.

It was an alien breed of panic that exploded in her veins. *Run*, it said. *Run, run, run, stupid!* She had to get away, had to tell someone, had to –

She was running before her brain could give her legs the order, plunging through the dew drenched grass, struggling against the woven mat of dead stalks that tangled around her boots.

Be careful, Walsh had said.

Be careful, I'm a murderer.

A solid weight landed against her back. "Oof!" The air went out of her lungs and the weight pushed her down, down, until her knees buckled and she collapsed flat on the grass.

The panic roared; it was all she could hear, see, taste, feel. It was tangy like metal and loud as ocean waves crashing over her. Crashing and *turning* her, flipping her onto her back. She saw stars and a human shape above her. She'd managed to hold onto her flashlight and she aimed it upward, shooting her attacker in the face with the beam.

It was Walsh, eyes closing against the brightness. "Jesus, turn that thing away."

She kneed him hard as she could, aiming for his balls, hitting his thigh instead.

"Shit!"

"Get off me," she hissed, struggling to crawl from under him. "Get off!"

She knew she had to get away. If she didn't, she'd be as dead as that shrouded man beside the freshly dug hole in the ground. Hell, they might save time and chuck them together into the same grave. She'd been naïve, sleeping with this man, trusting him, letting him into her home, but she knew what happened to people who happened upon crimes. She knew what these men would do to her. What *Walsh* would do, and that broke her heart.

He snatched both wrists and pinned them to the ground beside her head, pressed his knee into her stomach and held her down like an insect specimen. She was going nowhere.

Shapes were closing in, his brothers coming, circling them like wolves in the dark.

Emmie closed her eyes and gritted her teeth. *Let it be quick*, she prayed. *Whatever it is, let it be fast.*

~*~

"Who in the fuck is that?" Ghost's voice vibrated with contained fury. It was the voice he usually reserved for Aidan's more spectacular screw-ups. Walsh couldn't remember a time when he'd been on the receiving end of such censure, and it stung. But it was no match for the dread pulsing through him. He wasn't sure what Emmie was to him at this point, but he wasn't going to let her get treated like collateral damage, that was for damn sure. He'd drive her to Canada himself if he had to.

"Just let me talk to her." Walsh heard the pleading in his voice and didn't care. "She won't be a problem."

"Merc is talking to her."

And he was, looking giant looming over her, laughing at his own jokes. Emmie sat on the tailgate of the truck and stared up at him, expressionless, her hair silver in the moonlight. Walsh thought he saw tremors in her throat, little tells of fear.

"And you're talking to me," Ghost continued. "Who is that?"

Walsh forced himself to look away from her, took a deep breath. "She works for me. She's the barn manager."

"And your girlfriend."

"She's...it's complicated."

"Oh, complicated," Ghost scoffed. "We've got a dead body, an illegal burial, and a civilian witness. *That's* complicated."

"She isn't going to say anything. Let me talk to her," he said again. "She won't squeal, I promise you."

Ghost inhaled deeply through his nostrils like an angry bull, hands settling on his hips. "I haven't liked this farm bullshit

168

from the beginning. But I trusted you" – he dropped his voice so they wouldn't be overhead – "because when it comes to this kind of stuff, I always can. But this – Walsh, this a problem. Understand? It's a big fucking problem."

"I know." He stole another glimpse Emmie's way. Mercy was talking animatedly to her and she was still as stone. "But, please…" It was all he could say. What else was there?

~*~

The man in front of her was terrifying. Rather like her horse, huge and dark-haired and powerful in a way that inspired automatic fear. But Emmie had never been afraid of Apollo, and she refused to be afraid of this man, even if her hands were shaking in her lap.

"…I bet he'd love to see the horses," he was saying, his accent something she couldn't place. "He's only a year, but he pays real close attention to stuff. And my old lady, you'd like her."

He was trying to distract her, and he was talking about his son and his pregnant wife, and beneath the glazing of shock and imminent disaster, she was struck by the sweetness of his words, the way he couldn't stop gushing about his family.

But her sole focus was Walsh up by the front of the truck, talking to a man who was clearly in charge of this whole operation. She caught the tight whispers of their conversation and felt sure her life was being decided. Could she run? They'd catch her, like they had before, damn her short legs.

Could she shoot a few of them? Doubtless men carting around dead bodies were armed to the teeth, and she didn't relish the idea of a shootout. Plus she wasn't sure she could bring herself to shoot a person. Silhouette targets were one thing, living flesh another.

"…maybe, I dunno, pet them or something?" her captor was saying.

"Sure," she said woodenly. "That's fine."

When he grinned, his teeth were so white they almost glowed in the dark.

Rustling in the grass signaled an approach, and Walsh drew up to the tailgate, braced a hand on it, bringing them closer together than she wanted to be at the moment. His expression was indecipherable.

"Come on, love. I'll walk you back."

Love. She didn't want him to call her that after he'd tackled her. There wasn't an ounce of *love* between them.

"Aren't you going to execute me?" she asked, shocked by the coldness in her voice.

It was hard to tell in the ambient headlight glow, but it looked like he frowned. "No, pet. Let's go home."

Yes, home, the place he'd invaded and made his own, the place that was no longer safe.

A scream was building at the back of her throat, but she clamped her teeth down against it, hopped off the tailgate and set off through the grass, toward "home," Walsh a half step behind her. She felt the eyes of the other men and refused to acknowledge them.

It felt like it took forever to get back to the barn. Across the overgrown field, through the gate, down the run. Nothing but the sounds of swishing grass and their breathing. Her legs wet and filthy, her boots full of dew. She kicked them off at the base of the stairs and went barefoot up to her apartment, her anger mounting with every step Walsh took in her wake.

He followed her into the loft, across the floor. There wasn't room to escape him, so when she reached the foot of the bed, she rounded on him, hand gripping her satchel hard, drawing on the knowledge of the gun to still the awful shaking in her limbs.

The sight of him struck her hard, the regret stamped into his features, the dark terror in his eyes. It wasn't what she'd expected, and it knocked the breath out of her, the naked emotion in his gaze.

"Who was that?" she asked in a choked voice. "The dead man. Who was he?"

"A friend."

"A friend you were burying in an empty pasture?"

"One who was murdered."

"Walsh, when a friend gets murdered, you call the damn police! You don't dig a hole and roll him in it!"

He had no answer for that, and her eyes filled with tears.

"It's all true, isn't it? All the stories they say around town. The killing and the drug dealing and all the terrible, awful things they say."

Again, no answer.

"Right." She took a deep, shuddering breath. "So that would make this the part where I get 'bumped off.' Right? Isn't that what they call it? I saw something I shouldn't, and now you have to kill me." A thin, hysterical laugh bubbled in her throat. "You said to be careful. Be careful *of you.* Of what you'll do to me, huh?"

"I'm not going to kill you."

"Then what's to keep me from going to the cops?"

"This farm."

She lifted her brows.

"If I get arrested, this farm gets seized, gets sold. And then what would you do?" His brows snapped down low over his eyes, expression hardening. "You've got no plans, no man, no escape route, and no future. You've got nothing except this farm." His voice was like a knife as he threw her words back at her. "You said it yourself – you've got nothing to live for except a barn and a few horses, so you can't afford to tell the police anything." He took a step toward her. "You're gonna keep your mouth shut, because that's all you can do. Hear? You didn't see shit tonight, and you aren't gonna *say* shit."

The worst part? He was absolutely right.

He wasn't going to see her cry, though. She sucked up her tears, blinked, and straightened her spine. "Of course not. I wouldn't want to get fired, would I? *Termination* means a whole other thing in your world."

He stared at her one unreadable moment, then turned and left the apartment without a word, his footfalls steady on the wooden steps.

The tears broke through, filling her eyes, spilling down her face.

Nineteen

"Did you read it?" Sam asked, tapping the cover of their latest assigned writing manual.

Across the table, Ava wrinkled her nose. "Yeah. God, I hate manuals. Why does one person who doesn't even write novels feel qualified to tell me how to do it?"

Sam chuckled. "You would say that."

"And you wouldn't?"

"Touché."

They were at the Lécuyer house, making use of Remy's very brief nap time to sneak in a little study guide pow-wow before the next day's exam.

Both of them, in their months of grad school, had commiserated about the seeming absurdity of going for their masters in Creative Writing. Ava was about to be a mom of two. Samantha had a mother and little sister to worry about, and a regular class to teach. Neither of them needed to be chasing these writing dreams.

But need was a relative term, after all. And at this point, they only had a semester left.

"I thought it was generic," Ava said of the book. "No room for imagination at all."

"Hmm," Sam murmured in agreement. "I thought—"

Sound of a bike rolling up into the driveway.

Ava could identify a bike by sound. "Aidan," she said, and Sam's stomach clenched. Not a big girlish butterfly clench like it used to, but a quick squeeze to remind her that she was always going to be devastatingly attracted. It helped that they were on friendlier terms now. That he indeed remembered her from high school. She didn't know that she'd call them "friends," but he greeted her by name and was kind to her.

When Ava started to heave her pregnant self up from the table, Sam got to her feet. "I'll go let him in. You stay put."

"Thanks," Ava said with a sigh. "It'll take me five minutes to get out of this chair."

Aidan was in the process of knocking when Sam answered the door, and just like always, she was flooded with a wave of *holy hell, why does he have to look like that?*

With the sun behind him, his hair stood up in messy dark curls, his wide shoulders limned in warm afternoon light. He wore his usual uniform of obnoxious band t-shirt, cut, jeans, boots, and too much man-jewelry. He needed to shave.

He was stunning, and that was before he smiled.

"Hey, Sam." He gave her the lady-killing grin, the one that no doubt dropped panties all over Knoxville. "Are you guys ever not studying?"

"Nope. Summer semester is killer." She stepped back and let him come in, relocking the door after to keep things safe...and to situate herself behind Aidan for the ass view on the way back to the kitchen.

"Sis," he greeted Ava, and headed straight for the fridge.

"Bro. Why've you always gotta eat my food?"

"Drink your beer," he corrected, uncapping a Bud and sitting down at the table. "I wanted to..." He made a face. "Get a...ah, a female opinion. I guess. Yeah." He glanced over at Sam. "Both of you, I guess, since you're here."

Sam took her seat and propped her elbows on the table, curiosity piqued more than it should have been, pulse thumping just a little.

"Somebody mark this down on a calendar," Ava said.

"Female opinion on what?" Sam asked.

Sensing that she was the more receptive of the two, Aidan directed his strained expression toward her. "I've gotta...I mean, I'd like to..." He took a deep breath and blurted out the rest on the exhale. "I need to take a chick on a date, and I haven't ever really done that, so I need to know where to take her so she won't laugh my ass out of the restaurant."

She couldn't have heard right, could she? "A date?"

He fiddled with the label of his beer. "Yeah. Like, a real one."

"Is there some other kind of date?"

174

"There's the Aidan kind," Ava said, smirking, "which tends toward condoms and backseats rather than candlelight and roses."

"Oh, like you're so romantic," Aidan told her.

"When my back's killing me and I can't sleep" – Ava laid a hand on her round stomach – "Merc reads Dickens to me in bed. Let's not compare levels of romance."

Aidan muttered something and took a swig of beer. "So, can you help or not?" His expression softened as he turned back to Sam. "Any ideas?"

Yes, I have an idea, she thought. *Why don't you ask someone, anyone else about this? Anyone but me.* "Well, Doug took me to that boutique steakhouse by campus a time or two." Guilt tugged at her, briefly, as she thought of her coworker. Not her boyfriend, no, they'd only been out a few times, and it was obvious to both of them that things weren't going to get serious. "It's got the ambiance, but isn't as pricey."

"You probably can't dress like that, though," Ava said.

"I don't have anything else to wear."

"Well, dig something up. And no cut. A place like that won't appreciate you flying colors."

He made another face and downed more beer.

"Who is this mystery woman?" Ava asked. "She must have the best rack in the world to get you to go legit."

"It's not like that."

"Jesus." Ava leaned over and tried to feel his forehead. "Are you sick?"

"Leave off, brat."

Sam might have laughed at their antics if her stomach hadn't been churning. "Where'd you meet her?" she asked quietly, and both siblings looked at her, as if startled by her tone.

Ava's brows crimped, like she was worried. *What's wrong?* her eyes said.

But Aidan couldn't read her the same way, because she wasn't someone he paid attention to, just his little sister's friend, and some girl he sort of knew. "At the farm where Walsh is living. That big place, Briar Hall."

Sam nodded like she knew. She'd seen the name on corkboard fliers around town, ads for riding lessons and horse boarding.

"Poor girl," Ava said.

"If you take her flowers," Sam said, "take lilies. Everyone gives roses. She won't be expecting lilies."

It killed her, just a little, the way his smile was without heat or interest. "Thanks."

Twenty

He woke with the thumping of helicopter blades in his ears. The sound faded as his eyes opened, an old echo of memory that brought with it the sting of kicked-up sand against his skin, the hot desert air full of the smells of livestock and too many humans crowded together.

He didn't dream of Afghanistan often. He didn't like to think of that simple mission and how horribly sideways it had gone.

It was Emmie. She was dredging up old guilt and heartbreak, prodding at scabbed over wounds. She was something good and innocent, and he was failing her, hurting her. And that in turn was hurting him.

I gotta get furniture, he thought as he rolled off his mattress and his joints protested the movement. Thirty-nine wasn't that old in regular years, but in ex-jockey, ex-RAF, current-biker years, that was ancient when it came to knees and shoulders.

His phone started ringing before he could get fully upright, and he cursed as he scooped it from his jeans pocket and answered it. " 'Lo?"

"We'll be there at noon," Ghost said without greeting. "Have your manager at the house, alone."

~*~

"Don't tell me you're going out with him."

From Chaucer's back, Tonya shrugged. "So what if I am?"

Emmie took a deep breath and told herself to be patient. She hadn't slept well, and was exhausted. Still shook all over when she thought about what she'd seen last night. And shook even harder when she remembered the cold flatness of Walsh's eyes, the way her lover had turned into her captor and overlord in a blink.

But it wasn't Tonya's fault. She knew nothing about the Lean Dogs or what they'd been doing in that empty field next door.

"So, you've got a lot going for you," Emmie said carefully as Chaucer walked in circles around her. "And he's got…pretty much nothing going for him."

"He's hot," Tonya said matter-of-factly. "And he'll make my father furious."

Ah, it always came back to that with heiresses, didn't it? Pissing Daddy off, as a way to rebel against all those handouts they seemed to resent so much. The pressure of living up to expectations of perfection is so difficult, Emmie had always heard. *Yeah, well, try working sixty hours a week for minimum wage and dragging your deadbeat dad off bar stools. Let's compare lives and then we'll see who needs to rebel against something.*

"Be careful," Emmie warned. "These guys aren't pretend outlaws. They're the real deal."

Tonya gave a haughty sniff and collected her reins, heeling Chaucer off around the arena.

"We'll work on tempis next lesson, okay?" Emmie called to her back.

Tonya acknowledged her with a quick whip salute.

Emmie slumped back against the rail and shut her eyes. They felt full of sandpaper. The soreness between her legs had nothing to do with riding – horses, anyway. And she hated the physical reminder of her stupidity.

The sound of multiple bikes approaching brought her head up, and there they were, a whole pack of Dogs sweeping up the driveway, headed for the house. Sinister in their black and white.

As the ringing faded, and then shut off, someone cleared his throat behind her. Even his wordless murmurings had an English accent.

"You need to come up to the house with me," Walsh said, and his voice was low and careful.

"Not like I have a choice, do I?" she asked, bitterly, and he didn't respond because he didn't have to.

Damn him, his club, his…everything. And damn her for letting it get to this point.

Walsh seemed to want her to walk ahead of him, motioning her forward when she turned around. Like he was a gentleman or some shit. Whatever. She folded her arms across her middle and marched up the driveway, boot heels striking loud against the asphalt, chin lifted. She wasn't going to skitter around like a frightened mouse. If she had to face down this criminal club, she'd do it with her head held high.

Walsh opened the front door for her when they reached the house, and she walked past him without acknowledgement, determined not to show fear as she headed for the din of voices echoing around the living room, heart knocking against her ribs.

There was still no furniture, so they were standing, and that made them seem twice as tall and intimidating. The uniformity of their cuts, the wallet chains, the boots – they were like a military regiment. They looked at her with blank appraisal. Nothing sexual or leering, just an emotionless evaluation. Military again, she thought.

There was the super tall one with the long black hair. The young ones who'd been by the arena – Tango, Carter, and the one who had the hots for Tonya. RJ and Briscoe who she'd met outside of Bell Bar. A few she didn't know. And the one whose cut read *President*. He was by far the most frightening, and it was him she looked to, tilting her head, clenching her teeth so her jaw wouldn't tremble.

He gave her a small smirk, like he could see through her façade, but appreciated the effort.

A hand touched her back – Walsh – between the shoulder blades, and then he stepped around her, moving to stand beside his president. Making it very clear that they were on opposite sides of this issue.

She hated herself in that moment for ever letting him touch her.

The president stepped forward. "It's Emmie, right?" There was a semblance of a smile on his face, but it went nowhere near his dark eyes. He extended his hand for a shake. "I'm Ghost."

She put her hand in his, and didn't wince when he squeezed hard. "Nice to meet you."

His smirk widened. "Walsh speaks highly of you."

She lifted her brows. "Just trying to do my job."

"And save your farm, right?"

A cold chill rippled across her skin. "Right. Since I have nothing else in this world to live for."

She flicked a glance to Walsh, and saw him blink. No other reaction, though.

"I'd like to think we understand one another, then," Ghost said. "You have something to protect; I have something to protect." His chin tipped, making his eyes look darker, harder. "It's in both our interests for you to keep what you saw last night to yourself."

Or he'd have her killed. There was no misunderstanding him. And he'd brought his entire club with him to drive home the point. To scare her.

Asshole.

"I didn't see anything last night," she said. "So I'm afraid I don't know what you're talking about."

A slow, malicious grin brought out the lines in his face. "That's a good girl."

She'd never wanted to slap someone so bad.

But she held her composure. "Was that all you needed from me? I have lessons coming in."

Ghost dipped his head in mock chivalry. "Yeah, we're done."

She kept it together until she was halfway down the driveway, and then the shaking started. It began in her hands and traveled up her arms, turned her thighs to water so she had to stop and lean against an oak tree, palms pressed to the sturdy trunk as she struggled to catch her breath.

The problem with letting the devil into your bed, she reflected, was that the devil always had friends.

And she had no one.

~*~

"What did you say to her last night?"

Everyone had trooped out of the house save Ghost, and he stood on the other side of the massive kitchen island from Walsh.

Walsh poured a generous dollop of whiskey into his coffee and slid the bottle across in offering. "I reminded her she's got nothing to live for 'cept this place, and that if we get busted, the farm gets taken away from her."

"And this place is enough leverage?"

"It is for her. Bloody loyal, obsessive thing," he said sourly, disgusted with himself, with the spectacle that had just taken place. He was all for a show of club strength, flexing some muscles to drive home a point, but to a five-foot girl? Who'd done nothing but be in the wrong place at the wrong time? That made him sick.

"I'd like to believe that's true," Ghost said.

Walsh gave his president a level look. "It is."

The man twitched a smile. "You like her. Kingston Walsh *cares* about somebody."

"She's an innocent in all this. I don't like collateral damage."

"Me neither, but sometimes it happens."

"No offense, prez, but that answer's not gonna cut it with me this time."

Ghost snorted. "If these were the old days, back when Duane first got patched, I'd tell you to tattoo your name across her chest, chain her to your bedpost, and give her a few good licks with the belt so she understood she was your property, and she didn't speak out of turn."

"But these aren't those days."

"Thank Christ for that. Look, she's a little doll to look at. And I give her credit for putting on a brave face just now. But you know I can't afford to overlook a loose end that's this loose. What she saw, that could put all of us away for the rest of our lives. I won't let that happen. You're my number two guy, Walsh, and I trust you more than anybody else, but brother, I will not let this club, and all the families tied to it, get destroyed for one girl. I can't. Family comes first, and she's not family."

Walsh nodded. He understood – the brotherhood, the family built around it – that was the first priority. It trumped anything personal, and it crushed any outside threats.

He remembered Michael's tortured expression at the table a year ago, when he'd thought Holly would wind up a casualty of the club. Walsh felt some of that bile pushing up his throat now. He was invested at this point, and he couldn't just…

Wait.

Light bulb moment.

"What if she *was* family?" he asked. "What if she was my old lady?"

Ghost affected surprise. "It would be better for her. Doesn't change the fact that I can't let her squeal, you understand."

"Yeah, but…"

The wheels were turning now. Make her his old lady, bring her into the fold, let her meet the women and see the softer side of things, let her have a taste of being part of the kind of family she didn't have now.

Of course, that was assuming she'd even be willing to talk to him.

But she was a smart girl. If he explained it to her…

Yeah. He could make it work.

He hoped.

~*~

Aidan spotted his brunette as he walked to his bike. She was down in the arena, hands loose on the reins as her horse walked around in laps, staring out across the rolling fields with that picturesque thoughtful expression models always had in catalogues.

"Catch up with you back at the shop," he told Tango as he walked past him down the driveway.

Tango rolled his eyes. "Yeah. Good luck, Romeo. I'll have some ice ready for the burns."

Aidan flipped him the bird over his shoulder and then pushed his hand through his hair, tugging the unruly curls into place. He hadn't shaved that morning – shit. But he was wearing cologne. And his clothes had only been worn once, and not the usual three times.

He popped a piece of gum and buffed his sunglasses on the hem of his shirt. Before he slipped them back on, he checked his reflection in them. Same old sharp jaw and dark eyes that always looked back at him in the mirror, a younger version of his dad's face. But suddenly he was looking at it more critically. Should he start using a fancier shaving cream? Something with moisturizer? Get some of those teeth whitening strips?

Fuck it, chicks like your face, he reminded himself, popped on the shades, rolled his shoulders a couple times, and approached the fence.

Tonya noticed him with a slight turn of her head, but she made him wait, completing her lap around the arena before making her leisurely way toward him. The horse was tired, chest and neck lathered with sweat, its nostrils flaring wide and pink as it caught its breath.

"Are you supposed to look that beautiful while you're riding a horse?" Aidan asked, giving her his best, most devastating grin.

She gave him only a small smirk in return. "Does that line ever work?"

"All the time, sweetheart."

"Ooh, impressive."

This was a first for him. Except for his sister, the ladies never gave him a hard time, criticized his game. It threw him off.

"My mistake, then." He rapped a hand on the rail and took a step back. "I was thinking you'd like to come out with me, but I guess I'll have to find somebody who's impressed."

She shrugged.

He turned around and made it three steps before she said, "Go out where?"

Aidan grinned. *Still got it.*

~*~

"You did awesome today," Emmie told Kelsey, grinning, and held up her hand for the girl's firm high-five smack.

"That was so fun!" Kelsey bounced on the toes of her little black paddock boots. "Can we jump the big one next time?"

"Maybe the time after that." Emmie shot Kelsey's mom a covert wink, and the woman nodded in relieved thanks.

As mother and daughter headed for the entrance, side-by-side past and present versions of one another, Emmie felt the old stab of longing. Where was her mother these days? Where had the last Christmas card come from? Fresno?

Would her mom come to her funeral after the Lean Dogs killed her? Or, more likely, there would be no funeral, because she'd be in that pasture next door. God, how many bodies were there?

"You're good with the little ones," Walsh said behind her, startling her.

She spun, forcing a blank expression to cover her surprise.

He was wearing this awful faded short-sleeve button-up shirt that made him look extra farmer-ish. But it clung to him, and his hair was messy, and he needed to shave – and her stomach pulsed with heat as she imagined putting her hands on him.

She couldn't do that, though, because he had used her and then threatened her.

"Kids are easier to teach than adults," she said stiffly. "They listen better. Not that you have any experience with kids, though, I'm guessing."

He shrugged. "I like kids. Lots of the guys have 'em."

"Oh? You mean the lumberjack? Or the Godfather back there?" She nodded toward the house.

184

Walsh smiled. "Both of them, actually. The Godfather's the lumberjack's father-in-law."

"So?"

"Sooo," he said slowly, wincing to himself as he walked toward her, "it's all a big family, the club."

"It's going to kill me," she said. "I don't need to know anything else about it."

"Well, actually you might."

It felt good to be stubborn, gave her the only satisfaction she could have at this point to stand still and let him come to her, looking uncertain and awkward. "Why?"

"Because you need to join it."

She took a deep breath and choked on air, half-coughing and half-laughing.

He thumped her on the back. "You okay?"

"Hell no," she gasped, stepping back from him. "*Join it?* What the hell does that mean? I'm getting press-ganged into your freaking biker club?"

"No, nothin' like that. Women can't be in the club."

"Oh, what a *fucking* relief!"

"Em, calm down—"

"Like hell!"

"I'm trying to help you, okay? I'm trying to keep you safe." The low rough urgency in his voice gave her pause, forced her to quiet and collect herself a little.

"And whose fault is it that I'm not safe?" she asked.

"Mine. All mine, I know that, love, I do."

"Stop calling me love. I'm nothing but a pawn to you, so don't pretend otherwise."

His head reared back like she'd slapped him.

"What do you mean by join the family?"

"The club is a family," he repeated. "It looks after its own. If you were a part of it – a loyal part of it, mind – you'd be protected, looked after, included. You'd be trusted, and kept safe. You'd be" – be dampened his lips, leaned in close to her, eyes bright – "you'd be a part of something. You'd have something besides a bloody barn full of horses."

"Poor little me," she said quietly. "Nothing but some horses."

"That's not what I mean–"

"It's exactly what you mean, you said so last night. The only reason I'm not a threat to your club is 'cause I'm so pathetic and have no life."

"Em–"

"But that's okay, because you're going to give me a family and a better life, right? Pray tell, Walsh, how do I go about joining your little family? Do I have to fill out paperwork? Or is it a tattoo situation?"

He drew himself up so he seemed taller than normal, took a big, steadying breath. "You become my old lady. You marry me."

~*~

If only women were as simple as businesses. When it came to a bar, a garage, a strip club, hell, even a horse farm, he could run the numbers, calculate profit, account for risk, and come up with an airtight plan in a matter of minutes.

But women were complicated, subtle, and so much stronger than men always wanted to give them credit. They could swallow hurt whole and let it eat them from the inside out in a way none of his brothers ever could. And when they fought, their claws were sharper.

"I didn't think it was that funny," he said dryly, propping a shoulder against the rough outer wall of the barn.

After he'd made his big suggestion, she'd blinked at him a few times, and then burst into hysterical, pealing laughter. She'd laughed until she couldn't breathe, and he'd steered her outside, around the corner where Fred or Becca wouldn't walk up on them.

She gasped and fanned her face, tipping it back to the sky as she blinked at the tears her fit had brought on. "Oh my God." Her voice was hoarse as the last few chuckles died away. "It was possibly the funniest thing I've ever heard. Lord." She cleared her throat, dabbed her eyes, and glanced over at him, smile fading.

"Marry you," she said. "You actually think I'm going to marry you?"

No, he thought. Why would anyone ever want to do that?

But he said, "It's the best option."

Her brows lifted, but it was a limp gesture. The emotional upheaval had tired her.

"If you're my wife, the police can't question you about me. Can't compel you to answer, anyway, and can't take your testimony all that seriously."

"It's the best option for keeping you guys out of jail."

He gritted his teeth. "It's…ah, Christ, woman, can't you see it? It's best for *you*. If the cops can't get to you, Ghost won't want to. You marrying me is a show of good faith with the club, yeah? They'll trust you more. If it comes down to it, they'll protect you. I'm thinking about *you*, Emmie, and just you right now. No one will bother you, on either side of the law, if you're my old lady."

She grew quiet and stared at him a long moment. He wondered what she was seeing in him, what she was looking for. "Was this your plan all along? When you bought the farm? Marry me and trap me?"

Shit, he hadn't even anticipated she'd go there. "No. Not at all, I swear."

Her small smile was sad. "You know, the worst part is, I want to believe that. Because the *very* worst part is, before last night, I was starting to think that…well, it doesn't matter. Because now we're here, and…yeah." She let her head tip back so it rested against the wall. "What if" – she sucked at the inside of her cheek and it plucked her mouth at a pretty angle – "what if I didn't want the barn to be the only thing I ever had? What if I wanted a husband and kids?"

He smiled grimly. "Well, you'd get one of those things, at least."

"A real husband. One who loves me."

It was like there was a fist in his chest, gripping his lungs. "Well…if you meet someone, down the line…we can get divorced."

She glanced away from him, and her hair fell down off her shoulder, hiding her face from him. When she spoke, he could hear the tears in her voice. "I don't have a choice, do I?"

He wanted to touch her, put his arms around her. But he knew he was the last source of comfort for her right now.

"No. I'm sorry, you don't."

Twenty-One

There were sheets. And then there were *these* sheets, Egyptian cotton with an astronomical thread-count. *I have to stop this*, he told himself, the same words that filled his mind each morning he woke in this bed. In the early days it had been a scream. Now it was a whisper, a faint kiss of a thought.

Behind him, the lush, cream, *perfect* sheets rustled – even the sounds they made were expensive – and a hand landed on his back. One slender fingertip traced the knobs of his vertebrae, bump-bump-bump down to the small of his back.

"I have to go," Tango said into his pillow.

"You said that twenty minutes ago."

He had, but then Ian had said, "Do you really?" and as it always did, the sound of that voice had made it impossible to crawl out of bed. Because here, wrapped in Egyptian cotton, time was reversed, and he was Kevin again, and that cultured, English-accented voice was the only voice he could associate with pleasure, all others bringing pain, so much awful pain. Because before he was Tango the Lean Dog, before Jasmine and the other groupies, and the girls stuffing panties in his cut pockets at parties, he'd been Kev the dancing boy, raped every night of his life, made to dance for his owner. And the only respite had been the kidnapped English boy with the gentle hands and whispered endearments.

But he couldn't keep coming here, not for any reason.

He sat up suddenly, head spinning as his eyes adjusted to the dim room. The sun wasn't up yet, and he wanted to be well away from here by then. His brothers could never know. *Never.*

In a single brief flash of awareness, the haze of the night burned off and left him sick and shaking, hating himself, hating – a little bit – the club.

He heard Ian sit up behind him, felt his slender hands on his shoulders, thumbs finding the two precise knots of tension at the back of his neck. Ian's lips at his ear, his long hair falling forward and landing against his back like silk. Heard the soft clink of teeth against one of his earrings.

Tango closed his eyes. "No. I'm leaving."

"Suit yourself, darling." Ian pulled back with a deep, dramatic sigh.

Tango hated the way dizziness grabbed at him when he stood – too much cognac last night – but he forced it down, gathered his clothes up off the floor, the grungy jeans and t-shirt like refuse against the plush smoke-colored carpet. Everything about him was like a stain against this new life of Ian's.

Well, it was the life Ian had been born to, and in which he would have remained, had he not been snatched from his bed as a child.

Life seemed doomed to preordained cycles that way. Tango was born to shit, and now he had, appropriately, shit.

He dressed quickly, facing the wall. He couldn't look at Ian until he was fully clothed, too raw and exposed in nothing but his inked up skin.

When there was nothing else to do, he took a deep breath, and finally turned toward the bed.

Ian sat propped against the headboard, the sheets around his waist, his exposed torso a work of slender marble-carved art that belonged in a ballet museum somewhere. His heavy auburn hair fell in sleek sheets down his shoulders, like he hadn't slept on it. There was a true sadness in his face, his pale eyes large and soft.

"I don't like it when you leave," he said quietly, and it was the true Ian shining through the shell of Shaman, the version of the man who'd once loved Kevin. Perhaps still did.

"But I have to," Tango said, because that's all there was to say.

Ian nodded. "Come tell me goodbye."

He crossed to the bed and leaned down to brace his hands on it. Lifted his face when Ian captured it between his hands. A kiss he knew better than any other, that tasted of childhood trauma and first love and shattered dreams. A punishment, a promise, and a poison.

~*~

Holy fucking shit. *Hello, big break, I'm Harlan. Nice to finally fucking meet you.*

Six-ten a.m. and here came Kevin Estes out of the swanky high rise complex he'd been parking his bike in front of for weeks. He'd done it over and over and over again, arriving after nightfall, leaving before dawn, there for what could only be a sexual liaison. Harlan had assumed some rich bitch had decided to take a walk on the wild side.

That was true, but the rich bitch in question – not of the female variety.

This morning, as Harlan watched slumped behind the wheel of his department issue Explorer, Estes stepped off the elevator into the parking garage like normal. But then someone had come out after him.

A man.

A man with long flashing hair and a Hefner dressing robe. Tall and thin, he'd caught Estes by the wrist and turned him, and there had been nothing of the victim about Estes as he'd gone into the other man's arms and they'd kissed.

Fucking kissed.

The guy with the long hair finally let the biker go, and as he turned back toward the elevator, Harlan got a good look at his face.

Holy shit number two. This guy's picture was on the corkboard back at HQ, a rising star among the underground players who called himself Shaman, and who was so far untouchable. All the women in the office thought he was dreamy, with his sharp features and his long hair and his fancy suits.

Ha! Like he'd give a shit what any of them thought.

Harlan had been in a frenzy to get his long range camera in his hands, snapping picture after picture.

This was his ticket. This was gold!

It had begun in Georgia, an open-and-shut, easy-as-pie case of milking intel out of a pampered brat before finally putting the little shit away and moving on to the bigger fish he'd given up in his confession. But the Georgia chapter of the Lean Dogs had fucked all that up. And where had that gotten him? Nothing but a demotion, and a year skulking around the office until he finally convinced the higher-ups that he could be trusted with a new informant, a new assignment, and another go at bagging a big one – this time, the Lean Dogs. It hadn't had anything to do with revenge. No, of course not. He wasn't petty like that.

But that idiot Ronnie, and that even dumber idiot Mason – those two had ghosted on him, and had he been able to pin it on the Dogs? No. That would have been just too easy.

"Stick to paperwork," his supervisor had told him. And that had been it. His career as a field agent had been toast, thanks to two blown assignments, and one motorcycle club.

No. Fuck that. He wasn't going out like *that*.

His surveillance had begun on accident; he'd ended up behind one of the leather-wearing losers on the interstate, and just followed him into town, watched him go home, parked across the street for a bit.

Then it had hit him: if he could catch them in something criminal, he'd have the hard evidence he needed.

His therapist would have called it "obsessive behavior." His therapist was full of shit, though.

So far, he'd watched a lot of cooking, TV-watching, and fucking through curtains and the gaps in blinds. The fucking he didn't mind so much – some of these chicks were hot – but he was getting nowhere with his case. His unassigned case. His personal case.

He liked to think of it as a crusade.

But finally – *finally* – he had something.

Everyone knew MCs didn't allow gay members to fly the colors.

That's what you called *leverage*.

Twenty-Two

It was hard to beat a full-color sunset, the sun sliding like melted sherbet down over the burnished tree tops, fading into cricket whispers and the fast rustle of night things. Especially in the summer, when it was a salute to the day that had passed. It tasted like expensive wine and smelled like the faint crackled edges of autumn. But if something could beat it, it was a sunrise.

Emmie had been waiting for this one almost an hour, hands shoved in the pockets of her hoodie, head tipped back against the barn wall. She was sitting in the damp grass and didn't care that her shorts were soaked clean through to her ass. This was the best spot, and she needed a sunrise, desperately.

Her breath plumed like smoke, and she knew summer had passed the halfway point, that it would be cold soon. Would that make it easier or harder to pretend to be someone's wife? Someone's biker old lady? Harder, she thought. Too much time trapped indoors together.

The first rosy glow ignited along the tree line like a gas burner turning on, and she pushed the unpleasant thoughts from her mind. Just the sunrise, for now. Plenty of time to contemplate the ruin of her life later.

She was on her feet and halfway through feeding the horses when Fred and Becca arrived; she gave them smiles and waves, forced herself to act normal. Walsh stayed away, thank God – probably getting that marriage license he'd said they needed.

Jesus.

She had evening lessons that day, so the morning was blissfully quiet. She dragged a saddle stand to the center of the aisle, turned on the radio, and lost herself in the mindless, soothing process of cleaning and then waxing tack.

She wasn't sure how long it was before the sound of a throat clearing startled her.

A young woman stood on the other side of the saddle rack, wearing a simple navy column of a summer dress that showed off a distinct baby bump. She was brunette, slender-faced, pretty. She held a child on her hip that was somewhere between a baby and a toddler.

Emmie's professional side kicked in. "Hi." She stood from her stool, wiped the beeswax off her hands onto the sides of her breeches. "Can I help you?" She glanced down at her hands, winced, and decided a shake was a lost cause.

"Are you Emmie?" the brunette asked, and Emmie was instantly suspicious.

"I am."

The girl smiled at her, and there was something too old about the gesture. It was in her eyes, a dark flash like she knew so many things. "You met my husband recently. Mercy." She held a hand up above her head. "Real tall and long hair."

"Ah." Emmie's heart pulsed in a sequence of anxious beats. "Yeah. I guess you'd call it 'met.' " Or *was detained by*, either way.

"He's kinda hard to miss." The girl smiled again. "I'm Ava. And this is Remy," she said of the baby. "Merc said maybe we could come by and pet the horses."

"Ah..." Technically, she wasn't doing anything critical. The student saddle she was working on could wait a few minutes. It was the idea of doing something for the club, even something as small as showing a wife and her terribly cute dark-eyed baby a few of the horses, that set her teeth on edge. She felt so, so helpless in all this. A little protest couldn't hurt her too much, could it?

But she wasn't programmed that way. She always obliged, always did the polite thing.

Which was exactly why she'd never moved on from this farm and was now embroiled in an illegal, heartbreaking mess.

"Sure," she said, motioning for Ava to follow her. "I've got Sherman and Champ in one of the small paddocks back here."

She was surprised to hear the click of boots heels, and glanced over her shoulder to catch the blunt black toes of a pair of boots beneath the swirling hem of Ava's dress. Biker's wife, she reminded herself, and led the girl down the aisle and out the back doors.

"This is a very nice place," Ava said, and she sounded sincere.

So had Walsh, though. And he'd been sleeping with her out of pure manipulation.

"When I think about a barn," Ava continued, "I don't think about it being this fancy."

"There are barns much fancier than this," Emmie assured her. "This is a moderate, local level farm. You should see the stuff around Lexington."

Those gorgeous Kentucky equine palaces where Amy had moved her horses, after abandoning Briar Hall.

God, she was just full to the brim with bitterness today.

"You should see the craphole barns I'm used to," Ava said with an easy laugh.

Emmie didn't trust any of it. Why was this woman bringing a child this small to see horses he wouldn't remember? Why was she being polite?

Sherman and Champ were cropping grass in their paddock, tails swishing slowly at flies.

"Remy, look." Ava hoisted the boy up higher as they approached the paddock. "See the horses? Aren't they pretty? They're beautiful," she said to Emmie. "Yours?"

"They belong to the farm." Emmie wiggled her fingers and clucked, and both geldings lifted their heads and ambled over.

"Oh," Ava said. "So yeah, they're yours now."

Emmie glanced over, startled, and found the other woman smiling at her.

"Walsh said you two were getting married." Again, there was a knowing, ageless light in her eyes that left Emmie unsettled. "Congratulations. I think."

"Um…" Sherman nudged her, looking for a treat, and she pressed a hand to his velvet muzzle.

Ava glanced away, steered Remy's small hand toward Champ's nose and helped him pet it. Champ blew air through his nostrils and the child giggled in delight.

"What a nice horsey," Ava said to the boy. Her face was soft with maternal warmth when she glanced over at Emmie again. And sympathy, too. There was an understanding in the slow curve of her lips. "We're not all that scary, once you get to know us."

Emmie frowned. "I'm afraid I don't know what you're talking about."

"Yeah, you do."

Emmie swallowed against the dryness in her throat. "Look, I don't know what Walsh told you, but–"

"His exact words were, 'She's a special one, yeah?'" She did a decent job imitating the accent. "And the thing I know about Walsh is that he doesn't throw the word *special* around. Ever."

Flustered, Emmie glanced away. "He hasn't known me that long."

"It doesn't *take* that long to know something like that."

She snorted. "Guess I'll have to take your word for it."

"You ought to."

~*~

"The girls'll show her the ropes," Mercy said, leaning back in his chair, crossing his long legs and propping his boots up on the porch rail in front of him. Walsh couldn't have reached that far with his feet if his life had depended on it. "They'll tell her how it all works, give her the whole old lady initiation speech or whatever the hell it is they do."

"There's a speech?"

"No idea. But if there is, Mags and Ava can handle that." He sipped his beer and glanced over toward Walsh. "But you, my English friend, have got some work to do."

Walsh lifted his brows, inviting explanation.

"Brother," Mercy chuckled, "she's a brave little thing, I'll give her that, the way she held up the other night, but you jumped on her, and there's no way it was her idea to get hitched."

Walsh frowned, and Mercy shook his head.

"Hand to God, I ain't gonna tell that to Ghost. He ever asks me, she's got nothing but mad love for you. But just between us, she's gotta be freaked. And she'll go along with this plan for a little while to keep herself safe. But in the long haul, being loyal to the club – that's gotta come from you. We're committed to the club because it's our club. Our girls are committed to the club because they're committed to us. It's like a chain, bro."

He sighed and nodded. "Shit. Yeah. I know. And she...hates me right now."

"You give her a reason to?"

Let's see: tackled her, threatened her, proposed to her. "Yeah."

"But if she hates you, that means she gives some kinda damn. And that's better than nothing."

Or so people said.

Mercy took another long sip of beer and sank down lower in his rocking chair, looking good and comfy. Ava had said she'd text when they were done looking at the horses, and clearly, Merc was content to wait.

"It's not totally selfless though, is it?" he asked thoughtfully. "Making her yours officially. You're hoping it'll turn real."

Walsh wouldn't admit to that. It felt too unlikely and stupid a hope.

~*~

"Thanks," Ava said as they walked back through the barn. "Sorry we took up your time."

"It's fine," Emmie said, voice hollow. She felt a little shell-shocked. Yeah, Walsh had said she would join the family, but she hadn't thought that would start so soon. Why, she didn't know – Walsh had walked right in and taken over her entire life. Why would the rest of his crew be any different?

"Hey," Ava said as they reached the doors, voice going quiet and serious. "Walsh is a good guy." Her eyes were wide and imploring. "Probably the best of this bunch, really. Just…don't think too badly of him, okay?"

"Sure," Emmie said, arms folding across her middle. Because she couldn't shake her Southern manners, she said, "It was nice meeting you."

"You too." Ava flashed her a wide smile and then walked off, boots clicking.

She was driving a truck, Emmie saw, as she went across the parking pad to a black Ford. Another unexpected point in her favor.

She didn't quite know what to make of the woman, but she wasn't a ditz, and she wasn't easy to read. Both good signs…

In this world of badness into which she'd been thrust.

She sighed and went back to her saddle.

Twenty-Three

It was her wedding day.

It had taken three days to procure a marriage license, and now it was time.

She'd never held any ridiculous expectations when it came to weddings, but she'd envisioned a dress, a small bouquet, a modest cake. The gentle background murmurings of happy guests.

None of her girlish dreams had involved a threat to her life, a biker who'd lied to her, a courthouse ceremony, and a new family of outlaws.

Emmie dressed in jeans and flats, a pale pink sleeveless linen shirt. No dress; she would make no further mockery of this marriage by clothing herself appropriately for it. She twisted her hair up and pinned it to the back of her head, wore light makeup and simple studs in her ears. She looked like she was going shopping.

The horses were already out and Fred and Becca were busy mucking stalls, so when she went down the steps to the barn aisle, she was alone. Thankfully. Her fellow employees had been openly shocked and dismayed to hear her news. Becca had started to protest, but Fred had silenced her with a gentle touch on the shoulder. His eyes said that he knew this wasn't what she wanted. That she had to do it, for reasons he didn't want to understand.

Emmie propped a shoulder against the doorframe and waited for her groom, sliding the toe of her shoe through a stray clump of shavings until the black suede was dusty.

Wrong, wrong, all of it so very wrong.

She didn't hear him approach and suddenly his voice was right in front of her, startling her.

"Hi."

She glanced up with a jerk, no chance to hide the devastation on her face.

And then she took real notice of him.

Walsh's hair was still wet, and he'd tried hard to tame the thick spikes, though they were rebelling as they dried. His face was faintly pink from a close shave and the cologne smell reached her from a foot away. His shirt was plain black, clean, pressed, fastened at the cuffs instead of rolled, as usual. Dark jeans. His boots had been polished. The rings on his fingers shone from a thorough cleaning.

He wasn't dressed like a man on his way to a wedding, but the effort he'd taken was obvious. He'd tried to look nice for her, and she felt a reluctant stirring of tenderness deep in her chest.

No, she thought. *Don't be fooled by him anymore. He's nothing but a pretty liar.*

A pretty liar who was holding something matte, black, round, and head-sized in one hand.

"What's that?" she asked, but she already knew. She wore one every day, after all, even if the styling was different.

He extended the helmet toward her, and when he did, she saw the faint white detailing along the edge, little flowers with swirling leaves. "I got you your own," he told her, and almost sounded hesitant. Like Jack Cooper asking her out that time in the tenth grade. "I looked at your hardhat for size."

"That was...thoughtful." It was, it really was.

She took the helmet from him, turned it over in her palms, smelled the new plastic stink of it. Lifted her eyes to his. "But I don't care about riding on the back of your bike."

He might have looked less affronted if she'd slapped him.

His jaw tightened. "If you're my old lady – my real old lady – they'll expect you to be behind me some of the time. Might as well start things off right now," he said firmly. "Get it over with."

"The bike part? Or the married part?"

He made a face. "Both." He pulled his shades from the neck of his shirt and turned toward the bike. "Let's go, love. We're doing this." A gentle one, but a command none the less.

She hated him.

And her feet propelled her forward and she popped the snug helmet down onto her head, wincing as it pressed the hair pins into her scalp.

She faltered when she reached the black Harley, taking one deep breath after another as she watched him swing aboard and don his own helmet. She was still standing there when he turned to her, and she watched his gold brows drop down behind his sunglasses.

"What?"

"I–" She wanted to say something clever, but the truth came tumbling out. "I'm scared," she admitted in a small voice. "I've never been on one of these and..."

His grin was startling and wide, flashing two bottom teeth that were just a little crooked. "Are you really?"

"Yes." She folded her arms, scowled at him. "Everybody ought to be. They're freaking dangerous."

"And that giant horse of yours isn't?"

"Not to me, no."

His smile was infuriating...and adorable. "Every day you get on those animals, but this – with no brain of its own, which I'm controlling – scares you. Pet, you don't have to do anything. Just hold on and trust me."

"That's the scariest part," she said. "Trusting you."

His smile dimmed. He glanced away from her, cleared his throat. "Yeah, well..."

Time stalled out, and the jarring awkwardness filled the small space between them.

He wasn't going to force her, she realized, the longer she stood there. He knew she had to do this, that she had no other option, but he could have been an ass about it. Barked orders. Instead he waited. She didn't want to give him credit for that, she really didn't, but she had to.

She took a deep, shuddering breath, an apology on her tongue, and Walsh said, "I know you don't want this, and you don't want me, and it's awful for you. If it makes it any easier, I don't want it either."

Ah, there it was, finally – the truth. He didn't want to be saddled with her. He'd only ever been playing a game, and dipping his pen in the company ink had led him here, to some loveless sham of a marriage they both had to feign at the risk of her death.

She nodded. "Right." And swung onto the tiny bump seat behind him, feet finding the pegs.

"Em–" he started to say, twisting around.

"Let's just go, okay? I have lessons later."

He frowned. "You're gonna have to hold on."

She leaned forward and wrapped her arms around his waist. The contact kicked off a mental slideshow of memories, those two tumbled nights, the strain of his back beneath her hands, the sounds he made in her ear.

She closed her eyes, trying to shut out the sudden flood of heat.

The bike came to life with a sharp snort, shaking between her legs.

~*~

It made more sense now, why men gave their lives up to the road. A half mile from the farm, all her fear evaporated, pushed out by sheer exhilaration. It wasn't possible to be frightened with the wind in her face and the sun warming her back. With Walsh's solid strength in front of her, between her tightly clasped arms. Looking over his shoulder, it was impossible to tell where the front tire left off and the pavement began. The cars they passed seemed to be standing still.

If she was honest with herself, it was a wonderful shock to be pressed against him like this. When it came to the men in her life, it had only ever been sex and a few awkward dinners. There had never been this kind of touching, this occupying of the same space. And deep down, she wanted to be held, to link hands, to lean against one another. She wanted cuddling and all the sappy things that entailed. But she would never ask for it, because those were things men didn't want to give to her.

Reality returned when they reached the courthouse. Like a slap, her circumstances made themselves known, and she scrambled off the bike the moment she could, taking a few steps away, putting some distance between herself and yet another man who had used her.

He gave her a long moment, as she stared at the shining tops of the cars around them and caught her breath. But finally, it was time. "You ready?"

Emmie closed her eyes, pressed her fingertips to the corners. "Yeah. I'm coming." When she joined him, she was confident her tears were gone.

~*~

It was a perfunctory ceremony, the judge reciting the vows in disinterested tones, she and Walsh staring at the short-napped carpet, not touching. No rings. The kiss was a fleeting, emotionless thing, and he pulled back before she did. Figured. This was just as painful for him, only he'd never had any real sentiment involved, the way she had, so the ruse was becoming harder and harder to keep up.

Bastard.

It was unreal, the walk back to the parking lot, the weightless feeling in the pit of her stomach. Married. Emmaline Nadia Walsh, wife of Kingston Rutherford.

She couldn't breathe. They were all the way to the bike when she realized that the emptiness inside was a lack of oxygen, that her lungs had seized up, and she was gasping.

Her skin was full of needles, her eyes full of tears, and she couldn't draw a breath, couldn't form any words in her throat.

Married, married, married.

To a criminal.

To someone who didn't love her.

She saw it all unfold, her future, like a soggy Chinese takeout box coming apart. The loneliness, the desperation, the drinking. No children, no laughter, no life at all...

Strong hands latched onto her arms. "Hey." Walsh leaned down and put his face into hers, his eyes unusually wide, and bluer than the washed out summer sky above them. "Are you – yeah, shit." One hand moved to the back of her neck. "Head between your knees."

She obeyed because she had to, because if she didn't take a real breath soon, she'd pass out. His hand stayed at her neck, and on the pavement, their shadows linked to form some strange four-legged monster.

"Easy," he said, thumb rubbing a soothing little circle against her nape. "Just breathe. Nice and slow. It'll pass. You're alright, love. Easy."

The delicate vein of gentleness in his voice moved across her skin, made her shiver, brought up a memory of a darkened room and his hands on her in a different context – and her lungs opened, the breath pouring down into her with an awful gasping sound.

"That's right. Just take it slow," Walsh said above her, and it was like his voice commanded the oxygen, sending it where it needed to go.

Just like he was in command of her now, wasn't he? Because bikers *owned* their women.

"I can't do this." It was a whisper that became a chant. "I can't do this, I can't, I can't, I can't!"

This wasn't supposed to be her life. It wasn't supposed to end like this, right here in the courthouse parking lot.

His hand moved to her back, between her shoulder blades.

She couldn't let him see her like this. She couldn't seek succor from the source of her pain.

She jerked upright, stumbling a step back, breathing erratic, but at least happening.

Walsh's expression was wretched, full of sympathy and sadness. *I'm sorry*, it said.

She cleared her throat, wiped at her face, and said, "I should get back."

"Yeah." He handed her helmet over.

~*~

Walsh couldn't remember ever feeling like such an asshole. When your bride had a full-on panic attack ten minutes after the wedding? Yeah, that pushed him into asshole territory.

He was mad as hell she was doing this to him, laying on all the despair.

And he couldn't blame her, because in her eyes, he was this manipulative liar who'd wrecked her life.

It was all fucked up, and he had no idea how to fix it.

He watched her from the porch of the house, tiny all the way down in the center of the arena as a bouncy kid trotted in circles around her on one of the plodding old lesson horses.

He knew where she was coming from – had been in the place where he realized that the only thing getting him up in the morning was the idea that one thing would change for the better. That those dreams would get just a little easier to reach. And then when all possibility was taken away, you wound up broken on the floor. That's where she was now: the phantom family, the killer career, all her ephemeral maybe-somedays had been dashed to bits. And then he'd stomped on them.

Really made a man feel like a man.

The sound of bikes startled him, and he cursed. When in the hell had he not wanted to hear that sound?

The frightening truth was that he hated the sight of two Harleys pulling up at the barn, because he wanted to spare Emmie dealing with his brothers.

Bring her into the family? Ha!

He hustled down the driveway until he was in sight of them, and then he slowed, played casual, hands in his pockets.

It was Ghost and Michael who'd come, the former shooting him a dark grin, the latter being his usual stone-faced Terminator self.

"Here for the reception?" Walsh asked dryly. "'Fraid we're all out of champagne."

"Just well-wishing is all," Ghost said, still grinning. "Where's the blushing bride?"

"Teaching lessons."

Michael reached into his cut and withdrew something wrapped in white tissue paper and tied off with pink ribbon. He shoved it toward Walsh without ceremony. "Here. Hol got you a present."

He bit down on a sudden, impulsive smile as he accepted it. "That was sweet of her."

"She's sweet," Michael said, like he was daring an argument.

Ghost's brows jumped: *this guy over here…* He sobered. "Actually, I need you at the compound. New York's in the house with our Texas shipment."

"Ah." Which meant he'd spend the next six-some-odd hours cataloguing each barrel, scope, and magazine, creating a total inventory of the product they would move as initial payback for their giant loan. "Just let me…" He gestured to the barn, not sure what he meant to do.

Ghost nodded. "We'll wait."

Walsh entered the cool interior of the building, and ground to a halt. What was he going to do? Walk out to the arena and say, "Darling, I'll be home late tonight?" What would she do? Besides give him another of those *you ruined my life* looks.

He stepped into her office instead, set Holly's present down and found a notepad and pen. It took him longer than it should have to leave a note. And as he left, for the first time since he'd patched in, he felt a pull stronger than the club.

The useless tug of responsibility toward a woman who would never love him. An old habit that hadn't died after all.

~*~

"Should I stay?" Fred asked.

Emmie shook her head and massaged her lower back. "No, go on. I'm just gonna go up and crash." The horses were all bedded down for the night and the last lesson had just left.

"Dinner's probably waiting on you anyway." She gave him a tired smile.

Fred nodded, but lingered a moment, watching her.

"I'm fine. I swear."

He left with obvious reluctance, and then she was blessedly alone, the barn full of soft sounds around her, the cool of evening lifting in through the doors on a light breeze.

In the office, she collapsed into her chair with plans to jot down notes on the day's lessons. Two things caught her eye: a white-wrapped package, and the sticky note pressed to the blotter beside it.

The note was from Walsh:

Em,
Had to go into work. Will be late getting home. Am at Dartmoor if you need me.

Two phone numbers were listed, one labeled *mobile*, the other *clubhouse*.

If she needed him. She didn't want to think about any possible meaning behind those words, so she turned to the package, sliding the pink ribbon off and opening the paper at the corners. It wasn't a gift from Walsh – the handwriting on the note that fell out was tidy and feminine.

Dear Emmie,
Congratulations on your wedding! Walsh is very kind and always polite to me; I hope the two of you will be very happy together. I can't wait to meet you, but I know from experience how intimidating it is to walk into this great big family of ours. I wanted to send you a photo – list of names included! Looking forward to getting to know you.
Holly McCall (Michael's wife)

Emmie had no idea which one Michael was, but this was a point in his wife's favor. For whatever it was worth.

She looked at the silver-framed photo. It was a portrait, all of them standing grouped together, the ones in the back obviously standing on chairs. All the guys in their black cuts, the women prettier and happier than she'd expected.

And there was Walsh, in the front row because he was short, his expression tight and guarded, nothing like that wide-eyed look he'd given her outside the courthouse, when he'd told her to breathe.

The question was, which Walsh was the real one? The attentive lover, the caring new husband?

Or the man who'd tackled her in an open field, while his friends buried a body?

Twenty-Four

Too many people in too small a space, smoking too many cigarettes, and laughing at too many stupid jokes. That's how it always was when an out of town chapter was in the house, but tonight it bothered Walsh more than normal.

All the back slaps, congratulations, and innuendos didn't help. Most of his brothers thought he was some kind of monk, because he didn't play with the groupies and because he didn't bring girlfriends around. They were delighted by this sudden turn of events, the bastards.

It was a relief to turn off the crowded roads and hit the rural routes outside the city. He felt his stomach unclench when he turned in at the stone entrance to the farm. Emmie wouldn't be happy to see him, would no doubt be in her loft. They'd have to move her into the main house for the sake of the charade, but that could wait. Tonight wasn't about consummating or working past their hurdles. All he wanted was his mattress.

But something was wrong.

He saw the graffiti on the face of the barn as he started past it and pulled up short, killed the engine and left the headlamp on.

BURN IN HELL STUPID JUNKIE BITCH

"Shit." He started into the barn, and nearly stepped on a small black pile just inside the entrance. The stink told him what it was, but he didn't stop to look, just stepped over it and kept moving, taking the steps to the loft two at a time.

He banged on the door with the side of his hand, not caring if she was asleep, only worried she was something worse than that. "Em? Emmie!"

A seam of light appeared beneath the door and then it unlatched, gapped open. Her eyes were puffy with sleep, hair a mess down on her shoulders. "What?" She squinted at him.

He was breathing like he'd just run a footrace. "You've been sleeping?"

Her face said *duh*.

"You didn't hear anything?"

"Hear what?" She sounded annoyed, and he didn't blame her.

But he wanted to show her, not because she needed to see it – God, he wanted to spare her that – but because he needed her input.

"Come with me." He grabbed for her hand. "Someone left you a message outside."

Her eyes flew wide, instantly alert, and he saw the tremor move through her. "Oh God, what?" She was already stepping into her clogs, grabbing a hoodie off the rack by the door.

He put an arm around her waist when they reached the bottom of the stairs and she didn't resist; he felt her trembling.

"What the hell–" she started, and he steered her around the little pile and out the door. "Okay, seriously, what is…" She gasped. Both hands came up to her face as she stared up at the spray-painted words above the double doors.

Walsh tightened his arm, gave her hip a squeeze. "I saw it when I drove up just now."

She let out a deep, shaky breath. "Brett. This was Brett."

"I was afraid of that."

Her eyes dropped to the doorway. "What's that?"

"Something you don't want to see."

She turned to him, expression hardening. "I saw a dead body. How much worse could it be than that?"

Walsh sighed. "I think we ought to call this in. Let Fielding's people come take some pictures and go pick up the little wanker for questioning."

She nodded. "Yeah."

"You comfortable talking to the cops?"

"Absolutely."

~*~

She was brilliant with the police, his Emmie. The responding officers were a pair of thick-necked former footballers gone soft, nothing but buzz cuts and beer guts, and she handled them deftly. "Thank you for coming, officers. Emmie Walsh," she said, with only a slight hiccup on the name. She shook their hands, used her flashlight to point out the graffiti.

"The previous owner's grandson isn't stable," she told them, "and he's having trouble accepting the fact that this is my husband's farm now."

Both cops had given him the usual contemptuous looks when they spotted his cut, but Emmie hadn't let them get stuck on that, insisting in her polite, firm little way that she wanted the perp charged, that this was a respectable place of business, and she wasn't going to tolerate *any* illegal activity of this sort. She suggested animal cruelty charges be applied considering there was the digestive tract of *something* piled up in the entryway to the barn.

The cops called in a lab guy, thanked her, and dismissed both of them, saying they needed room to work, paint scraping samples or some such.

"Come on, lovey." Walsh put an arm around her again, steered her up toward the house. "Let's leave 'em to it."

She didn't argue but fell into step alongside him, arms folded against the night chill, head down as she chewed her lip and stayed rooted in her thoughts.

It gave him a moment to appreciate the warm smallness of her tucked up against him, the way she was little enough to be his perfect fit, the way the moon played across her hair and turned it silver. She smelled faintly of soap and something floral. Her clogs made clomping sounds on the asphalt.

"I'm sorry," he told her, and it felt like insufficient compensation for not just tonight, but everything she'd been through.

She didn't respond.

The emptiness of the house was an acute reflection of the two of them, he noted as they entered and he locked the door behind them. Empty vessels, wanting to be filled, yearning for small comforts.

Emmie lifted her head and stared out the big picture window down at the dancing flashlight beams at the barn. "It's funny," she said in a low, reflective voice. "I was eleven when I started working here. Not on the books, no, but Amy asked if I wanted to walk her horse for a little tip – he'd bowed his tendon – and I jumped at the chance. And then I was scrubbing water buckets. Carrying cold water bottles to the older girls during their lessons. I cleaned tack, and then stalls, and then exercised horses. I worked, year after year after year, and then Amy asked me if I wanted to run the place. I never asked for any of it." She glanced toward him, eyes full of a deep sadness. "I just worked, and I used to think working hard paid off. But now everyone hates me, and everything's wrong, and all that work was for absolutely nothing."

"Em." He stepped toward her. "Don't say that. Nobody hates you."

She turned her face away and it pulled at the deep center of his chest, propelled him toward her. She made him restless with inaction, desperate to right her wrongs. But most of them were emotional, and he had no tools for that, no methods or plans. All he had was himself, and that had never been good enough for anyone.

"I'm so tired," she whispered to the glass in front of her. "I'm exhausted."

Walsh touched her shoulders first, and when she reluctantly turned toward him, a rejection on her lips, he reached to her throat, her face, cupped her warm cheeks in his hands and tipped her chin up, so her eyes were on his.

"I know you are, baby," he said, and felt her shiver again, a low surge of energy under her skin. Even if she loathed everything about him and this situation, he held a physical sway over her, their bodies communicating of their own accord. "And I can't change anything that's already happened. But it doesn't have to be cold and lonely between us. We can be a comfort to each other."

Or more, so much more, he thought, *if you'll just open the door to it.*

Her hands lifted and closed over his wrists, but there was no resistance to them. He felt the liquid give of her neck as she relaxed into his hold.

"I can't love you," she whispered. "All you'd ever do is hurt me."

"Not on purpose."

She closed her eyes and tried to turn away from him.

He held her fast and kissed her.

She stilled, but she didn't pull away.

He teased at her lips with his tongue, a gentle sweep. Asking. Encouraging. She trembled against him, drawn tight, resisting in her silent, unresponsive –

Her mouth opened, and something a lot like joy surged in his chest. It was like she fell into the kiss, sighing deeply, melting against him, hands curling around the back of his neck as her lips welcomed him.

He was almost forty, and he was a detail guy; it wasn't just about the race to the finish with him. He liked every part of the sex, liked taking the time to wind a woman up and listen to all the little pleased sounds she made.

And this was not simply a woman, but his new wife, who he'd frightened and damaged. So he kissed her for long moments, thumbs stroking gently across her cheeks, gentle and careful, but hotly focused on tasting every inch of her mouth.

And she slowly came undone. Her nails bit into his neck; her breasts pressed against his chest. She gasped between kisses. Mrs. Walsh? She wanted him. And that was the single hottest thought to ever enter his mind.

He walked her backward until she hit one of so many blank stretches of wall. Slid his knee between her legs, let his thigh ride against the seam of her flimsy shorts.

A deeper sound, a wordless murmur as she shifted her hips and rubbed herself against him.

Walsh turned loose of her face, because he had to touch the rest of her. He unzipped her hoodie in a fast sweep, pushed it

213

off her shoulders, and she was helping him, ditching it in a hurry. He whipped her shirt off her head, sent her shorts to the floor.

She was beautifully curved, and golden, and naked, and she was all his, and only his.

Comfort, he'd said. This had nothing to do with comfort.

He picked her up, hands latched on her thighs, and pinned her back against the wall with his hips. Her legs wrapped around him, and tightened on a fast squeeze when he took her budded nipple into his mouth.

It was a moan that left her lips this time, a full-throated feminine sound that went straight to his cock.

Emmie was the one who reached between them to open his belt. He managed to snag a condom out of his back pocket and gave it to her, let her do the honors.

Sliding into her was exquisite. He fought to hold to a thorough, grinding rhythm, breaking out in a full-body sweat under his clothes from the effort. All he wanted was to finish, the urge urgent and painful at this point he was so excited by her. But she was watching him, her head kicked back against the wall, the breath heaving in and out of her, her eyes heavy-lidded and drugged with arousal.

She wasn't pretending he was someone else, wasn't kidding herself. She wanted him. *Him.* Even if she hated him and even if he was her husband.

He worked her until she came with a high, breathy gasp, her sex tightening around him like a fist.

She was his. He knew it, and the way she arched against him – she knew it too.

~*~

"I had a dream about you," she whispered. She felt cracked open like an egg, every emotion emptied out of her, so nothing was real save the mattress beneath her in the moon-silvered room and his naked warmth beside her. She lay on her side, resting against his shoulder, his arm a comfort around her waist. "Right after we met. A sex dream."

He chuckled. "Did you now? That's the best kind to have."

"Hmm. It was nice."

"That's encouraging. Tell me: do you normally fantasize about your bosses?"

She was playing with his chest hair and gave it a sharp tug. "You know I'm not that kind of girl."

Another low laugh moved through his chest. "All I know is, you were enjoying yourself downstairs a bit ago."

Yes, she'd been enjoying herself, because God, it was just so *good* between them. Thinking about it heated her skin, but it was easier now to remember all the reasons it should have never happened.

"I shouldn't be–" she started, trying to roll away from him.

His arm tightened, and he caught her loosely by the hair with his other hand. "None of that now," he said softly, drawing her face to his. "It's my wedding night, and I married this lovely, lovely girl, and I really need to hear her come again."

The words propelled her heart up her throat for so many reasons. She had to wet her lips. "If I try to leave the bed, will you let me go?"

He sighed and it ruffled her hair. "I'll always let you go, love. I won't make you be my wife. But I want you to be."

He was a smart man, wasn't he? Force would never have worked, but his earnest admission left her with melted knees and a throbbing pulse.

"It's my wedding night too," she reminded, and pressed her lips to his.

It might be her only wedding night, she reflected, because even if he let her go, who would want a biker's cast-off old lady?

The sudden bloom of sadness made the kiss all the sweeter. She gave herself over to it completely, leaning into the stroke of his hands, shifting onto her stomach at his gentle urging. She arched her back when he entered her from behind, and curled her fingers tight in the sheet as he rode her.

"Ah, good girl, pretty love, you feel so good around me," he murmured, the accent making the words darker, heavier.

It was the most acute pleasure of her life. It was what she'd hold onto, she decided. An uncertain, terrifying road lay ahead of her, but she had this fantastic well of passion between them, and she'd drink from it, long swallows here and there, to ease the burn of losing the life she'd always wanted.

She pushed everything practical from her mind and concentrated on the sex. Just the sex. The gorgeous sensation of her man inside her.

Everything else could come later.

Twenty-Five

"Dude! What part of 'feed the hose' didn't you get?"

"I thought you were doing one of your stupid joke bits again."

"Bits? I don't have bits!"

"Bro, you have bits, and they suck. FYI."

"Children," Walsh said with a tired-sounding sigh. "Can we not just do this?" He gestured to the front of the barn with the pressure washer's wand.

To be fair, he probably *was* tired, and didn't just sound that way. Emmie was on her second cup of coffee and still battling flagging eyelids.

Side-effect of so much awesome sex.

Stop thinking about it.

Aidan and Carter had shown up about fifteen minutes ago with a pressure washer, lots of detergent, and a bad case of being mentally twelve. She stood off to the side, not really caring that her hair was still wet and she was wearing Walsh's faded denim shirt over her sleep shorts. They were married, not like it was a big scandal.

Her eyes flicked up to the words painted above the barn door. They were just as tall and poorly punctuated as they had been the night before, but held no power to frighten her now. Her husband was taking care of it – he and his brothers. He'd called, and they'd come, simple as that.

Like family.

There was a warmth in her veins that had nothing to do with the coffee, and everything to do with the sight of three male friends fumbling through a simple task, giving each other shit.

She loved it.

Carter got the hose situation fixed and the washer started with a roar. Walsh manned the wand, and it became quickly apparent that all the mist rolling off the blast zone was going to soak him through. Not that she minded the idea of damp clothes sticking to him. Not at all.

The machine was so loud she didn't hear Tonya's Mercedes SUV pull up. The brunette heiress was suddenly standing beside her, outrageously beautiful in mocha colored breeches and a black Ariat polo. She folded her arms and nodded toward the guys.

"Enjoying the show?"

Emmie sipped her coffee. "I'll neither confirm nor deny that."

Tonya sent her a smug smirk. "Hmph. Well, not that I blame you. They do have a certain animal appeal. Purely physical, though." Feigning boredom, she examined her manicured nails. "Aidan's taking me to dinner tonight."

"Really?" Emmie tried not to look too curious. "Where are you going?" Which meant, where could he possibly afford to take you that you'd deign to eat?

Tonya shrugged. "Don't know, don't care."

Aidan leaned down to adjust something on the washer and caught sight of them standing there, straightened up and flashed Tonya a truly dazzling smile that, beneath the playboy charm, had a true boyish delight crinkling up his dark eyes.

Emmie was surprised by the little spark of worry that ignited in the back of her mind...and in her chest. It was an emotional reaction too. "Tonya...I think he might actually like you. Not just in a hookup way, I mean." She glanced over at her student and frowned in reaction to the self-satisfied expression on the woman's face.

"I know," she said. "Isn't it funny?"

~*~

Vince didn't get paid enough to deal with this shit. He really didn't. "Agent Grey," he said firmly. "Tell me why you're here – none of that mustache twirling you do, the facts, man – and then kindly get the hell out of my office. I have work to do."

The FBI agent in the chair across from his desk frowned, and it emphasized the new heaviness of his face. He'd been a little tired and worn around the edges the last time Vince saw him

– a young, attractive man worn down by stress – but now, he had that bloated, doughy look of a drunk.

"Fine," he said tightly, "the facts. The main *fact* is that I've got intel on the Lean Dogs that could tear them open from the inside out."

Swift punch of déjà vu. "Yeah, you said the same thing the last time. Remember? When you were gonna get Ava Lécuyer's boyfriend to find some dirt for you."

Grey glanced toward the wall, face creasing with disgust. "Ugh. That little bitch. Nothing but a goddamn cat in heat."

Talking about the Lean Dogs was one thing; picking on Maggie's only daughter was another. He frowned. "Leave Ava–"

"I've been watching them."

"Excuse me?"

"I've been watching them," Grey repeated, without an ounce of shame. "They're boring as hell, mostly, but there's two things going on." He pitched forward in his chair. "Big things."

"Do your supervisors know you're doing this?"

Ignoring the question – which meant "no" – he clamped his hands on the edge of the desk. "Did you not hear me? The Dogs are up to something, and I've got a grenade to throw in the middle of them. You could end up putting them all away with this intel."

With a deft movement, Vince reached over with one hand and pulled up a Word doc on his computer, poised his fingers over the keys, ready to take notes. He needed to make a call to the feds, report Grey as rogue. Request they pull him out of Knoxville. But before that, he needed to know what the guy was going on about with the Dogs. So he could decide if it had merit, or needed burying.

Things had been quiet lately. The last Dog-related trouble had been stirred up by the former mayor, his concocted war with the Carpathians that had damn near caused a revolution in this city.

But the Dogs had put that down, and since, things had been peaceful. A little too peaceful, at moments, signifying the Dogs' control of the underground. Damn them.

"Go ahead."

"Okay, for starters" – there was a delighted glint in Grey's eyes, something like the dilated wonder of a junkie who'd just shot up – "the club bought that big horse farm. Briar Hall."

Vince nodded. "Walsh did, yeah. I knew that."

Grey made a face. "But why? They don't have a reason to do that. What the hell do a buncha bikers want with a place like that?"

"What do they want with a nursery?" Vince shrugged. "They own a lot of businesses. It's what keeps them from living hand to mouth. Kenny Teague likes money. That's no secret."

"Oh, wake up the hell up, Fielding. These guys don't give a damn about business. It's all money laundering. They're smuggling stacks out in the hay or something. Or" – he snapped his fingers – "they're using the horses as drug mules. Coke balloons." He made a motion with his hand that was clearly meant to simulate shoving said balloons up a certain part of a horse.

Vince bit down on a grin. "Wouldn't that make them drug horses instead of drug mules?"

Grey sighed. "I'm telling you–"

"I've grown up in this town," Vince said, "which means I've grown up around the Dogs, and I've spent more time with them than I ever wanted to. But I know for a fact that the Dogs don't deal their own drugs. And they pay their taxes, and there's not a damn thing on the books that so much as smells illegal. If you try to use this farm against them, you're gonna come up empty."

"Walsh. The English one? He married that girl yesterday. The one who works there."

"I know."

Grey's brows went up, like he was asking him to give a damn.

"Emmie's a nice girl, but she's really practical and hard-nosed, and she works too much. If she and Walsh get on, then good for them. Her family life's shit, and I always thought she was lonely as hell."

"Jesus Christ, you sound like you're on their side."

"I'm on Knoxville's side," Vince said, frowning. "I care about my city, and the people in it. I don't give a shit about a demented fed's spying games."

Grey puffed up.

"You brought a spy to my city, and you were involved in starting a fucking street war that got innocent bystanders killed. I hate the goddamned sight of you. Now, either you have orders to be here, or you don't. And since I'm guessing you don't, I'm kicking you out of my office. Now."

Grey flushed purple with rage, veins standing out in his neck. "Estes is queer," he snarled. "Did you know that?"

Vince sat back. "*What?*" He shook his head. "Nevermind. Why would I care?"

"We both know outlaw MCs are backward as shit. There aren't gay members. And Kevin Estes? Very gay." He pulled a digital camera from the pocket of his sweatshirt and handed it over.

Vince looked at the photos only because he felt he had to, to confirm that this wasn't another of the man's lies. He shoved it back. "I don't care what Tango does. It's nobody's business but his."

Grey smiled. "Yeah, except all his brothers. You drop this bomb on Teague, and it'll start a civil war with those losers."

Vince sighed and pinched the bridge of his nose. "Remember what I said about getting out? I meant it."

~*~

"Fucking moron," Harlan muttered to himself as he left Fielding's office. The sergeant made him sick sometimes. Sure, there were protocols to follow and all that, but when it came to guys like the Lean Dogs, no one frowned too heavily upon a little blurring of the lines. Putting away an entire outlaw organization, one that bullied and evaded law enforcement, and that ran this city – and one that had humiliated him, personally – should have been top priority. Fielding should have been kissing his shoes right now, thanking him profusely for those photos he would have never otherwise seen.

Dumbass.

But he'd worked with dumbasses before, and he'd always found a way around it.

A commotion drew his attention, a young man walking out of an interrogation room, a woman who was obviously his mother screaming at the officers around her.

"He didn't do anything! I will sue this place! I'll sue the badges off all of you!" she railed, gesturing wildly with manicured hands, eyes flashing in a way that was more insane than it was compelling.

Meanwhile her son, scowling and muttering under his breath, stormed out of the precinct.

"My father is turning in his grave," the woman continued to fume. "Never in my life – accusing a Richards of vandalizing his grandfather's own farm?"

"It's not his grandfather's farm anymore, ma'am," one of the officers said in a bored voice.

"No, you're just gonna let that goddamn biker have it!"

Biker? Richards? Farm? Vandalism?

A dozen thoughts clicked together in Harlan's head. He took off at a jog, exiting the precinct, hustling down the front steps. The young man was headed for a BMW SUV in an exaggerated, swaggering punk walk.

"Mr. Richards!" Harlan called, catching up to him.

The young man paused, turned, expression set in a superior sneer. "I'm not under arrest." His voice was petulant, childish.

Why did he always end up working with the spoiled rich brats?

"You're Brett Richards?" Harlan asked, and when he got a slow nod, he extended his hand. "Agent Harlan Grey, FBI."

Brett wouldn't take his hand, eyes widening. "Dude..."

"I understand your grandfather was murdered," Grey continued, tone professional. "And that you might have been showing your emotion about that. A little spray paint?" He lifted his brows as if to say *don't deny it.*

Brett made a face. "Man, they can't prove shit. I—"

"I wouldn't blame you if you did," Harlan said, quickly. He lowered his voice. "If I'm being perfectly honest, I'd do just about anything to get those damn Lean Dogs off the streets. It seems like we've got a mutual problem in them, don't we?"

Brett studied him a moment, expression cautious, but finally smiled. "Yeah." He accepted the handshake at last. "We do."

~*~

The siding on the barn was rough-cut, and the paint had soaked in. The pressure washer faded the graffiti, but it was still there, a hint of something foul. "We'll have to paint it," Walsh said, frowning as he surveyed it. "Stain it. Something."

"Bleach?" Aidan asked.

"Nah. That'll burn the wood."

"Right."

Without turning his head, Walsh glanced over to where Emmie had been standing. She wasn't there anymore; probably went in the back door of the barn so she could properly dress and get to work.

He was exhausted, deeply satisfied...and worried about her, still. She'd stayed through the night with him, face peaceful and lovely in the first light of dawn, her hair wild across the pillow. She'd murmured and snuggled against him when he'd kissed her forehead. She'd thanked him for the coffee when she came down from the shower, wearing his shirt. And she'd had the distinct look of a woman who'd been fucked well and liked it.

But they hadn't talked about anything.

"...to do?" Aidan was saying beside him, and he refocused.

"What?"

"I can hang around for a while, if you need me, if there's something you want me to do?" The guy looked hopeful, almost, energetic.

"Okay, no offense, mate, but why would I need you to do anything?"

Aidan made an exasperated sound. "It's like I said before. I wanna help you run this place."

Walsh frowned. "Is this just to be closer to the rich girlie? I think she'll let you bang her whether you're around or not."

"No." He rolled his eyes. "I want to manage something. Co-manage."

"What about the shop?"

"Merc's taken that over, and we both know that."

"Aidan, bro, you know nothing about farms. Or horses. Or managing."

Aidan pressed his lips together in obvious frustration. "Yeah, you're right." It sounded like it took tremendous effort to say it. "But how the hell do I get better at managing if no one will let me manage anything?"

I have my own problems to sort, Walsh wanted to tell him. *I got married yesterday, and I got people calling my wife a junkie bitch, and I'm trying to hold onto this farm so the developers don't get it.* The club's burial ground was in danger of being discovered, and here was Aidan worried about finally becoming a man at age thirty-two.

But Walsh knew that his accident last year had shaken him up, gotten him thinking about the bigger picture. Because he was still Aidan, it was a skewed view, but nevertheless, bigger than it had been previously.

So Walsh said, "I need to hire a new groundskeeper."

"What, like, mow the lawn?"

Walsh shrugged. "Or find me someone who can." Before Aidan could interrupt, he added, "Look, I appreciate what you're trying to do. I get it. You want to step up. But around here, Em runs a tight ship and I've got all the financial stuff handled. I don't need a co-manager."

Aidan glanced down at the toes of his boots, blowing out a tired-sounding breath.

"I'm not trying to hold you back," Walsh said. "It's just the way things are right now."

"Yeah. I get it."

Maybe a kinder VP would go after the guy as he ambled back toward the truck to help Carter load the pressure washer, but he was too distracted for that.

He found Emmie in the feed room with Becca, adjusting the rations on the whiteboard with eraser in hand. Both glanced his way.

Becca's expression was stricken, like she wasn't sure whether to give him a cheeky atta-boy grin, or a vicious, friend-supporting scowl.

Emmie looked at him with a clear-eyed, unreadable calm.

"Give us a minute?" he asked Becca.

"Sure." How a teenager could pack such attitude into one word, he'd never know. She clapped the eraser down on a feed can and left with her nose stuck up at a defiant angle.

"Take it she doesn't approve of our new living arrangement."

Emmie shrugged and capped her marker. It had left black smudges on her fingertips, and he found that cute and real, for some reason. No flawless manicures for his woman. She was all work and sacrifice.

He loved it.

"She doesn't approve of a lot of things. Right up until she does," Emmie said. "She'll come around."

He took a few steps further into the room. It smelled like molasses and feed pellets, and he'd always loved that smell; he took a deep breath of it now and fixed his old lady with a questioning glance. "And you? You coming around?"

When she didn't answer right away, he said, "I thought we ought to talk about some things."

She nodded and moved to sit on an upturned bucket, booted toes tucked together. "Living arrangements, for one thing." Her voice quavered with sudden nerves.

"Yeah. You know you have to stay up in the big house with me."

"For appearances."

"And so…"

"We can have more of last night." She blushed. "I…" A line of tension appeared between her brows and she rubbed at it with her ink-smudged fingers. "I've been thinking," she started again. "Really thinking." Her eyes lifted to his. "If we're going to make this work – living together, trusting each other, me being your old whatever."

"Old lady," he supplied with a slow grin.

"Right. That. If I'm going to be that, I need to know more about you. Real, deep, where you came from, who you are kind of stuff."

He nodded slowly.

"Is it so wrong to want to know who I married?" she asked quietly.

"No, love." He felt a tingling across his skin, apprehension at the idea of breaking himself open the way she was asking him to. "It's not too much."

Twenty-Six

There were so many things she should have been thinking about as she packed several days' worth of clothes in a duffle bag. The lessons she had to teach the next day. The flexion exercises she needed to work into Apollo's routine. The fact that Brett was clearly trying to imply that she was the source of the heroin that had killed Davis, and therefore the killer. The fact that she hadn't heard from Dad – or Bell Bar – in a few days, and Maryann would no doubt leave soon, throwing her back into the role of DD.

But those were the things she'd thought of every day, for as long as she could remember, with no time off, no vacation, no relief. So Emmie wanted to think about the big house on the hill, and the man waiting for her inside it.

Her man.

She had showered, and dressed now in a loose white tank top and clean cutoffs, rolled a coat of gloss across her lips before she doused the lights and headed up to the house.

There were honest to God butterflies in her stomach.

She went to the front door, because that was the one Walsh seemed to use most, and found it unlocked, let herself in. The scent of food hit her first, and when she stepped into the cavernous living room, she spotted a dinky leather sofa, a chair, a little table...and Walsh.

"You've been busy," she said, because she didn't know how she wanted to greet him just yet.

He shrugged and scratched at his chin stubble in a self-conscious movement. "I brought over some stuff from my old place. And there's frozen potato skins in the oven." He jerked a thumb over his shoulder toward the kitchen. "If that's alright."

She nodded, and inwardly, took a deep breath, bracing herself for whatever the night held. "Sounds good."

~*~

Mags and Ava both had funeral dresses. And sometimes, if she was going to school or some sort of writing meeting, Ava would wear slacks and pumps. But none of the women in Aidan's life dressed like *this*.

Across the white tablecloth and flickering candles, Tonya looked poured into a wine-colored dress that hugged every graceful line and swelling curve of her body. She was flashing a lot of cleavage, and a trio of diamonds on a silver chain disappeared down between her breasts, drawing his eyes there again and again. Her lipstick was dark, her eyes ringed in black, her hair a spill of shadow down her back.

Aidan had been staring at her for a solid minute, all his charm drying to dust on his tongue.

"Everything alright?" she asked, slicing into her tiny serving of chicken-whatever-the-hell.

This was the third time he'd ground to a conversational halt since they'd sat down. It had to stop.

"Yeah." He pushed a grin across his face, hoped it was cocky enough. "Just thinking I ain't dressed right for this place."

Her dark eyes moved up and down him, taking in his carefully pressed plaid shirt, the unholy amount of gel in his hair. Her smile was small, didn't show any teeth. Predatory, almost, and how weird to think that about a woman. "You look fine." There was a purr in her voice, and something that was definitely her foot slid up the inside of his leg under the table.

Okay, so that answered the first date question.

He felt his grin become easier, more natural. "I always wonder why chicks wanna get so dolled up all the time."

She made bold eye contact. "I wanted to look nice for you."

She was a seductress, this one. Like the more forward groupies, but with more style, and a better wardrobe. The thrill, though, is that she wasn't part of his usual string. This was a classy girl, one with money and power and influence. She was unlike anyone he'd ever bedded before.

A change, his father had said, and this was a change. Boy, was it ever a change.

228

"I don't think 'nice' covers it, sweetheart."

Her foot reached his knee, heading between his thighs.

"Well then you'll have to elaborate," she said, smiling wide, "later."

~*~

"So what do you want to know? Or shall I just start at the beginning?" Walsh asked as he dragged two greasy potato skins onto his paper plate and then licked his fingers. He'd forgotten napkins, damn it.

Emmie didn't seem to mind that. She popped a speck of bacon into her mouth, touched her tongue to her fingertips – a potent reminder of all the things he still wanted to do with her. Her brows tucked together over her eyes. "I swear you look nervous."

"Hmm. Only a bit."

She grinned. "Well that's nice for a change." She squared up her shoulders, gave him a serious face. He loved that about her, the way she could be all business. "Okay. Well, I think the beginning is best. And then you're welcome to my beginning, however lame that is."

Never, in his entire life, had a woman offered up her beginning to him. Her history. The little horrors that had brought her to his bed. He couldn't squander that. Couldn't hold anything back.

He ducked his head over his plate, took a deep breath and said, "Well, Mum was easy to fool. You ought to know that…"

The words poured out of him, faster and smoother than he'd thought possible. He told her about the squalid London flat into which his husbandless mother had brought him home. About them being hungry, the rare treat of a sweet, the elbows and fists from the other boys bigger than him.

"I was a tiny thing," he said, hearing his accent deepen with remembrance. "Everyone picked on me."

Her face was full of sympathy. She was small too. She understood.

And so he moved onto Rottingdean, his grandparents, Gramps with his vicarious dreams. To Brighton Racecourse, and his short-lived time as a jockey. His epic failure after the rider beside him went down. And died.

"Oh God," she breathed. "But you didn't mean to. You were defending yourself, and it was an accident." She slapped her plate down like she wanted to storm off and track down the officials who'd banned him. "They couldn't just do that to you!"

"Can and did, love."

He didn't tell her about Rita, because he didn't want to spoil things. He didn't want to tell her about a woman rejecting him, and his seed. Didn't want to give her any ideas.

But he told her about finding out that Phillip Calloway, the then VP of the London chapter, was his half-brother. How he'd joined the RAF instead. He faltered in the middle of the Afghanistan story, and she stared at him, deeply concerned, but didn't press. Didn't ask him about that medivac mission, about the woman garbed in black who'd been used as a human shield for the rat bastard who'd gunned down the two injured soldiers he was supposed to be rescuing. He didn't tell her about killing that woman, as he'd put a bullet in the scum behind her; she seemed to know it, though, and her hand covered his on the tabletop.

It was a short sprint to the finish after that. Back home he'd prospected, been patched, then been sent to Knoxville for a job, and stayed.

"The Money Man. That's what they call me." His gaze was fixed on her tiny fingers, the way they stroked mindlessly across his knuckles again and again. "They send me in when a chapter needs to make some cash." He offered her a half-assed smile. "The strip club fixer, that's me."

Her frown was concerned, curious, but not disapproving. "The farm fixer too, apparently."

"This place was my idea. I thought we ought to make a go of it."

"Because you hate high density condos? Or because you hate high density condos next door to...however many bodies are over there?" Her fingers stilled, and then closed tight over his, asking. There was fear in her eyes, but there were bright shards of trust, too. She was giving him a chance to help her see, and that was sweeter than anything a woman had ever given him.

He turned her hand over, cleaved his palm to hers. Chose his words carefully. "The club works a certain way, pet. Some things have changed a little, over time, but most haven't. It's not modern, but that's how it is."

"It's a crime ring," she said quietly.

"It's protective. Of itself. It's self-sustaining. Which means there are some things I can't ever tell you. Only a man with a patch on his back and a seat at the table can know all the secrets. The club doesn't go around trying to break the law, but club comes first – club law trumps city, and state, and country law. Yeah? We protect it, and it protects the people who belong to it. The men who wear the patch. And the women we love, and the children they give us."

Her lips parted and she inhaled deeply. "Walsh–"

"When someone tries to hurt us – any of us – we put 'em down. Simple as that. It's what we have to do to keep everyone safe."

"How many..." She swallowed. "How many people are buried over there?"

He squeezed her hand. "I'll tell you as much as I can, but there's some things you can't know. You'll have to trust me on that."

"That's going to be difficult, given the circumstances."

"I know, love, I know." He threaded his fingers through hers. "But I promise you – I *promise* – that I won't let you get hurt. You're my wife, and even if it's just pretend, it means something to me."

Okay, time to look away now; he couldn't drop all that on the poor girl and expect her to handle it well.

But he couldn't. His gaze was riveted to hers, and he was shocked by the softness in her face

She twitched him a bare smile. "My turn now, right?"

~*~

When Tonya asked if he wanted to come up, as they stood at the base of her expensive high-rise building, he accepted, and he ran through the advice his sister had given him. He needed to compliment her place, say the sorts of ridiculous, flowery things chicks always wanted to hear. He should be sure not to track mud onto her floors, and hold the doors for her, and...

All that well-meaning shit fled from his mind the second they stepped into the elevator and Tonya turned the most unmistakable look his way.

He moved toward her, but she met him partway, and when he caught the back of her head in his hand, she reached behind him and gripped his ass. The kiss was a crashing together, and it didn't feel hesitant, or tender, or like a first kiss at all.

She bit his lip hard, and he hissed, pulling back. "Shit." He touched the spot with his thumb and drew back with a drop of blood. "Are you serious?"

"Very." Her hands moved up his stomach, smoothed across his chest. She leaned into him, pressed her breasts against him. Her face was flushed, eyes heavy-lidded. "That's not a problem, is it?"

If she wanted to play rough, he could play rough. "Nah." He grinned. "Just wanna make sure you don't get hurt, darlin'."

"Trust me. I won't."

~*~

"Mine's not very exciting," Emmie said, a self-conscious blush warming her cheeks as she sank down low against the back of his cracked leather bachelor pad sofa. She wouldn't admit it, but she'd always loved old leather couches like this. They were so cool against her skin in summer, and the leather never really lost its earthy smell.

Walsh was beside her, his arm thrown over the back, so that if she wanted to, she could lean sideways and lie against him.

That felt too intimate somehow, in this moment of secret-spilling, so she stayed in her slouch.

"The farm I already know about," he said, helpfully.

"Right. And that's most of it. Pretty much all you need to know about me is that I live, breathe, and sleep Briar Hall." She sighed. "But here goes. Mom left when I was eight. Right after she put me in riding lessons. Dad didn't drink then, but he was a sappy kind of guy. A bit of a nerd, incurably uncool. He was sweet, though." She sent him a wan smile that he returned. "He always brought her flowers, and he had these hokey pet names for her. He adored her.

"And she ran off with a minor league baseball player who called her 'bitch' and treated her like hell. She needed excitement. She needed danger." She snorted. "She would love that I'm here with you."

"Hey now. I don't call you names."

"No, you're a perfect English gentleman," she agreed, and laughed at his frown.

Then sobered. "She's married to some kind of nine-to-fiver now. They have kids. She sends me Christmas and birthday cards sometimes." She shrugged. "Dad never got over it. And I'm afraid he wasn't ever much of a dad afterward." Another shrug. "That's all there is to tell, really. I buried myself in this place. I didn't have friendships or long-term relationships because I was so dedicated to the horses. And now…"

"And now," Walsh said quietly, smug smile pulling at his mouth, "you live in the big house, and it's half yours."

She sat up straight. "I thought the club bought it."

He rolled his eyes. "Well, yeah. But Ghost ain't gonna live out here and muck stalls for you. Far as the club is concerned, this place is yours and mine, to do what we want with, so long as it turns a profit."

"You're not serious."

"Completely."

Emmie took a deep breath. It was the sort of dream she'd never allowed herself, because it had been too big, too far-fetched.

"Em." Walsh leaned toward her. "You're not *just* the manager, love. Not anymore."

No, she was the mistress of this place she'd poured her life into. She was married to the owner. The sweet owner, who'd shown her more affection and care than anyone related to her, than anyone she'd worked for, than…anyone.

She lunged forward and threw her arms around his neck.

Twenty-Seven

"You don't need to keep walking me out," Tango said, rolling his eyes. "I'm not going to get mugged."

"Don't think me too practical, darling," Ian said beside him, reaching up to play with the row of hoops going down Tango's ear. "It's just that I'm never quite done with you."

Tango bit down hard on his lip as deft fingertips tugged at one piercing and then the next, moving down to the sensitive lobe. He wanted to tell Ian to stop, but he knew that if he turned to face him, the words would never get a chance to leave his mouth.

So he turned his head, and the kiss was consuming. Ian could be utterly soft and feminine in his manner, or he could be dominating, and this kiss was of the latter variety, his tongue shoving roughly into Tango's mouth, his hands gripping the sides of his head.

The elevator reached the parking garage level with a soft ding, and Tango shoved away, breathing ragged.

Ian smiled rather smugly, wiped the moisture off his bottom lip with a quick flick of his thumb. "One last taste," he said, and turned to face the frosted stainless doors as they slid open.

Tango took a huge breath and tried to tidy his hair. He didn't say goodbye; words always seemed to evade him at this moment. He stepped out into the chilly underground garage and made it about five steps toward his bike when Ian caught up to him, his slippers silent on the concrete, long-fingered hand curling around Tango's wrist.

"Wait," he whispered, stilling, his breath halting as he scanned the rows of cars around them. "We're being watched," he said.

"What?"

Ian ignored him, reached over his shoulder and made a fast hand gesture that made no sense.

"Ian—"

"Shh. Kiss me again."

Tango frowned. "What in the—"

Ian grabbed his head, brought their mouths together, and kissed the hell out of him. When he pulled back, Tango heard a scramble of feet on the tarmac, assorted shouts, grunts, and a loud, "Get your hands off me!"

He shook away from Ian completely and saw that two of the Englishman's no-necked security thugs were pulling a man out a black Explorer across the way. Tango was good with faces, and he recognized this one immediately. "Oh shit."

"Go," Ian told him with a little pat on the shoulder. He turned toward the captive, squalling man and straightened the lapels of his robe. "Go on, darling. I've got this."

Like he'd always been so good at doing, Tango followed orders, and left.

~*~

They were going to have to make a serious furniture run, Walsh decided as he moved around the kitchen the next morning. He'd never been much of one for material aesthetics, but he'd awakened that morning with a deep sense of purpose in his gut, one that was personal and had nothing to do with the club. He'd decided some things, in the dark, with his woman curled against him. And for starters, he needed to make this place comfortable. He didn't want them going into winter with one sofa and a floor mattress. This needed to be a home.

"This house is going to spoil me," Emmie said with a dreamy sigh as she came into the room, twisting her hair up into a curly blonde knot. "Did you know the tile floor in the bathroom is heated?"

"It is?"

"And it's divine." She wiggled her bare toes against the kitchen tiles in demonstration, smiling.

She was dressed to ride and she was...well, bugger it, she was cute. She was beautiful and she was sexy and all those things, but she was cute too, and that was the thought that struck him as he stepped to her and dropped a kiss on her lips.

"You okay?" he asked as he pulled back.

Her smile took on a softer, almost embarrassed cast. Like she was remembering the way they'd tested out the Jacuzzi tub last night and found that it was a perfect fit for two. "I'm fine." Her eyes dropped to his mouth, like maybe she wanted another kiss.

His phone chimed with a text alert, breaking the moment. She turned away, going to the coffee pot.

"Hey, there's something I've been thinking about," he said as he checked his phone.

Ghost: *Come in to the clubhouse.*

"Yeah?" she asked as she poured. They were using Styrofoam cups, and that was another thing to remedy.

"Two things, actually." He turned around to face her, hands braced back on the counter. "One, we need furniture."

"I've got a few things in the loft."

"Real furniture. Enough to fill this place up."

Her brows popped in surprise. "Okay."

"And the other thing is…" He winced. "My mum."

Interest sparked in her eyes. "You're thinking of bringing her here, aren't you?"

He'd told her about his mother's poor decisions when it came to Devin Green, the way he couldn't trust that she wouldn't get hurt again. "Yeah. There's plenty of room for her here. If you're okay with it."

She smiled and it did things to his insides. The simple act of giving her a say pleased her so much, and he loved that he could do that, include her and make her happy. "Yeah. To be honest, it's super adorable to hear you say 'mum,' so I'm totally on board."

He had to grin. "Just to warn you, though. She's going to love you to death."

Her eyes crinkled up she smiled so wide.

His phone chimed again. "I gotta go check in with the boss. You're teaching this morning?"

"Yep."

"I'll be back in a bit."

"No rush."

It felt like some suburban cliché, both of them off to work, the smell of coffee swirling around their expensive kitchen.

He grinned, suddenly, at the absurdity of it. The way life had taken such unusual turns to get to such a commonplace moment.

"I know," she said, nose scrunching up. "Let me call you 'honey' and they can slap us in a Rockwell calendar."

~*~

When he pulled up to the clubhouse at Dartmoor, he caught the bright gleam of sunlight on a black Jag XF. Black luxury sedans were kingpin-required. But a Jaguar? That could only belong to one person.

"Shit," he muttered, hustling off his bike.

Inside, his brothers were scattered at the tables, a few at the bar, Ghost lounged back on a sofa with deceptive calmness, squared off from Shaman, who was seated in a deep leather chair across from the president.

The man was in a tailored suit, his hair smooth and shiny, like he used a straightener on the damn stuff. His shoes were square-toed, saddle-colored things that cost more than the chair in which he sat.

Fancy bugger.

"Alright, VP's in the house," Ghost said with a sigh. "We're all here. You gonna tell me what this is about?"

The Englishman had a tumbler of what looked to be Scotch and he held it up to the light, highlighting a dozen water marks on the glass that hadn't come off in the dishwasher. He frowned. "Well that's not very hospitable."

"You're in my house. I don't have to be hospitable for shit."

Shaman sighed, set the glass down, and took in the room with a fast flick of his eyes. Everyone listening? Everyone paying attention to me? Self-absorbed prick.

Walsh stole a glance at Tango, to get a read on the guy, but he was staring at the toes of his boots, hands knotted together.

"Your club's under FBI surveillance," Shaman said, and a round of disbelieving curses rippled through the room.

"How do you know?" Walsh asked, and Shaman smiled, like he'd been hoping for that question.

"Because I caught him outside my building this morning surveilling *me*. He had a camera, and I looked through it while Bruce had him...detained." He motioned toward the hulking black-garbed bodyguard standing behind his chair. "There were photographs of all of you, at your homes, with your families." He held up a hand and Bruce pulled a folder from inside his jacket and handed it over.

Shaman sat forward and laid out the glossy photos on the coffee table in front of him. There was Maggie standing at her kitchen sink. Holly watering the azaleas. Rottie having dinner at the table with Mina and the boys. Ava and Mercy in bed together, and Ghost flipped that one face-down with a disgusted sound.

Then Walsh spotted Emmie, and a chill skittered up his back. It was her standing at his side, the night they'd discovered the graffiti, illuminated by his bike's headlamp. The camera was an expensive one, because it was a surprisingly clear shot to have been taken at night, without a flash.

"Jesus Christ," Rottie murmured, as all the guys crowded over the table.

"Oh, he's dead," Mercy said. "He's fucking dead."

"Also, you need to get some blinds," Dublin told him.

Ghost picked up the photo of Maggie, face a mask of contained rage. "How do I know you didn't take these?"

Shaman sighed, rolled his eyes and reached inside his gray suit coat. He came out with a man's wallet, and tossed it onto the table. "I didn't just fall off a cartel truck. Give me some credit, Teague."

Ghost snatched up the wallet.

"Harlan Grey's your man," Shaman said. "You've had dealings with him before, yes?"

"Yeah." Ghost ground his jaw as he studied the driver's license.

"I checked with my contacts," Shaman said, casually, "and he's not on assignment in Knoxville. So what he's doing is completely off the books with the Bureau."

"You have FBI contacts?" Ratchet asked wistfully. "Dude. Respect."

"He's gone rogue?" Walsh asked, gut tightening.

"It would seem so."

Walsh glanced at his prez and they shared a fast, silent communication. If the guy wasn't acting as a fed, he was fair game.

~*~

The sight of a squad car pulling up to the barn went a long way toward dampening Emmie's mood. It was easy to forget, when she was alone with Walsh, talking and tangling together in bed, that the only reason any of this was happening was because Davis Richards was dead.

She felt a fast stab of guilt for her deceased boss – here she'd been enjoying his deep tub last night – as she climbed over the arena fence and walked to meet Sergeant Fielding.

"Emmie, hi," he greeted with a smile and an awkward half-wave. Thanks to Brett's constant shenanigans, she'd encountered the sergeant a lot over the last few years, when he was dropping Brett off and unhooking his cuffs. Fielding had always been a likeable, serious sort.

"Morning, Sergeant. How's the investigation going?"

"Well," he said with a sigh, hands going on his gun belt, "we talked to Brett, and there's no doubt in my mind he did it. Unfortunately, he's got an alibi and we don't have the incident on tape." He shrugged and made an apologetic face. "That's how these kinds of things go, I'm afraid. We rarely charge anyone."

"Oh, well that stinks. But I meant about Davis. The…" Should she say it? "Murder."

His brows twitched. "I'm sorry, but you know I can't talk to you about that."

"I know." She nodded.

"But since you brought it up, how've things been around here?"

"Except for spray paint and cat guts?" she asked with a dry chuckle.

Fielding was serious. "You seen anything that was off? Anyone been by? Found anything up in that house?"

She frowned, thinking of the night a noise in the barn had awakened her and Walsh, thinking about the door being ajar the night she found Davis. "It's nothing concrete."

"Tell me anyway."

"I…" How to put it? "I get the impression, just this feeling – and there have been some sounds in the barn – that something's not right. Like there's somebody skulking around after dark." After she said it, she realized just how strongly she believed it. She'd been pushing it down, in hopes it was her imagination, but now she felt a new rush of fear. "I guess I sound paranoid."

"Not at all. When people get that kind of gut feeling, they're usually right. Listen to it," he said, "and please be careful. Call if you feel like you're in danger, okay?"

"Yeah. Okay."

~*~

Aidan walked into the cramped central office expecting to find Mags, and instead encountered a very different blonde. Samantha sat behind the desk, Remy in her lap, turning the pages of a picture book as she read aloud to him.

" 'And then the rabbit said–' " Her head lifted as his shadow blotted out the light from the door. Her expression cycled through a series of emotions he didn't understand, and then settled into a flat neutral. "Oh hi."

241

"Hey. Mags isn't here?"

"Ava had a doctor's appointment and she was feeling a little under the weather, so Maggie went with her. I offered to keep Remy."

"Oh. Cool." He rapped his knuckles on the doorframe and started to back out of the office.

Sam's voice stopped him. She was a professor, and she had one of those pleasant voices a person could listen to all day, always pitched at just the right volume to carry, but never to startle. "Did you need something?"

When he turned back around, she was shifting Remy to a better seat in her lap. "Not that I know where anything is, but I could look."

He hesitated. He'd been coming to ask about an advance on his next check, because last night's date had seriously depleted his cash. "Nah," he said finally, "nothing you can help with. Paycheck shit."

"Ah." She nodded. "Right. Can't help you there."

He started to turn away, but didn't, struck suddenly by how very sad she looked. He'd noticed Sam before in the last year or so that she'd been friends with Ava, because anything blonde and female deserved a good look. But her attitude was all wrong, sort of shy and awkward and too quiet. He looked at everyone, but it was the woman with a hair flip and a sly smile that really grabbed his attention. Chicks like that knew what he had to offer and wanted a slice. Chicks like Samantha were a minefield he had no idea how to navigate.

"Hey, are you alright?" he asked, and felt kind of stupid for it.

Her face smoothed over with surprise. "Yeah. I'm fine."

"You just...I dunno. You looked upset, or something."

She gave him a wistful smile. "I'm not upset."

See, that right there. He had no idea what the point of that was, when their faces said one thing and their lips another.

He decided to make light of it. "It's cool if you are. Writers are supposed to be all moody, right?"

She exhaled sharply through her nose, smile turning wry. "Right."

It was time to walk away now. "Okay. Well. I'll see ya."

"See ya."

But she called him back again. "Hey, Aidan?"

"Hmm?"

"Have you been on that date yet? The one you needed advice about?" A tense notch formed between her brows, mouth tucking down in the corners. Was it unhappiness? Disapproval? Or just a general sourness?

"I have, yeah. Went last night, actually." He couldn't stop the smile at the memory.

Sam's brows twitched above the rims of her glasses. "Lucky girl." More of that wistful look that wasn't really a smile. "What's her name?"

Not a question he'd expected, but not a strange one, considering.

"Tonya. Tonya Sinclair. Her dad owns the bank or something."

Sam's expression went totally blank.

"She's a nice girl. Not one of those..." Hmm, no delicate way to say it. "Tell my sister I'm not just doing what I always do." He grinned, imagining the face Ava would make. "I've got a real girl this time. She ought to be proud."

"Yeah. I'm sure she will be."

~*~

Tonya Sinclair. Aidan was finally dating someone age appropriate, and it was *Tonya Sinclair*.

When he was gone, Sam closed her eyes and let her chin rest against the downy soft top of Remy's head. The baby was a warm, squirmy burden in her arms, grounding her to this chair and this moment. But with her eyes shut, it was so easy to lose her mind to the past.

Tonya's parents had made a go at exposing her to "the regular kids," or some such, when she was young. Tonya hadn't been in her class, but Sam had encountered her at the elementary school playground. The wealthy, beautiful, haughty girl all the other girls had wanted to be friends with. And by "friends," they'd meant "toadies," offering to carry her lunchbox, braid her hair, giving her barrettes and curiously shaped pebbles and assorted trinkets they thought would win her favor. She'd held court at the top of the slide, already perfecting that lifted-nose posture that signified her unquestionable superiority.

Nothing had changed in the intervening years. Tonya had been pulled out of the public school system and sent to a private academy, breezing through town in her silver drop-top Mercedes the day she turned sixteen, berating poor coffee shop girls and grocery baggers for the hell of it.

Sam opened her eyes and took a big breath, because it was too painful to think about the girl who got everything taking something that she herself had always wanted.

"This has to stop," she murmured, and Remy babbled in response.

"Yeah, I know, buddy," she said. "Your uncle's a damn stupid dream for a girl to have, isn't he?"

So she was done with him, she decided then and there in Maggie Teague's chair. It was time she moved on.

For good.

Twenty-Eight

One week, two trips to Macy's, and four delivery trucks later, the Walshes had some furniture, a stocked fridge, and something like a daily routine.

Emmie approached her unexpected marriage as if she were getting to know a new horse that was in for training. Observing, taking note, reacting here and pushing there, working with and around him so that there was a flow to their interactions. She didn't want to fight, fuss, or struggle, and instead absorbed every little detail about him, so that she could know him, and live with him. And maybe...

Too early for that yet.

He'd been a bachelor so long that he wasn't hesitant in the kitchen. If he was up first, he put the coffee on. He was fine with scraping together eggs, or something frozen, or sandwiches. But he was happy to stand back and let her have a go at roasted chicken and spaghetti with real meatballs.

He spent a lot of time on his computer and phone, and she had learned that unlike his brothers, who were mechanics and laborers by day trade, he worked solely for the club, moving money around, consulting, acquiring, and selling. She learned that his shoulders got tense, and that he groaned in delight when she worked the knots out of them with her fingers.

And the sex. God, the sex was incredible. In bed, in the shower, in the tub, on the new Oriental look-a-like rug.

It was Sunday and she was done at the barn for the day, all her lessons taught and her Apollo spoiled with a good curry and a mash. Fred had offered to do the evening feeding – his in-laws were driving him up the wall and he was glad for the chance to stay at work – and so she was relieved of the business end of Briar Hall until the next morning.

In days past, that would have been less of a gift and more of a burden. Time off had always been spent watching old test videos to see where she could improve her score, or cleaning her loft, or going generally stir-crazy because she was nothing without her work.

But today she was in the cozy suede chair at the living room's picture window with a cup of tea and a romance novel. Wondering when Walsh would get home. Wondering what they'd have for dinner. Idly enjoying the words on the page and the hopping of birds in the grass outside.

It was like she was a married person or something.

The sound of the doorbell startled her. Badly. The thing was loud, and she guessed that was because Davis had been old and hard of hearing, but *damn*.

There was a woman waiting on the front step, a napping baby in a car seat/carrier clutched in one hand, a sack full of groceries in the other. She was brunette, vaguely familiar, and had the biggest, greenest eyes Emmie had ever seen.

She was someone from the photograph, Emmie realized. This was –

"Hi!" she greeted. "I'm Holly. And this is Lucy." She hefted the carrier. "And I'm hoping Michael remembered to give you my gift, or you're going to think I'm a crazy person."

"Holly, right. Michael's wife." Emmie smiled, but the bag of groceries had her worried. "It's nice to meet you."

They stared at one another a moment.

"I brought stuff to make dessert," Holly said, and the grocery bag rustled. "Brownie trifle. It's a little rich, but Michael likes it…" She trailed off as Emmie continued to stare at her. "Walsh told you we were coming, didn't he?"

"We?"

A flash of brilliant blonde hair out on the sidewalk caught her eye. A woman she didn't know walked alongside Ava, both of them loaded down with more bags, and baby Remy.

Behind them were two more women.

"Um…" Emmie said.

The blonde reached the top of the porch steps and flashed Emmie a cool smile. "Hi, darlin'. Which way's the kitchen?"

Realizing it was let them in or get run over, Emmie stepped aside. "Straight back through the living room," she said numbly.

The woman waved a hand in acknowledgement and breezed right on in, smelling faintly of gardenias, managing to look imperial in a gauzy top, jeans, and ballet flats.

"Maggie," Holly explained as she slipped past. "Ghost's wife."

Which made her the *president's* wife.

"Got it," Emmie whispered back.

"You don't mind if we barge right in, do you?" Ava asked, rolling her eyes as she went past.

"Um...no..."

"Mina," the next one said with a smile.

"And Nell. Can't miss me 'cause I'm the old bat," the one with the sun-lined face and the smoker's voice said with a rough laugh.

"Don't say that about yourself," Mina said.

"Well, if the flu shits, ya know."

Emmie checked that there was no one else coming up the walk, then shut the door and hastily followed them into the kitchen. They seemed to be making themselves right at home.

Maggie unloaded a heavy grill pan from her canvas tote and then began pulling out packages of steaks. The way she took the prime position in front of the six-burner stove, the way everyone seemed to be a satellite around her, her authority was a silent, unquestioned thing. "You've got the tongs?" she asked Mina.

"Right here."

"I'll get started on the potatoes," Nell said, pulling Yukon golds from her bag.

"You know, I could make more than just salad," Ava said. "I can cook now. Sort of."

"But you make such pretty salad," Maggie told her.

"After I get this put together" – Holly was slicing up a pan of brownies – "I can help anyone else."

247

The baby she'd brought in fussed in her carrier, like that wasn't part of her plan. Lucy – the baby's name was Lucy, Holly had said.

Emmie stepped up to the vast island and cleared her throat. All eyes turned toward her, and she wanted to squirm beneath them. Down in the barn, she was all boss, mistress of her domain. Here in the house, not so much.

"Not that it isn't lovely to meet you all," she began.

Maggie smirked. "But what the hell are we doing in your kitchen?"

"I would have left out the 'hell.'"

The smirk turned into a true smile. "We're having a club dinner. Welcome aboard, sweetheart, this is your crash course."

~*~

Walsh remembered to warn Emmie about dinner about a half hour too late. And then he didn't call because he was afraid he'd get his ass chewed. Part of him loved the idea of his woman waiting at home pissed off. And part of him worried that she didn't care enough about him to even bother with reaming him out.

So he was a jumble of uncharacteristic emotions when he pulled up to the big stone Briar Hall house with his brothers.

Mercy was beside him as they took off their helmets. "You think she's handling it alright?" he asked with a half-grin and a lifted eyebrow.

"I expect so," Walsh said vaguely. "Got a level head."

"You didn't tell her ahead of time though, did you?"

When he didn't answer, Mercy laughed. "So wise, and yet so dumb."

"Piss off," Walsh said in a mild voice. "I'll worry about mine and you worry about yours."

"Yeah, but mine grew up in the life," Mercy reminded, becoming serious. "Yours is gonna take more convincing."

Walsh frowned to himself and swung off his bike. So far, he'd felt he'd done a pretty good job with the convincing. The furniture shopping, the spectacular sex. But nothing had been happening. It had just been them, the house, getting to know one another.

And tonight was all about the club flexing its social muscles. *Look here, little girl, you're a part of something bigger than yourself. You gotta learn to fit in.*

And she hadn't asked for any of it.

Everyone dropped back as they approached the door, even Ghost.

"Master first," the president said, and all the guys chuckled.

Walsh rolled his eyes. "Master of what exactly? Getting bitched at?"

The front door opened as he was reaching for the knob, and Emmie looked like she always did…except for the eyes. Those were too big, and full of that dissociated look soldiers got during wartimes.

"Hi, love," he said carefully, hyper aware of his club brothers crowding on the porch behind him, watching their interaction.

Emmie's gaze skipped across all of them before coming back to his face. "Hi." Her tone was guarded. "We're hosting the big dinner thing, huh?"

He winced in apology. "Yeah."

She stepped back and opened the door wide. "Okay, boys, beer's being iced down on the back porch. Dinner will be ready in just a bit."

Walsh lingered, watching all the Dogs greet her with nods, hellos, and a couple handshakes. When they'd moved deeper into the house like a herd of wildebeest, he reached for her, laid a hand on her waist.

She jumped a little. Her expression was still detached and frazzled when she turned to him. "You didn't tell me in advance."

"I'm sorry."

She exhaled deeply. "Nothing to do about it now, I don't guess."

He flashed her a wide, cheesy grin. "Make it up to you later?"

She snorted. "With interest."

~*~

There were half a dozen collapsible tables in the back of Ava's truck, and they set them up end-to-end to form a crude dining table that was shamed by the room around it. But since a dining table hadn't been at the top of their shopping list, it made do. Dinner was a hit: the food was good, the alcohol flowed freely, and there was too much talking over one another for Emmie to have to worry about socializing.

She studied instead, learning their faces, their speech patterns. Mercy was the big loud storyteller, and the way he outwardly adored Ava was staggering. When Ghost spoke, everyone listened. RJ was a douche, and everyone thought so. Tango and Carter were gorgeous blonde sweethearts; Aidan the overconfident ladykiller. Michael was aggressively quiet, if such a thing were possible, but his face softened when he spoke to his wife or looked at his daughter.

Walsh had called them a family, all of them together, and as she watched them laugh, talk with food in their mouths, pass around the green beans and potatoes, she could think of no better way to describe them. A big, boisterous family, with obvious love for one another.

She'd never been a part of anything like it.

After dinner, the men migrated to the back porch with fresh beers, and Emmie wound up in the kitchen with the women. Ava was told to go sit down and get off her pregnant feet. Holly excused herself to nurse Lucy, and Nell and Mina set about disassembling the tables in the dining room and recruiting some of the younger members to carry them out to the truck.

With a crawling sensation of dread, Emmie found herself rinsing dishes and passing them to Maggie to be loaded into the dishwasher. They were alone.

The biker first lady took a breath that sounded like the start of something. Emmie lifted her emotional walls and braced herself.

"It's a lot to take in, isn't it?"

Growing up on a farm, she'd had no experience with being anything besides brutally honest. "It is," she admitted. "Y'all make for a big group."

Maggie snorted. "Be glad nobody spilled anything tonight."

"I will."

There was a pause filled by the rushing of water on plates.

"I wasn't talking about dinner, though," Maggie said. "That's the easy part."

Emmie sighed. "I figured."

"Has Walsh filled you in yet?"

"I got the 'club comes first' speech, if that's what you mean."

"Good."

"You're okay with it then? Knowing your husband's a part of something so...archaic?"

"Honey." Maggie snorted. "It's not archaic. It's tradition. Kids nowadays can think what they want, but there's something to be said for tradition."

The part of her that watched the evening news wanted to argue. The part of her that employed classic German training techniques in the arena agreed wholeheartedly.

"I get that," she said, though there was a nervous fluttering in her chest.

"Do you?"

"You obviously aren't all that familiar with dressage training."

"Decidedly not."

The last dish was done and Emmie turned off the tap, staring straight ahead, trying to push down her sudden surge of temper.

Maggie finished with the dishwasher and clicked the door into place.

There was no way to stall. "I know what you're doing," Emmie said, turning to face the woman.

Maggie's mouth lifted at the corners, but her face was otherwise blank, controlled. This was a woman with the sort of aura Amy Richards had always craved. That total ownership of her identity and her superiority. "And what's that?"

"Establishing the hierarchy. You're the boss mare, and I'm the new member of the herd. You're thinking that Walsh is blinded by the sex, because he's a man after all, and you want me to know, female to female, that there are rules. This is the 'don't fuck with me' spiel, right?"

Maggie stared at her, unreadable.

"I don't scare easy," Emmie said, feeling like she'd stepped in it royally, and not caring.

Maggie was still a moment longer, and then twitched a smile that said *be careful, girlie,* but wasn't without a bit of approval and humor. "Thank God for that."

~*~

"The brass have gotten nowhere," Ghost said, looking to Ratchet for confirmation.

The secretary shook his head. "The prints they pulled were all from his kids, and from Emmie." His eyes flicked over to Walsh for a second. "No syringe, no needle, no scrap of evidence from anyone who wasn't normally in here."

"Which means one of his kids killed him."

"They all have alibis."

"Or the girl did it." Ghost shot a half-smile to Walsh before he could protest. "Not that I think that. What about the other two who work here, though?"

"No," Walsh said. "They were devastated. And their prints weren't on the doorknob."

"Right," Ratchet said.

"Had to be the grandson," Walsh said, grinding his molars in frustration. "He's the one who left us a spray paint present a couple weeks ago."

252

"But nothing since?" Ghost asked.

"No."

They were all on the back porch, bellies full; the sky was netted with stars and the smell of cigarette smoke blended with pine sap. But unease tickled at the back of Walsh's neck. It was going too well. He and Emmie, the farm, the loans working out, the cattle property still a secret. In his experience, things didn't stay serene for long. Especially not when it came to his personal life.

"Obviously," Briscoe said with an officious throat-clearing, "we walked into an episode of *Dallas* with this fucked up family. But they're gone. They didn't get what they wanted. What's the sense in worrying about 'em now? They ain't gonna shoot any of us up with H."

Nods of agreement.

"You talked to Sly Hammond?" Ghost asked Walsh.

"Yeah. He and Eddie had to pick up a car for a client in West Virginia. They gotta pass through, so they're gonna stop by tomorrow afternoon."

"Good. Get the scoop on *our new friend* Agent Grey. They know him better than we do."

Before Walsh could answer, Hound said, "I wanna know what the hell happened to Fisher."

Many murmured agreements.

"What'd your lab guy say?" Mercy asked Ratchet.

"No prints or skin cells, which meant the guy wore gloves. And the DNA on the doorknob was, in his words, 'a big fucking mess.' Which leaves ballistics. Striations match a nine mil used in a convenience store holdup from two years ago in Detroit."

Ghost exhaled loudly, words swirling with smoke. "Which means jack shit."

"The gun was stolen or sold before it got here, unregistered. So we've got basically nothing."

Aidan started to flick his butt over the railing, caught Walsh's eye, and thought better of it, dropping it into his beer bottle. "What I don't get," he said, "is why Fisher, of all people. I know that kinda shit happens. But Fish? Could you get more harmless and pathetic?"

"He's never late with deliveries or payments," Tango said. He snorted. "He was always 'Dealer of the Year.'"

"It was about us," Ghost said. "A message."

"Message of what?" Aidan asked, irritated.

Ghost looked to Tango. "What about Shaman. Is he the type to do shit like that for fun?"

Tango glanced down at his toes and shrugged, clearly uncomfortable being asked about…whoever the hell Shaman was to him. "Nah. I really don't think so."

Ghost sighed deeply, took one last drag off his smoke, and ground it out on the sole of his boot. "We'll deal with it when it's time to deal with it," he said with an air of finality. He glanced at Michael. "Holly made dessert?"

"Yeah."

Walsh knew that was all the business they'd be conducting for the day and he let his thoughts drift. And then himself, sliding back into the house with the others, branching off from the living room-bound group and going in search of his old lady.

She was on the front porch, hands wrapped tight around the rail, head tipped back, breathing deeply toward the stars.

He closed the door quietly behind him and took careful steps toward her. She had to have noticed him, but he didn't want to break the spell. She looked lovely with the moon pouring over her face and unbound hair.

She looked sad, too.

When he reached her, he traced a single finger down the ridge of her spine and was rewarded with a shiver. He spread his hand and pressed it to the small of her back, stepped into her, until her shoulder was against his chest. "Too crowded, hmm?" he asked against her ear, and she shivered again and leaned into him.

"I think – no, I know – Maggie's trying to play Big Bad Queen Bee with me. That's the annoying part. Everything else is just your general overwhelming too-many-people type stuff." She turned her head to give him a thin smile. "You really weren't kidding about the family part."

He grinned. "Nope."

She went utterly soft, and molded herself against him, face pressed against his chest, arms going lightly around his waist. "I haven't ever had that," she said, like she couldn't believe it. "A real family."

"I know, love." His hand found the back of her head, held her to him. "I know."

Twenty-Nine

With a home base in Georgia, Ray Russell ran a security operation that complemented the MC, aided them at times, but was on the other side of the outlaw spectrum. Outlaw Light, with no artificial sweeteners. His two best guys, Sly and Eddie, were classic car mechanics by day, professional badasses by night, and Sly in particular was one of Walsh's favorite non-club people.

They arrived at Briar Hall around lunchtime, when Walsh had the house to himself. He was on the front porch with his laptop, feeding Dolly scraps from his sandwich when a gorgeous burgundy Barracuda and a black Dodge Ram pulled up.

Sly was driving the client's car, and tossed Walsh a fast wave as he climbed out and hooked his shades in the neck of his plain white t-shirt.

"I'm driving that the rest of the way back," Eddie said as he got out of the truck. "Nobody said you were in charge."

Sly pulled up short and glanced at his friend with a tiny amused smile. "I did."

"Fuck you."

"When you say twelve-thirty, you mean twelve-thirty," Walsh called in greeting.

"Old habit," both men said together, and joined him on the porch.

Walsh stood and handshakes were passed around. He went inside to fetch them beers.

Sly waited until they were all settled to cast an appraising eye up the front of the house. "So."

"Explain the mansion," Eddie said, grinning. "Did you marry an heiress? Is it like in those books chicks like?"

Walsh snorted. "I married a broke-ass barn manager with no mother and an alcoholic shit for a father."

Eddie's grin widened. "Is she hot?"

"Very."

"That's all that counts."

"Explain the house, though," Sly said. "I thought we were here on fed consult. Didn't know we'd be staying at the Four Seasons."

"Don't expect a mint on your pillow, mate."

Walsh gave them the abridged version of things, brief and comprehensive.

When he was done, Eddie whistled. "Talk about your unforeseen complications." He leaned over and tapped Sly in the arm with his knuckles. "You know all about that, dontcha, man?"

Sly exhaled sharply through his nostrils, like a horse. "She handling it okay? That's a lot of change in a short amount of time," he said seriously.

Walsh thought about that morning, about waking up beside her and throwing an arm across her waist, her snuggling back against him. "Yeah," he said. "She's smart. She's adjusting."

~*~

"Anybody need a salt block, do you know?" Emmie asked, surveying the row of white and brown mineral licks lined up on the floor beneath the halter display. Given the chaotic turn of her life, she didn't know when she'd be back in the feed store with time to shop at her leisure. Walsh said friends would be in for dinner, and there was already an anxious grinding in her gut at the prospect. She wasn't a social person, and wasn't sure she wanted to become one.

But the store was working its magic on her, like always. Something about the tang of leather, the pungent herbaceous scent of sweet feed, the strike of boots on an old stained concrete floor. It was like a drug to a horse girl, the racks and racks of saddles, the stacks of fluffy saddle pads, the shelves of spurs, color-coded braiding bands and brushes with stiff neon bristles.

Lawson's had been her favorite tack and feed shop since she was nothing but a little mouse following along behind Amy. It was delightfully shabby, unpretentious, and sold everything under the sun, all of it crammed into an old converted warehouse space, and smelled charmingly of the coffee and cookies the owner's wife provided fresh daily.

A trip to personally pick up feed with Becca was just the way to unwind after an evening of hosting too many bikers to count.

"Champ does," Becca said as she sorted through the nylon halters, searching for something hot pink no doubt. "And maybe Tally. He licks that stuff like he's a salt junkie or something."

The mention of a junkie put to mind drug dealers, and criminals, and nefarious deeds, and the dead man's face Emmie had seen in the pasture next door.

She shook her head to clear the memory. "Right." She bent down to heft the blocks up into their cart. "I'll have him deliver some of the big ones for the pasture when he brings the pallet of shavings."

"Yeah," Becca said distractedly, "hey, what's it like being married to a biker?" Then, in a rush, "Ooh, they have a pink *and* purple one. I have to have that."

Emmie dusted mineral grit off her palms and glanced over at her student, noting the bright tinge of Becca's ears as she tried to untangle the halter from its hook.

She grinned. "Seeing as how I don't have any experience with being married to more than one, I don't know. But being married to Walsh is…surprisingly okay. It's kind of…nice," she finished lamely, no idea how to describe it properly.

"Is he good in the sack?"

"Do you really want to know?"

Becca's entire face went red. "Um…no?"

Emmie laughed. "He knows what he's doing. Let's leave it at that."

Becca sighed dramatically. "I wish Todd knew what he was doing," she said of her boyfriend.

Emmie was about to respond when –

"Excuse me. Emmaline Johansen?" a deep voice asked behind her and she whirled around.

A man stood on the other side of her cart, dressed in a t-shirt, jeans, and a windbreaker that was much too hot for the weather outside. Certain things about him – the buzzed hair, the way he held himself, the breadth of his shoulders – signified a young man around her age, fit and confident. But his skin was pale, his face puffy and lined. Eyes shiny, like maybe he had a fever. He wore gloves, a thin pale leather, which she found strange, but she wasn't up to speed on every cop habit.

He pulled out his wallet, and then flashed her a badge. "Detective Hanson with Knoxville PD. Do you mind if I ask you a few questions?"

That explained the puffiness, then. Cops were stressed, worn down, stuck at desks. Fatigue could kill a man.

"It's Emmie," she said. "Emmie Walsh." She nodded. "Sure. Becca, will you take this up to the front? Have them put it on the farm tab."

Becca gave the detective a long look, then said, "Sure thing," and wheeled the buggy away. She glanced over her shoulder twice before she was finally around the corner.

Emmie focused on the cop. "This is about Davis? Mr. Richards, I mean," she added, remembering she'd only ever called him by his first name in her head.

"I'm afraid so," Detective Hanson said gravely. He gestured to a stack of feed bags that looked sturdy enough and she sat.

He stayed on his feet, right in front of her, closer than she would have liked him to be. "Miss…Walsh, you said?"

He was slipping his badge back into his pocket and fumbled it, dropping it between her feet.

She picked it up and handed it to him. "Yes. Recently married."

A concerned frown etched lines in his face. "He's a member of the Lean Dogs, isn't he? If I remember from your vandalism report."

She nodded. "He is."

"Does that worry you?"

259

"Why should it?" she returned. Tell her a few weeks ago that she'd be evasive and worried about her outlaw husband, and she would have laughed someone out of the room. But now, she was seeing it all from a different angle. The one from which Walsh was good to her, and she wanted to hold onto that goodness.

At the cost of being cooperative with the police.

He gave her a patronizing smirk. "Your husband is a member of one of the largest international criminal organizations, and that's not something you worry about?"

She shrugged. "Walsh is a businessman. He's hardly threatening. Detective," she said, frowning, "I thought this was about Davis."

"It is." His smirk became a tight smile, less cocky. He didn't like the way she was responding to him. "Very much so. You see, the way I look at it, *Mrs. Walsh*" – he turned her new name into a mockery – "what we have is a local legend in Mr. Richards. A man with lots of money, lots of respect, lots of influence in Knoxville. He's well-liked, frequently donates to charities, and is seen as a pillar of the community."

"Yes." She lifted her brows as if to say *so?*

"A well-liked man without enemies, without any grudges, killed in his own home. Nothing stolen, no robbery, no break-in. Who kills a man like that?"

He was giving her the stink eye, and she gave it right back. "I think you ought to talk to Amy Richards about that. She's the only one I know of who stood to gain anything by his death."

Look at her, condemning her former mentor and defending her one-percenter husband. My how times changed.

Detective Hanson snorted. "His grief-stricken, doting daughter, the one he built a farm for? Yeah, that makes about zero sense," he sneered. "What *does* make sense is an outlaw walked into the picture, and a couple weeks later, the guy owns the place, and Richards is dead. An outlaw who's part of a club notorious for dealing drugs, I might add."

"Check with the bank if you want, but the paperwork was already finalized. Walsh owned the farm before Davis was killed."

He stepped in closer, crowding her. "So you're telling me you truly believe that the man you worked for *for years* winds up dead of a heroin overdose, and his daughter did it? Not the crack-dealing white trash thug you're living with."

Emmie surged to her feet, forcing him to take a step back. "Okay, take me down to the station if you want, but I'm not going to sit here and listen to you insult my husband."

She made a move to step around him, and he caught her with one meaty hand on her shoulder. His face grew serious, less mocking. "Did he tell you why he left London? Why he really left?"

The menace in his eyes sent her pulse tripping, panic unfurling deep in her gut. "He hated the big city," she said, but couldn't hear any conviction in her voice. "He came here for a job and liked it so much he stayed."

Hanson snorted, but it wasn't mean. Almost like he was sorry for her. With his free hand, he reached into his jacket pocket and withdrew a photograph, turned it toward her. It was a mug shot, Walsh, holding the little plaque with his name on it, giving the camera the dead eye. His face was smooth and maybe ten years younger.

A cold chill moved down her back.

"It was a turf war," Hanson said quietly. "There's a bar in London the Dogs own, and some other club tried to come in. A fight broke out, and three civilians were killed in the mayhem. When the police arrived, your husband had blood all over his hands, literally. No witnesses came forward, the case stalled out, and he jumped ship to America before any real charges could be pressed."

Emmie swallowed with difficulty.

"The civilians? Two of them were women."

Her eyes lifted to his face.

"I'd be very careful about where I put my loyalty, Ms. Johansen." She didn't correct his use of her maiden name. "The Lean Dogs sell illegal weapons, drugs, and contract kills.

Wherever they go, they leave bodies in their wake, and they don't care if outsiders get cut down in their quest for power. Why do you think they wanted Briar Hall? Did he give you the old story about how he was a jockey? How he wanted to be around horses? It's a lie. Everything any of them ever say is a lie. They destroy lives, and they take what they want. It's what they do."

He tucked his chin, eyes softening. "I'd hate to see you get hurt in all this. Or worse."

Then he withdrew his hand and the photo and stepped away from her.

Emmie had to grab hold of a shelf to keep steady on her feet.

~*~

She lingered at the barn longer than she needed to, well after Fred and Becca left. She clipped Apollo into a wash rack and gave him a thorough bath, counting on the lathering of sleek horse hide to serve as its usual balm. But Detective Hanson's words were a poison in her bloodstream, working on her though she tried to ignore the effects.

Her horse swung his head around to look at her, sensing her energy. "What am I gonna do?" she asked quietly, running her fingers through his short mane. "When will it stop?"

When she could put it off no longer, she hiked up the hill to the house and found two foreign vehicles. A classic car of some sort she didn't care about, and a black Dodge truck, parked in front of the garage.

She'd forgotten all about Walsh's friends, and glanced down at herself. Tank top spotted with water, gummy shampoo residue on her arms. Her boots were filthy and she had spatters of mud or something all over her shins. She could feel the hair sticking to the perspiration at the back of her neck and on her forehead, the tendrils come loose from her ponytail.

What a picture she must make.

Whatever.

They were in the living room and Walsh stood and walked over to greet her. As he reached her, it was devastating to realize how strongly he affected her physically, and to know how wrong it was for her to feel that way.

Hand on her hip, he leaned in for a quick kiss that tasted like cigarettes.

"Hi." His smile was small and said he was pleased to see her.

Her stomach knotted. "Hi."

His arm slid around her waist as he turned to the men holding up either end of their new sofa. "Em, this is Eddie" – scary handsome and tossing her a lazy, bad boy grin – "and Sly" – God, the blue eyes and the blonde hair on a face that could turn people to stone, a little like Walsh in that regard – "guys, this is Emmie."

"Hi." She gave them a scant smile and ducked out of Walsh's hold. "I really ought to go clean up. I stink like a wet dog." She didn't check to see if they thought she was rude, just went, hurrying around the edge of the room, down the hall to the back staircase.

Her heart was in her throat by the time she shut the door of the master bedroom and leaned back against it. Maybe she was having another panic attack, like at the courthouse. Or maybe, she thought, as she surveyed the very lived-in room, she was just a willing accomplice.

"Everything any of them ever say is a lie. They destroy lives, and they take what they want."

Was this a lie? His jeans slung over the bedpost and her flip-flops on the floor in front of the dresser. His razor and her makeup in the bathroom drawers.

God, they were *living* together. Was that the lie…or was that what he wanted?

A hot shower eased some of the tension in her muscles. And afterward, as she dried her hair, she caught sight of the little pile of stuff Walsh had dumped out of his pockets last night: a paperclip, a handful of change, part of a fast food straw wrapper, lint, and a Werther's caramel.

She smiled faintly. Whatever else he was, he was a man too. A human, with pocket change, who ate McDonald's and liked old lady hard candy. Could he really be the stuff of nightmares?

Dressed in clean shorts and a top, smelling worlds better, she headed down the stairs with the resolution to act more normal. She'd gotten spooked, it happened. It was undoubtedly going to happen again.

She paused on the first landing when she heard voices below. There were more than just three of them in the living room now. A fourth voice, one sharp with authority, even when he laughed, one she'd heard before. Ghost.

"Zel clocked him so hard, I'd be surprised if he didn't have brain damage," Sly or Eddie said. There were a few low chuckles. "That woman could find a way to kill you with a bottle cap. Give her a frying pan, and you're talking frontal lobe damage."

"But they cleared him to go back to work," Ghost said.

"Oh yeah, but it was a big demotion. Throw in what you guys did to the poor bastard" – more chuckling – "and he's one bad hair day away from being completely off the reservation."

"So this is personal, then," Walsh said. "Vendetta type shit."

"That'd be my guess. Your guy said he wasn't on assignment, right?"

"Not my guy," Ghost said, "but yeah, if Grey's after us, it's because he's gone rogue."

Low murmurs she couldn't hear at that point. She clutched at the bannister, heart pounding. She was eavesdropping, but couldn't make herself stop.

"Ego's his thing," Sly/Eddie said. "Without it, he's got nothing."

"And becomes very dangerous, apparently," Ghost said.

Who in the hell were they talking about? Whoever it was, she most certainly wasn't supposed to hear it.

Emmie sat down hard on a step and waited, listening to Ghost thank the two newcomers and then leave.

"There's more beer in the fridge," she heard Walsh say, and the voices seemed to move that way, growing more distant.

She strangled a surprised yelp when Walsh appeared at the bottom of the stairs, looking up at her with a mild expression. "Had your shower?"

He knew she'd been listening. He had to. But he was the picture of serenity.

"Yeah." She stood and brushed her shorts down to hide the shaking of her hands. "I was just…" *Totally spying on you.*

"I told the boys you'd had a long day, so we ordered pizza. It's on the way."

"Oh. That's good." She'd anticipated he would ask her to cook for his guests. Not that she really minded. Not that it would be unfeminist to do so.

But she'd been searching for some sign that he was this domineering jackoff the detective had described to her, and he just wasn't. Whatever else the other club members were, Walsh couldn't be a killer.

Could he?

She had reached a dangerous point of self-reflection, one in which she couldn't have been reasonable if she wanted to be. She wanted a drink. Hated that she had her father's urge to drown her worries. She didn't want to be worried about all this.

But she was.

~*~

Sly and Eddie might as well have been furniture for all the attention she paid them during dinner. After, she left her dish in the sink and headed for the hallway.

Walsh started toward her, and she kept going. "I'm going to take a walk," she said, and slipped out the front door before he could say anything. She struck off at a fast clip, short legs working
double time to get her down the steps, around the bend in the walk and headed for the barn.

The air was still hot and it felt good filling her lungs, chasing away some of that inner chill she'd carried since Lawson's. Walsh had done nothing to her – well, save that whole tackling incident – and had given her no reason to be afraid of him personally. Then again, he'd turned her entire world on its end. Shouldn't that spook a girl?

Shadows lay in long fingers across the pavement, collecting in tide pools between the trunks of trees, the breeze like the low roar of ocean surf.

Emmie walked faster. What sort of delusion had she been operating under? How could she have thought sex, a little cuddling, and what was probably pretend tenderness would somehow serve as worthwhile counterbalance to the fact that she was married to a damn criminal?

She was breathing in ragged gasps when she reached the doors of the barn, and she paused to collect herself.

It didn't work. Especially not when Walsh materialized beside her, slightly winded from having followed her at her powerwalking pace.

"Just a walk, huh?" He propped his hands on his hips and looked down his nose at her. "Not, let's say, a nice running away?"

"If I was going to run away, I wouldn't do it on foot." She patted her pockets, kicking herself for not going for a drive instead. She didn't even have her truck keys.

Then again, she hadn't truly meant to bolt. She was only thinking that now, as she saw the serious light in his blue eyes and was struck anew by the fact that she was married to this man. Who she didn't know, and who had wed her on the pretense of keeping her from a shallow unmarked grave.

"Em," he said. "What's got into you?"

When his hand reached for her she sidestepped it, going into the shadowy interior of the barn. The urge to confide in him was overwhelming, and that frightened her. How quickly she'd become dependent upon him, leaning into his support as easy as breathing.

"Nothing, I just want to be alone is all." She put her back to him and walked down the aisle, wanting some distance.

He followed her. "Emmie."

She got halfway down, right in front of Apollo's stall, and spun to face him. He was covered in shadow, his eyes shimmering like a wolf's, the dark making him seem taller, more threatening than he'd ever looked. She could believe it, looking at him right now. Could he have killed Davis, forged the paperwork, worked some outlaw magic, and then pretended to care about her? Absolutely. It happened all the time.

"Did you kill Davis?" she asked, proud that her voice was firm though she was shaking on the inside.

"What?" The incredulity in his voice almost sounded real. "Didn't we already have this conversation? Love, what in the bloody hell—"

"Answer the question, Kingston. I'm your wife, right? So no one can force me to testify against you. So tell me, for real this time. Did you kill my boss?"

He stepped toward her, boots scraping across stray bits of hay that had escaped the night's sweeping. "I don't know what's got into you," he said calmly, "but I already told you, I didn't kill the poor bugger. He sold the place to me. Why would I pop him off?"

She swallowed hard; her pulse thundered in her ears. "Maybe he was trying to renege."

"Or maybe his junkie fucking grandson did it." A thread of steel creeping into his tone, layering in aggression. "You know me now. You know I wouldn't have done that."

"I know you?"

"I told you everything."

"Or so you say."

He dragged in a deep breath. "You're right. There was one thing I didn't tell you."

She knew it.

She bolted.

Tried to, anyway. Walsh caught her by the back of her shirt and hauled her around, pushed her back against the metal bars of a stall and pinned her there with his body, his hands locked on her forearms.

"Let me go!" she gasped. "You said you would. You said you wouldn't make me stay." It was almost a sob, burning in the back of her throat. "Let me go."

His breath was warm across her face. She could see nothing but the glint of his eyes, could only feel the shape of him pressed against her. "Don't you want to hear it, though? The big awful secret I didn't tell you before."

She couldn't swallow down her fear so she could tell him that yes, she did want to know, underneath the terror that he might be about to throttle her.

His head dipped low, his breath fanning across her throat. His lips touched her jaw, just beneath her ear. "I got a girl pregnant once," he whispered, and she stopped breathing. "Her name was Rita, and she was the daughter of someone important, and I was a banned jockey."

Her hands curled into the front of his shirt, and she tried to push him away…

"I bought a little hat, a little white lace thing, and I thought if it was a boy, I might name it for my grandfather."

She froze.

"And Rita couldn't stand the idea of being attached to me like that. So she had the doctor take it out of her. Like it was a tumor. My child."

Her heart stuttered and then started up a slow, throbbing rhythm.

"That's what I didn't tell you, pet. That women think I'm a disease." His chuckle was dry and bitter. "Guess you're no different, then."

She took a deep breath, and then another. She didn't want to ache for him, but she did. It could be a lie, but the harshness in his voice told her it wasn't.

She wet her lips. "A detective came up to me at the feed store today," she whispered, and felt his hands tighten on her arms. "It was…it was like he was trying to scare me."

"About us." His voice hardened.

"I didn't tell him anything."

He sighed and let go of her. Stepped back. Shoved both hands into his hair and scrubbed hard. "Bugger all."

"I don't want to be frightened," she added, "but I am. I don't know what to do about that. I never expected...any of this." It was a relief to be honest, but it filled her eyes with tears.

Her phone rang, and she was almost glad for the chance to answer it, and break up this moment.

"Hello?"

"It's Joan," the bar owner's wife greeted. "And yep, you guessed it. Daddy's in the gutter again."

Emmie groaned and slid the phone back in her pocket without acknowledgement.

"Your father?" Walsh asked.

She pushed her hair back, pressed hard at her scalp with her fingertips, like she could contain the headache that was coming on. "Yeah."

He made a frustrated sound, and then sighed deeply. "I'll go with you."

"You don't have to—"

"Well I'm not very well going to let you drag a man out of a bar by yourself, am I? Even if you do think I'm worthless."

"I never said—"

"Just get yourself together and let's go. I don't want to talk about it anymore."

~*~

Patrons shifted in and out of Bell Bar in waves. Inside, the crowd was overwhelming the AC's ability to keep things cool, and Emmie felt sweat break out across her chest the moment they pushed inside.

"Jesus," Walsh muttered.

"It's orientation week for the college," she told him, having to shout to be heard. "They overrun all the bars."

It took a full minute to work their way up to the bar, getting elbowed and trampled-on the whole way. Karl sat perched on his favorite stool, staring down into his empty tumbler, neck limp as overcooked pasta.

"Dad." Emmie wedged herself between his stool and the next one over, laid her hand on his shoulder. "Dad, come on, let's get you out of here."

He turned a sightless glance on her, eyes glazed over. "Esther's gone," he said miserably, and her stomach clenched at the sound of her mother's name.

"You mean Maryann. Maryann left again, didn't she?"

"Esther," he repeated. "My beautiful, sweet Esther."

Emmie sighed. "Yeah, Dad, she's gone. Very gone. But what about Maryann?"

"I hate that bitch," he said with a scowl, and raised his glass to his lips though it was empty.

"Dad–" A touch on her arm brought her head around. There was Walsh.

And there were two uniformed police officers.

"Emmaline Johansen," one of them said in a booming voice that transcended the bar noise. "We need you to come down to the station with us for questioning."

"What?"

Walsh put himself between her and the officers. "She's not going anywhere. Questioning about what?"

Emmie grabbed onto the back of his cut, willing him to stay in front of her. Not that it looked like he'd be willing to budge.

"Theft of police property, for one," the second cop said. "Come with us, ma'am, or we'll be forced to place you under arrest."

"Arrest?" Walsh asked, an obvious, emotional outrage in his voice she'd never heard before. "What police property? She didn't steal shit."

The noise level in the bar dropped suddenly as people started to take notice of what was happening. The prospect of a police brawl was too tempting, and they cut off conversations, turning to watch the exchange. Emmie saw a few phones aimed their way.

Beneath her hands, the muscles in Walsh's back locked up tight. Each breath pushed at his ribs, drove the bones hard against her knuckles. He exuded such calm all the time, but he was clearly ready to flip the switch on her behalf.

She took a deep breath. "I'll go."

He half-twisted toward her. "What? No you won't. They've got nothing against you."

"Actually, we do," the first officer said. "Let's go, Miss Johansen, and they'll explain everything down at the station."

Fear threatened to choke her, but she nodded, and stepped around Walsh. "Look after my dad, please," she told him.

He shook his head. "I'm—"

"Walsh, please. I'll be alright."

His eyes tracked across her face, wide with helpless panic. It was real fear she saw in their depths. Fear for her, worry, anger on her behalf.

Then his jaw hardened and he looked at the two cops. "I'm calling her a lawyer."

"You do that," Cop Two said. "And we'll see what she has to say for herself."

Thirty

Bugger this. Bugger *all* of this. Buggering cops, buggering drunken fool, buggering woman who couldn't stop worrying.

Walsh had managed to wrestle Johansen out onto the sidewalk, where the man had then puked up his guts and sent a group of college age girls running in all directions with shrieks and curses. The gin-soaked wanker now lay face-down on the concrete.

Time for reinforcements. Both for physical, and moral support, at this point.

Mercy answered on the third ring. "My British brother," he greeted, and Walsh heard Remy babbling away in the background.

Guilt needled him. It was after dark, Merc was enjoying his family time at home.

"Ah...I had a favor to ask," Walsh said, wincing. "If it's not too late."

Mercy didn't hesitate. "Where are you? I'll be there in five."

Walsh sighed gratefully. "Tell your girl I'm sorry to drag you away."

"Walsh says sorry to deprive you of my magnetic sexuality," Mercy said, voice more distant as he spoke away from the phone.

Ava laughed. "Yeah. I bet he did."

Walsh smiled to himself as he disconnected. He'd grown up without that kind of banter, and the first time he'd heard it between a couple it had shocked him. It had excited him, too. Not in a sexual way, but in a warm, fizzing way, like when he was a kid waiting for Christmas morning. It made him want to smile like a dope, hearing a husband and wife give each other sweet hell. He'd never experienced it for himself...until Emmie.

Who was probably going to get arrested for God knew what.

Her father moaned on the sidewalk.

"You and me both, mate," Walsh told him grimly.

~*~

A paper cup of water landed on the table in front of her, alongside the granola bar that had already been offered. The detective who'd brought it had an ugly yellow tie studded with blue diamonds, and one of those slack, beefy faces that lifted up in all the corners when he offered her a tight smile.

"Would you please tell me what this is about?" Emmie asked, massaging the back of her neck and trying to find a comfortable spot in the folding chair. They unbalanced the things on purpose, didn't they? To put you on edge? She'd read something about that in a crime novel.

Her whole fucking life was a crime novel now.

"I will," the detective said, sitting down across from her. He had a folder that he opened and turned toward her, displaying two photos, and two blue-ink fingerprints on white cards. "Do you recognize this?" He tapped the photo on the left.

"A doorknob."

"The doorknob to Davis Richards' back door. The one we dusted for prints. This" – one of the fingerprints – "is the print we took from you, for elimination purposes in the Richards investigation. It matches this print" – the other one – "that we pulled off of this. Do you know what that is?"

"A police badge," she said, and her stomach turned over.

"It's my police badge," he told her with a small, helpful smile. "I'm Detective Hanson."

"No." She shook her head, but he was nodding. "I met Detective Hanson yesterday, at Lawson's Tack and Feed, I met him…"

The man across from her pulled out his wallet and showed her his driver's license. Mark Hanson, age forty-eight, right there in front of her.

"God," she breathed, "who did I meet? Who *was that?*"

The real Detective Hanson heaved a deep breath. "How about instead, you tell me how your prints got on my stolen badge?"

~*~

"Just makes you feel all welcome, doesn't it?" Mercy asked. He hauled Johansen's unconscious weight from the backseat and slung the man over one shoulder like a bag of laundry, with no visible effort. He gestured toward the house with his free hand. "Take it your Emmie wasn't living here with him."

"Nah, she had the loft above the barn."

"Hell, I'd live in the stall *with* a horse 'fore I lived here." Mercy adjusted his burden. "You lead the way, son-in-law."

Walsh grimaced and headed up the walk, stepping over stray candy bar wrappers and plastic takeout cups that the wind had carried into the yard and the homeowners hadn't bothered to collect.

The front door was unlocked, but he had to fumble around for a light switch. When he found it, the foyer chandelier sputtered a few times before deciding half its bulbs would work.

"Nice," Mercy said as they mounted the steps into the main part of the house. "You sure this isn't Fisher's long lost brother?"

"We shouldn't speak ill of the dead."

Mercy snorted.

Because searching for a bedroom in this hell hole sounded like a stupendously bad idea, they dumped Emmie's father on the couch.

"Let's get outta here before we die of gin fume inhalation," Walsh grumbled, one last contemptuous glare thrown at his father-in-law's sleeping back.

In the moment, he hated the man for making Emmie's life difficult.

"Who in the hell are you?" a shrill, female voice said behind them, and they whirled at the same time.

The stepmother, Maryann, stood at the top of the stairs, bloated face pinched with anger, dress fitting her broad shape with all the elegance of a tablecloth.

"You robbing me?" she demanded. "What the hell are you doing in here?"

"Bringing your husband home," Walsh said, stepping toward her.

Her eyes widened with recognition. "You! It's you, you foreign asshole! Get outta my house!"

"Ma'am," Mercy said, stepping forward with a few swaggering steps that emphasized his height. "Personally, I can't wait to get out of your fucking landfill of a house."

She took a step back, managing to bristle and cower at the same time.

"But maybe you oughta think about thanking Emmie's husband for bringing your half-dead old man back in one…very smelly piece."

The woman's beady eyes darted around Mercy, zeroing in on Walsh. "*Husband.*"

"That's right." Walsh grinned darkly for her benefit – God knew he didn't feel like it. He advanced on her at a slow stalk. "Which means you're gonna want to be a lot nicer to Em."

"We'd hate to have to make another visit," Mercy said with a giant grin.

She looked between the two of them. Pursed up her mouth and shoved between them. "Always knew that girl was trash," she muttered. "Always knew she'd end up married to more trash."

Mercy started to say something else and Walsh shook his head. "Bigger fish, mate."

~*~

A sharp knock sounded on the interview room door before it swept open to reveal Sergeant Fielding. His face flushed with anger when his eyes landed on her.

"Hanson," he snapped. "What's going on in here?"

The detective got to his feet, face reddening. "Interviewing a suspect. In the interview room. Where we interview suspects," he said with a pointed glare that meant he didn't want to have this discussion in front of her – said suspect.

Fielding's lips compressed. "Give me a minute with her."

Hanson made an unhappy sound, but obliged, leaving them alone.

The sergeant shut the door and leaned back against it, posture non-threatening. "What's going on?"

She told him, growing calmer in the telling because without Hanson interrupting and trying to trip her up, the story sounded plausible. At least she hoped it did.

"And you'd never seen him before?" he asked of the fake Hanson.

"Never. But I haven't had a lot of dealings with the police, so…" She sighed. "I had no reason to believe he wasn't legit."

"Your student Becca saw him too?"

"Oh yes, she was all suspicious, so she got a good look." Relief flooded through her, and then another wave of it. "And they've got cameras at Lawson's, ever since those guys stole that roping dummy, so I bet he's on film."

"I bet he is too." He looked at her a long moment, studying her. "Walsh is out there, waiting on you, 'bout jumped down my throat when he came in."

She could envision his shoulders braced with tension, his scowl intense and cold. For her.

She wanted to cry and bit at her lip instead. "I didn't steal that badge. I might have married a Lean Dog, but I swear, I didn't steal it. I had no reason to. And that's *not me*."

"I know. Let's get you home."

Detective Hanson was standing in the squad room, looking pissed off by the loss of his chew toy. "I sent her *old man* out front," he told Fielding as they passed. "He was all riled up like a little Chihuahua."

276

Emmie shot him a dark glance as they passed, resentful on so many levels. When it came to Dogs, her husband was anything but a trembling neurotic lap warmer.

"Thanks," Fielding said with a sigh, and propelled her forward with a respectful grip on her elbow.

Walsh paced the width of the stairs outside, smoke trailing over his shoulder as he worked on the last nub of a cigarette. He tossed the butt away and turned to her. Fielding cleared his throat about the littering, but Walsh ignored it, coming to her, pausing just short of reaching for her with his hands.

"You okay?"

She nodded…and tears flooded her eyes. She lifted her hands to shield them and Walsh's arms wrapped around her, pulled her into the comforting warm solidness of his chest. She choked silently, biting her lip, closing her eyes, but the tears were pushing at her, trying to get loose.

"No charges?" he asked over the top of her head.

"No." Fielding sounded troubled and exhausted. "I'll look into what she told us and get back to you."

"She didn't steal anything, and you know it."

"Hmm. Take her home." To her he said, "Get some rest, Emmie. It'll be alright." Then his shoes retreated across the concrete, the door opened with a hiss of released air pressure.

Emmie burrowed her face into the leather covering Walsh's shoulder and willed herself to stop shaking. She shouldn't seek comfort from him, because he was the reason for all of this. But all she wanted was the strength of his arms around her, his hands gentle against her back, her neck.

"I didn't tell them anything," she said through chattering teeth. "About you, about the club—"

He stroked her hair. "Ah, love, I know you didn't."

~*~

"What'd he look like?" Walsh asked when they were in the truck and she'd calmed down a little. He gripped the wheel hard, veins standing stark in his forearms, illuminated by the dash lights. "Your fake cop."

Emmie relaxed back against the seat. "He was young. My age, probably. He looked like one of those fit, douchebag gym guys who'd missed a buncha sleep and drank too much. Like an echo of somebody who thought he was hot once."

He glanced over at her. "What? I meant eye color, height, weight, did he have a big nose? That kinda thing. They didn't have you talk to a sketch artist?"

"No. But you couldn't see that anyway."

"No, but they should have done it. So they could catch the guy." His jaw tensed as he stared through the windshield. "How did Fielding react when you told him?"

She shrugged. "Concerned. But he would, wouldn't he?"

His brows tucked low over his eyes, his scowl fierce. "I know what's going on. And my guess is Fielding does too."

"What?" She sat up straighter.

"Be thinking about what that guy looked like, and when we get home, I want you to describe him to Sly and Eddie."

"Okay…"

"They wanna crash on my couch, they can sit up and listen for a bit."

He was terrier-like, she reflected. Even-keeled for the most part, his tenacity was an impressive sight.

A thought formed, and she tried to push it down, but it was a stubborn one. "Walsh, there was something the fake cop told me. Something that happened at a bar in London. Pub, whatever you call it – he said civilians were killed during a confrontation. And he said – he said you had blood on your hands when they found you."

A glance showed that he was frowning, expression thoughtful as he dug back through the layers of the past. "I did. We were at Baskerville, and these wannabe tossers were trying to stir shit up. One of 'em pulled a knife."

She dampened her lips. "He said you killed a woman."

Walsh's gaze slid across the cab, challenging, but uncertain. "Do you believe that?"

Did she believe the man she'd married, the man who called her "love," the man who had been waiting for her on the precinct steps just now was the kind of man who killed women?

"No," she said, and felt a final loosening inside her. The Gordian knot that had formed early on relaxed at last, the tangles slipping free, the hollow relief bursting through her like joy. "I don't believe that," she said with new conviction, because, God, she didn't. She couldn't. She was with Walsh, bound to him by law, by the humming rhythms of her body and its desires – they belonged to one another, and that was too precious to waste because of the dark nasty things tied to his club. This was the choice fate had set before her: love the man and take on the club, all the violence it entailed, or be alone and ultimately stagger beneath the weight of her demons. Skeletons were going to own her either way – it was just a decision between his or hers.

And the thing about Walsh's blood-drenched, terrifying skeletons? The love made them worth it.

She grinned suddenly, and flopped her head back against the seat. "No," she repeated. "You didn't kill her. You couldn't have."

"Sure of that, yeah?" he asked.

"I didn't marry a murderer."

He was quiet a moment, then, "I told you I was a medical evac pilot."

"Yeah."

"I wasn't a medic, but I'd seen them do their thing enough. I put my hands on her to try and stop the bleeding." His voice stretched thin, growing fainter. "There was too much, and my hands weren't enough."

She laid a hand on his forearm, that crinkly dusting of hair she loved to pass her fingers across, squeezed him and willed comfort. "Walsh…"

"Just be thinking about your fake copper."

It was three when they got home, and the exhaustion hit her halfway up the sidewalk. When Walsh put his arm around her, she leaned into him.

"You aren't really going to wake them up, are you?" she asked as they passed into the dark, quiet house.

He snorted like he couldn't believe she'd said such a thing. "Of course I am. I got rogue FBI agents harassing my old lady, and you think I care about beauty sleep?"

She wanted to smile, even as tired as she was, at the protectiveness in his tone. But then the rest of the sentence permeated her foggy brain. "Rogue FBI agent?"

"Why don't you put the kettle on, love? I'll get the boys."

Since they had no kettle, and the only tea in the house was the orange-flavored crap she put in microwaved mugs of water, she put coffee on to brew and busied herself in the kitchen lest she fall asleep on her feet. The dinner mess had been sort of cleaned up by the guys, but in typical dude-fashion, they'd overlooked sauce drips on the counter and the pizza boxes were halfheartedly crammed into the garbage.

When the coffee was done, she filled four mugs, set them on a cookie sheet to serve as a makeshift tray, and headed into the living room.

Their houseguests were bleary-eyed, but awake, dressed in an identical uniform of undershirts and wrinkly jeans.

"Sorry," she said as she set the tray down and passed out mugs. "Walsh didn't think it could wait."

"It can't," he insisted.

Sly nodded his thanks for the coffee and dug a pack of Marlboros from his back pocket. "Mind if I smoke in here?"

Emmie was too tired to be nervous, or polite for that matter. "Yeah, I do actually. This isn't the sort of house for that."

Sly looked over at Walsh, lifted his brows, got a small smile in return.

Sly tucked the smokes away and shot her a tiny, wry grin. "You sound like my wife."

"I'm gonna assume that's a compliment."

"It is." He took a long swallow of coffee. "Alright, doll, tell us all about him."

She gave them as much detail as she could remember, and by the end, they were both nodding.

"That's Grey," Eddie said with a grim smile. "And this is a whole new level of asshole for him."

"Why's he rogue, though?" Emmie asked.

"It's some kinda personal shame bullshit," Eddie said. "It started with us…"

"And moved on to us," Walsh said. "He's on some kind of demented crusade against the Dogs."

"Why? Not enough human traffickers and homegrown terrorists to keep him busy?" Emmie asked.

Sly snorted.

Walsh gave her a warm smile that was full of masculine pride. It was an *atta girl* smile, no mistaking it, and it sparked little fireworks in her stomach. "He's off the clock," he said. "His bosses have demoted him twice now, and it's wrecked his head. He isn't undercover, and he doesn't have clearance to talk to any of us."

Fear skipped down her back. "A desperate man does desperate things."

Walsh leaned forward, braced his forearms on his knees. "Which is why I don't want you out alone anymore. Becca doesn't count," he added when she started to protest. "And I'm getting you a gun. No argument on that point." He actually shoved his index finger at her, all school headmaster-like.

Emmie pressed her lips together so she wouldn't smile. "A gun? I don't know, Walsh…"

"It's happening."

~*~

She remembered her dad with a fast stab of guilt as they were climbing into bed. "How difficult was he?" she asked, wincing.

Walsh flipped back the covers on his side and slid in beside her, wearing nothing but boxers. "I called in reinforcements."

"Oh no."

He flopped down onto the pillow and looked over at her. "Nah. Merc probably needed the exercise."

"Mercy?" She didn't know if she should laugh. "He didn't go into my father's house, did he?"

"He thought it was lovely."

She laughed and groaned at the same time, slipped down so she lay flat. "I'm an awful daughter," she said. "I ought to go in there and clean that place up."

"You're busy with work."

"Everyone's busy with work." She sighed. "That's no excuse. First Mom abandoned him, and then I did."

Walsh made a disagreeing sound. "He's a grown man, able-bodied, when he's not piss drunk, and he's married. You can't always save them from themselves, love," he added quietly. "You shouldn't give away another part of your life just to take care of him."

She closed her eyes, like concentrating would keep the sweet, supportive words inside her mind longer.

Thirty-One

"Sir, Kenneth Teague is here to see–"

"That's alright, sweetheart, I'll see myself in," Ghost said, pushing past the desk clerk and into Vince's office.

Jessie, pale and nervous, backed out, pulling the door to behind her, leaving them alone together, outlaw and law enforcement officer.

Vince took a deep, steadying breath. A simple conversation with Kenny Teague was like going a round in the ring. "This is about Emmie Walsh, isn't it?"

"What? No coffee? No 'please have a seat'?" Ghost smirked and dropped into a visitor chair. "Straight to business then, like always, Vinnie. Alright, yeah, it's got something to do with Emmie, because she's an old lady, and I take threats against all our women very personally."

"Threat? From what I gather, someone impersonated an officer and spooked her about the club."

"Someone? Don't be cute, it doesn't suit you." He reached inside his cut, withdrew a sheaf of photos, and tossed them onto the desk. They landed with a *splat* sound and fanned out, sliding over one another. "Someone's spying on my people, and you know exactly who it is, don't you?"

The pictures were of the Lean Dogs at home, with their wives, their children, having dinner, having...oh hell, he didn't need to see Mercy and Ava doing *that*.

He pushed them to the side and glared at Ghost. "What the hell?"

"My question exactly. A...*friend*...brought those to me. Said he pulled them off your buddy Grey."

"And I'm supposed to take your word for it?"

Ghost twitched a smile. "Well, if he's taking pictures through windows, I'm guessing he was planning on doing something with them. Like, say, showing them to you."

"So I could do what?"

"Well, in my case, I dunno – arrest me for not eating all my vegetables." He reached forward to flick the corner of one photo, one that showed him and Maggie at the kitchen table.

Vince's stomach clenched at regular intervals that had him itching to reach for the Tums in his top desk drawer.

"Oh yeah." Ghost pulled something else from his cut. A man's wallet. He flipped it open to reveal Grey's ID.

Vince reached for it and Ghost recoiled. "Aw nah. I'll hold onto this for now."

"He's not on assignment, I already checked," Vince said. "But I'm guessing you already knew that."

"Yep."

"God, the implications of this…" He rubbed at his forehead, willing away the pounding ache building behind it.

"I don't give a shit about the implications. That's the problem with you and your rules," Ghost said with a sneer. "You logic yourself to death. This is simple. Grey is batshit fucking crazy, he's doing very illegal things to try and hurt us, and it's going to stop."

"I know." He couldn't believe he was agreeing with the man about something, but stranger things, and all that. "I'm going to report him. I'll put a call into his supervisor."

"Do whatever you want," Ghost said, standing. "This is your warning, Vince. If you want to do something about him, do it before I get to him."

Thirty-Two

"Okay, now, it's gonna kick some. The trick is to hold firm, but be relaxed. Got it? Firm, but relaxed."

Emmie nodded gravely, biting down hard on the inside of her cheek to keep from laughing. "Got it."

"You're sure?" Walsh settled his hands on his hips, one booted foot propped on a tree stump. In his clinging buffalo plaid shirt and jeans, the determined set to his brows, he looked like a miniature lumberjack.

A smile almost got loose and she pressed her lips together. "Sure."

"What's wrong with you?"

"Nothing." She wiped her face clean of all expression. "Are we shooting, or talking about it?"

He grumbled something and reached down to pull the earphones out of the bag he'd brought.

"What was that, sweetie?" she asked.

"Nothing."

As the alarm had sounded that morning, Walsh had pounced on her, bearing her down into the mattress as he hovered above her, lips against her ear as he'd awakened her with, "We're going shooting."

At any point during her zombie shuffle routine as they prepared, she could have told him about the guns she owned, the concealed carry permit she possessed, or her decent aim. Instead, she dragged on clothes and let him haul her across the pasture, over the gate, and back to the dead body property.

So far, she'd been too bombarded with instructions for the vibes of the place to creep her out too badly.

"Start with the target on the left" – he stepped up behind her and set the muffs over her ears, muffling the rest of his words – "just one shot, and then we'll see where we need to go from there."

She nodded.

285

When he'd secured his own ear protection and stepped back behind the firing line, she lifted her arms and set up her shot. He'd arranged three paper targets, affixed to old straw bales. The gun in her hands was one of his, a nine millimeter semiauto with only a moderate recoil.

Easy as pie.

Emmie squeezed off a round at the first target and moved to the second, the third, then back to the first. She dropped her arms as the echoes faded, and turned to face him, not quite restraining a smug smile.

Walsh stared at her with open confusion, shock, maybe even a little admiration.

"I own three handguns and a shotgun," she told him. "I know how to shoot."

His mouth opened twice before he spoke. "You didn't say anything."

"You didn't ask. You just assumed."

Slowly, he took off his headgear, dropped it down into the bag, like he was in a daze. "I don't know if that makes me feel stupid, or incredibly randy all of a sudden."

Emmie handed him the gun as he reached for it, pushed her earphones down around her neck. And grinned. "Either is acceptable."

He gave her a smirk from where he couched, loading the bag back up. "Take it you don't need more practice?"

"Nope. And I need to get to the barn."

"Gimme your ear thingies, then."

She did, and he zipped the bag up, giving her a view of the top of his head, the crazy cowlick in his thick hair she couldn't see when he was standing. It was the sort of thing a mother would have spent long minutes trying to tame with water and a comb before he went off to school. The sort of thing that made a wife want to run her fingers through the thick thatch of golden spikes.

Emotion surged through her slowly, a tide of warm, tender things she didn't normally feel toward humans.

"Hey, Walsh," she said softly, and his head lifted immediately. "What does your mother call you?"

He blinked, face unreadable as she stared at her. "King," he said at last. "She always calls me by my first name."

"It suits you."

He forced a dry laugh and stood, bag slung over his shoulder. "No it doesn't. I can think of a lot of blokes more kingly than me." He made an impatient gesture that they start walking and she fell into step beside him.

"And what makes them more kingly? Mink capes or crowns or something?"

"Try height, weight, and just your general meanness."

Emmie stared at her feet, stepping high to keep from getting tangled in the tall, unkempt grass. "That has shit-all to do with being king."

He snorted, unconvinced.

"I'm serious. Take horses, for example. There's always that asshole horse who gives me hell, gives his pasturemates hell, holds the others off the water trough and kicks and bites any chance he gets. Around here, that's Zeus. That palomino in the end stall. Total, incurable jerk. But you put him in the pasture with Apollo, and he straightens up. He doesn't bully anyone else when Apollo's around, because he knows he'll get his ass kicked. Because Zeus," she explained, "is like that wild stallion who never gains a herd of his own. And Apollo is the true lead horse. The real king."

She glanced over at her King. "A king is responsible," she said seriously. "He takes care of his people. Even when they already know how to shoot."

He darted her a wary glance, and she smiled at him.

"I'm complimenting you here."

"I know. Just not used to it."

His phone rang, and he sighed. "Oh, what in the bloody hell now?"

"See? Responsible," she said as he dug the offending device out of his pocket.

"Not every king is worth a damn, you know. Henry VIII, hmm?"

"I was talking about good kings. Why even talk about the bad ones?"

"Because the bad ones," he said as he checked his phone, "are the ones that get you killed, pet."

~*~

"That was quick," Walsh said as he joined Ghost in the precinct parking lot.

The president stood leaning back against the brick wall of the building, arms folded, head tipped back like he was enjoying the sun on his face. "I've never seen ol' Vinnie's face look like it did this morning. He was good and freaked out."

"Good." Walsh mirrored his pose, putting his back to the wall. "Surprised he called you though."

"I gave him some incentive, you might say."

"Hmm."

The front doors of the place opened and out came two agents in jeans, t-shirts and FBI flak vests walking a fuming Harlan Grey between them. He wasn't in cuffs, but they had firm hands clamped on his biceps, and they pushed him down the steps and out toward a waiting black Suburban.

"...unbelievable," Grey muttered. "I wasn't doing–" His gaze landed on the two of them, up against the wall. "You," he snarled. "Fucking bastards. You're gonna let them just stand there, career criminals, and you're reprimanding *me*?!"

Ghost gave the agent a wave and a dark, satisfied smile.

Grey continued to bitch until he was shoved unceremoniously into the back of the SUV.

Fielding appeared at the top of the stairs and started down them slowly, looked troubled and tired. "He was staying at the Marriott. When my guys got into his room, he was looking through more photos on his computer. His bosses aren't happy," he finished, drawing up beside them. He glanced toward the

Suburban as it backed out of its parking spot. "He'll lose his shield for this."

"Regrets?" Ghost asked.

"None for him." Fielding took a deep breath and let his shoulders slump afterward. "How 'bout *you guys* try not to make me regret anything."

"Wouldn't dream of it," Walsh said.

Ghost gave the man a salute.

Another deep, bone-weary sigh. "Why don't I ever believe you?"

~*~

Aidan scrubbed at his chin in silent frustration and surveyed the interior of the Briar Hall maintenance shed. There were two ancient Snapper mowers, a push mower, an aerator, spreader, and a tangle of garden tools. The place smelled like rotted grass and mold. Pallets of seed, fertilizer, and mulch took up the far wall. And beneath a tarp, he finally found a shiny green John Deere lawn tractor, which appeared to be the largest mower around.

A necessity, since he was going to mow this goddamn place.

His initial reaction to Walsh's comment about a groundskeeper had been to give the guy the mental finger. Stepping up didn't involve sinking to new lows in his book.

But then had come that night in Tonya's apartment, and he'd tasted her mouth, and felt her wet and tight around him, and his priorities had begun to shake out.

He hadn't found a groundskeeper yet, and the grass around this place was getting bad shaggy, so he was going to mow the lawns himself.

He yanked the tarp the rest of the way off, coughed at the dust it stirred up, turned to throw it over his shoulder –

"Shit!" He snatched it back just in time, barely avoiding Walsh's old lady. He'd almost thrown the nasty thing over her like a shroud. "Damn, I didn't see you."

Emmie swiped a hand through the glittering dust cloud and shook her head. "Just walked in. What are you doing?"

"I'm gonna mow."

She stepped deeper into the shed, the sunlight behind her flaring around the halo of her bright hair. "You're serious? Did Walsh put you up to it? Did you lose some kind of bet?"

He checked the face he wanted to make. She was somebody's woman, even if he wanted to react to her the same way he would Ava. She threw off that sister vibe for him. "Nah. It needs doing, so I'm gonna do it."

She tipped her head to the side, studying him. "Are you just trying to impress Tonya, 'cause no offense, but she's not going to be into the whole yard man thing."

He smirked. "I already impressed Tonya enough, trust me."

"Ew."

"I just…look, do you not want me to or something?"

"No. Please, that would be awesome. It needs cutting badly and Fred shouldn't have to."

Right. Because a horse groom was too good to put his ass on a lawnmower. "Too cliché for him?" he asked.

"He's got more important stuff to take care of."

"Gee thanks. I feel so valuable."

She shook her head, face scrunching up like she was mad at herself. It was cute enough to dispel some of his temper. "Okay, I didn't mean it like that. I meant Fred has prior commitments, and our clients will be pissed if he doesn't fulfill them. It would be wonderful if you mowed the grass, Aidan. Please." She threw in a cheesy grin that he couldn't help but find charming.

He nodded. "Yeah. But just this once. Until I can find you a guy to do it all the time."

"Deal."

So that was how ten minutes later, the son of the Lean Dogs president, and the city's most sought-after bad boy chick magnet, ended up puttering alongside a horse arena on a bright green John Deere lawn tractor. He was pretty sure his balls were trying to crawl up inside his body.

And that was before Tonya spotted him.

She was walking her horse down to the arena, and paused to inch her sunglasses down and examine him over the tops of them, mouth curling up in disgust.

He cut off the mower. "Hey."

"What the hell are you doing?" she asked.

He flashed her his patented shark smile and spread his arms to encompass the mower and the acres of barnyard lawn around them. "What's it look like?"

"It looks like you're...*mowing the grass*." She might as well have said *eating* the grass, for the total disdain in her tone.

"It's my day off at the shop, and I thought I'd help out around here," he said proudly. Women loved that – doing extra work, taking responsibility.

But Tonya didn't look impressed. "Emmie's supposed to hire someone to do that."

"I'm looking for a groundkeeper," he said, less proudly this time. "But until I find one, I thought..."

She turned away from him mid-sentence, leading her horse through the arena gate. "Wash the grass smell off yourself before you pick me up later. I don't have gardener fantasies, Aidan."

Thirty-Three

"Tomorrow?" Emmie followed Walsh into the bedroom, trying not to let the sinking sensation in her stomach bleed into her voice. "For how long?"

He started undoing the buttons on his denim shirt – she'd thought at first it was the same shirt, then realized he had four *identical* shirts while she was doing the laundry – and shrugged. "Couple days there, couple days back, maybe three days layover. Long as it takes to…" His face twitched. "Conduct business."

The business part wasn't what bothered her. This was a purely emotional reaction on her part, and she wasn't going to do a good job hiding it. "Why didn't you tell me sooner?"

He shrugged out of the shirt and tossed it on the hamper, started in on his belt. "Just found out this afternoon when I saw Ghost. Texas needs to step up the timeline, and since I can't very well tell them no after this" – gesture to the room around them, the house, the farm – "I've got to head out in the morning."

All the way to Texas. She thought she must feel exactly like an anxious wife. "You're not traveling alone, are you?"

He gave her a little smirk as he ditched his jeans. "Worried about me?"

"Um, yeah! You don't need to be riding halfway across the country by yourself. What if something happens to your bike? What if you get attacked?"

"Attacked?"

"Well I don't know how many enemies you have. It could be like a bad eighties movie out there."

He laughed.

"Walsh–"

He stepped up and took her gently by the arms. "Love, I'm not going alone," he said, sobering. "There's a whole group of us going, with a truck, in case something happens to a bike. I'll be fine. The trick will be you not getting into some kind of massive trouble while I'm gone."

"I am *not* a troublemaker."

"Beg to differ." He kissed her and stepped back. "I've got to shower 'fore we go."

"Go where?"

"Oh." He paused on his way to the bathroom. "Club party tonight. A send-off before we go tomorrow."

"Club party." Her chest tightened. "And what does that entail, exactly?"

He grinned. "Guess you'll find out."

~*~

Aidan caught his reflection in the frosted elevator doors, and noted his vicious expression. He looked like his father: brows drawn low, jaw set, eyes bright and dark like an animal's. A hungry predator, one that was tired of being treated like a Golden retriever.

He hated Tonya's building, he decided, as the elevator arrived and dropped him into a terrazzo hallway identical to the one on the first floor. Everything spoke of restraint, from the clean lines of the wall sconces to the exact angles of the apartment numbers, to the walls the color of eggshells. Someone else might have called it masculine. Tasteful. Expensive. He called it pretentious and douchey. He'd grown up in rooms crowded with furniture, full of warmth, laugher, and color. What must Tonya think of his skin, if she lived someplace like this? All his ink, his roses, the scars on his forearms where the tats had been power-sanded off by the asphalt.

He rapped loudly on her door when he reached it, drawing a disapproving glare from a passing resident. He stared the guy down until he looked away.

The door opened and out rolled a cloud of subtle, high dollar perfume. Tonya braced a hand in the open doorframe and angled her body in a way that showed off her lithe figure, tonight wrapped in second-skin green silk.

"Hi," she greeted in a low purr.

The picture she made did everything for him physically: the fuck-me shoes, the glittering jewelry, the glossy coiffed hair, the perfect makeup.

But Aidan had a coldness in his gut. He'd thought this was a strong woman, self-possessed, driven, who knew what she wanted. He'd thought she might be a little like Mags, that quasi-sister stepmother female figure who reigned supreme among his ideal thoughts of women.

He'd thought wrong, though. This was an expensive bitch who liked to fuck bad boys.

"Hey," he returned, voice bored, face locked down as before.

Her head tilted, seductive smile freezing a second. "Hi," she repeated. She leaned in close, her hand came down off the doorframe, and she reached for him –

Her nostrils flared. "You didn't shower." Her eyes flooded with accusation, distaste, disapproval.

He grinned, and he knew it was nasty. "Nah. I'm all dead grass, motor oil, and sweat right now, baby doll. Come here and take a good whiff."

Her eyes narrowed. "I told you–"

"And I'm telling you that you gotta get your fancy ass in gear if you're going out with me tonight. Otherwise, see ya around."

She glared at him, eyes shooting sparks, and her lips worked like she was forming insults to throw at him. But ultimately, she slammed her apartment door behind her and set off toward the elevator at his side.

"You stink," she said, and her voice was full of leashed excitement.

So she was one of those, the big bad bitch who secretly wanted to be dominated. Ugh.

"You like it, don't you?" he accused. He faced her as they stepped onto the elevator, and the energy shimmering off of her danced across his skin like electric currents. "You wanna act like a guy's supposed to dress nice and act right and take you to expensive dinners and shit. But really…" The doors slid shut on them and he leaned into her face, saw the spark of arousal in her eyes, watched her dampen her lips. Her breasts heaved as she sucked in a breath. "Really," he said softly, "you just wanna be put up against a wall and have your brains fucked out. You're nothing but a bitch in heat."

Her hand hovered over the emergency stop button. "I ought to hit you for that," she said through her teeth, but her expression gave her away; she was thrilled.

"But you won't," he said smugly. "'Cause tonight, I'm gonna give you the real biker experience, and you can't fucking wait for it. Your panties are already damp, aren't they?"

She licked her lips again. "I'm not wearing any."

~*~

Walsh had never brought a woman to the clubhouse before. It didn't matter that he was almost forty, that the woman in question was his old lady, and that no one was going to razz him about it – he was nervous as a kid on the way to prom.

"So this is the clubhouse," he said, though that had to be self-explanatory.

It was a small party, but some of the New York guys were still in town, so the lights were strung up beneath the pavilion and the music was thumping.

Beside him, Emmie had an arm looped through his, but didn't seem frightened. Just curious. A little tired maybe, after a long day's work.

"You've met all the local guys," he told her. "But there's some from out of town."

"Okay."

"And there's probably some stuff going on in there. Smoking. Lots of drinking. There might be a stripper. And the club girls will be there, for sure."

Emmie turned a laughing look up to him. "Are you worried I'm going to freak out?"

He shrugged. "No."

She laughed. "I've made it this far. Do you think a little smoke and tit show is going to send me running?"

"You never know." Because much less offensive things had sent others running.

She leaned in closer, propped her chin on his shoulder. "Well, it's not."

He'd have to trust her on that, because there was no going back.

~*~

"You're stuck in your head again tonight." Jasmine was sitting so close, his arm wedged against her breasts, that he felt the slick slide of her freshly glossed lips against his ear.

"Just tired." He took a long swig of his beer and wished it was something harder.

Or maybe red wine.

Fuck him.

"You're tired a lot lately." True concern in her voice, in her touch, as she reached to push a stray piece of his hair back. "Something on your mind? Someone?"

They were sitting on a couch against the wall, as the party rocked around them. Blaring music, clink of pool balls, barks of laughter. No one was paying them any attention.

He turned his head and saw the concern in her face.

She'd spent hours on her hair and makeup: the big barrel curls, the exact black eyeliner and shadow, the glistening sheen of her lips.

"I don't tell you how beautiful you are enough," Tango said quietly. "You are, you know? Absolutely gorgeous."

She smiled and batted her lashes. "Well thanks for noticing, baby." Then grew serious again. "But I'm worried about you. I don't see you much anymore."

Regret speared through him. "I'm sorry."

She pressed in closer, so their lips were almost touching. "Do you still like girls?" she whispered.

"I always liked girls. Always will." And that was the truth. He'd wanted women from the beginning, to know the secrets hidden beneath their clothes and taste their impossibly soft skin, but life had dealt him a different hand, and he'd spent those developmental teenage years having his sexuality explored for him, by force most times. He'd been conditioned, until pain and pleasure became the same thing, and attraction something that was only about his cock and the tangling of bodies, and nothing emotional.

There had been times, though, even during the dark days, when a man would bring his girlfriend into the club with him. Times when both of them had wanted to use him.

And then there had been Jazz, and the club girls, and he'd been awkward and fumbling at first, because he hadn't known what to do with his muddled proclivities.

Jasmine's hand landed in his lap; she cupped his cock through his jeans. "I miss you when you're not around, you know."

"I know."

She grinned. "And you never did ask Aidan, did you? You promised me." She pretended to pout, and smiled again. "Cheer me up, and maybe it'll cheer you up, too."

Tango glanced across the room to where Aidan stood with his furious-faced, model-looking rich girl. "I think he's got his hands full tonight."

Jazz snorted. "She's pretty, I'll give her that. But you can smell the crazy bitch on her from all the way over here."

He laughed and it felt good; God knew when the last time had been.

Jasmine's hand tightened on him. "That's what I like to hear." She reached for the button of his jeans.

He moved to stop her, and she swatted his hand away. "Jazz, not in front of everyone…"

"Relax, baby," she said as she reached inside his jeans. "No one's watching."

But they were there, though. In the same room, just feet away, as her fingers curled around his cock and gave it a firm tug.

297

The laughter died away in his chest, the smile sliding off his face. He pressed his boot heels into the floor and lifted his hips because his body wanted her touch, any touch, all touches.

But he was still nothing but an exhibition, a cock that needed stroking, and not much of a man at all.

It was killing him. Slowly, since the beginning, an acid eating away at every foundation.

It was only a matter of time before there was nothing left.

~*~

"I've never seen Walsh with a chick!" the brunette with the huge breasts and the excessive eye makeup said, leaning in closer. Chanel, she'd said her name was, like the perfume.

Emmie hadn't quite known what Walsh meant by "club girls," but when this woman had plunked down beside her, she'd learned. These were groupies, who performed menial tasks because they were hooked on bikers.

"He doesn't ever give us the time of day," Chanel went on, waving her hand like she couldn't believe Walsh would have done such a thing. She grinned at Emmie. "But he's married! Oh my God. I totally don't believe it."

"Yeah…um…we're married. So yeah." She sipped her wine to fill her vocabulary void. She wouldn't say that she was spooked, and she for sure could handle the atmosphere, but she would admit to being a touch overwhelmed. The music was louder than she'd thought, the jostling bikers rowdier, and there was in fact a stripper, though she appeared to be one of the regular groupies, because RJ reached up, grabbed one of her nipple tassels and pulled her down into his lap, at which point she squealed in delight and shoved her tongue in his mouth.

The wine was at least decent. Walsh had headed for the bar to get her a second glass, and that's when Chanel had swooped in.

Across the coffee table, Briscoe said, "Girl, don't be bothering his old lady. She don't wanna talk to you."

"She does too," Chanel insisted, hands going on her hips, chest thrusting forward.

"No, she doesn't," a female voice said, and Maggie Teague appeared, standing on the other side of the groupie, somehow making a plaid shirt, jeans, and boots look like Fashion Week's finest. "Go see what the beer situation is, Chanel. I'll keep the new Mrs. Walsh company."

The groupie hustled to obey with a fast "yes, ma'am."

As the queen sat beside her, Emmie didn't know who she would have rather been subjected to. Chantel was…well, it wasn't nice what she was thinking. But there was no agenda there. No cunning.

"How's it going?" Maggie asked. Light. Casual.

Emmie stepped carefully regardless. "Good."

"Ever been to anything like this?" She gestured to the party with her beer bottle.

"Not since high school. There were topless girls then, too, but they weren't getting paid with anything besides gonorrhea."

Maggie snorted. "RJ, meanwhile, gives a girl such a great compensation package."

Across the way, he was pulling the stripper astride him, and it was obvious his jeans were undone.

Emmie felt her cheeks warm, but she kept her cool, turned to give the other woman a raised-brow look. "Don't you just love the way he respects her?"

They both laughed together, and Maggie's smile looked genuine, her eyes dancing. "God," she said with a sigh, "I remember my first club party. Waaaay back. I was sixteen," she said with a glance that was wondering if Emmie would judge her.

Emmie didn't.

"And the second I walked in, there was a guy laid out on the pool table, and a girl was going down on him, and I freaked the hell out." She laughed again, quietly. "I was halfway down the street before Ghost caught up to me."

"He convinced you to come back?"

"No, he took me to an all-night diner and we had chocolate chip pancakes." Her smile was directed inward, toward her memories. "And he made me a promise. He said no matter what I saw, no matter how crazy things got, none of that would ever touch me. 'You're not a conquest,' he told me. 'You're my girl, and no one else's.'"

"They've all got a sweet side, don't they?" Emmie asked.

Maggie nodded. "The good ones do."

~*~

Aidan dropped his head to whisper in Tonya's ear. "Wishing that was you and me?"

Up close, he could see her cheeks flush, see her skin prickle with gooseflesh. Her eyes were trained on RJ, where one of the naked club girls straddled him, working herself against him, the trailing tail of his belt proving this wasn't a dry-humping situation.

"This place is disgusting," she whispered, but her eyes told a different story when they flashed to his face. Her gaze said *Fuck me.*

"Then let's get out of here."

Her hand was trembling when he took hold of it, and he knew it had nothing to do with nerves. He led her through the crowd and out of the clubhouse, the clean air punching down into his lungs. He hadn't even had a drink yet, but he was buzzing.

Tonya ran her hands up and down his back while he unlocked the bike shop. She pressed her breasts up against him as she followed him through the dark lobby and out into the garage bays.

The lights came on with a loud thrum, flooding the space with harsh fluorescent light. The customer bike he'd been working on earlier was still parked in the center of the first bay, and the sight of it gave him an idea. One that got him hard.

When he turned to Tonya, she braced her palms on his chest, leaned forward on her toes.

"Kiss me," she said, breathlessly.

"No." He hooked his hands in the front of her dress and gave a sharp tug. The silk split down the middle with a tearing sound, and she gasped, but didn't move to cover herself.

She wasn't wearing a bra, and her nipples were hard, aroused points, rosy thanks to her full-body flush. Aidan pinched them between his fingers, harder than he should have, until he heard her swift intake of breath.

He bent his head toward her, hovered his lips above hers; her neck softened and she tried to melt against him. He held back, not quite kissing her. "Turn around, and put your hands on the bike."

"No, I–"

"Do it."

The light in her eyes was feral as she turned to comply, bracing both hands on the bike seat, arching her back and popping her ass toward him. She glanced over her shoulder in silent challenge, egging him on.

She was going to regret that.

He pushed up the hem of her dress, all the way up, over her ass, bunched it up at her waist. The rustle of the silk wound him tighter, made his hands jerkier, crueler. She'd told the truth about the no-panties thing, and visible in the dim glow of the garage lights, her sex was already wet and glistening with arousal.

There wasn't a drop of blood in his brain at this point, all of it funneling down his body, pounding in his cock with each heartbeat. Nothing in the world mattered as much as getting inside her. He tore at the fastenings of his jeans, freeing his erection. He didn't take the time to test her with his fingers, stretch her, ready her. He braced a hand on the small of her back, aligned their bodies, and drove into her. Hard.

Tonya made a sound that was part-yelp, part-moan, and it electrified him. He latched onto her hips and started moving, let the need to thrust into her again and again take over.

He was rough, hammering into her, digging into her hips with his fingers until he knew he'd leave dark bruises. Her hands slipped on the bike and she almost fell, catching herself at the last moment. He didn't relent, just kept up the driving rhythm, until he could hear his skin smacking against hers; his hands and her hips were so slick with sweat he could barely hold onto her.

It wasn't about Tonya. As he fucked her like a club groupie in the goddamn garage where he worked on bikes, he knew that this moment had nothing to do with her. He'd wanted it to. He'd been attracted to her. Physically, yes…but he'd liked her fire. Had thought that meant something. That maybe she was…special. Something. He didn't know. She was supposed to be different, the cool, calm, classy broad he needed in his life.

But she was just a slut with issues, like every girl he'd ever fucked before.

She let out a high, keening cry as she came, and he didn't care, bearing down on her harder, working those last hard thrusts to his own release. And that's all it was for him – a release. Because there was no satisfaction in it.

He pulled out and turned away from her, straightened his clothes, zipped up. Pushed his sweat-slick hands through his hair and took a deep, shuddering breath.

He hadn't changed at all, had he? Same old fuckup Aidan. Same habit, different pussy.

Tonya's breathing slowly evened out behind him. Her stilettos clipped across the concrete, and her hands latched onto his triceps. "Aidan." Her voice was deep, ragged, satiated.

"We're leaving," he said. "We're done."

~*~

"Were you the first one to leave?" Holly asked, grinning, as Michael braced a hand on the arm of the couch and leaned down to kiss her. He tasted like smoke and whiskey, and stank of cigarettes, the scent falling off his leather jacket and cut.

His mouth twitched as he pulled back. "Yeah."

"You didn't have to. We're fine here. Lucy's been down for about a half hour. And that guy who was looking in the windows is gone now, right?"

He sighed and dropped down beside her, arm draping absently across her lap, one hand curling around her knee. "Yeah." He glanced at the TV and frowned. "What the hell are you watching?"

She covered his hand with hers. "It's this cooking competition. They're making cupcakes, but they have time limits, and they have to use certain ingredients."

"Exciting."

"It's fun," she defended. "And it's given me some new recipe ideas. How do you feel about maple bacon cupcakes with buttercream frosting?"

He glanced over and gave her one of his little twitchy Michael-smiles. "You're a wild woman, Mrs. McCall."

"Wilder than you. Why'd you leave the party early?"

He shrugged and his eyes went back to the TV.

"I thought things were better. With you and the guys." Much to her delight, he'd been making friends with all of them. He was never going to be a high-fiving, what's-up-bro kind of friend, but he had bonds with his brothers now, Mercy and Walsh especially. She and Ava had even managed a double dinner date a couple of times.

"They are."

She stroked his knuckles. Even in summer, they were chapped from the wind, all those hours on the bike. "You're just not a party animal, are you?"

He didn't comment, but his hand tightened on her knee.

"That's fine with me." She leaned sideways, so she could rest her head against his shoulder. "I'd rather have you home, watching cupcake competitions."

He snorted, and she knew it meant *me too*.

~*~

Ava was far enough along that she was in the habit of talking to her belly. Partly because at eight months, the baby felt very much a part of the family, but also because he was a kicker, and their voices seemed to quiet him. "There's Daddy," she said as Mercy

303

came in through the back door. "Do you hear him?" She laid a hand on her stomach. "It sounds like there's a water buffalo shuffling around in my mud room when he takes his boots off. Daddy's loud," she added in a stage whisper as Mercy stepped into the kitchen.

"In Daddy's defense, so's Mama when she gets worked up." He grinned and stepped in to kiss her, put an arm around her and tucked her against him. Even when she was hugely pregnant, he made her feel small. "Baby, why are you on your feet? Go sit down."

"He's restless," she said, rubbing her belly. "So I'm walking laps. How was the party? You smell like a Marlboro manufacturing plant, so I'm guessing there was a good turnout."

"Meh." He shrugged and steered her toward the living room, and the sofa. "The usual. Walsh brought his girl."

"How'd that go?"

They reached the couch and he helped her lower down, sitting beside her afterward and pulling against his side. "I didn't talk to her, but she seemed alright, actually. Some of 'em get that look, you know? Like they can't believe any of it. But she seemed cool. Saw her sitting with your mom."

"The hazer, you mean?"

"She's just gotta break 'em in. You'd do it, if Mags didn't."

"I wouldn't."

He chuckled. "Oh yeah, you would."

She rolled her eyes. "*Anyway*. So Emmie's gonna stick around, do you think?"

"For Walsh's sake, I hope so. Not that he'd ever say it or anything, but he's got it bad."

Ava smiled. "I've always had this theory about Walsh."

"What's that?"

"I think he's a total closet Romeo. I think he's secretly romantic as hell."

"I'm telling him you said that."

"No, don't!"

Mercy laughed. "Too late, it's out there. I can't un-think it, and I can't not say it."

"Don't embarrass him, Merc."

"You're bossy when you're pregnant." He squeezed her shoulders and grinned. "I like it."

"You're a doof." She settled against him more fully, the fatigue washing through her now that she was off her feet. "And now I'm gonna have two doof sons."

"Aren't you the lucky lady."

~*~

Walsh realized, as the party began to wind down and the local members dispersed, that he'd been waiting for something to happen. His nerves had danced all evening as he waited for Emmie to be offended, to be outraged, to stomp up to him with eyes flashing. It had to be too much for a respectable girl like her – his club world. But he watched her talk to Maggie, saw the tension leave her small shoulders. He'd heard her laugh, had watched her wave a hand through a cloud of cigarette smoke and smile rather than frown.

It was midnight, and they sat side-by-side on a bench out in front of the clubhouse, the damp night air clearing the secondhand smoke from their nostrils. Their elbows rubbed together, and it was a casual, familiar, comforting touch. It felt like the beginning of coexistence, something more lasting than just sex or protection.

She took a deep breath that sounded tired, but wasn't a sigh. "So that's a club party."

"Yep."

"Holly and Ava were home with their kids?"

"Yeah. Ava usually comes when she can."

"But she's very pregnant."

"Yeah." He cleared his throat. "It's not always like this. Some parties are wilder. Some are more like family dinners. Just depends."

305

"Hmm." She nodded, and it sent her shimmering blonde curls falling forward along her face. She pushed them back and gave him a searching look. "Walsh, why do I get the impression you're still nervous?"

"Ah..." He exhaled loudly. "Shit." He faced her, feeling stupid, feeling exposed, unsure how else to do it. This normal, decent, dedicated girl was prying up the veneer of club, getting to the Kingston beneath, and that was terrifying, and he was ill-equipped to handle it. So he had to be honest, for lack of any other plan. "I'm waiting on you to disappear on me," he said, grimly. "I'm waiting on you to decide it's too much, load up your horse, and get as far away from all of this as you can."

She smiled faintly, and her shoulders slumped. "Glad to hear you're so confident in my loyalty."

"I've never seen loyalty anywhere outside the club."

She studied him a moment, absorbing the statement. "That might be true, but I wish it wasn't. Because loyalty exists in other places. It has to...I want it to." Her voice faded and she glanced away, across the dark parking lot. "Walsh, I've spent my whole life working toward something that was never really there. I didn't ever have a goal, really. I was just loyal. Sometimes I wish that was a habit I could shake." Her eyes came back to him. "But I can't. I'm hardwired. And my life may have taken a turn, but I haven't. I'm your wife. I'm an MC old lady now. And I never thought I'd be one of those, but I'm not one to back down from a challenge," she said, firmly. "So I'm telling you right now that I'm not going anywhere. I'm not your Rita. And I'm not my mother. I'm here, Walsh. And I'm staying."

When he put his arm around her, she came up into his lap; she opened her mouth against his when he kissed her.

His. Like a benediction inside his head: *his, his, his.*

Thirty-Four

The woman patting him down was stunning: African-American with caramel hair and a body of feminine curves not disguised by her jeans and casual t-shirt.

"Careful there, Foxy Brown," he told her as her hands slid to his front pockets. "You might find something there you can't handle." He laughed.

She glanced up at him through her lashes as she felt down both his legs, face expressionless. "Call me that again, and I'll handle it right off your pasty-ass self with a dull knife and feed it to you."

Harlan forced the smile off his face. "Noted."

She stood, which put her a good inch taller than him. She was a large woman, and her gleaming arms were padded with muscle. She wasn't an attack dog, or a bodyguard, or one of the hired guns, was just an assistant of some sort, but was threatening, and whatever else she did for her boss, she took care of herself too.

"Come with me," she said, and led him forward down the hall, between a matched pair of thugs with biceps the size of Christmas hams.

Don had beefed up security since their last encounter. Beefed up his entire enterprise, by the looks of it. From a tumbled-down house to this place: an abandoned, renovated strip mall, four storefronts converted into one giant office, all but a few of the streetside windows bricked up for safety's sake.

Foxy led him down a tight hallway that switched back again and again, forks splitting it here and there. Another security measure. They arrived at door with a key card which she swiped them through, and into a spacious room tricked out with plush chairs, couches, tables arranged with magazines, potted plants. A wall-mounted TV was playing CNN without the sound.

"Wait here," she told him, and used her card to go through a second door, leaving him alone.

Sort of alone. Four cameras, one in each corner of the ceiling, watched him.

Okay, so Don was doing *well*.

The second door opened and Foxy stuck her head through. "You can come in," she said, with obvious contempt. She pushed the door wide and motioned him through it – damn, she smelled nice. Like vanilla and flowers.

But then all thoughts of her vanished, as he got a look at the room, and the man behind the desk.

They were in Nashville, and somehow, the office reflected that. Bright red plush carpet, black and white Victorian wallpaper. Sleek chrome and glass furnishings, and on the walls, lit up with playbill bulbs, were country music concert posters. It was like the lobby of a theater. Flashy, tacky, but somehow fitting, given the city. And Don Ellison – a complete contradiction.

Tall, built like a bull, square-jawed, he looked like a lineman, or an escaped convict who'd enjoyed his yard time, rough, grizzled, and out of place in his sport coat and open-throated oxford.

"Grey." The man's voice was a whole truckload of gravel dumping out into the room. "I heard you got canned."

Harlan ground his molars. "Word travels fast, then."

"I have eyes and ears."

Which was exactly why he was here. You went up against the Lean Dogs, and by proxy, Shaman, then you needed to bring the big guns to the table.

"So do I," Harlan said. "And I hear you'd like to move into east Tennessee."

Don shrugged. "Who doesn't want to expand?"

"I hear you're thinking of taking on the Dogs. Maybe even your old boss."

For about five years, Don had worked as one of Shaman's most successful dealers, before he'd decided to break out on his own. According to the rumors in the Bureau, the split had been a nasty one, and now there was no love lost between the two men. No one truly understood how many pies Shaman had his fingers in, or what his ultimate endgame was. But Don was a straightforward guy. He wanted to make money, and he wanted to expand.

"I hear you took out one of Ghost Teague's dealers, and the dumbass doesn't even know it was you."

Don's face creased heavily as he frowned. "You've been talking to that Richards kid. That little shit."

"I have." Harlan stepped closer to the desk, growing more excited as he drew on his research. "He's got a bad case of talking too much, and he told me some things. He said you've got ties to the Gannon & Gannon development firm. That you were going to use that condo village to get a toehold in Knoxville, fly in under the radar."

The lack of reaction meant Harlan was right, and he grinned triumphantly. "Are you gonna take out Teague's dealers one at a time? Is *that* how you think you'll get him to sit up and take notice of you?"

No comment.

Harlan braced both hands on the desk. "Let me help you, just one old friend looking after another. You want into Knoxville, you want that land, and I can help you get it."

The dealer popped one eyebrow. "What's in it for you?"

"I get to watch Ghost Teague's world fall apart."

Thirty-Five

He woke her at two, hands skimming over her skin in the dark, turning her toward him. "Say goodbye to be properly." A smoky whisper against her throat.

It was a slow, lingering joining, in their married bed. *Lovemaking*, she thought fleetingly, before the pleasure crashed over her. Is that what this was?

He left before dawn and she kissed him on the front porch, clasping onto his shirt as he drew away, not releasing him until the last moment. He called her *love* again and her chest squeezed.

How could she miss him before he was even gone?

By noon, the daily grind had distracted her, so she wasn't a total sappy mess of emotion. Becca was sick, and the extra work kept her running.

At least until lunch, when Walsh called her from a gas station on the Alabama/Mississippi border.

"How'd you sleep after I left?" Walsh's accent was magnified through the phone, for some reason. Deeper and rougher; it made her toes twitch inside her boots.

"Like a baby." She held the phone between her cheek and shoulder while she oiled a bridle. "You know, for a no-account outlaw, you have the softest mattress."

"Hmph."

She laughed. "Well not no-account really. I can account for you."

"When you're not sleeping like a baby."

She grinned to herself. "Are you worried I don't miss you enough?"

"No."

"Are you lying right now?"

"Maybe a little."

It warmed her, inside and out, to hear his voice, to know that he disliked their separation. So many little things other women took for granted, that she'd never had, that Kingston Walsh was giving her.

"I miss you plenty," she said, putting him out of his misery. "How's the trip going?"

"We're making good time. Aidan caught the biggest bug right in the mouth," he said, a laugh teasing at his voice. "It was brilliant."

"Poor Aidan," she said, chuckling. Tonya had already been by that morning, unusually subdued, and Emmie had gotten the impression things between the princess and the biker hadn't ended well last night.

"How's it going there?" he asked. She could hear voices in the background, a bike engine starting, and figured he couldn't talk much longer.

"Fine. Same old same old. Becca's sick, and Fred went to get lunch, so I'm cleaning tack."

There was a pause. "You're there alone?"

"Yes, and I'm fine, Walsh."

An engine revved on his end of the line.

"Do I need to let you go?"

"Uh, yeah, actually. But I'll call again next time we stop. You *be careful*. I'm serious. I don't like you there all alone."

"I know, I know." She heard the low drone of a car engine outside. "Look, I've gotta go, too, that's my next lesson pulling up."

They traded goodbyes – there was a distinct sense of something missing when neither of them said "I love you" – and she slipped the phone into her pocket, put the bridle away, stood.

"Hello," she called as she stepped out into the aisle. "How are you–"

Amy Richards stood in the middle of the barn, mouth set in a firm line beneath her giant sunglasses.

"Amy. Hi." There was a knot in her throat, suddenly, and she swallowed it down. "It's…nice to see you."

"Hello, Emmie." Amy adjusted her sunglasses, probably because they were about to slide off and take her nose with them.

"Um…" Old habits, it turned out, were indeed hard to fight. The part of her that was Emmie Walsh, who lived here, and presided over the place, and who hated what this family had done to her wanted to throw this bitch off the property, call the cops if necessary. But the part of her that had followed Amy like a devoted lap dog cringed at the idea of being rude to her mentor of almost twenty years.

"You've made yourself right at home here, haven't you?" Amy asked coolly. "Living in the house, fucking that biker, running my barn like it's yours."

A bright spark of anger flared to life inside her, and Emmie grabbed onto it. She was no one's lackey anymore, and she was done acting like one. "It is mine. You were all ready to throw it away, have the whole thing bulldozed, and then you want to act like I've taken something from you? I know all about your fiancé's connection to the developers."

Amy stiffened.

"I never did anything but work for you. I took care of your horses, cleaned your tack, groomed for you at shows, handled all your emotional meltdowns, and I did it all with a smile on my face. You know what, Amy? I'm not smiling anymore. What you did to me was awful, and I'm not going to say 'yes, ma'am' and take it anymore.

"And we both know what happened to Davis," she said, taking an aggressive step forward, ramping up. "I loved your dad like a grandfather, and you accuse me of pumping him full of heroin? Killing him? There's only one druggie around here, and it's your worthless son."

"Shut up," Amy hissed through her teeth. "Shut up, bitch."

"Or what? You'll fire me?" Emmie laughed. "No, I've bottled this up for too long. You're selfish, and petty, and you're a user. And Brett is nothing but a complete waste of oxygen. He's offensively useless as a human being." She laughed again, a high giggle. "God that feels good to say. Do you know that? I've been the dog you kicked for so long, but you can't kick me anymore, Amy."

Amy trembled with rage. "You'll wish you hadn't said any of that," she bit out.

Emmie rolled her eyes –

And something struck her in the back of the head. The pain flared white and brilliant.

And then black, and she was falling, falling, falling...

~*~

By the second gas stop of the day, Walsh was reminded that age and distance rides didn't go so well together. Reminded also that the MC life aged you rapidly, made you sore and stiff in ways that desk jobs never did.

He'd never trade it, though. His face had that good, sandblasted feel after too many hours of being pummeled by wind; his body quivered with subtle vibrations, even though he was off the bike, and he could taste the grit in his teeth. That's what freedom tasted like: dirt and asphalt.

"Oh my God," Carter said, resting his forearms on the seat of his bike and leaning forward to stretch out his back.

"You're ten-years-old," RJ told him. "Don't be a puss."

"It's those handlebars," Aidan said. "What were you thinking with the apehangers? Your arms'll fall right off going distance with that shit."

"I know that now," Carter groaned.

Tango patted him on top of the head as he walked past, and earned chuckles for it. "I need something to drink. Anybody else want anything?"

"I'll go in with you," Aidan said. "I gotta take a leak."

"Be in in a minute," Walsh said, digging his phone out of his pocket.

He had seven missed calls, all from the same number. Fred.

"*Señor*," the man gasped when he answered the return call. "I tried to reach you."

"What's wrong, Fred?" An awful prickling tingled across his skin. She'd been alone, she said. All alone...

313

"Emmie. She's gone. Her truck is here, but she is not. She's gone, and I tried to call her, and she won't answer. I went into the house, and she's not there. She's gone, and she left the beeswax out, and her drink is warm where she left it in the tack room, and there's blood..." He was babbling, but it made all too much sense to Walsh.

"Wait. Slow down. There's blood? Where is there blood?"

"On the floor. Not much blood, but it's blood, and she's gone!"

Walsh's gut doubled up on itself. His breath jammed up in his throat. He tried to sound calm though. "Okay, Fred, listen to me. I want you to think, really think. Is there anywhere she might have gone on foot? Did that bloody horse jump the fence again and she went after him?"

"No, Tally is here–"

Beep.

"Hold on, Fred, that's my call waiting. It's probably her."

He swapped the line over. "Em?"

A masculine voice he didn't recognize flooded his ear. "Kingston Walsh."

"Yeah, that's me," he snapped. "What–"

"I have something that belongs to you. Something I'm guessing you want back." Low, rough voice, very deep. "If you want to see your wife again, you need to follow my instructions."

Time stretched. The moment expanded, until it filled every corner of his mind, halted his breathing, drained all the blood from his head. He saw the boys coming out of the convenience store with bags full of sodas and chips, heard the flow of traffic on the street behind him.

He must have been making some kind of face, because Aidan frowned and said, "Hey, what's wrong?"

There was no label for the terror and fury that welled inside him. He didn't recognize his own voice when he said, "Who the bloody fucking hell is this?"

"You'll find out. Wait for my text, and we'll make arrangements."

The line went dead.

"What?" Aidan repeated.

Walsh swallowed. God, he couldn't breathe. "We have to go back."

Tango and Carter crowded in around him.

"Walsh, dude…" Aidan said, reaching toward him.

"Someone took Emmie." His voice seemed to be coming from a long way away. "We have to go back."

Thirty-Six

More than halfway to Texas and back, and he didn't feel the miles, didn't feel the hunger, didn't feel the exhaustion. Littlejohn had been driving the truck behind them, and he'd called ahead to let everyone know. The clubhouse blazed with light. Dawn was coming up, dovetail gray hanging over the river. It should have been a relief to be back home, but it felt like a start. Like the hours on the road had been nothing but a stall-out, and only now could he start *doing something*.

Someone had Emmie. Her name was a chant in his head. He imagined every horrid possibility, felt her fear, screamed inwardly because he couldn't reach her fast enough.

Ghost walked out of the clubhouse to meet them, and the sight of his president grounded him. He could do nothing for his girl if he was this frantic.

Deep breath. Focus. Get her back, solve the problem. Be the Money Man, and everything would work out, because he was bloody good at his job.

"Have we had second contact yet?" Ghost asked as he reached the bike.

Walsh swung off and pulled out his phone. "Yeah. Text came in a couple hours ago. Wants to meet at three this afternoon." He tilted the phone so his boss could read the address.

"Right. I assume we're not waiting for that." He gave Walsh a level look, one that was just man-to-man, and not president-to-VP. "This is your old lady, and it's your call, VP. What do you wanna do?"

"I want Ratchet to find out where Brett Richards lives."

~*~

The relentless, throbbing pain in the back of her skull woke her, finally. Opening her eyes proved difficult, but she managed to pry the lids up by sheer dint of will. Panic coiled tight around her throat, and her instinctual need for safety propelled her out of the dark, into a state of pained, chaotic awareness.

She lay on her side, hands bound behind her, feet secured together. She was on the floor, cheap carpet scratching at her cheek as she tried to tip her head back. She smelled pot smoke and musty gym clothes, and when she caught sight of the two people standing a few feet away, she realized where she must be: Brett's apartment.

"...that wasn't what we talked about," Amy snapped, arms crossing like armored bands across her chest. She stood with shoulders squared and one hip cocked, feet propped at fighting angles. The anger hummed off her, carried through the carpet.

Brett took a long drag off a cigarette and scowled at his mother. "Don't worry about it, Mom."

Amy leaned toward him, tone vicious. "I said we could do this, but only when I thought it was just us. You can't just invite people into our business, Brett! What if they go to the cops? What if they rat us out?"

"They won't go to the cops, they're drug dealers," he sneered. "God. You're so stupid."

"Don't you dare—"

"It wasn't my idea anyway. Grey asked where I got the H, and it was his idea to get Ellison involved. He said they'd take us more seriously if Don was backing us."

"Ransom is one thing, but the dealers—"

"Oh my God!" he groaned. "Stupid, *stupid*. Ellison gave the Gannons the loan they needed to get started. Do you not know that, dumb bitch? Your man belongs to the dealers. All of us do!"

"Don't call me that." Her voice shook.

"Then quit being one!"

Damn. And Emmie thought *she* had family problems.

Her head was pounding, so she closed her eyes and tried to make sense of it. So they were trying to ransom her, no doubt so the Dogs would sell the farm to the Gannon brothers. And Agent Grey was in on it? Should have figured – the boys hadn't been kidding when they said the guy was completely nutso at this point. And then there was someone named Ellison. A drug dealer?

God, her head hurt.

Sound of a door opening, footsteps coming in.

Emmie opened her eyes again and fear rallied in her bloodstream as she saw the fake Detective Hanson, the real and former Agent Grey.

"Don's people are on the way. She's secure?"

Amy turned a flashing glare on him. "You didn't tell me we were giving her to someone else."

*Oh God, oh God…*Being held captive by Amy and Brett was more pathetic than scary. But someone else? Someone she couldn't guilt and use time and past history against?

"It'll be better this way, trust me," Grey said. Then his gaze came straight to Emmie. "She's awake? See, this is why I can't trust you people," he grumbled, pushing between mother and son and coming toward her.

"Don't worry, sweetheart," he said, grinning as he crouched down in front of her. "I'm sure they won't hurt you much."

"Can't say the same for you," she retorted. "Not when Walsh gets hold of you."

"Oh, honey. It's cute you think that. He was only ever after your silence. The pussy was just a door prize." He grinned again and shoved a handkerchief into her mouth, turning her next insult into a muffled grunt.

A loud knock sounded on the door and Grey stood. "Get that," he told Brett.

He complied, letting in two colossal thugs in black tees and jeans, heavy combat boots, with matching bored expressions. There was a woman with them, a tall, pretty black woman similarly dressed, but with a crisp blazer over her shirt, and spike heels. Her eyes zeroed in on Emmie.

"This is her?"

"Emmaline Walsh, all ready for transfer," Grey said.

"Good." The woman gestured to the thugs and one stepped forward, coming toward her.

Emmie bit down hard on the handkerchief and fought the urge to scream. It wasn't supposed to go like this! It was the Richards family who hated her, who wanted the farm. Drug dealers with meatnecked henchmen had never been part of the picture.

The man took her by the arm with one giant paw-like hand and dragged her upright, caught her around the waist with one arm and threw her over his shoulder like so many potatoes. She landed on the unforgiving flat of his shoulder and it forced the air from her lungs.

No, a voice in the back of her head shouted. *No! No!*

Thoughts of the farm, her horse, Becca and Fred filled her mind, brought tears to her eyes. She thought of Walsh, of his gentle hands and his rough, accented voice. Where was he now? In Texas? Partying it up with his club brothers there? No one knew she'd been taken, no one knew where she was.

"Hey," Brett said as she was being toted out the door. "What about my money?"

"Excuse me?" the woman asked him, coolly.

"My money." He had that indignant, spoiled brat lift to his voice. "I did the work for you, I got her here, and if I don't get to ransom her, then I should at least get paid for it."

"No," the woman told him.

"What do you mean 'no'?" Brett demanded. "This ain't charity! I ain't doing Don's work for free!"

The woman sighed – Emmie couldn't see it, but she could hear the sound, and imagine the expression that went along with it. "The answer is no. Don't make a big deal about it."

"Fuck you!" Brett shouted.

Emmie heard a scuffle, a grunt. The woman said, "Don't touch me."

"Bitch!" That was Brett.

Then there was a gunshot.

Emmie stared down at the carpet as her captor held her, helpless, gasping against the cloth in her mouth, shivering, as she listened to the shot echo in the small apartment. Listened to Amy's awful shrill scream.

"You shot him! You shot him!"

She heard Brett's body hit the floor.

And she could do nothing but pray, as she was carried out into the hall, and toward new terrors.

~*~

"This one," Ratchet said as they drew up to the door of number fourteen.

Walsh glanced up and then down the long hallway, saw that it was clear, and gave Mercy The Nod. The single gesture that unleashed major chaos.

The big Cajun grinned hugely, hefted his sledgehammer in a two-handed grip, and went through the door into Brett Richards' apartment.

Or, rather, he used the sledge and all his body weight as a battering ram, knocked the lock through the doorframe hot-knife-through-butter style, and the door swung back on its hinges and buried itself in the inner wall, sheetrock dust flying.

Merc didn't hesitate, but kept going, momentum propelling him forward into the apartment, the rest of them crowding in behind him, guns raised. It was a tactic that shocked and terrified, and it always worked.

When whoever they were trying to shock and terrify was alive.

"Oh, Jesus!"

"Damn!"

"Shit!"

"What the fuck?!"

They tripped and staggered over Brett Richards' sightless corpse where it lay sprawled just inside the entryway. Mercy executed a leap that got him clear, but he tracked blood onto the cheap cream carpet. Aidan slipped in the stuff and almost went down, grabbing at the back of Tango's shirt, the wall.

"Merc, clear the rooms," Walsh barked, and leaned over to inspect the body.

He'd been shot in the head, nice and clean in the forehead, a bloody buggering mess in the back, where bone and brain matter had blasted the wall in a sick collage.

A fleeting hope touched his mind. Had this been Emmie? Had she shot him and escaped? The girl was a great shot –

"Walsh!" Mercy bellowed from deeper in the apartment. "It's Grey! He went down the fire escape and he's going for his car. He's got a woman with him!"

"Come on," Walsh told the others, and he heard them follow him, feet pounding as they left the apartment, went down the hall, the stairs, hit the emergency exit.

Mercy was already there, sprinting across the lot when they reached it; he'd taken the fire escape, same as Grey. But they were all too late, the black SUV turning out onto the street with a sharp squeal of tires.

Walsh pitched forward at the waist, braced his hands on his knees and tried to draw in a deep breath. "Was it Em?" he asked, gulping air. "The woman he had, was it her?"

"No." Mercy was slightly less winded, but not by much. He rubbed at his bum knee with a grimace. "It was a brunette."

Walsh's neck went limp; he let his head hang. "Brett's mother, then. Amy Richards."

"Jesus, what the hell's going on?" Aidan muttered.

The wail of sirens began as a low sound, and swelled.

"Someone called the cops when they heard Brett get shot," Tango said. "We need to move."

~*~

Vince knew the security cameras clocked him approaching the Lean Dogs' clubhouse, so he was prepared to walk into one of them the moment he crossed the threshold. Ghost met him in the foyer, blocking the way with his body. Voices echoed around in the common room behind him, the energy urgent and restless in the clipped tones and muffled murmurs of the conversation.

The president's face was harsh with impatience, and he lacked all his normal cop-bothering swagger. "What?"

"Brett Richards is dead." Vince didn't feel like playing attitude games either. Then again, he never did. "Murdered. He spray paints the front of your barn, he turns up dead. That brings me here."

"If you know who killed him, we'd love to know, because whoever it is has Emmie Walsh and is holding her for ransom."

Okay, he hadn't been expecting *that*. "How – how do you know? They made contact?"

"No shit." Ghost snorted. "They want Walsh to meet them at three. The boys went by Brett's place and saw Harlan Grey fleeing the scene, Amy Richards with him."

"She's an accomplice?" His blood pressure was sky rocketing and he rubbed at the back of his neck, unable to ease the sharp prickling of unease.

"Or a hostage."

"Damn," he murmured.

"Where would Grey take someone?"

"I have no idea. I've never dealt with anyone like him."

"No psychotic asshole pricks in your life?"

"Only you."

Ghost twitched a humorless smirk. "This is bigger than you and me and our bullshit right now."

"Yeah." Vince nodded. "I can put an APB out on Grey, but it's a long shot. Hold on."

He unclipped the radio from his lapel and put the order in with dispatch, while Ghost watched and rolled his eyes.

When he was done, he frowned and said, "What about Emmie? What can you tell me about her kidnappers?"

"We've got nothing, which means our meetup has to go well, which means we don't need your boys crashing the party and scaring these guys off."

"I need to listen to the voicemail, read the text, whatever. I need a statement from Walsh. I have to go through the proper channels, so it's above board," he said stubbornly. If he was going to bust someone for a kidnapping, he wanted the charges to stick, not be thrown out because of shoddy detective work.

"No," Ghost said. "You do things your way, we'll do things ours."

"Ghost, I can help you find her."

"And do what with the people who have her? Arrest them?" he sneered. "Nah. We're good."

Vince opened his mouth to argue further-

His radio squawked to life. *"Sergeant Fielding, I've got reports of a vehicle matching your description and plate number, traveling south on 129, doing eighty-five. Officers in pursuit. Do you read? Over."*

Ghost perked up.

"Tell them to follow, but hold back," Vince said. "I'm on the way. Over."

"I'm coming with you," Ghost said.

"Like hell…"

"My VP doesn't have time to wait on the wheels of justice," Ghost barked. "That asshole knows where Emmie is, and I'm getting the intel out of him, one way or another."

~*~

Vince kept in contact with his officers as he drove to rendezvous with them. About a half mile from their last given position, they radioed to tell him they'd run up on a massive accident, six cars piled up, one vehicle aflame. They had to stop, clear the road, radio in for fire rescue, control traffic.

"I'll pursue," he said, "and radio in if I need backup. You take care of that accident. Over."

"Understood."

At the next red light, he caught up to Grey, picking the guy's black Explorer out of the lineup of other vehicles, subtly pulling in two cars behind him and following.

All the while, Ghost stayed within sight in the rearview mirror. The bastard.

Grey went nearly five miles, turning again and again, getting into a rural part of town, finally turning onto a hard-to-spot gravel drive and disappearing behind a screen of trees.

Vince gave the guy a head start, then put the cruiser in gear again, heading up the driveway. The way was narrow, oak and maple branches slapping at his windshield. One nearly took off his radio antennae.

Tension coiled tighter and tighter in Vince's gut, until he was breathless when the drive dumped him onto a gravel parking pad outside a ramshackle clapboard house. The black Explorer was parked in front of it.

When he killed the engine and popped his door open, the drone of bees filled his ears, and a sense of finality washed over him. Something was happening in this moment. Something big. But something he couldn't walk away from.

The Harley hadn't arrived yet, and he wasn't going to wait for it, instead drew his weapon and crept up to the sagging porch, tip-toed up the steps and peeked in the windows.

Amy Richards sat, unbound, in a chair in the center of a room walled in rough-hewn planks, surrounded by hunting trophies and cracked leather furniture. Grey paced behind her chair, talking into his cellphone, rubbing at his forehead like it pained him.

Vince tested the doorknob and found it unlocked. Slipped inside, gun raised.

Grey spun to face him, startled. He dropped the phone to the floor – it clattered on the boards – and made a reach for his hip, toward the gun he must have at his waistband.

"No," Vince said firmly, gliding deeper into the room, gun leveled on the man's chest. "Harlan, just no. Take a step back and think about where you are, what you're doing. You don't want to shoot me."

Grey's fingers twitched and he stared at Vince a long moment. His face was slack with exhaustion, deeply grooved with stress, eyes glassy and feverish. His expression alone indicated that he'd gone off the deep end…and cracked against the bottom of the pool. Vince had seen suspects like this before: running on fumes, possessed of a hair trigger. One wrong move, one thoughtless word, and the powder keg would blow.

"I just want to talk," Vince said calmly. "Okay?" Just you and me."

"Now?" Grey sneered. "*Now* you wanna talk?"

"I talked to you before, didn't I? I listened to you, looked at your photos. But you know there was nothing I could do with them. You weren't on the case, and I can't take ill-gotten evidence and get a warrant with that."

Grey made a face and began to pace again, behind Amy's chair. His hands stayed loose at his sides, though, gun forgotten for the moment.

Amy lifted pleading eyes to Vince, and he pressed his finger to his lips, told her to keep quiet.

"Like you're so squeaky clean," Grey said, pivoting and pacing the other direction. "You know you let stuff slide with those Dogs. Don't deny it." A sharp glance dared him to. "So what's wrong with sliding back the other direction a little? Turning the screws on them."

"Because that's not how I operate."

"Bullshit. That's how everyone operates. If we all did everything by the book – if we all had some sort of...personal code...we'd never lock anyone up. You're dealing with career criminals, sergeant," he said, coming to a halt and glaring full-on at Vince. "Lock them the fuck up, for God's sakes, in any way you can."

"Even if that involves kidnapping innocent women?"

"I didn't kid–"

"What do you call this?" Vince asked, gesturing to Amy. The woman quivered head to toe, her face streaked with mascara and shiny trails where her tears had cut through her makeup.

"I call it leverage," Grey snapped. "That thing you won't utilize."

"Where's Emmie Walsh?"

"She's wherever biker sluts go. Somewhere you'll never find her," he said with a snort.

"Someone's trying to ransom her from the Dogs. Who's helping you?"

"*Him* helping *me?* Ha! That's rich. I just invited him on board, and he took the wheel. This is his show now, not mine."

"Whose?" Vince insisted. "Who's stupid and ballsy enough to try and manipulate the Dogs?"

"Someone way above your paygrade," Grey said smugly.

Vince clenched his jaw tight, teeth gritting together…and then an idea struck. It had always been an ego game with this man. What better way to get him talking than to belittle his influence, and appeal to his crazy.

"You think? Because what I think is that you're running this whole little game by yourself, because you don't have a friend in the world."

Grey's satisfied smile froze. Slipped.

"I think you stashed Emmie somewhere, and you invented some powerful boogeyman just to spook the Dogs. Because you know that you yourself couldn't spook a kitten."

Grey snarled, actually *snarled* like an angry canine. "You stupid son of a bitch! You think I don't have contacts? You think I can't get shit done? It's Ellison. Don Ellison, that's who has the little bitch."

Don Ellison. He filed it away. And since it was the only bit of info he needed, it was time to wrap this party up.

"I believe you," he said. "I do. Why don't you come back to the precinct with me and you can tell me all about him. You can be the hero in this one, Harlan. You can help us get Emmie back, and who knows, maybe the Bureau will—"

A floorboard creaked, back behind Grey, in the hall that led to the bedrooms.

Ghost materialized from the shadows, giving credence to his club name, the dark breaking over him and falling away, revealing him standing with gun in hand, gaze dark, flat, and shark-like where it rested on the disgraced agent.

Grey spun toward him, and the breath exploded out of his lungs in a sound that was both gasp and growl. "Him!" he yelled. He turned back to Vince, face flushing crimson. "You're here with *him*? You *asshole!*"

"Harlan, Harlan, calm down," Vince said, making a staying motion with one hand, gun trained with the other. "I'm not here with anyone. He just followed me here." He shot Ghost a pleading look.

Which the Lean Dogs president blatantly ignored. "He gave you a name?"

Vince sighed. "Yeah."

Grey started pacing again, movements jerky, breath sawing erratically through his open mouth. "All your shit about the rules," he raved, "and you're in that bastard's pocket! You're not righteous, you're in the MC's corner!"

Amy Richards cringed, curling in on herself, covering her ears with her hands as Grey's shouting grew louder.

"I'm in nobody's pocket!" Vince shouted back. "Look, just calm down–"

Grey let out an animal roar, and reached for his waist, for his gun.

Ghost took three aggressive steps into the room.

Amy screamed and jumped to her feet, fleeing.

Vince tuned all of it out, and his training took over. Grey's gun was out, and it was turning toward him.

It was all a blur, this fast tangle of movement and sound in the dim cabin, floor cartwheeling with dancing leaf shadows from beyond the windows.

Vince fired, and two bodies went down, instead of one.

Amy Richards fell facedown, boneless, unable to catch herself as she hit the floor with a sick thud.

Grey went down backward, yelling, blood blooming on his shirt down low, too low, not a direct kill.

Vince dropped to his knees and grabbed Amy by the shoulders, turned her over. "Amy. Shit, Amy, can you hear me?"

Her eyes darted across his face; her lips worked, blood spilling from the corners of her mouth, trailing across her tear-stained face. She gasped, and she tried to speak, but it was only a wheezing, whining sound. A hiss of air.

327

"Amy...oh, shit, oh shit, oh shit...

Pulse thrumming in his ears, skin electric with dread and shock, he reached for his radio –

But she was gone, already slipping, slipping...silent.

Her eyes froze, pinned to his face, wild and sightless.

Dead.

Vince couldn't move, couldn't speak, couldn't think, couldn't breathe.

Another gunshot sounded. *CRACK.*

Vince jumped, gasping, air raking his throat as it funneled down to his lungs.

Ghost stood over Grey, who was now very still, gun trained on the man's chest. With total calm, utter control, Ghost looked at him and said, "Do you have backup on the way?"

"B-b-backup?"

"Yeah, backup. Are there other officers on the way? Did you call for help?"

Had he? Had he... "No," he mumbled. He sucked in another breath. "Oh Jesus, I killed her."

"Yeah, you did." Ghost stowed his gun away. "And unless you want to lose your badge for it, you're going to do exactly what I tell you to."

He was too stunned to do anything but nod.

"You're going to come back to the clubhouse with me, and I'm going to get a cleanup crew in here."

Another nod.

"Come on. I got you."

And with nothing else to do, he let the man pull him up to his feet.

Thirty-Seven

"This has to be a first," Walsh said.

Sergeant Fielding accepted a mug of coffee from Dublin, but didn't acknowledge the man, or the beverage, holding it in both hands and staring off into space.

"For us, and for poor old Vinnie," Ghost said, taking a swig of his own heavily-liquored coffee. As they heard the door of the clubhouse open, he lifted his brows and said, "And he's about to have another first."

Shaman entered with graceful, superior drama, shoulders back, head lifted proudly, wearing yet another bespoke suit and designer shoes. His muscle, Bruce, came hulking in behind, a wall of beat-your-ass trailing his boss.

"Gentlemen," he greeted, grinning wickedly. "So nice to see you again so soon. I came as quickly as I could. Always happy to ride to the rescue."

"Just…can it, alright?" Ghost said. "I ain't got time for you to gloat, Mary Poppins."

Undeterred, the Englishman glided toward them. "Oh, but I want to, my friend. It's not every day I can claim I've handed out a favor to the surpassingly capable Ghost Teague."

Ghost sighed and rubbed at his eyes, pinched the bridge of his nose. "Shit. This is a bad idea."

"It's our only idea," Walsh reminded. And there was a clock inside his chest, tick-tick-ticking away, counting the time that Emmie had, fretting away the minutes that they couldn't find her.

Shaman drew up to the bar and braced an elbow against it, struck a model pose with hair tossed behind his shoulders. "This is the favor, I'm assuming." He looked between the two of them. "Yes?"

Ghost nodded. "Yeah. We need to know everything you can tell us about Don Ellison. Where he'd keep a hostage, for instance."

Shaman's brows went all the way up his high, aristocratic forehead. "Hostage?"

"He has my wife," Walsh said, and it was hard to swallow afterward.

"Ah." He nodded gravely. "I see." He inclined his head toward the sofa where Fielding was still doing a killer impression of a mannequin. "And we're talking about this in front of our friend in blue?"

"He's got his own shit to worry about," Ghost said.

"Very well. Bring me a cuppa and I'll tell you all I know." He gestured to Bruce and pulled out a chair at one of the tables, sat. The bodyguard moved in behind the chair and planted himself there.

Dublin went for the coffee and Walsh went to sit beside his countryman, as always struck by the stark differences between them. Shaman, whoever he'd been before he'd become Tennessee's premiere outlaw, had been born in Mayfair, or thereabouts. One of the wealthy districts, where parents bought their children braces, knee socks, short pants and new Jags.

Ghost joined them, then Ratchet, laptop at the ready. Dublin brought the coffee and a little pitcher of milk.

Tango wasn't here, thankfully, off handling Fielding's mess with Aidan, Rottie, Mercy, and the "kids," as they called the three newest members.

"Don Ellison used to work for me," Shaman began airily. "He was just a thug, really, straight out of prison. But he was a persuasive salesman." He sipped his coffee. "A little too persuasive, at times. He had a penchant for kneecaps, and he ran off as many customers as he gained. In the end, he became too insubordinate, and I let him go."

"Yeah, I bet," Ghost said. "You just fire people, and that's it."

"There are parting conditions, of course." He shrugged. "But more or less, yes, I let him go. He went to west Tennessee, and I kept the east. Along with my other areas of interest."

"Where is he now?" Walsh asked.

"Nashville, principally. Though I'm sure he has safe houses scattered at satellite intervals."

It felt huge and impossible to Walsh. Too much ground to cover, too many unknowns, too little time to find her.

He'd promised her she wouldn't get hurt, and now…

"I can find where they're keeping her, of course," Shaman said.

Walsh leaned back in his chair. He and Ghost said, "What?" at the same time.

"I can find her," Shaman repeated, sipping his coffee. "I'm not sending my people in – that would be in poor taste. But I can locate her. That will of course constitute the aforementioned favor. After which, you will owe me."

Walsh locked eyes with his president, wondering.

Ghost tipped his head in silent communication. *This is on your head*, he said. *If this goes badly*. But there was love, trust, and sympathy in his gaze too.

"Fine," Ghost said with a deep exhale. "We owe you one. Just find her."

Shaman nodded, his smile pleased. "There's something else you ought to know about Ellison. He's in the business of funding companies that appear very legitimate, and for the most part are, excluding their initial capital."

"Such as?"

"Gannon & Gannon Developers, for instance."

"Are you shitting me?" Walsh asked, startled.

"I'm afraid not, friend." Shaman loved this, was delighted and completely in his element. "It's not merely homebuilders trying to move into your city, boys. There's another turf war brewing, and you're one of the chief players, whether you know it or not."

~*~

"So let me get this straight," Mercy said in the passenger seat. "Ellison backs the developers. Amy is set to marry one of the developers. Ellison sells H to the kid. When the old man

331

wouldn't sell the farm to them, mother and son planned to kill the old man, and have Amy and her siblings sell to the developers."

"Right so far," Walsh said, hand white-knuckled on the wheel. He didn't have the patience for this conversation. For driving, at this point.

"When they couldn't pin it on you or Em, they decided the best thing was to kidnap her. How am I doing?"

"You're right." He sighed. "Christ, it's all a mess. There are no bloody coincidences, are there?"

"Not in my experience."

Shaman's trackers made Hound and Rottie look like kids with magnifying glasses playing Sherlock Holmes. They'd pinned down a location within an hour. A new safe house, they'd said, on the outskirts of Knoxville, and a prime spot to keep Emmie. So that's where they were headed. Ghost would handle the three o'clock meeting. He had a plan for that.

"Walsh," Mercy said beside him. "We're gonna get her back, man. You know that."

He hoped it. But all he knew now was that he was slowly being torn in two, and he wouldn't be able to breathe again until she was in front of him, unharmed.

~*~

The house they'd brought her to was cheaply furnished, but at least she was sitting on a bed and not the floor. Although the mattress beneath her left her panicky about the ideas her captors might dream up to occupy their time.

The bedroom where they held her was narrow and windowless, more of a closet, really, and it smelled like there was mold somewhere behind the wallboard. Her wrists were bound in front of her with duct tape, and they'd taken her shoes, presumably to make her less likely to kick the walls or try and make a break for it on foot. Not that making a break was an option – one man stood right outside her door, the other watching TV somewhere, judging by the low drone of canned applause.

A laugh bubbled up in her throat and she swallowed it with a struggle. It was absurd, to think she was being held hostage. Terrifying, awful, pulse-pounding – and yes, absurd.

If she'd packed up Apollo and left Briar Hall, she would have found some other farm, made a new start, never been hit on the back of the head and taken.

And she'd still be alone.

And she wouldn't have Walsh.

The trade-off. There was one in all things in life, some were just a lot more life-threatening than others.

"What time is it?" the guy outside her door called to the other one.

"One-fifty," his friend hollered back.

Emmie shifted on the bed, leaning from one hip to the other. The bed frame squealed loudly at the slightest movement, and it protested as she resettled.

The thug outside shoved his head through the open door. "What are you doing in here?" He had one of those heavy, Cro-Magnon brow ridges that made him look like he was scowling. When he frowned, like now, the effect was magnified.

She pressed her head back against the wall, chin lifted. She was determined not to let these people see her shivering. "Nothing."

He stared at her a moment, dull eyes sharpening suddenly. "You bored?"

A sensation like fingertips moved across the back of her neck. "No. I'm fine."

He pivoted around the doorframe and stepped fully inside, his bulk filling up the jambs. He was nearly as tall as Mercy, but thicker all over, his face jowly. His gaze swept downward from her face, lingering on parts of her body she suddenly wished weren't so noticeable. She was dressed in a white tank and tan breeches, neither of which left much to the imagination.

"Nah, you gotta be bored by now," he said with a grin that turned her stomach over. He approached the bed. "I can think of something for you to do, sweetheart."

Emmie pulled her knees up as far as she could, given her hands were in the way, shrinking back against the wall.

He braced one knee on the bed, and the mattress dipped, springs squeaking horribly. When he reached for her, she ducked away, falling onto her side and tucking into herself.

He laughed, and she heard the jangling of his belt as he unfastened it. "What's a matter? You scared? You ain't never seen anyone hung like me, have ya, honey? You're married to that little guy they got." He laughed again, and she wanted to gag.

"It won't hurt," he said. "Much." The mattress bucked as he climbed onto it, springs shrieking like crazy.

Will it hurt, Emmie thought, *when I kick the shit out of you?*

The thing this man didn't understand about her, was that beneath her quaking fear, her violent disgust, her despair and panic – she was a woman who'd been raised with horses, and she'd put bigger animals than him on their knees. Figuratively. For him, she was going to make it literal.

He moved up over her, braced on his arms. "Let's see that pretty face."

"Al, what you doing?" his friend called from wherever the TV was.

The man on top of her ignored the question, and took her by the wrists with one huge hand, turned her onto her back, so she was facing him.

Emmie was compliant, holding still, letting him manipulate her into the right position.

He'd pulled his cock out, and it was standing tall.

She kicked it as hard as she could, with both feet.

~*~

The house was small, trimmed in brown siding and flanked by overgrown trees, one of dozens like it on a crowded, residential street. Corner lot, more conspicuous. But not impossible to approach. Michael clocked one guard in the front lawn, sitting in a chair beneath one of the trees, trying to look like he was reading the paper, plainclothes dress.

Michael slid his sunglasses into place. Pulled his hat down low. Adjusted the empty pizza box on one flattened palm, and headed up the front walk. The direct way was usually the best way, because no one ever anticipated it. And in this case, the trees were dense enough to keep the neighbors from seeing much of anything. Privacy for the thugs meant privacy for them, too.

He was almost to the door when the guy in the chair surged to his feet. "Hey, what are you doing?"

He paused and half-turned, letting the guard approach. He knew once the guy got within range, he'd realize that Michael was shit at feigning emotion, and that he in fact wasn't a pizza delivery guy.

"Pizza," he said, lifting the box for emphasis. "Pepperoni and mushroom."

The man's thick brow creased. "We didn't order a pizza."

"That's what it says on the receipt – 4357 Windham, right?"

He came closer. Closer. "Nah, we didn't–"

Michael tossed the empty box at his face. Startled, the guard grabbed for it, eyes closing out of instinct as he fumbled.

Michael caught him in the belly with the Taser. The man let out a strangled sound, stiffened, and went down like a felled tree.

No casualties, Ghost had said. Just restrain them, get the girl, and get the hell out, no reason to rile Ellison beyond repair. A war was the last thing any of them needed.

The guy was still twitching and Michael was moving quickly, pulling the duct tape from his back pocket, tearing off a strip.

Behind him, the squeal of tires pulling up at the curb snatched his attention. Reinforcements, and not his.

"Shit."

~*~

"This is a lot less fun than it could be," Mercy complained as he secured the two backdoor guards with duct tape. Their legs still twitched with spasms from the Taser.

"Yeah, well, we don't need another war in Knoxville." Though honestly, that was the last of Walsh's worries at the moment. If one of these guys gave him a reason to, he'd put a bullet in him. He was feeling a lot like his Cajun companion at the moment – it would have been fun to spill a little blood.

He reached into one thug's pockets and found the house key. "Here we go."

"I don't hear anything up front, so Michael must have handled things," Mercy said.

Walsh slid the key into the deadbolt.

And gunshots sounded from the other side of the house.

~*~

It didn't matter how big and strong a man was, you kicked him right in the cock, and he was going to fall to pieces, simple as that. The man on top of Emmie howled and collapsed onto her; his weight forced the air from her lungs.

She gasped for breath, turned her head, and bit his ear. Sank her teeth as deep and hard as she could.

He bellowed and rolled off her, landing on the floor with a tremendous *thump* that shook the bed.

Emmie sat up, scrambled toward the foot of the bed on her knees. There was another one waiting for her out in the living room, but it gave her some small measure of hope to get past this one. To –

He backhanded her across the face. One moment he was moaning on the floor, and the next he'd staggered to his feet. His knuckles bit into the soft flesh of her cheek and the blow sent her sprawling back across the mattress. Her vision clouded with white lace, and pain shot through skin, flesh, bone, hitting her in the brain.

"Fucking bitch," he snarled. "I'm gonna make you hurt for that."

Emmie closed her eyes and rolled to the side, landing hard on her knees on the carpet, the jolt snapping her teeth together.

He grabbed the back of her shirt and hauled her back, ripping the thin cotton of her tank top at the seams with rending pops.

Never stop fighting. She'd heard that once on some self-defense PSA. Never stop fighting back against your attacker. She believed that wholeheartedly...but no amount of belief was going to ensure that this huge man didn't beat her senseless and rape her. Because in truth, she was small, and she only had so much strength, and her hands were bound together. And eventually, he was going to succeed, and pin her down, and violate her body.

But she wasn't going to make it easy for him.

She curled in on herself, knees drawn up tight to her chest, total dead weight as he dragged her back onto the bed by her shirt, shredding it completely down both sides so it was only a scrap of cloth hanging over her breasts.

"Bitch," he kept saying to her. "Stupid fucking bitch."

He hit her again, on the side of the head, and her skull filled with the pealing of bells.

"What the hell are you doing?" the other man asked from the door, and Emmie squeezed her eyes shut against the pain, and the fear that they would both try to take a turn with her.

Oh God, please...no...

Gunshots.

She held her breath. The man above her froze, fingers loosening their death grip on the back of her shirt.

"What?" the other one asked.

No, she wasn't imagining it – those were gunshots!

An image of Walsh filled her mind, and she was afraid to let herself hope.

The man let go of her and he and his companion hurried from the room. Only a second later, she heard a sharp crack, like wood splitting. Angry shouts.

"Drop your weapons!" someone roared.

A gunshot.

Another.

Emmie clambered off the bed and staggered toward the door, floor seeming to tilt beneath her feet.

She heard thundering footsteps, the clomp of heavy boots.

"Merc!" someone yelled.

"On it!" someone yelled back, and that Cajun accent was unmistakable.

Then another accent reached her ears, this one heaven-sent. It glazed her eyes with tears and kicked her heart into a gallop.

"Em? Emmie!" There was only one British man who would call her name with such panic and emotion, and she tried her best to get to him, fighting the dizziness, moving down the hall.

"I'm here!" she shouted back.

There were sounds, so many fleshy, grunting, fighting sounds. Noises that would normally have filled her with terror. Horses kicking at one another sounded a whole lot like men beating each other to a pulp, she reflected, and both were terrifying prospects. But right now, that racket was her salvation.

"Walsh!"

And there he was, in front of her, gun in one hand, grey sweatshirt dotted with blood. Eyes pale and frantic.

The most beautiful thing she'd ever seen.

"Jesus," he breathed, snatching her into his arms, crushing her against his chest. "You okay? You hurt?"

"No, I'm fine." She took her first deep, rattling breath since the whole ordeal had started. "I'm fine."

Thirty-Eight

Ghost stood slouched back against the door of his favorite club truck, the '99 Ford, smoking and counting the pigeons that swooped down to peck up the bread crumbs a group of children were spreading. Rats with wings, but the kids giggled and shrieked with happy laughter at the sight of them bobbing and cooing.

He'd brought Aidan to this same park, when he was just a little scrawny thing, in the dark time after Olivia had left and before Maggie had come along. He'd had no idea how to be a father to a small child. A teenager he could have bought bike parts and taken to the races. A small, sensitive boy he'd had no tools to handle, and so they'd come to the park a lot. Aidan had always wanted to feed the birds, tossing handfuls of Ritz crumbs at them and laughing, the sun glinting off his glossy dark curls.

Ghost had sat on a bench, smoked, and felt useless. It was Maggie who'd thought to teach Aidan how to fly a kite, to make paper boats they pushed out onto the pond. Maggie who'd sat cross-legged on the sidewalks and drawn chalk pictures with him. Who'd thought to pack sandwiches, sodas and a blanket and have lunch in the shade of a tree, counting ants and talking about the airplanes that glided overhead.

When he started bringing Maggie around the club, his brothers had laughed and peppered him with lewd comments; they'd thought she was a juicy little piece of jailbait to him. They hadn't seen her with Aidan, hadn't realized, as he had, that there was a wealth of thunder lying quiet inside that girl. She'd stood on the cusp of a womanhood fit to bring men to their knees. They hadn't seen the queen buried just beneath her skin.

They saw it now. Everyone saw it.

He thought he heard faint echoes of that thunder in Walsh's Emmie, not as strong as Ava's, but there all the same. And so he stood against his truck, and smoked, and waited, as a long black Mercedes rolled down the park driveway and cruised to a stop alongside him.

The man who climbed from the passenger seat looked like a day laborer stuffed in a suit that badly needed tailoring. If Shaman was clever, deft, charming, and wicked, this man was blunt, obvious, and dull. Didn't mean he wasn't an effective enemy, only that his motives would be easier to decipher, and the negotiations much simpler.

"Afternoon," Ghost said, flicking his cig away as Don Ellison and his driver/bodyguard joined him.

Don gave him an up/down inspection, tugging at his suit lapels. "You're not who I was expecting see."

"Yeah, no. That'd be my VP. He's a little busy getting his old lady back."

Ellison frowned and gestured to his guard, who pulled out a cellphone and stepped away to make a call. "You found my safe house, then."

"With a little help from a mutual friend." Ghost quirked a smile.

"Shaman."

Ghost shrugged.

It never failed to amaze him: the civilized meetings between outlaws, the way talking about death, theft, kidnappings and shootings took on the language of business mergers.

"Whose idea was it to take the girl?" he asked.

Ellison's turn to shrug. "That was Grey and the Richards kid. I tried to do things through G&G. When that didn't work, they decided to get a little leverage. I decided to ensure they weren't fucked over, because they're both totally fucking incompetent."

"So are your safe house boys, apparently."

"I need to be more careful in my hiring," the man agreed.

"And you've got some hiring to do. I think next you check, you'll find yourself a few guys short. Given my VP's old lady was stripped half naked and covered in bruises, you'll want to consider us even. One wife is worth about three and a half of your thugs."

Ellison ground his jaw, but said nothing, gaze resolute.

Ghost gave him a level look. "Knoxville belongs to me and mine. You're not getting in."

"Is that a fact?"

Ghost reached over his shoulder and tapped the truck window. On the other side, Fielding popped the door and climbed out, gun belt jangling as he walked around to join them.

Ellison's eyes widened.

Fielding wore an expression Ghost had never seen before, one of resolute sadness, and total aggression. His head was wrecked over what had happened in the hunting cabin, and he was channeling that self-hatred into something useful.

"I want you to meet my friend Vince," Ghost said. "He's a Knoxville PD sergeant."

Ellison frowned.

"You see, the Lean Dogs don't just own the city, we own the police force too. So like I said, you're not getting in."

Ellison considered a moment, finally gave Ghost a tight smile. "Not for now, anyway. You play the game well, Teague, I'll give you that." He stepped back and touched an imaginary hat brim in salute. "I'll be seeing you."

When the Mercedes had slipped out of sight, Ghost turned to the cop beside him. Fielding had one hand braced on the truck, staring at nothing, complexion waxy like he might be sick.

"Ah, cheer up, Vinnie." Ghost clapped him on the shoulder. "It won't be so bad. You might even like being my puppet."

~*~

"Thank you." Emmie wrapped both hands around the coffee mug Dublin offered her and he smiled in return.

"You're welcome, darlin'."

On the coffee table in front of her, Tango had left aspirin, Aidan had left a bottle of wine he'd dug from beneath the bar, and Carter had found a bag of Hershey's Kisses, saying, "Sometimes sugar helps when you're in shock."

It was hard to recall that she'd found these men frightening only a few weeks ago. The night in the field, in the flare of headlights, running for her life and seeing them close around her like hunting dogs – only to end up here, waited on by them, consoled and comforted.

And rescued. She still couldn't believe it. It was too big to digest at the moment, and her head hurt too badly, and so she sat with her coffee, beneath all their gazes, letting Walsh shine a light in each eye to check her pupil response.

"Did you heave?" he asked, retracting the flashlight, eyes bouncing across her face with clinical scrutiny.

"No."

"Still ought to get you to the ER and have you checked. We'll tell them you fell off a horse."

She nodded, the lie not bothering her in the least.

What *was* bothering her was the man seated across from her. Strikingly pretty, tall and elegant, with long hair and a thousand-dollar suit, he would have looked less out of place in the clubhouse if he'd been in full clown face paint.

He noticed her staring and gave her a little wave with the tips of his fingers, smile straight, white, cutting. "So you're the one all the fuss has been about. I see you're in one piece."

Crap – he was English too.

She glanced over at Walsh, and he made a negative gesture: not going there.

Then she looked down at herself. She was wearing Walsh's sweatshirt, the bloody one, breeches ripped from carpet burns. She didn't want to know what her face and hair looked like.

"I'm Emmie," she introduced herself, without much in the way of politeness. "And you are?"

He chuckled. "Take it they didn't kick the claws off you. Cheers, darling." He stood, straightened his suit jacket. "I'll be taking my leave, then. Kev, walk out with me."

Tango sighed deeply, massaged his forehead.

"Just go," Aidan told him. "And get him the fuck outta here."

Walsh gathered her attention again. "Soon as Ghost gets back, we'll head to the ER and get you looked at, love."

She smiled faintly. "It's just a little headache. I'm alright." She wanted to say more, so much more, but she was afraid she'd cry, so she pressed her lips together and tried to smile again.

~*~

Nerves chased across Tango's skin as he followed his lover out of the clubhouse and across the parking lot toward the black Jaguar.

"I hate when you walk behind me like that," Ian said over his shoulder. He halted as they reached the car and turned to face Tango, frowning in a way that made his face somehow more beautiful. "I want you beside me, always."

"That's not happening here," Tango said, firmly. His voice was dark, nasty even; it didn't sound like his own. He was angry, he realized, furious that Ian would show him any sort of partiality or affection here at the clubhouse, in front of his club brothers. "Not now, not ever."

Ian's brows lowered over his eyes, their blue depths soft with emotion. "I don't want you to pretend to be someone that you're not, just for their benefit."

"I'm not. I like girls."

"So do I. But that doesn't mean I don't want you in my bed every night."

Ian took a step forward, and Tango took one back. "I'm not gay," he said through his teeth.

"Of course not, darling," Ian said softly. "Do you think there's a label for what we are? We are ruined, love. Inside and out, forever and always. We've been destroyed, and I see nothing wrong with taking comfort where we can. You shouldn't either."

"I have comfort. I have a family now."

"Yes. You do." The caressing voice and the tender smile were mocking.

Tango turned to walk away.

"Tell your president I won't forget that favor he owes me," Ian called to his back.

"No, that would be too much to hope for," Tango muttered under his breath.

Baskerville Hall
Pub and Eatery
London, England
Fifteen Years Ago

Candles flickered in glass lamps on every table, electric light pooling on the ceiling from the rustic fixtures hanging from the low-beamed ceiling. It was a classic basement pub, a honeycomb of nooks and dining rooms, air shimmering with the greasy scents of fish and chips and hops. A quiet afternoon, only a few patrons tucked away with beer and heaping plates of food, the tellies rumbling to themselves in low voices.

Walsh wiped a thumb down the condensation on his pint glass, revealing a stripe of golden beer through the haze of frost. "Every year it seems I meet a new brother," he said to the foam on his beer, frowning to himself. Then he lifted his gaze to the man in the Lean Dogs cut across from him. "You're the first that's impressed me."

Phillip Calloway smiled, revealing crooked bicuspids. "Now there's a compliment if I ever heard one." He sipped his beer. "I wondered if your mum would ever send you my way."

"She didn't. She told me about you. I'm the one who decided to come here."

"Just because you're curious?"

"Because…" He took a deep breath and when he let it out, he released a bit of the tension he'd been carrying between his shoulders for so long now. "I've got nowhere else to go," he admitted. His jockey dream had tanked with the death of that other rider; Rita had ripped his blood out of her body; he'd killed a woman in Afghanistan; and now here he was, jobless, broke, and living with his mother.

"I have no money," he told Phillip, bowing his head. "I can't find a job." He heaved another deep sigh. "I know I'm supposed to come to you and tell you I've got dreams of riding a bike in your army, that I want to join the Dogs more than I want anything in the world. But I figure I owe you the truth. And the truth is, I don't have nothing much to offer, but I will work. I'll work hard as I can, to be what you need me to be."

That said, he sagged back in the booth, depleted of all mental and physical energy. All he could do now was hope his newly discovered half-brother didn't boot him out of the pub.

Phillip studied him a long moment, gaze thoughtful. "I do like for a man to be excited about it," he said, and Walsh felt his chances crumble to dust. "A young tosser comes in here, loaded with ink, with the rings in his nose and his hair all standing up. And he just bought a new Triumph, and he can't wait to join the brotherhood. It's all he thinks and talks about.

"And you know what? Three weeks later, he's puking at the sight of blood, and he's running his mouth when he shouldn't, and he can't even gain his prospect patch."

He leaned forward, grinning. "Excitement means nothing, King, my boy. It's a man who comes to the club out of desperation that finds his heart and soul there, on the road, with his brothers. You come to the MC a broken man, and it'll make you whole again, mark my words."

Thirty-Nine

Emmie slept and slept, and Walsh knew he ought to wake her, but he couldn't bring himself to. Her face mottled with bruises, she lay curled tight beneath the covers, eyes darting beneath her lids as she dreamed, or battled nightmares.

Walsh slipped from bed and went shirtless down to the first floor, made himself tea because he felt nostalgic, fed Dolly. The sun was just lifting over the horizon, lancing the trees with spears of golden light. He followed the porch around to the side of the house for once, where his view was not of the barn and arena – the business side of the place – but of an empty dew-drenched field.

A pair of does stepped cautiously from the wood and began to crop at the grass, large ears swiveling. Bright red cardinals fluttered through the shafts of sunlight, wings translucent as the rays passed through the feathers.

Never in his wildest dreams had he thought to end up here, not after the path he'd taken.

You come to the MC a broken man, and it'll make you whole again.

That Old World wisdom of Phillip's, something deep and true that reached through the outlaw superficialities and struck wholly human nerves. The scary part of being broken, though, was that you never realized how badly until the pieces started fitting back together again, the new happiness so fragile it took your breath.

Fragile as soft skin and little woman bones, breakable and vulnerable as the dying spark in a girl's eyes.

He didn't hear Emmie approach, but felt her small hand on his shoulder, his automatic startle soothed by the scratch of her nails at the back of his neck.

"We never sit on this side of the house," she said as she settled in beside him on the bench, legs tucked up beneath her. He thought she looked beautiful in her pajamas, her hair loose.

But she looked tired, too, still a little frightened around the edges. And her bruises made him murderous.

"We ought to," he answered, eyes trained to her. "It's lovely."

"Hmm." She braced an elbow on the back of the bench, cupped the side of her head in her hand, and winced when she pressed against a lump.

"Are you hurting? Do you need some aspirin?"

She motioned for him to stay put. "It's not as bad if I don't touch it."

"You probably should have stayed overnight in hospital."

"I didn't want to." Her gaze was fixed on the field, the birds, the does. "Oh, look at the deer."

"I want you to tell me if you feel nauseas," he told her. "Or if your vision goes wonky."

She sighed.

"I'm serious."

"I'm fine."

"No, you bloody well aren't," he said, more harshly than he'd intended. He was angry all over again. "You go through what you went through, you aren't *fine*."

She turned to face him finally, and the light in her eyes wasn't anything he'd expected. Maybe it was the rising sun, but he didn't think so; it was an inner shine, pouring out toward him.

"Walsh, you came for me."

He stared at her, not understanding.

"You *came* for me."

"Yeah, I did."

"Someone took me away, and you and your friends, your brothers, you found me – I don't even know how – and you came in with guns – Mercy had a damn *sledgehammer* – and you *hurt* and you *killed* people, and you got me out of there. You got me back." She took a deep breath and her lips quivered; her eyes filled with tears. "In my life, I can't even get anyone to cover at work for me, and Walsh, you *saved my life*. You…" She shook her head and drew in another shuddering breath.

"I'm the reason your life was in danger," he said, throat aching because he knew it was true.

"No," she said firmly, through the tears. "No, you're not. Those people – people I poured all my time and energy into – they put me in danger. My mentor and her son – I meant nothing to them, and they…" She sniffled hard, dabbed at her eyes. "They used me, and they didn't care if I…"

"Em–"

"I don't have a life, or options, or a husband, or children," she said miserably, "because I don't know how to have those things. Because no one's ever loved me before. Ever. And maybe you don't really love me, but that's what it feels like–"

He slid across the bench to get to her, took the side of her face in one hand and leaned in. She was crying too hard now for him to kiss her, crystal tears sliding down her cheeks. So he tangled his fingers in her hair and pressed his forehead to hers.

"Em, love, I am completely, devastatingly in love with you. You have to know that by now."

She nodded, her forehead pushing against his. "I know you said you'd let-let-let me go…"

"Not on your life, sweetheart."

It was like she'd been holding a tight check on her tears, and she let them loose, melting against him and dissolving into deep, racking sobs.

He gathered her close and let her soak his skin, hand clasped gently to the back of her head. This was her catharsis, and she had to cry through it, cry all the poison out.

The warmth of her body seeped into him, through the skin, warming him to the bone. It spread, filled him up, softened a thousand tensions.

He closed his eyes and thanked God for his club. It had given him the means to support himself and his mother. Had brought him here to this moment, brought him this woman…and given him the tools to defend her.

~*~

"...it's our belief at this time, based on forensic evidence, that a member of Davis Richards family injected him with the lethal dose of heroin. His daughter Amy, and his grandson Brett, are missing at this time, and we believe they are fleeing police custody."

On the small screen of the kitchen TV, Vince Fielding looked grave, drawn, and empty-eyed as he stood on the precinct steps, talking into a reporter's microphone.

Maggie turned away from the morning news and set a plate of scrambled eggs and toast in front of Ghost, frowning. "Baby, what did you do to Vince?"

"Why do you think I did anything to him?"

"Because you're smiling right now. Smiling *evilly.*"

"Is that even a word?" he asked, reaching for the pepper. " 'Evilly'?"

"Don't dodge the question."

He shrugged. "Nothing he didn't deserve."

She studied him a moment, lips pursed. "We're okay, aren't we?" And he knew she was talking about their family, and the club. *Are we safe? Are we still on top?*

"Yeah, we're okay, baby," he said, meaning it down to his bones. "We're fine." Because for the time being, they were, thanks to Walsh's insane farm scheme. He forked up a bite of eggs and saluted the air with it, grinning. "All hail the Skeleton King."

Forty

Fall was coming. It was in the evening shadows, in the cool undercurrent of the breeze, in the tangy stink of the water. The river had a different smell for every season, distant in the winter and heady in summer. Autumn was nipping at summer's tail, and Aidan felt the old excitement stirring in the pit of his belly. He loved the cooler weather, the cloudless skies, the crackle of party fires in fifty-five gallon drums. It was a subdued elation this year, one tempered by time, more thoughtful and less exuberant.

Yes, it was time to grow up. The correct way, not the way he'd tried. Because none of his leadership efforts had ever gotten him anywhere. It was time to accept that his role within the club was that of a follower.

He sat on the bench in front of the deserted shop, working on the last of a cigarette, letting the depression of realization wash over him.

When his phone rang, he almost didn't answer it, but dug it out at the last minute, putting it to his ear without checking the caller ID. "Yeah?"

"Aidan?" Female voice. Hesitant. Maybe even reluctant. Definitely not Tonya.

"Yeah."

"This is Sam. Sam Walton."

"Oh." A strange lightness blossomed in his chest, a release of the tension he'd held when he first answered. "Hi."

"Yeah, hi. I called over at the auto garage and they said they were swamped, but that they thought you could help me. I was on my way home from school, and I've got a flat."

He flicked the rest of his cigarette away. He felt that instant compulsion to start moving, the same as if Ava or Mags had called for help. "Yeah. Where are you?"

"I managed to turn off at the Waffle House parking lot."

"Gimme ten minutes."

"I've got nowhere else to be," she said with a faint, humorless laugh.

"Hold tight. I'm on the way."

The guys at the auto garage were busy, but the trucks weren't, so he swiped the flatbed and headed to Waffle House.

He spotted Sam from a full block away. Her Caprice was backed in at the street side of the parking lot, and she sat on the curb, wind playing with the length of her golden hair while the late sun burnished it. The picture she made – in her prim black slacks and white shirt, sleeves rolled up, glasses perched on her nose, with all that rich honey hair – softened him in unexpected ways. She looked like someone's sister, daughter, friend. She wasn't a vixen; she was human.

She stood when he double parked the truck in front of her car, dusted off the seat of her slacks in a normal, self-conscious, un-sexy maneuver. He wasn't used to being around woman who did normal, self-conscious, un-sexy things, he realized. Any woman who wasn't related to him was nothing but batted lashes, tossed hair, squeezed-up breasts and model poses.

Sam was neither his relative, nor one of his usual females.

And the thought of Tonya sitting on a curb made him want to laugh.

"Thanks for coming," she said, but didn't quite meet his stare, looking somewhere over his shoulder.

He didn't understand her awkwardness, so he said, "Which tire is it?"

She showed him. "I could hear it, while I was driving."

When he crouched down to look at it, she bent forward at the waist and looked along with him, like she was waiting for him to unveil something she'd missed in her earlier examination. Her hair swept forward and brushed against the side of his face.

"Oh, sorry." She pulled it back, tossed it over her shoulder.

When he glanced up at her, several things hit him at once. One: he'd never seen her hair loose like this. Two: it smelled amazing. Three: when her glasses slid down her nose, like they had now, she had the biggest, brightest, most colorful blue-green eyes he'd ever seen. And four: bending forward like this, he could see down her shirt, the swells of her breasts held snug in the lace cups of her bra.

Like he was seeing her for the first time, or through a different set of eyes, it dawned on him: Samantha Walton had grown the hell up and she was beautiful.

"Aidan."

"Uh – what?"

"I asked if you can tell what happened to it."

"Oh...uh..." He was stammering like an idiot. At least until he refocused on the tire. "Yeah, you don't have a flat, you've got dry rot, babe. The tread just fell off this thing. I'd bet the rest of your tires are in this shape." He turned a frowning look up to her. "Hasn't your dad or boyfriend noticed this?" He didn't care if anyone thought it made him a chauvinist: keeping the cars in good running shape was a man's job, and he felt suddenly pissed that the men in Sam's life weren't keeping up with what was already a pretty shitty ride.

She captured her lower lip between her teeth and again her eyes refused to meet his. "I'm not dating anyone seriously. And my dad's been dead for a while."

"Oh."

She shrugged. "I should have been paying better attention. It's my fault."

"Nah. This is a dude area." He gestured to the car.

She suppressed a laugh behind one ladylike hand. "Dude area? How progressive you are."

"I ain't progressive for shit. Pardon my French." He tapped the rotted tire with his knuckles. "You oughta set up a regular oil change appointment with the shop. They'll check your tires while you're there."

"Yeah." She nodded and sighed. "That's a good idea."

"I'm serious now. You can't get busy with work and just forget to keep up with your car. You don't wanna be a pretty girl stranded on the side of the road. Some creep-ass outlaw biker'll throw you on the back of his Harley and take you to Sturgis with him." He waggled his brows at her and she burst out laughing, like she didn't want to, but couldn't help it.

353

He grinned; he hadn't gotten too many female laughs lately.

She calmed with a groan. "Okay, so, how much is a new set of tires gonna set me back?"

He winced on her behalf.

"That bad, huh?"

He sat back on his rear end, legs extended before him beneath the car. "They're gonna cost you more than this sniper-mobile is worth."

Her distressed expression stirred something in his gut, regret blended with sympathy. He didn't like giving her the bad news.

"Why do you drive this thing anyway? You'd get way better gas mileage if you drove a chick car."

"Chick car?" Her brows lifted above the rims of her glasses, and her mouth puckered up in patented disapproval.

It was hot.

"You know, a Camry or an Accord or something. Women don't care about the cars they drive."

"You're seriously oh-for-two on the sexist comments thing," she said, but it looked like she was trying not to grin.

"I'm cute enough to get away with it," he said, throwing her his best smile.

She snorted. "Yeah, you are, that's the worst part of it." She sighed and sobered a bit. "I used to have a chick car, actually. I had a little Corolla."

He cocked his head, inviting her to explain.

"My parents bought it for me before I turned sixteen. It was going to be a surprise. My dad took it to the shop to have it all freshened up for me. He was T-boned by a truck on the way home. And it killed him."

"Shit," Aidan breathed. The bottom dropped out of his stomach as he watched her expression grow dark, the light in her pretty blue-green eyes dimming. "I didn't know. I'm sorry."

She offered him a thin non-smile. "It was a long time ago." She heaved a deep breath. "Anyway, the Caprice was his car. I haven't been able to part with it."

"Damn."

"Like I said." She shrugged. "So, you can change this? And quote me some new tires?"

"Tell you what: I'll change this. And the new tires are on me."

She coughed in surprise. "What? Oh, no. I can't let you do that. That's too—"

"Sam, let me." He gave her the smile again, the softer, more sincere version. "It can be my good deed for the week."

"I…" Her eyes were bright with argument…and an unmistakable gratitude. "Are you sure? I would feel terrible about taking advantage—"

"No arguing. I'm the tire fairy, and you're just gonna have to deal with it."

She smiled, a tired, thankful smile. "Thank you."

"My pleasure."

She stared at him a moment, maybe a moment too long. Then shook herself. "I'm gonna run inside for a second. I'll be right back."

"Take your time."

She was back about five minutes later, as he was pulling the ruined tire off, with a takeout container and two foam cups. "Sweet tea and a whole mess of bacon," she explained, sitting down on the curb again.

"Thanks." He took the offered cup and watched her pop the lid on the takeout container. Inside was nothing but a pile of bacon. He chuckled. "You weren't kidding."

She lifted a piece between two delicate fingers and blushed. "I had them drizzle it with maple syrup. Hope that's okay."

"Never say no to syrup on bacon." He let her hand him three pieces, so he wouldn't get his greasy hands all over the rest of it, and crammed it into his mouth gracelessly, watching her nibble at her own.

"Why are you single?" he blurted, before he could catch himself.

She choked on her bacon.

"Shit, I didn't mean to kill you."

She coughed a few times and took a slug of tea. Her voice was hoarse. "Why would you ask *that?*"

"I…dunno." He felt his face heat and turned away from her, picking up the spare and fitting it into place. "Just curious, I guess."

"Curious why I'm single. Why wouldn't I be?"

"Because people aren't single."

She huffed a laugh. "Lots of people are single, Aidan."

He reached for the lug nuts he'd set aside and sent her a pointed glance. "Good looking girls aren't single. Why are *you* single?"

She shrugged, and again avoided eye contact, cheeks flushing crimson. "I'm a geek. I dunno."

He grinned. "You're bad at flirting, aren't you?"

"I'm not just bad at it, I don't do it. Ever."

"Why the hell not? Ditch the glasses and smile a little bit, and you'd have dudes lined up down the block."

She sighed. "I don't want dudes lined up down the block."

"Why the—"

" – hell don't I want that?" she finished. She sighed. "Because I don't like dating. I hate putting on a show and hoping someone will like me, and doing it again the next weekend and the next, with someone new. I don't want 'dudes.' I want a man, who's all my own. I want 'the one.'" She gave him a halfhearted smile. "But you probably think that's lame, don't you, playboy?"

That elusive "one," the partner his father had been telling him about. The stand-beside-you woman who never faltered, and carried you when you weren't strong enough to stand on your own conviction. He'd actually been searching for that this time, but he'd been so far off base. He'd thought the bad bitch would make a good queen. But bad bitches were just that – bad.

"No, I don't," he said softly.

Her brows lifted. "You don't?"

"Nah. It sounds pretty nice, actually." He turned back to her tire, securing it into place.

"The spare's pretty rotted out too," he told her when he was finished, and had strapped the ruined one to the back of the flatbed. "So you'll need to come in as soon as you can to get the new set."

She nodded. "I'll do that."

He was getting ready to climb into the truck when her hand on his arm pulled him up short. He glanced down at the sight of her white fingers on the messy scars of his forearms, the distorted lines of tattoos that would never make sense again.

"Aidan," she said quietly, and when he met her gaze, she was looking directly into his eyes this time, her pretty irises turquoise in the fading light. "You don't have to settle for what's readily available either, you know. You could have your 'one,' if you wanted to."

He rolled her words through his mind all the way back to the garage. He needed to talk to Mags, he decided. It had been too long since he'd sought her wisdom.

~*~

He got the chance two weeks later, when he walked into the hospital with a blue teddy bear tucked under one arm, ready to meet the newest Lécuyer.

He'd missed all the rush beforehand, the delivery itself, the cleanup afterward. He didn't want to see any of that, to be honest. He just liked showing up as Uncle Aidan. They had a private room, and Ava was dozing in the bed. Maggie had Remy on her lap and Mercy was holding the new little bundle, showing him proudly to the grandparents.

Aidan eased the door shut behind him. "Hey." Whispering felt like the thing to do.

Mercy glanced up at him with a smile that made him embarrassed for some reason, the naked joy in the other man's face more than he wanted to bear, as a non-parent. "Hey, bro."

Calvin Louis Lécuyer was placed in his arms, a tiny red-faced human beyond his wildest comprehension.

357

"Y'all named him for Uncle Cal?" he asked, glancing over at Ghost, whose younger brother had died as a child in an accident.

"Yeah," Mercy said. "Him and my Gramps."

Ava stirred. "That fuzz on his head is blonde," she said, smiling tiredly. "He's got some recessive genes in him."

"That's your story anyway, huh?" Aidan asked.

"Hey, I'm blonde," Maggie said, tossing her hair. "And your grandfather was, right?" she asked Mercy.

"Yeah. He was real pale. And he's where the nose comes from." He tapped his own.

Aidan looked down at the baby in his arms. "He does have a beak, I'll give him that."

As if he'd heard and been offended, little Cal started to squirm and whimper.

"Uh-oh."

"He's hungry, bring him here," Ava said, sitting up higher against her pillows.

Mercy took the baby back and went to the bed, which meant breastfeeding was about to happen, which meant Aidan didn't want to stay in the room.

"Hey, Mags? Can I talk to you a sec?"

"Sure, baby." She stood and passed Remy to Ghost. "Here, Poppy. I'll leave you in charge."

"Come here, man." Ghost took the kid with an ease that always amazed Aidan. Crappy dad, good grandfather. That's just how it went sometimes.

Maggie slid her arm through his as they left the room. Ghost headed down toward the vending machines, and she steered Aidan the other way, toward the window pouring warm light into the cold tile hallway.

"It's been a while since you asked to talk to *me* about something. I feel honored," she joked, bumping him with her shoulder. "You usually go to your sister for female advice these days."

"Well, sometimes…"

She chuckled. "That's good. She's a woman now. She's a good source of womanly wisdom."

He snorted. "Maybe about some stuff."

"But not other stuff?" She gave him a lifted-brow, penetrating glance.

"Not about...well...I mean." He sighed. "She was born into the club. And she knew she wanted Mercy all along. Which is gross, by the way, when you think about it."

Maggie made a disagreeing sound.

"What I mean is, she doesn't know much about being outside the club and coming into it."

"Who are you wanting to come into the club, baby?" she asked, giving his arm a little tug so they stopped in the patch of sunlight and she moved around to face him. She had a seemingly innocent stare that could have forced a confession out of a mob boss.

"Not a new member," he said, rubbing at the back of his neck, wanting to shift his feet. "But..." He exhaled. "That girl I brought to the party a few weeks ago."

"Ah." Her expression tightened. "The princess."

"Yeah, her. Well, I was thinking, when I asked her out, that since she was different from some of the other girls–"

"Collections of dead braincells."

" – I've been out with–"

"Screwed around with."

" – that she might be, I dunno...a good old lady."

"Are you serious?" Her hazel eyes widened.

"I know she's not," he rushed to say. "She's a bitch, and a brat, and I don't ever wanna see her again."

"Thank God."

"But I was trying this time, Mags. Really I was."

She smiled sympathetically. "That's good. I'm proud of you."

"So how do you know" – an image of Sam popped into his head, her pretty eyes behind her glasses, the unbound waves of her hair, her tea and syrup-drizzled bacon, the catch in her voice when she talked about her dad – "when someone's *really* old lady matieral?"

"Oh, sweetie." She smiled again. "It takes time to know that. Women don't come with resumes."

"Unfortunately."

She chuckled. "You've got to find someone who sees Aidan underneath the cut, who's got her eyes open wide, and who doesn't run when she gets scared. The good ones are always harder to catch," she said. "But they'd never think of running once they're caught."

Forty-One

Three Weeks Later

"Dad, the longer you delay, the later it's going to be when you get done. And I'm not going to hold dinner for you."

Karl gave her the most wounded look, and for the first time in her memory, his eyes were clear, his gaze sober. AA was working. So far. Falling off the wagon was a distinct possibility, but given how grouchy and uncooperative he was, it was a safe bet he'd stuck to his pledge today, at least.

"You're cruel, Emmaline," he told her. "Trying to let me go hungry."

"Not trying, Dad, no. I'm trying to get you to implement a little time management. If you're the groundskeeper around here, then you have to stick to the farm schedule. And Miss Walsh is coming in tonight, and she'll be starving, so I won't hold dinner just because you wouldn't get your butt in gear."

He glared at her, grumbled under his breath, but finally started the lawn tractor and rolled away.

Emmie folded her arms and watched him ride off a moment, feeling a sense of pride in her father for the first time in...ever. He was just mowing the grass, but that was worlds better than what he'd been doing – which was nothing.

It was Walsh who'd started Karl on the proper road. They'd gone to drag him out of Bell Bar and Walsh had put his foot down. Dumped ice water down his back and gotten in his face when Karl started to go on a drunken rampage. "You're breaking your daughter's heart, you sod! Bloody step up and be a man for once."

He was three weeks sober, and he was the new Briar Hall groundskeeper. Small steps, but positive ones.

The sound of a car engine on the driveway drew her attention, and she saw Walsh's truck swing past the barn and head up to the house, three heads silhouetted in the back window where before there had been one.

She took a deep, shaky breath, nerves jumping all at once. It would have been terrifying enough to meet a boyfriend's mother, but to meet her mother-in-law? That typically wasn't done in this order. *Hi, I married your son almost two months ago, nice to meet you!*

Ugh, what was this woman going to think of her?

She ducked into the tack room and glanced in the mirror above the sink. "Oh, shit." Her hair was coming loose, curls clinging to her damp neck. A big smear of horse slobber marred what had been a clean polo shirt, and there was an inexplicable smear of dirt across the bridge of her nose.

She did the best she could with damp paper towels, called herself a lost cause, and took three huge deep breaths that did nothing to calm her.

"She'll love you," Walsh had insisted, but she wasn't real popular with mothers, given that her own had seen no reason to keep being her mother.

"I'll be back at feeding time," she told Becca on her way out of the barn.

Becca gave her a sharp grin. "Good luck."

When she got to the house, she went in the back door, through the library, where they were in the process of amassing a book collection; Ava had made some donations and gifted her some others. She paused in the hallway just outside the living room, listening to the voices.

"King, it's just lovely!" a light, chirpy female voice exclaimed, bright with an English accent, charming as a period film. "Look at all the light coming in! The windows! Oh, you must have more furniture. And maybe lace doilies for the tables. Yes, you don't want to ruin them with candles."

"Candles, Mum?" Walsh asked dryly.

"You must have candles. Much more romantic that way."

Which would be her cue. Emmie took one last shivery breath and stepped around the corner. She didn't make a sound, but Walsh's mother whirled toward her instantly, smile catching, and then doubling in size, her small dark eyes sparkling.

She was a tiny thing, dressed in a simple, modest dress, with a short cap of blonde and gray hair. Her face was heavily lined from smiling. A happy woman, despite her shit luck with men.

"Oh my," she said with a laughing gasp. "You must be Emmie."

"Yes, ma'am." Emmie moved toward her, hand extending for a shake. "I'm sorry I'm such a mess. I had lessons this morning, and I'm dirty from the barn, and – oh."

The woman bypassed her hand and pulled her into a tight hug. She pushed her back at arm's length after, giggling to herself. "You're beautiful, dear! Such a classic face. Isn't she classic, King? And the hair – you must let me braid it for you. I've always wished I had curls like these."

"She's gorgeous," Walsh agreed, and Emmie thought she'd blush to death.

Walsh's half-brother, Shane, introduced himself next. He had Walsh's blue eyes, and there was a certain similarity in his face, but he had dark, close-cropped hair, and his dark brows gave his face a more shadowed look. She read him as shy, and quiet, but his smile was sweet and his handshake warm.

"Call me Bea, dear," Walsh's mother said, taking her by the hand and patting the back of it. She had smooth, cool hands, the flesh loose with age, the veins little ridges along the backs. Maternal hands, full of love and affection.

Emmie felt a lump form in her throat.

"Now," Bea said, drawing Emmie's hand through her arm. "Show me your lovely home! I can't wait to see all of it."

~*~

The house was made for a crowd. For a big family, laughter and chatter filling up all the vast corners.

The Lean Dogs MC was that family. The brothers and sisters she'd never had. And tonight she had her father with her. And Bea Walsh had established herself as surrogate mother in a matter of hours.

Before the party, when she'd been tossing together buffalo chicken dip in the kitchen, Emmie had thrown her arms around Walsh. "I've never had a mom," she'd whispered against his throat, and felt his arms close around her. "I love you so much, you wonderful man."

He'd turned the color of ripe radishes.

He hadn't been embellishing, or trying to manipulate her, before their courthouse wedding, when he'd promised her a family. The bikers crowding her dining room now – they were family, in all their ragtag, leather-covered glory.

Emmie glanced around the table. Ava ate one-handed while she held Cal in one arm. Mercy had Remy in his lap, and was tearing bits off a roll for him.

Michael leaned toward Holly to hear what she was saying, and he twitched the tiniest of smiles, one Holly responded to with a beaming, adoring grin.

Nell said something that made Maggie laugh so hard she almost choked on her wine.

Under the table, Emmie laid her hand on Walsh's thigh and squeezed, a silent thank you, greeting, show of affection. His hand covered hers, his rings warm and smooth on her knuckles.

At the head of the table, Ghost pushed his chair back and cleared his throat, lifting his beer bottle. All heads turned toward him, conversations grinding to silence. "I want to raise a toast," he said, voice officious, impressive. "To the Walshes." His eyes came to them. "For holding down this particular fort, keeping our club safe."

Emmie felt a little shiver move down her back. This was her presidential seal of approval.

"Emmie, welcome to the family," Ghost continued. "And Walsh, brother, you never let us down."

There was a hearty round of applause. Even Bea clapped along vigorously, saying, "How nice!"

Emmie's face warmed; all of her did. This was hers now: this house, this farm, this man, this life, this family.

Hers. And she wanted for nothing else.

~*~

Aidan prowled around the island in the kitchen, scanning the dessert plates, trying to decide which was tempting enough to force into his full stomach and risk a bellyache.

Emmie stepped into the room, expression hesitant. "Aidan, Tonya's at the front door. She walked up from the barn and she wants to talk to you."

He sighed dramatically. "Nah. Not gonna happen. Don't take this the wrong way, but your star student's a superior bitch."

"No argument there," she said with a snort. "But, she was pretty insistent. Maybe you ought to at least see what she wants."

He groaned. "Yeah. Sure."

Tonya waited down at the base of the porch steps, arms folded, hair slicked back in a severe bun. She turned at the sound of his footsteps on the boards, and watched him with cold dispassion as he descended.

She was dressed unusually – for her, anyway, in a loose silk shirt and jeans. Her flats probably cost five-hundred bucks, but they were flats instead of spike heels.

"What?" he asked when he reached her, digging out a cigarette just to annoy her. "I've got apple pie waiting on me, so make it quick."

She sniffed hard, face pinched up with cold displeasure. "Alright then, fine."

He stuck his cig between his teeth, dug out his lighter.

"There's something I need to tell you, and trust me, I don't want to. But I thought you ought to know, so you don't make the same mistake in the future."

"Will you just get to the point?" he asked as he lit up.

She took a deep breath and let it out in a fast rush through her nostrils. Her eyes were totally dead as they latched onto his. "Yes, Aidan, I'll get to the point."

"So do it."

One last sigh. "I'm pregnant. And it's yours."

THE END

~*~

The Lean Dogs, and their old ladies, will return for Aidan's story in:

Secondhand Smoke

Coming Soon

~*~

Get Connected:

Facebook: Lauren Gilley – Author

Twitter: @lauren_gilley

Blog: hoofprintpress.blogspot.com

Email: authorlaurengilley@gmail.com

Keep up to date with new releases, gain access to exclusive teasers and bonus material, join the Dartmoor discussion group on FB, and enter giveaways. Lauren loves to hear from readers, so don't hesitate to Like, Follow, leave a comment, or send an email.

Lauren Gilley writes Literary Fiction which is sometimes mistaken for Romance. She's the author of fifteen novels and several short stories. When she's not writing, she's at the barn, plotting stories and cleaning horse stalls. She lives in Georgia.

Other Titles from Lauren Gilley

<u>The Walker Series</u>
Keep You
Dream of You
Better Than You
Fix You
Rosewood

Whatever Remains

Shelter

<u>The Russell Series</u>
Made for Breaking
God Love Her
"Things That Go Bang In The Night"
Keeping Bad Company
"Green Like the Water"

<u>The Dartmoor Series</u>
Fearless
Price of Angels
Half My Blood
The Skeleton King
Secondhand Smoke (coming soon)

56407114R00223

Made in the USA
Lexington, KY
21 October 2016